Praise for

Simply Starstruck

★★★

"*Simply Starstruck*, debut novel by author Aspen Hadley, sparkles with all the elements of a classic love story. Kate Evans is the perfectly flawed heroine, struggling to figure out the future for her and her son, Ethan, after the tragic death of her husband. Movie star Jess Sullivan is the classic leading man, a hero in every sense of the word. Sparks fly as the two collide, then slowly, they learn how unexpected love can be the most magical of all. Delightfully witty and clever writing, unforgettable characters, and a beautiful setting will pull the reader into the story and make you hope it never ends. Destined to become a fan favorite, don't miss *Simply Starstruck*."

—Michele Ashman Bell, best-selling author of The Butterfly Box Series and *A Candle in the Window*

"Stunning debut from a genuinely talented new author! I read *Simply Starstruck* in one sitting and loved every minute. Compelling characters drew me in, and the storyline never let me go. I look forward to many, many more great reads from Aspen Hadley!"

—Kerry Blair, award-winning author of *This Just In*

Simply StarStruck

Elaine -
To an earthly angel!!
Happy reading
AHadley

Simply Starstruck

Aspen Hadley

SWEETWATER
BOOKS
An imprint of Cedar Fort, Inc.
Springville, Utah

ISBN 13: 978-1-4621-2240-0

Published by Sweetwater Books, an imprint of Cedar Fort, Inc.
2373 W. 700 S., Springville, UT 84663
Distributed by Cedar Fort, Inc., www.cedarfort.com

LIBRARY OF CONGRESS CATALOGING-IN-PUBLICATION DATA

Names: Hadley, Aspen, 1978- author.
Title: Simply starstruck / Aspen Hadley.
Description: Springville, Utah : Sweetwater Books, an imprint of Cedar Fort, Inc., [2018]
Identifiers: LCCN 2018026743 (print) | LCCN 2018029458 (ebook) | ISBN 9781462129232 (epub, pdf, mobi) | ISBN 9781462122400 (perfect bound : alk. paper)
Subjects: LCSH: Widows--Fiction. | Motion picture actors and actresses--Fiction. | LCGFT: Romance fiction.
Classification: LCC PS3608.A29 (ebook) | LCC PS3608.A29 S56 2018 (print) | DDC 813/.6--dc23
LC record available at https://lccn.loc.gov/2018026743

Cover design by Wes Wheeler

Edited by Jessilyn Peaslee and James Gallagher (Castle Walls Editing LLC)
Typeset by Kaitlin Barwick

Printed in the United States of America

10 9 8 7 6 5 4 3 2 1

Printed on acid-free paper

For Steve,
who saw the real me and believed,
long before I believed in myself.

Chapter 1

It's funny in life how you never recognize a big moment when it's actually happening. It takes time to realize that there was a fork in the road, that something seemingly normal about your day ended up changing the entire course of your life. The real brain squeezer is wondering how you would have done things differently if you had known that you were about to stumble into a pivotal moment. Take me, for example; I probably would have put on something, anything, other than sweatpants that afternoon.

Although I wasn't terribly picky about my outfits, I wasn't without standards. But about every fifth Wednesday, I'd get this gripping desire to exercise. So I'd bunch up my hair in a messy bun high on my head, dig those sweats out of the laundry basket, and sort of meander for an hour or so around the hills backing my aunt Cassandra's property.

And while I'd never spent that much time worrying over what size pants I wore, or how short my legs were compared to other women's legs, all that changed the day that Jess Sullivan—famous actor, model, and all-around media darling—appeared in the hallway outside the kitchen of Aunt Cass's house.

As I was returning from one of those rambling hikes, I noticed a sporty little car parked on the side of the house. Other than the fact that it was a car rather than the usual trucks and SUVs that Aunt Cass's friends and associates drove, I didn't think much of it as I entered the kitchen through the back door. I was looking for my son, Ethan, who always managed to leave our cozy little guest cottage the minute I turned my back and was most often found digging in Aunt Cass's treat stash. I was hoping to catch him before he got to the point where I'd be up all night giving him sips of ginger ale and doses of children's Tums.

When I entered the kitchen, it was empty, but signs of both Ethan's raid and some sort of rushed food prep were in evidence. Candy wrappers near the garbage can, but never quite in, were enough to confirm my suspicions about where Ethan had been. But the rest of the mess was a mystery to me. Aunt Cass usually told me when she was having guests over. She acted like she did this to be polite and considerate of the fact that I lived on her property. I believe, however, that she did it as a warning for me to keep Ethan out of the big house on those nights. She'd mentioned no gathering when we'd had lunch that day, so I mentally shrugged and used one of my feet to ninja-kick open the swinging door leading into the hallway. It didn't matter how many times I'd been asked to open it gently—ever since I'd been a child, I'd gotten an extreme amount of satisfaction out of karate chopping it open at lightning speed. I considered it an all-out success if I could kick hard enough for the door to hit the wall behind it. The tough hinges didn't let it happen often, but that didn't stop me from hoping.

As the door swung open, I raced through it. It was another game of mine to zip through before the door started to swing closed. This time, things didn't go as smoothly as they normally did. I'm not entirely sure how it happened, but as I hurried through the door—all the while watching its progress—I felt something solid slam into me. The slam was followed by a loud crashing sound and then I was wet. I looked down in confusion to see that the front of my shirt and top half of my sweats were getting darker as some mystery liquid seeped into the absorbent material. The next thing I noticed was a gasp and then mumbling, frustrated sounds coming from somewhere in the puddle on the floor.

I looked down to see Aunt Cass's housekeeper, Zinn, doing her best to pick up pieces of shattered glass while simultaneously mopping at the mess with her apron.

"Oh, Zinn, I'm so sorry!" I immediately knelt beside her and began picking up pieces of what used to be glass—I was praying not crystal—goblets. "I didn't know you were out here." I was focused on not cutting my fingers and double focused on not attracting Cass's attention as I slipped and slid on my hands and knees.

"Okay, okay, get away." Zinn swatted at my hands as I fumbled to help her. "You'll cut yourself and just make it worse." Then Zinn mumbled something under her breath about me being a dumb karate-chopping infant. At least that's what I was choosing to hear, because the reality of what she was mumbling was most likely worse.

"Seriously, Zinn, I'm so sorry! Let me help you. Where were you headed?"

"I was trying to serve drinks, but I forgot the lemons. I was coming back to get some," she grumbled. "If I'd known you were coming, I would have just kept going and gotten the lemons later."

"You go get new drinks and I'll clean this up. I'm already a mess. Look at me." I drew her attention to my less-than-stellar outfit, which was now sopping wet.

Zinn gave me a once-over and then rolled her eyes. "You're right. You couldn't look much worse," she agreed.

I bit my tongue to keep a sarcastic retort from flying out and gave her a grimace, which I was hoping would pass for a smile, as I nodded. "Yep. So you'd better get going before Cass comes to see what all the commotion is about."

That seemed to be the right thing to say, because Zinn looked behind her, toward the parlor, and straightened back up. She said nothing more as she stepped around me and the jumble of glass before pushing the swinging door and letting herself back into the kitchen.

I took a second glance at the mess before deciding I'd need a mop and a bucket to properly deal with the destruction. I pushed back up from my knees and was about to follow Zinn into the kitchen when I heard a soft chuckle behind me. I froze in place.

In that moment, I knew two things. First, the person behind me was a man. The chuckle was low and soft. Second, the person behind me was a stranger. Any of Cass's typical friends and associates would be familiar enough with her ditzy niece to ignore loud crashing noises. And they certainly wouldn't take the time to stand in the hallway chuckling about it.

I didn't want to turn around. I wanted to take my soggy self into the kitchen and stay there until Zinn got back out with the drinks and I knew that this stranger with the sort of gravelly chuckle was gone. But I've never been one to do what's smart, and I've always been horribly curious.

I turned slowly, feeling the weight of my sticky, soggy, used-to-be-light-pink sweatpants clinging to my thighs. And there, standing in the hallway with a grin the size of Texas on his handsome face, was Jess Sullivan.

It was my greatest dream turned nightmare. Handsome man, in my home, straight from the cover of *Hunky* magazine, laughing at me standing in a puddle of broken glass and—I glanced down—some mystery liquid. Have I mentioned I was wearing sweats?!

My baby-blue T-shirt didn't even have the decency to match my pink sweats, and my hair, which badly needed a day at the salon, was pulled up on top of my head like Pebbles from *The Flintstones*. My shoes squished as I shifted my feet. I couldn't even bring myself to think about the status of my makeup, or the fact that tweezing hadn't been a priority since I'd moved in with Aunt Cass the year before. Perhaps the whale-sized blush that crept up my neck and into my face was enough to take the focus off my unibrow. A girl can dream.

Speaking of dreams, I pulled my eyes off the floor and back up to his. Green. They were green. He had crinkles around his eyes and smile lines around his mouth. Darn it if he wasn't even more gorgeous in person. It was awful!

Luckily, I was saved by Zinn slamming the kitchen door into my back as she plowed through with her tray full of new drinks. No one could say Zinn didn't work quickly. I caught my balance by slamming my body into the wall and remaining there, eyes closed, praying that if I couldn't see him, then he couldn't see me.

"Oh, Mr. Sullivan, if you'll follow me, I have more drinks now, sir," Zinn chirped cheerfully.

"Sure thing, Zinn. Thanks," he replied in his deep voice. Even deeper than on TV.

Oh my heavens. He had to be the most attractive man I'd ever seen. Why hadn't someone, anyone, mentioned that a hunk of this magnitude would be gracing the big house with his beautiful presence?

I heard footsteps retreating down the hall, and when I cracked open my eyes to see if they'd gone back into the parlor, I was just in time to see Mr. Sullivan glance back and hold up his glass in a salute. Then he winked.

The wink was a little much, I told myself as I pushed away from the wall and scowled back at him. In my confusion and embarrassment, I decided he had to be a conceited man. I clung to that thought like a lifeline. No one who looked like that and made fun of women in distress deserved an adoring fan in me. He could have at least asked if I was okay!

Mumbling to myself about his obvious case of narcissism as I gathered cleaning supplies and got to work on the mess in the hallway made me feel marginally better. I refused to think about the fact that I was being childish. All that mattered was that it took the focus off the entire ridiculous situation being my own fault.

I'd completely forgotten about Ethan until I heard the sound of feet running down the hallway above my head and then pounding down the grand front staircase. Lovely. Leave it to Ethan to make an entrance. In his defense, my entrance had been even more grand.

He slid around the corner, followed closely by Aunt Cass's German shepherd, Wade, who upon seeing me began to bark in greeting and passed Ethan in an effort to continue the tradition of slamming me to the ground. I was the only one Wade seemed interested in squishing.

"Wade, sit!" I commanded sharply, worried that he'd step into the glass and cut his foot. Wade, trained by the best, stopped and sat on his haunches, his tongue lolling out and his head cocked to the side. "Good boy." I smiled and then glanced to where Ethan was standing slightly behind Wade.

"Hey, Mom," he said and gave me a toothy smile.

"Hey, yourself," I replied. "What brings you to Aunt Cass's house tonight?"

Ethan had the decency to look at his toe and smudge it around on the floor while softly saying, "Uh, I got lonely while you were on your walk."

"Uh-huh."

"And so I came over to visit Auntie Cass, but she had friends over. Mom, did you see who her friend is?" At this Ethan's head popped up and his eyes shone with excitement. "It's that guy who was in that movie about the lost treasure in Africa! He's so much bigger when he's talking to you than he looks on the TV." He was gushing. My eight-year-old son was gushing. "He shook my hand and called me 'Big Guy.' But then Auntie Cass said I could play with Wade in her upstairs TV room while I waited for you to get back from your wanderings."

"My wanderings?"

"Yeah, that's what Auntie Cass calls it when you go on your sometimes exercise."

I could just picture Jess Sullivan's face when Cass announced that her niece was out wandering on her occasional exercise while her eight-year-old son was left alone wolfing down every sugary sweet in the house. Great. Just how chubby did my short little legs look in the now-skintight sweats? But back to the task at hand . . .

"Right, well, how much candy did you eat before barging in on Aunt Cass's guest?" I decided to change the subject.

"Not much," Ethan shrugged. "What happened here?" In his own effort to change the direction this conversation was about to take, he pointed to the mess that I was about halfway done cleaning up.

I sighed for what felt like the hundredth time since I'd innocently entered Cass's house that night, and then I began mopping again. "Zinn spilled some drinks," I dodged.

"Zinn?" Ethan sounded surprised. Probably because Zinn had never spilled a drink in the thousand years that she'd been walking this earth. She was meticulously clean and graceful. It was the reason she and Cass had such a great working relationship. I often felt clumsy in comparison and knew that they both tolerated me, their complete opposite, with exasperated affection. At least, I liked to tack the word *affection* on at the end and hope that it was the truth.

"Yep." I refused to let him know what exactly had caused Zinn to spill the drinks. I preferred that he maintain some respect and admiration for his dear old mom. "But I knew she had a visitor to attend to, so I offered to help her clean it up," I explained. Ethan nodded, because it made sense and also because little boys don't like to overthink things. "Will you take that garbage bag around back while I finish up with the mop? Be careful with it; it's full of glass. I'll meet you at home."

Ethan didn't argue, for what may have been the first time in his entire life, as he gave Wade a farewell pat, grabbed the garbage bag, and hefted it back through the swinging door. I waited until I heard the back door slam before I quickly finished mopping.

After washing out the mop and putting it carefully back in its place, I exited the big house and followed the rock path to the guest cottage that Ethan and I called home.

Ethan was sitting in the main room with his sneakers up on the coffee table, flipping through channels on the TV. One of the advantages Ethan most loved about living with Aunt Cass was that she had satellite television and an endless supply of channels to flip through but never actually settle on. He could have made an Olympic sport of it. It was honestly surprising that the pointer finger on his right hand, the finger he used to flip channels, wasn't all bulked up and muscled after so much use.

"Homework all done?" I asked as I stepped out of my slightly soggy hiking boots and placed them by the door.

"Yeah." Ethan didn't even glance away from the television.

"Chocolate hangover coming on?"

This time he just shrugged. Super. That meant he'd taken down quite a bit and we'd have to wait it out to see what the aftermath would be. Next time I was taking him with me rather than seeking solitude. I knew better than to attempt to get Zinn and Cass to curb his enthusiasm for sweets.

"I'm getting in the shower, and then it's time for bed." I ruffled his hair as I walked by.

"Ah, Mom, it's only eight," he whined.

"Yep. And you're only eight. And it's a school night." I shot him my biggest, cheesiest smile, designed to let him know arguing was pointless. "You have fifteen minutes before it's TV off."

Ethan grumbled something designed to let me know that he was arguing in his mind. I smiled to myself as I walked down the short hallway to the bathroom we shared.

The cottage was small. One main area was kitchen, dining, and living space. Down a short hallway were two bedrooms and one bathroom. That was it. But it was all we needed, and I was grateful that Aunt Cass had offered its use during a time when I really needed a refuge.

Ethan and I had quickly grown to love the slower pace of the small community, and Cass and Zinn had been even quicker to love having Ethan's young presence around the place. Even though I understood the time was quickly coming when I'd need to make more permanent decisions, I was pretty sure they loved having me around too. But Ethan, well, everyone loved Ethan. He was a good kid. As I scrubbed the sticky liquid and sweat off my body, I thought again about how lucky I was to have him. I definitely did not think about Jess Sullivan and his green eyes. Not at all.

The next morning, after getting Ethan off at the bus stop and walking back to the big house, I decided to drop in on Zinn for breakfast. She seemed to be expecting me. Odd. I tried not to make a habit of bumming breakfast off her too often. Maybe I was slipping up and it was becoming the norm. I'd have to reevaluate my actions . . . over breakfast.

"Kate," she said before the door had even closed behind me. She didn't look up from whatever she was stirring. Just my name. Nothing more.

"Morning?" It came out as more of a question than a greeting, as if asking, Is it indeed a good morning? Is your mood okay? Should I back out quietly, or perhaps play dead? I opted for not fully entering the kitchen until Zinn looked up and I could see if she had a crazed look in her eye. I had, after all, caused her to spill for the first time in her 105 years of life on this earth.

Okay, in all fairness, she may not have actually reached the age of 105. But I wasn't exaggerating about her lack of spilling. The woman was amazing. And ageless. I really wanted to ask her how old she was, because she'd been gray and wrinkly since I'd met her when I was five years old. But I wanted her to keep feeding me even more than I wanted to know her age, so I lived with the gnawing question hovering in the back of my mind. She'd probably outlive me either way, so it didn't really matter. It just kind of annoyed. Like a mosquito bite.

When I was ten and had visited Cass a few times, I finally worked up the guts to ask her about Zinn. All I'd gotten was a raised eyebrow and this little nugget of information: "What could you possibly want to know about Zinn? We're lucky to have her." Huh. Not nearly enough information for an inquiring mind like my own, but I'd recognized a losing battle and had kind of given up after that. Also, Cass had mentioned my "interrogation" to her sister, my mother, and I'd been told in no uncertain terms to stay out of Zinn's business in the future. It was weird.

One summer when I was fourteen, I made up a life history for Zinn. I'd been tweaking and perfecting it over the past fifteen years, and the current version was that she was a refugee from Ireland who had emigrated in order to survive the Great Irish Potato Famine. She and her new husband had stowed away on a crowded ship bound for America with hopes of a better future. Through hard work and perseverance, they had made their way west to a new place called Colorado. But upon arriving in their promised land, her young husband had saved her from a rabid wolf and was fatally wounded during the heroic rescue. Sadly, she was childless. And because of her deep and abiding love for her husband, whom I named Callum, she never remarried but instead dedicated her life to serving others.

The only real problem with this current biography was that the potato famine happened in the eighteen forties, which was about 170 years ago. I was willing to overlook that, though, considering I was also willing to overlook lesser points such as her lack of an accent and the fact that I may have at some point heard Cass say something about Zinn's childhood in Utah.

Anyhow, until I got my chance to raid the attic storage area and dig for clues about Zinn, it was the theory I was operating under.

"You coming in or not?" Zinn, speak of the devil, speared me with a glance, pulling me out of my daydreams.

"Uh, yes?" Again, a question. I hadn't really gotten a good look at her eyes yet. Zinn kind of huffed and gestured at the countertop, where leftover breakfast items had yet to be cleared.

I shuffled slowly toward the food, all the time keeping Zinn in my peripheral vision. You couldn't be too careful around someone with a mystery past like hers. Maybe I'd rewrite her story to include a stint as a knife thrower in the circus. Better safe than sorry.

I grabbed a clean plate from the end of the counter, along with a knife and cup, and began perusing my options. Biscuits, muffins, some fruit. Clearly the best items were gone.

"No eggs or bacon today?" I questioned as I chewed my lower lip.

"'No eggs or bacon,' she says," Zinn grumbled in reply. She was probably speaking to some Irish patron saint. "She wanders in at nearly nine o'clock and expects that I've just kept the food waiting for her."

"Yum. This muffin looks great, Zinn. I'll just have one of these." I turned, flashed her a winning grin, and waved the muffin in her general direction before placing it on my plate.

After pouring myself warmish orange juice and spreading butter on my mystery muffin, I sat at the table and began chomping away. I should have retreated to my cottage, but I had to know about last night's guest, and I knew that if I played it right, Zinn would be more forthcoming than Aunt Cass.

"Really great muffin, Zinn!" I enthused, even as I sprayed crumbs out of my mouth onto the table. Dry little devil. I took a swig of orange juice to choke it down before offering yet another smile.

"I'll make sure to tell the baker at the gas station that you like it," Zinn huffed.

"Oh, well, sure, that would be great." I was confused. Zinn always, always, baked her own muffins. She was clearly still peeved with me. Did Zinn even drive? I was pretty sure there was no way that muffin had come from a gas station. Then again, it was dry as dirt and Zinn took pride in her food. I looked suspiciously down at the muffin . . . just how old was this thing? I knew that mentioning its age wouldn't win me any goodwill from Zinn, so I chewed in silence for a few more minutes, planning out my best angle, trying to figure out where Zinn's soft spot would be this morning.

I opened my mouth to offer up something about the lovely bun Zinn had pulled her flowing locks into when I was interrupted by Cass breezing into the kitchen and shooting me a glance. Sometimes no words are needed. She knew about last night. And she wasn't pleased.

"Morning," I mumbled into my orange juice.

"Morning, Katherine," she stated in much the same way Zinn had when I'd entered the kitchen. And I'd gotten the "Katherine" treatment as well. This wasn't looking promising. "How are you today?" Cass asked as she walked over to snag a plate out of the warming oven. A plate suspiciously filled with eggs, bacon, and even a pancake. And was that warm syrup that Zinn passed to her before Cass joined me at the table? I couldn't keep my mouth from dropping open as my eyes flew to Zinn's face. Zinn smirked at me and returned to washing dishes.

"Uh, I'm good, Aunt Cassandra." Two could play at the name game. But I was nervous playing that card when I was already in trouble, so I managed to turn my gaze to Cass and offer a small smile.

"I'm glad to hear it. And how is Ethan?" At this Cass's gaze warmed a bit. Lovely, lovely Ethan. He'd saved me from more than one spot of trouble with Aunt Cass.

"He's good. Off to school this morning. I believe he's doing his report on caterpillars today."

"Such a smart young man," Zinn offered up from the sink.

"Yes, he is a fine boy," Cass agreed before putting a forkful of fluffy, delicious pancake in her mouth, syrup dripping off the edges. I licked my lips. Cass must have noticed because she quirked her lips while she chewed.

As Cass and I ate, the kitchen was quiet other than the clanking of silverware on plates and dishes in the sink. Stalemate. I knew I should apologize. It was what they were waiting for. But it wasn't as though I'd purposely slammed into Zinn and caused the mess to happen. After spending large chunks of my childhood summers with Cass and Zinn, and then living with them for the past year, silences had grown comfortable. But this wasn't comfortable. I squirmed a bit. Cass threw me a glance. I tried to hold still. I took another bite of muffin and worked my throat to keep from choking. Zinn threw me a glance. Good grief.

"Okay! Jeez!" I swallowed my muffin and threw my hands in the air. "I'm sorry, okay. I had no idea Zinn was behind the door and I was trying to find Ethan!"

At my outburst Cass and Zinn shared a satisfied little look across the kitchen. Zinn dried her hands and turned to lean against the sink's edge while Cass swallowed her last bite of sinful-looking pancake and cleared her throat.

"We know it was an accident, dear. Don't worry about it. Just be more careful in the future." Cass smiled at me.

"Really?" That may have sounded more sarcastic than questioning. "After this awkward little punishment this morning, this horrid gas-station muffin and the smirks? You're just going to tell me not to worry?" I looked back and forth between the two of them. "No lectures on how to properly open doors or on my outfit choices?"

"Kate, it's just that your timing last night was stressful. We had an important visitor," Cass replied. I was back to being Kate. So that was good, I supposed.

"And I pride myself on running a smooth and clean home," Zinn added, still in a bit of a huff.

"Yes, I know, Zinn. You've never spilled in your life," I grumped.

Zinn smiled softly. "Quite right."

"Mr. Sullivan told me what happened. He found the entire thing amusing and wasn't at all upset about it," Cass added.

"Oh, well, goody then. Wouldn't want Mr. Sullivan to be upset about your spastic niece in the back hallway," I said softly. I looked up at Cass and she had flatlined her lips, letting me know that she didn't appreciate my thoughts on Mr. Sullivan. "Why was he here anyway? I didn't know you knew him."

"I didn't, until yesterday. Mr. Sullivan has decided to purchase the property next door. He's moved into a trailer and is looking to build a home where he'll live between projects. For now he's taken it upon himself to visit the neighbors and make an effort to be a part of the community." Cass's previously flat lips now flushed out into a soft, happy little smile, her eyes looking at nothing in particular. It looked as if she had fallen into the category of groupie where Jess Sullivan was concerned. Wasn't she a bit old and experienced to be falling victim to movie stars? In her career she'd known a few, and I'd never seen that look on her face when she spoke of them.

"It sounds like you enjoyed your evening with him," I said.

"Well," Cass started, and then cleared her throat and went back to her breakfast. "Yes, I did. He's a very nice man who works hard and needs a place where he can relax and enjoy a slower pace. I think he'll be a nice addition to the community. Better yet, he has the money to really make some improvements to the land he's purchased. I told him that we'd be happy to help with anything he needs."

"How neighborly of you. It must be terribly draining to smile at a camera and dance in clubs all over the world for a living." I'd seen the magazine covers. From where I was sitting, life as a star didn't look too exhausting.

"Kate, please. Stop being so sarcastic. Just because he's famous doesn't mean he isn't like any other man looking for a place to call home." Cass speared a piece of bacon and chomped on it in irritation. Cass didn't appreciate it when I accused famous people of being lazy. She'd known famous people, had been somewhat famous herself as a lawyer and judge in Denver and then Aspen, and she knew how hard they worked.

I sighed to myself. She was probably right, and I said so. "Right. Well, in that case, I wish him luck." I pushed my chair back and carried my half-eaten muffin to the garbage can before placing the plate, cup, and knife in the soapy sink water next to Zinn. "Now I'm off to do some work of my own."

"Oh, and Kate?" Cass called as I put my hand on the doorknob. I turned back to face her. "I let Mr. Sullivan know that if I'm ever not around and he needs something, he can come see you at the cottage. I'm sure you'll be pleasant and helpful. After all, we *all* need help sometimes." Cass had made her point. I was living in her cottage on her beautiful property because I had needed help and she had offered it. She expected that I would do the same thing in return.

"Of course," I replied.

Chapter 2

Two weeks later, I was sitting at my desk in the cottage and tapping a pen on my forehead while I stared out the window at the view of the creek running the length of Cass's property. It was so pretty that it was easy for me to forget work and just stare. Too easy to let my mind wander away and daydream about other things. Like Ethan. Yes, thinking about Ethan was a great way to kill time. I smiled to myself and thought about his spiky brown hair and big chocolate-brown eyes. The grin he always had on his face. Ethan was great, and being his mom was the best thing I had going for me. I loved the hours before and after school and on the weekends, when we could be together. The daytime hours were often lonely. Sure, I wasn't totally alone. Somewhere close at hand I always had Cass and Zinn. Then there was the gardener, Paul, and the handyman, Ken, who were almost as mysterious as Zinn. Only Zinn was more mysterious, because I saw her so much that I should know more about her.

Sadly, Cass and Zinn and Paul and Ken were busy with full lives. There had been a time when I'd had a full life too. But that was before. This was now. And it was still an effort to remember to face forward rather than always looking nostalgically over my shoulder.

I frowned to myself and looked back down at my computer screen. This thought process was wandering into dangerous territory. It was painful and frustrating to look back at all I had lost and not let it suck me into a dark place. I'd better get back to work.

I set down the pen and wiggled my mouse to get my computer screen going again. I was fortunate to have found three small local businesses who had hired me to do their bookkeeping. I couldn't afford to lose their business by daydreaming. But before I could get going again, darn it, I heard the sound of a loud engine coming down the long drive from the highway.

Well, shoot, I guess I'd be forced to investigate. Can't let someone get the slip on me. I mean, good heavens, it would be irresponsible of me not to check on our visitor.

I walked to the front window and craned my neck to see around the corner of the big house. There was a tiny strip of drive that came out of the tree line before curving in front of the big house and being lost to my view. I only had a matter of seconds to see what the car looked like.

The engine got louder as that same sporty little car sped around the corner before disappearing again. There was only one other time I'd seen that little car, and remembering it made my toes curl.

Regardless of my continued embarrassment over the first impression I'd made, I was about ready to sneak down the rock path and spy on Cass when I was saved the trouble by him coming around the corner of the house and starting toward the cottage. He was tall and lean and had lovely dark hair. He was carrying a big red folder and, oh man, it really was *him*.

It had been two weeks since my heart had stopped beating when Jess Sullivan grinned at me. Wait, just to clarify things, it hadn't stopped beating in a good way. I was no young screaming girl wanting his autograph. It was more like how it would be if you saw the ghost of your grandfather walking toward you down the hallway. That heart-stopping moment when you see something you never in a million years expected to see. Yep, that kind of moment.

Anyhow, it had been two weeks, and I was feeling fairly certain that I wouldn't have to deal with Mr. Sullivan myself. I was supposed to be thrilled by this, but I had found myself disturbingly disappointed. Not that I wanted to get mixed up with his rich and fabulous life, but Aunt Cass had seen him occasionally and I was kind of jealous. I was all messed up. Just because I didn't want to be a screaming groupie didn't mean I wasn't a red-blooded American woman who wanted her chance to meet a superstar.

But I didn't really have time to think about that, because he was headed my way.

I experienced that dreadful feeling again of my heart not working right. I figured that it's got to be normal to react that way to a famous person. Right?

I turned to look in the mirror hung next to the door for just such occasions. Who was I kidding? I didn't hang that mirror there on the off chance that a superstar might drop in. I was being ridiculous. That mirror was there because the previous cottage dweller had hung it there. Most of the time I forgot about it altogether in my rush out the door.

Aunt Cass had told me that Jess Sullivan was just like any other man. Well, fine, then I'd treat him like any other man and get my heart rate under control. But wait, was that a mascara smear under my left eye? Dang, dang, dang. I licked my finger and rubbed it off, leaving my eye looking red and like I was having an allergic reaction. Nice.

I froze as the man of the hour knocked. On my door. *My* door. Yikes! This was bad. I was acting like one of those crazed fans I always made fun of. I took a deep breath, squared my shoulders, and put on a smile that I hoped would convey a pleasant, questioning look. I forced myself to ignore the smudged mascara and swollen under-eye situation as I swung open the door.

Somehow, in spite of it all, I was still surprised to see Jess Sullivan standing on the other side grinning down at me.

"Oh, hello, Mr. Sullivan. This is a surprise." I continued to smile. At least I was pretty sure I was smiling. Thank goodness the mirror wasn't in front of me. I didn't want to know.

He raised his eyebrows and gave me a questioning look. I was guessing that meant I was grimacing. Best thing to do at that point would be to wipe all expression off my face and just bag trying to be normal. Yep. That was the new plan. So I stopped my grin/grimace, put my hand on my hip, and looked back at him.

"Can I help you with something?" I pressed when he didn't say anything.

"Yes, actually, you can. Cassandra told me to bring this folder to you if she wasn't at home when I dropped by." He held out the folder I'd seen him carrying.

"Right. Okay." I took the folder and began to close the door, wanting nothing more than to put my awkwardness out of his view. "I'll give it to her when I see her later tonight."

The man had the audacity to reach up a hand and stop the door from closing. Didn't he know when a woman was trying to hide under a rock? I swung it back open.

"Yes?" I said.

He shot me the smile that had made him millions. I'm not sure what he was trying to accomplish with that smile, but I kept the door open, so it probably worked.

"Actually, I didn't catch your name," he said.

"It's pretty hard to catch something that isn't thrown," I replied in a lame attempt at a joke. He chuckled. It hadn't deserved a chuckle.

"Good point. In that case, I'll just start from the beginning. Hi, I'm Jess Sullivan." He held out a hand.

"Kate Evans," I replied as I spoke my tragically unfamous name and shook his movie-star hand in greeting.

"Nice to meet you, Kate. So you're Cassandra's niece?"

"Yeah."

"And you and your little boy live here in the guest house?"

"Yeah."

"And his name is Ethan?"

"Correct again." I smiled. I should try to be friendly.

"And you make messes?" He grinned. Never mind. I didn't want to be his friend, even if it meant I couldn't send a braggy Christmas letter this year all about my new famous friend, Jess Sullivan.

"Ha, ha, ha," I replied sarcastically. He chuckled again. Then we both just stood there for a few quiet seconds before he pushed back away from the door.

"Well, it was nice to meet you. I'll see you around," he said. He turned and sauntered away down my little gravel drive. I was practically forced by the genetic pull of my ancestors to watch that handsome specimen walking away.

He paused again by the creek, and I was embarrassed when he turned around and busted me standing in the doorway watching him walk away. He waved toward the creek and called back to me, "You have a great view here," before continuing on his way.

I couldn't decide what I thought about Jess Sullivan. But I did know that things were going to be very interesting around Cassandra's place if he kept showing up. And it appeared I'd be along for the ride.

A few days later, Ethan wanted to take Wade on a hike along a trail that began at the northern edge of Cass's property, looped up the mountain, and then ended on the south side of her house, near my lovely creek. Good mothers don't send their eight-year-olds off into the woods alone, so I went along too. It was early May, and the air was still blissfully cool in the evenings, the temperature perfect, which I had found to be a necessary factor in my motivation to exercise. Plus, we had some time between dinner and dark.

Ethan and Wade scampered ahead of me, investigating each bush and boulder with superhuman energy and probably burning off every last piece of chocolate that Zinn had snuck to Ethan after dinner. I was content to walk at a more sedate pace, enjoying the picture that boy and dog presented to me. I'd smile and wave whenever Ethan turned to check on my progress. It was postcard perfect, which is better than picture perfect. See, pictures are great, but the majority of pictures I take aren't ever shown to anyone but me. But postcards, well, those are the ones that you print out and mail to everyone. Snapshots worth sharing.

We eventually came to the center point of our hike, which happened to be a lookout in the foothills above Cass's property. It was our habit, whenever Ethan could coerce me into leaving the comfort of my cottage, to pause at the lookout point and enjoy the view of our little slice of life.

About five minutes after we'd stopped, just before we were getting ready to move on, Wade's ears pricked up and he looked in the direction we were about to go. Then Wade turned and began barking. Ethan patted his head to quiet him down, and once he stopped, we could hear some rustling and voices.

"Who do you think that is, Mom?" Ethan looked to me.

I shrugged. "First time I've ever run into someone up here."

We waited quietly until two heads bobbed into view through the brush just below us. All I could tell at first was that it was a dark-haired man and a bleached-blonde woman moving gracefully toward us. Then the man looked up. Rats!

I did a quick spot check on my current look. Sweats, check. Ponytail, check. Spill from dinner on my shirt, check. Adult-onset acne suddenly sprouting, check. Great. I was as ready as I'd ever be.

"Hey, Mr. Sullivan!" Ethan and Wade were off before I had a chance to stop them. Part of me admired the ease with which Ethan could make friends. To my knowledge, he'd only seen Jess Sullivan two or three times at the most, yet he didn't hold back at all in greeting him and welcoming him into his world. It was a skill I seemed to have lost over the past couple of years.

Wade reached the intruders first, and Jess—*when did I start calling him that?*—greeted the big dog with a scratch on the head before smiling at Ethan and giving him a high five. They greeted each other with words I couldn't hear before Ethan gestured toward me and Jess looked to where he was pointing.

"Hi, Kate," he said, raising his voice to cover the distance and smiling. Then he turned to his hiking companion, who had been focused on Wade slobbering near her feet, and said something to her. She glanced up at me and my heart stopped . . . again.

The good thing about this was that it proved my heart wasn't just stopping for Jess Sullivan. That would have been awkward and probably painful in the end. The bad thing was that it meant I was face-to-face with the second famous face I had met in the past month. She wasn't quite in league with Jess's superstardom, but she was up-and-coming and definitely recognizable. And I was once again wearing sweats. Of all the bad luck.

"Holy cow, Mom! Do you see who is with Mr. Sullivan?" Ethan squealed in my direction.

"Um, yes, I do," I replied quietly, unsure of the protocol in a situation like this.

Ethan had no such reservations. He turned back to the beautiful woman and said, "You're that pretty lady who was in that same movie as Mr. Sullivan. My mom and I watched it just a few weeks ago. And now we get to meet you too. This is so great!"

The woman smiled kindly down at Ethan, and then her gaze met mine again. I started walking toward them and talking in an effort to look in control.

"Yes, well, it's nice to see you again, Jess." *Oh, man, did I just call him that to his face?* "And, uh, so nice to meet you, uh, Ms., uh . . ." I started to say her name but then hesitated when I realized I didn't remember her last name. I did remember her first name because it was so beautiful—Vivienne—but it felt overly-familiar to call her that when we'd never been introduced.

I'd even gone so far as to catalog it in the back of my mind, wishing I was a Vivienne rather than plain old Kate. Viviennes had flowing locks of blond hair, porcelain skin, and blue, blue eyes. Viviennes didn't wear sweats—heck, they didn't even sweat. And they had long, graceful legs and arms that could reach the high cupboards in the kitchen.

Kate was none of those things. Kate was five foot four in heels and slightly heftier than she would like to be, and she had wild, wavy hair that could be kindly described as auburn on a great day. Kate kept a step stool in the kitchen. I sighed to myself.

"Lawson. Vivienne Lawson," she spoke up. Her voice was dripping with ice. It was the strangest thing. I guess famous people, or at least people aspiring to be famous, don't love it when people forget their names. My mistake. I smiled at the ice princess.

"Right, Ms. Lawson. So nice to meet you. I hope you're enjoying your hike." I stiffly held my smile and glanced at Jess as I began herding Ethan and Wade toward the path.

"Don't leave on account of us," Jess said.

"No, really, we're just heading back down. Got to get home before dark." I was talking quickly and practically had Ethan in a headlock to get him to follow me.

"But, Mom . . ." he tried before I cut him off.

"Bye!" I chirped and nudged Ethan into the trees and out of sight.

I could have sworn I heard Jess chuckle. Vivienne sure had some thoughts to share. I didn't stick around for the monologue.

The next morning, there was knocking on my door at the awful hour of 7 a.m. I pulled myself out of bed and stumbled to the front door.

"There had better be a fire!" I grumbled as I opened it.

"That's probably what it would take to get you up any earlier," Cass replied in her typical composed manner.

As usual, she was totally put together and looked as fresh and cheerful as the sun itself. Cass kept her lovely white hair shoulder length, with soft waves. Her makeup always looked expertly applied, and she wasn't fond of crazy bright lipsticks like others of her generation. This morning she was wearing a long, flowing black skirt with a white button-up shirt and her denim jacket. She looked ready to go to town. Actually, she always looked ready to go to town. She often told me that in her line of work, appearance had mattered. She was probably right, as she continued to be highly respected even after retirement.

Cass, aware of my morning brain-functioning issues, gently moved past me into the cottage and took a quick look around before seating herself on the edge of a couch cushion. She had a large manila envelope in her hands and set it down on the coffee table. I took comfort in knowing I was a fairly tidy person, despite my fondness for accidents, and sat on a chair across from her.

"Good morning, little bird, what makes you rise so soon?" I questioned when Cass was quiet for a moment.

"Well, actually, I have a favor to ask of you."

"In all fairness, I have to tell you that waiting until after 9 a.m. would have yielded you better results." I yawned.

"You're probably right." Cass's eyes twinkled back at me. "However, I don't have the luxury of waiting until you rally yourself. I need to go out of town for a couple of weeks and have some things that I need you to handle for me."

"What about Zinn?" Usually Zinn kept loose ends going while Cass was out of town, and I was curious as to why things would be different this time.

"Zinn is coming with me."

"Wait, what?" This jolted me out of my sleepy state faster than anything else could have. Zinn never, never, never left Owens land. Okay, that was an exaggeration. I was aware that she occasionally went to church on Sunday. But I was fairly certain that she hadn't left the town of Clark Springs in at least eighty of her hundred years of life. "Why? Is she okay? Are you okay?" I was gripped with worry.

"Kate, settle down." Cass raised an eyebrow at me.

"I can't. Is everyone okay?" I really needed Cass and Zinn to be okay.

"Yes, we're okay."

"Are you sure? You're not hiding something, are you?"

"She isn't Charlie, sweetheart, and neither am I," Cass gently replied as she reached over and took one of my hands.

The reference to my deceased husband was both painful and calming. Cass knew why I was overreacting, and she was reminding me in the only way she knew how. Her hand felt warm and soothing on mine. I took a deep breath and nodded. I understood what she was saying. If something was wrong with one of them, she would tell me. She would never hide it from me the way Charlie had. They wouldn't blindside me. They would give me warning.

"Now, Zinn is coming along because I am going to Salt Lake City on business and her family lives nearby." She released my hand and sat back up. "She's getting older and feels like it's time to see them."

"Salt Lake City, huh? So that's where she's from?" Cass nodded. For the first time, something Zinn-related had been confirmed. It was enough to distract me momentarily from Charlie. "Just how old is Zinn?" I couldn't help pressing the matter. "And what do you mean 'it's time to see them'?"

"Really, Katherine, have some respect," Cass chastised. I was both shot down and *Katherined*. Darn it.

"So what is it that you need me to do?" I slouched down in my chair and accepted that I wasn't going to get any more information on Zinn this morning. Cass smiled at my tactical failure.

"While I'm gone, Ken is going to be working with a contractor to do some updating in the kitchen." Cass leaned forward and tapped one manicured finger on the envelope she'd set down. "In this envelope are explicit instructions on my tastes and preferences. Ken has the same paperwork. Please read over it, and do not allow him to vary from my list. If I come back to find my kitchen painted bubblegum pink, or worse, then I will hold you responsible."

I nodded, and Cass gave me one of her patented looks, letting me know that she didn't believe my commitment was real. It was really sad that she'd never been a mother, because she had some seriously good looks in her repertoire.

"No, I won't just throw the envelope on my desk and pretend to read it," I dutifully stated, pulling a fake annoyed face.

She smiled. "Thank you. Wade will also need to be exercised." I gave her a thumbs-up. Ethan would be more than happy to help with that. "And, lastly, Mr. Sullivan mentioned seeing you and Ethan up on the mountain trail last night."

“What? How have you talked with him between then and now? It’s 7 a.m.!”

Cass actually blushed a bit and chuckled before replying, which was highly questionable. “Oh, no. We spoke last night after he got back. He stopped by the house with that lovely woman, Ms. Lawson, to see if I’d had any luck with the information in the folder he left with you.”

“Oh. So you met Ms. Lawson then?” She’d called her lovely.

“Yes. But that’s not the point.” Cass’s lips thinned, and I wondered if she really had found Vivienne Lawson to be lovely, or if she was just being polite. “Mr. Sullivan mentioned that he’d like to become more familiar with the trails on his land for hiking and ATV riding. He’d also like to actually make up a map of sorts for future guests he’ll have staying with him.”

I didn’t say anything. I wasn’t sure if Cass was just making conversation or if there was a bomb about to be dropped at the end of that explanation. Rather than continuing, Cass looked at me as though I should know where this was leading.

“So . . .” I fished around a bit, assuming she wanted my input. “Why don’t you put him in touch with the local Boy Scout troop? They’re always hiking and getting lost and having to perform rescue missions in the area. If anyone should know their way around there, it’s the people always having to find their way out. Besides, they’d be really excited to help out a star.”

“Well, I suggested you.”

“Me?” I jerked up straight in my seat as my mouth dropped open.

Cass was quiet for another moment, almost as if slightly embarrassed to say the next part. “Yes, well, when you first came here after that terrible year of trying to muscle through everything, you used to wander around a lot and clear your head. I just assumed that out of all of us you would know the most about the area. And I didn’t want to suggest just anyone.”

“I see.” And I did. “You think I could use a friend and saw an opportunity.” As if Jess Sullivan needed a friend. He could have any friend he wanted. As if Jess Sullivan *wanted* me for a friend.

This was not about helping Jess. This was about me. This was about Cassandra Owens trying to make the wallflower get out a bit more. I was humiliated to realize that she was using Jess Sullivan to accomplish her task. I was being pawned off on the pretty boy. The cliché of the jock befriending the geek. I'd never be able to look him in the eye again.

Cass didn't say anything for a few moments. The multiple silences in this conversation were getting to me. I could hear the ticking of the clock over the sink and the sound of Ethan's alarm kick on from his bedroom. Time to get up.

Finally, Cass cleared her throat and started to stand. "I just think that you could help each other, that's all." She might as well have been saying, *He needs a math tutor, and I suggested you. He can make you popular, and you can help him with his homework.*

I nodded and stood with her. We walked the few steps to the doorway in silence, me looking at the floor, anywhere but at her.

"Listen, Kate, after Charlie—" Cass began. But I held up a hand and met her eyes.

"I know all about after Charlie," I said in a flat voice that I hoped conveyed my desire to keep the subject closed. I glanced at Ethan's room in what I hoped was an exclamation point at the end of my hint. Then I looked back at her. "I'll help him if he calls. Have a good trip."

Cass smiled softly at me. "I will." After a quick hug, she closed the door behind her.

As I sped through the morning routine with Ethan, my mind was unfocused and melancholy. It seemed like my life had been split down the middle. Everything was *Before Charlie* and *After Charlie*. Before Charlie got sick and died, I was a naively happy stay-at-home mom to a sweet little boy. After Charlie, I was an undereducated, struggling single parent with a slightly less sweet and hurting little boy. Before Charlie, I knew I was loved and cherished. After Charlie, I wondered if anyone found me beautiful and wanted my company above all the others. Before Charlie, I had been the one to stop and see the beauty around me. After Charlie, I had barely made it through that first year before Aunt Cassandra had shown up on my doorstep, said enough was enough, and packed me back to her home in Clark Springs.

Coming back to the present, I walked Ethan to the bus stop and waved him off. Then I trudged back up my little gravel driveway. I was too caught up in my own ponderings to take breakfast at Cass's house, and the beautiful creek held no interest for me. Instead, I threw myself onto the sofa, pulled an afghan over myself, and stared at the picture of Charlie that I had put on an end table near the sofa.

Charlie. Charles Evans. Sometimes when I saw his smiling face in that picture I would feel irrationally angry. It had taken me a long time to be able to see the beauty in the photo. To remember the park he'd been standing in. To remember that Ethan was behind me making faces while I snapped the shot. Charlie had a grin that split his face in two and made you unable to help smiling back. He had been all golden sunshine and happiness.

But he had betrayed me. Betrayed my trust. One day he had just died. He'd left me and Ethan without a goodbye.

Oh, I knew a lot of people died suddenly without any final goodbyes. But then again, a lot of people don't know beforehand that their life will be shortened and choose not to tell their loved ones. A lot of people hadn't already watched their wife grieve the sudden loss of her parents. He had known what sudden death did to me, and still he had chosen to put me through it again. It was the only selfish act he'd ever committed, and the most painful one he could have chosen.

I didn't realize what Charlie had hidden from me until I'd rushed to the hospital and heard the ER doctor say, "I'm sorry, Mrs. Evans, but in cases like these—" And I'd interrupted him.

"What do you mean, 'cases like these'?" I'd asked. Tears were streaming down my face and Ethan was shaking by my side. I had been a wreck, having flashbacks of being called to the hospital when my parents had been killed. I had held tightly to Ethan's hand as I somehow managed to keep from collapsing.

"Well, when there is a tumor on the brain like your husband had," he explained.

In response to my blank look, he'd had to explain a lot more. Like how several months before, Charlie had been seen by his regular physician because of headaches and dizziness. But Charlie had told me it was just a regular yearly physical. He'd had tests, and he'd known that he had a rapidly growing brain tumor. He had known his prognosis wasn't good, but he'd kept on living like everything was normal. Work each day, yard work, errands, and family fun time on the weekends. We'd had a great life. At least, I'd thought we'd had a great life. But he'd kept me out of the most important information. The fact that his life was winding down.

In the end, the doctor couldn't explain why Charlie hadn't told me. But our lawyer could. He handed me a letter shortly after the funeral. I hadn't even known we'd had a lawyer. While I had gone ignorantly forward with life, Charlie had been making plans. He'd only had a small amount of life insurance. We were in our late twenties and didn't feel it was necessary to bulk up on that while building Charlie's career, but he'd managed to arrange for the costs of the funeral to be covered. And he'd put a tiny amount into a nest egg for Ethan to go to college. But there was nothing for daily living. Nothing to help me pay our mortgage or car payments. And, most important, there was nothing that could help prepare me for suddenly finding myself alone.

Charlie had gotten to say goodbye, in the end, in the letter. He'd taken even that away from me. I hadn't gotten to say goodbye, and I was so angry knowing that I could have if only he'd let me. He'd tried to explain that he hadn't wanted our last months together to be burdened with the heavy knowledge that it was coming to an end. He'd wanted only good memories to be left behind, carefree and easy. I tried to understand, but I wished he would have trusted me.

For the longest time, I couldn't return Charlie's smile when looking at his picture. Instead, I saw the face of someone who could betray me and hurt me. Someone who taught me to question everything and had me running through hundreds of conversations in my head, not sleeping, wondering if he'd dropped hints, reworking events in this new light. Someone I wasn't sure I'd even really known.

Chapter 3

Two days after Cass and Zinn left for Utah, Jess had called about showing him one or two trails. During a somewhat forced and awkward phone conversation, at least on my end, he had suggested I go over to his place after dropping Ethan at the bus stop. That way we could get the exploring done before the weather warmed in the afternoon. I had been too embarrassed by my lingering thoughts over the geek-forced-on-the-jock situation and hadn't said much other than halfheartedly agreeing to be there.

As I left the main road and entered the clearing where Jess's camp trailer came into view, I was grateful to see that the only vehicle in the area was that little sports car. Maybe Ms. Vivienne Lawson had packed her ice-queen attitude back to LA. I hadn't mentioned her during my brief phone call with Jess, and neither had he. However, the knowledge that she may still be visiting prompted me to put on jeans, a new shirt, and the nicer looking of my two pairs of hiking boots. I'd had enough of being caught in my sweats and stained shirts. I had brushed my hair up into a high ponytail and even taken the time to put on some makeup. I just knew that in a hotel room somewhere Auntie Cass was smiling at her success. Me, out of the house, with a man. She was in heaven.

As I pulled my car to a stop and shut off the engine, Jess swung open the door of the trailer and stepped down into the dirt. He, too, was wearing jeans and hiking boots. At least I'd dressed correctly for the occasion. He had a baseball cap pulled low over his dark brown hair and a canteen in one hand. In his other hand was a piece of paper that was bending in the slight breeze. He smiled at me as I got out of the car and fumbled with my keys.

"Morning, neighbor," he said as he came to stand next to me.

"Hey," I managed in reply through my suddenly parched mouth.

"I got a map." He put the piece of paper down on the hood of my car and gestured for me to look. "It shows the boundary lines of my property so that we have an idea of the area we're working in," he explained.

"I see. So where do you want to start?" I asked.

"Well, what's your favorite area to hike?"

"Uh, all of it," I stupidly mumbled. Jess chuckled. It was low and quiet. It made my insides twist a bit, and then they twisted a bit more when I realized how silly I was being.

"Okay. So if you were to take a tourist hiking here, where would you take them?" he pressed. I thought about it for a few moments as I looked toward the foothills.

"Probably the waterfall."

"There's a waterfall? That's great!" Jess was super enthusiastic about this waterfall idea. In my opinion, he was too excited. He was probably used to tropical waterfalls. This was a Colorado waterfall. Big difference.

"It's nothing major. Small, but pretty." I paused to see if he was still interested.

"Where is it on the map?" He glanced down to where the map was resting on my car. I looked at it for a bit, made a guess, and pointed to one edge of the map, where the side of his property bordered Cass's land. "Great. Let's go." Jess smiled and folded the map before tucking it into his back pocket.

I shrugged and started hiking in that direction. Jess quickly caught up, his stride much longer than mine, as I looked for the head of the trail that would lead up to the small—had I already mentioned how small?—waterfall. In fact, I was beginning to feel a bit guilty for calling it a waterfall when he was probably going to think it was more like a trickle of water falling off a rock.

"So you've hiked around here a lot, huh?" he asked as he matched my shorter strides.

I glanced up at him and then back to the ground before answering. "Uh, yes." I thought the question was odd. Hadn't I been asked to guide him because of my knowledge of the trails?

"Great. So that should be really helpful."

I nodded, and a few moments of strained silence followed. Actually, I had no idea if Jess found it strained or if it was just me, but to me it was like the silence before a tiger jumps out of the woods and attacks you.

The area had grown over in the months since anyone had hiked it from Jess's property. Ethan and I had figured out a trail that accessed it from Cass's side and had stopped using this one. I paused in front of some overgrown brush and took stock of the landmarks. Then I walked a few steps to my left and then a few more. There it was. I pushed tree branches out of my way and stomped down the weeds.

"This is the trailhead. You want to mark it somehow?" I said as I turned to find Jess standing closer than I'd realized. He was stealthy. I wondered if all super-fit people were or if that was his gift.

"Sounds like a good idea." Jess grabbed a red handkerchief from his back pocket and tied it to one of the tree branches I was holding on to. Then he nodded at me to keep going.

Problem was that there was no way I was hiking with Jess Sullivan behind me. Not happening. Aside from the fact that he was much easier on the eyes, I wasn't going to be able to concentrate on hiking if I had to worry about how much of an eyeful he was getting.

"Why don't you take the lead?" I suggested.

"I'm good. I know it's my property, but you're the one who knows the trail. And besides, ladies first." He smiled. He clearly thought I'd be pleased with his gentlemanly behavior and deference. I was not. Our gazes held while I thought about what angle to play. In the end, he won. He grabbed the tree branch I was holding out of my hand and held out his free arm in a gesture for me to proceed. It was either do so or tell him I didn't want him hiking behind me.

I started hiking as he chuckled from behind me. Behind. Oh, dear heaven. This was going to be the longest hike of my life. I mean, I'd worn dark jeans to make my legs look slimmer and attempted to give myself a face-lift by putting my hair in an uber-tight ponytail, but there is no way to suck in your backside. None. There is nothing more honest about its shape than a bum.

The incline was steady but not overly steep until we cleared the foothills. At that point, it turned into a steep zigzag trail before leveling out and entering a ravine with a creek running through the bottom of it. At the back of the ravine was the much-touted waterfall. I was already prepared for him to be disappointed.

We didn't speak much as we hiked. I couldn't have even if I'd wanted to. It wasn't from the exercise but from the way my heart was pounding as I imagined Jess mentally measuring the breadth and width of my derriere. I was pretty sure he was comparing it to the size of Ms. Vivienne Lawson's tight little bottom. I just knew that he was wondering if I'd float if he threw me into the pool at the bottom of the falls. Having him behind me was worse than I'd initially anticipated. I was going crazy wondering what he could possibly be thinking.

"Nice view," Jess suddenly said from behind me. I froze midstride and sucked in a harsh breath.

"Excuse me!" I whipped around, prepared to smack him for his comment. Either that or cry. My hand was curled at my side, and tears had sprung into their holding queue behind my eyes. I was prepared for either reaction.

But Jess was looking out over the view of his building plot and not at me. The breath whooshed out of my lungs, and I couldn't help a relieved giggle from escaping.

"You don't agree?" he asked upon hearing my laugh.

"No, no. It's great," I replied awkwardly.

We finished the zigzag into the ravine, and I held my breath as Jess took his first look at the waterfall . . . correction, drizzle.

"It's small," I stated in an apologetic tone.

"Hey, things don't have to be big to be pretty," Jess commented as he walked toward the falls. I followed in silence, having no idea how to interpret that comment. Did that mean he favored small things over larger things? Fantastic. Bummer for my buns and thighs. But hey, bonus points for my height and shoe size.

Not that I wanted Jess to favor me in any way—it was just that here I'd been obsessing over the size of my caboose the entire hike and now he was telling me that small things are beautiful. I couldn't decide if I'd be calling Jenny Craig when I got home or swinging through the drive-through at the Shake Shack.

I stayed back a bit as Jess explored. The farther he got from me, the more I was able to relax and enjoy the serenity of the area. The trees were waving a bit, and the sound of the water falling down the rock face was soothing. It really was beautiful. Jess would have a great time bringing his friends up for picnics and, well, whatever it was that the rich and famous did when they were on vacation.

"Think an ATV could fit up that trail?" Jess called from beside the falls. I nodded rather than yell back. With some clearing, it would make a great ATV trail.

Before long, Jess decided it would be great to take off his shoes and socks and wade around in the pool. I sat on the sidelines and watched as he rolled up his pant legs and stepped into the shallow water. It only came to just above his knee at the deepest part. When he reached the center, he turned to me and smiled.

"This is great. You should come in." He motioned for me to do just that.

"No, thanks," I replied. I was still sour about my perceived chubbiness and my aunt Cass thinking that hiking with a movie star was the best idea ever. The last thing I was going to do was uncover body parts. Besides, I had worn clean clothes, but I hadn't gone as far as to shave my legs for the occasion.

Before I could follow that train of thought too far down the track, I was splashed in the face with a handful of water. I spluttered and wiped my hands over my face, shaking the excess water off before glaring at the culprit. Jess sported a grin the size of a million-dollar paycheck.

"Not cool," I said, wiping at droplets on my arms and hoping my shirt wasn't too wet. "I actually did my makeup today," I grumbled.

"Come on," he said. "It feels great after that hike."

I shook my head. Apparently that was his cue to cup another handful of water and splash me with it. This time it hit near the top of my head and worked its way down my neck as well. I jumped up.

"Mr. Sullivan, stop it."

"Mr. Sullivan? You can't be serious. That's my dad." Jess smiled at me. Then he splashed me again.

"What are you doing?" I cried as I fanned out my shirt to try to dry it a little. Was he so handsome and famous that he had a hard time understanding the word *no*?

Jess stopped his attack and put his hands down by his side. His eyes sparkled with amusement, but he had at least stopped grinning.

"I'm trying to have some fun." He shrugged.

"Well, what made you think I'd want to have this kind of fun with you?" I was maybe starting to yell a little bit on accident.

"Nothing, really," he admitted. His eyes were losing some sparkle.

Suddenly, I felt the humiliation of Aunt Cass's pawning me off on him, the embarrassment of walking ahead of him up the trail, and the mortifying realization that I was standing there refusing to have fun with a man whom most women regarded as an eleven on a scale of one to ten. I was such a stick-in-the-mud. And I was far too ashamed to apologize. So I let the feelings boil up into anger and I lashed out.

"Good. Because I don't know who you think you are. You don't even know me. I'm not one of your little groupies." I pointed a finger at him. "What do you want from me? Why am I up here? You could have found all of this without me." I gestured wildly around.

Jess was silent as he watched me throw my hands up in the air and stomp away from the water back toward the trail.

"You don't need me, and I don't want to be part of some weird little plan that you and my aunt came up with." I whirled around at the head of the trail and put my hands on my hips. "I'm not going to be the girl that gets pawned off on the jock! And I don't want you looking at my . . . fanny!"

And then I left him. I left him standing there in the sad little Colorado puddle as I stomped and huffed and kicked my way down the trail. I ranted and raved, letting the forest creatures hear my ramblings, until I reached my car and slammed the door shut behind me.

Then the horror of it all came crashing down on me. I had just told Jess Sullivan to stop looking at my fanny. My fanny! No one under the age of eighty-five used that word, and I'd yelled it at one of the most handsome and famous men in America while throwing a temper tantrum. It was too much to wish for a sudden and painless death to overtake me. I knew that. But I also knew that I could never, ever see him again without wanting to crawl into a hole.

Until that point I had never really seen how fast my little car could race down a dirt road. I'm telling you now, that baby can fly.

About an hour later, I awoke to the sound of knocking on the front door. I had fallen asleep after letting the tears burst from me in horrified sobbing. What on earth was wrong with me? I was used to feeling emotional—that was just part of my makeup. But it had been years since I'd allowed those emotions to boil over and scorch things. I sat up on the couch and rubbed my face. Another knock, this one more persistent.

"Kate? You in there?" a male voice called. It was Jess. Darn it. I couldn't face him. "Kate, please, open up. I came to apologize." He knocked again. "Please?"

"Go away!" I called back.

"I can't, Kate. Please?" he replied.

I started thinking about Ken and Paul overhearing and Cass finding out that Jess Sullivan had been banging on my door and begging to apologize. I sighed. Best to get it over with and get back to my normal life. Jess would want nothing to do with me now, which I had kind of wanted, but not in the way it had played out.

"Fine. Just give me a minute," I yelled back as I stood up. I went into the bathroom and did the best I could to wash my face and fix my hair before venturing back out.

When I swung open the door I was greeted with a bouquet of wildflowers and the top of a baseball cap. The flowers lowered and Jess was standing behind them. For once, he wasn't grinning. He was dusty and his pants were a little muddy at the bottom. He pushed the flowers toward me but didn't attempt to follow them inside.

"Hey." He tugged at the brim of his cap and looked out toward the creek before meeting my apprehensive eyes again. "For the record, I wasn't looking at your, uh, bottom," he began. I felt a blush rise up my neck and heat my face. This was terrible. I shouldn't have answered the door. Facing Aunt Cass would have been better.

"I hope you aren't expecting me to thank you for not ogling me," I retorted. The corner of his mouth twitched a bit, but he kept a smile from forming.

"No, I don't suppose you would."

"Thanks for the flowers, I guess. See ya." I started to close the door, but Jess stopped it with a big boot. New, I noticed. I hoped he had blisters so that I wouldn't be the only one suffering right now.

"Listen, I'm really sorry. I just thought that, well, I don't know what I thought. Cassandra made it sound like you could use a friend, and I don't really know anyone around here, so . . ." he trailed off.

"I see," I replied in a way that said a lot about how annoyed I was.

He fidgeted a bit. "It's . . . just . . . your aunt suggested you could use a friend, and I took that to mean that you'd asked her to make introductions. I thought the trail-guide thing was kind of a ruse. In my line of work, it wouldn't be the first time."

While I didn't exactly appreciate him adding that this stuff happened to him all the time, he had a point. I had thought the same thing about the trail guide being a ruse. But I'd never thought it came from him. I'd known all along that Cass was the mastermind. The fact that he'd thought I'd been looking for a way to meet him made the shame burn brighter.

I pushed out a sigh. "Look, you don't need help making friends, and my aunt told me that you needed a trail guide. I don't want to play games with you or be your little vacation girlfriend while Vivienne Lawson is your Hollywood girlfriend. I'm not interested. I have a full life." This was maybe a sort of lie. No woman who had eyeballs and was sucking air wouldn't be interested in spending time with him.

"I'm not looking for a vacation girlfriend." His brows creased together.

"Good. 'Cause I'm not looking for anyone of any sort!" Take that! Point for me!

"Okay. Now that we're clear on that . . ." Jess shook his head like he had no idea what had just happened. "I hope we can try to be friends."

"You tried to get me into a pond . . ."

"Puddle."

"Even though I had no desire to get soaked . . ."

"To wade."

"And you were being overly familiar with me. You're practically a stranger."

"Who was asked to be your friend," he stated.

"Excuse me?" The self-righteous anger seeped out of my rigid back, and I began to want to curl up and die.

"I thought your aunt wanted me to be your friend. She's been so helpful getting me set up with good contractors and local businesses that I thought I'd return the favor and befriend her niece." He shrugged like it was the most natural and nonhumiliating thing in the world.

“You scratch my back, I’ll scratch yours, huh?” I managed to choke out.

“Right.” Then he smiled. After all that had just happened he managed to give me a grin and look relieved, like we finally understood each other. But he didn’t understand anything. He didn’t understand that my cheeks felt hot with mortification and that my hands felt clammy with nerves.

“How very Hollywood,” I mumbled. His grin slipped. But I plugged on. “Okay. Well, consider your debt paid off. Thank you for the lovely hike today and these beautiful flowers. It was the beginning and ending of a beautiful friendship. It’s played itself out, and we can move on.” I managed to get the words out around a lump the size of a buffalo in my throat. My hands were shaking around the stems of the flowers, and I knew my face had to be as red as a cherry. “Maybe I’ll see you around sometime.”

Jess’s smile faded a bit as the words penetrated.

“I’ll make sure to let Aunt Cassandra know that you fulfilled your side of the bargain. Have a nice afternoon, Mr. Sullivan.” I gave him a huge, cheesy grin with trembling lips as I quietly closed the door on his handsome face.

I turned and slid my back down the door so that I was braced against it and leaned my head back. The flowers fell to my lap, and I looked up at the ceiling. *Well*, I thought, *that couldn’t have gone any worse.*

The next morning, I stood holding Ethan’s little hand as we waited for the bus. I thought for the millionth time of how grateful I was for this boy. When I turned to look down at him, he smiled up at me, and I couldn’t help but pull him into a tight hug as the bus came into view. He giggled and hugged me back, still young enough to want this kind of attention from his mother. I gave him one last pat on the back and watched as he climbed up the big stairs before choosing a seat. After waving as his bus drove away, I headed back to the cottage to spend a few hours buried in my bookkeeping work.

It was mind-numbing and routine and exactly what I needed to get my mind off the humiliating and immature episode involving Jess the day before. I gave myself a stern pep talk in which I reminded myself that I was a responsible mother and a grown woman. The entire thing had been a silly misunderstanding. I had said some pretty unkind things, and, obviously, as neighbors I knew I would see him again. I determined that I would handle our next encounter with maturity and grace. I hoped.

By the time I'd finished working, I'd decided I'd been negligent of the tasks Cass gave me and went to check on the work being done in the big-house kitchen. Also, I was running low on groceries and needed food after skipping breakfast. Really, I was doing Zinn a favor by eating any leftovers so she wouldn't have to clean out moldy old food after returning from a vacation.

Which reminded me, I needed to do some rewriting of her history now that I knew she had family and had possibly even originated in Salt Lake City. It didn't help me narrow down her age, though, considering Salt Lake City had been founded back in the mid–eighteen hundreds. Had she immigrated in a covered wagon? And I was still wondering what Cass had meant when she'd said it was time for Zinn to see her family.

My thoughts were returned to the present when I swung open the back door and walked into the biggest disaster zone I'd ever seen in Cass's home. Ken and two other men were standing amid the wreckage of what had previously been a gorgeous kitchen. Cabinets were on the floor, cut into big chunks. There was no countertop or sink or, *gasp*, refrigerator! White dust coated everything. I let the door slam up against my rear end and push me into the room before it shut with a bang. I'd been too surprised by the mess to remember to stop the self-closing hinges. The three men turned at the sound.

I tried not to laugh at the looks on their faces, or at the fact that they were coated with the same mystery dust layered over every surface. They looked like three gray-haired men, even though the two strangers were obviously young.

"Hello, Kate," Ken spoke first.

"Hello, Ken." I let a little laugh squeak out. I couldn't help it. They looked so funny. "This is quite a mess." I gestured around.

Ken nodded. "Yes. This is why Ms. Owens wanted it done when she's not at home."

"Obviously." I looked toward where the pantry used to be, my stomach not quite willing to give up on the thought of breakfast. "I don't suppose there's any food lurking around here?" I returned my gaze to Ken. He shook his head, but one of the two mystery men piped up.

"Sorry, but unless you like donuts coated in dust and warm milk to choke it down with, we can't help you." He smiled, revealing a nice smile and dust-free teeth. Our eyes met and, with a jolt, I realized that under that dust was a nice face. Possibly even handsome. And, even more important, no one had told him to smile at me.

An answering smile warmed my face as I replied, "How warm and how much dust?" Wait, was I flirting? This was new and unexpected. Both of the younger guys grinned, and the one who had spoken gestured to an area out of sight from the back door.

I turned to my right and found a box with two donuts left inside, sitting next to a mostly empty half-gallon container of milk. The lid of the box was sitting next to it. Typical. They could have taken two seconds to put the lid back on and those donuts would have been edible. They would have been a perfect pick-me-up. I sighed with longing as I picked one up with two fingers and examined it from every angle. Behind me I heard the two young guys laugh, and I turned, still holding the donut, to give them a frown.

"It hurts me to see a donut in such sad shape." I waved it at them.

The second guy, who hadn't spoken yet, piped in. "Well, it hurts us to see a lady starving. How about we make it up to you by taking you to lunch later?" He smiled.

I couldn't have been more shocked by that lunch invitation if it had come from a chimpanzee. I was ready to laugh it off and decline, which would have been the normal thing to do, but then I thought about Jess and suddenly I was totally on board with letting two young men take me to eat. I wasn't exactly a dinosaur. I mean, how much younger than me could they really be? As I opened my mouth to accept their invitation, Ken suddenly found his voice again.

"I'm not sure that's a good idea, boys. Ms. Owens wouldn't like you getting involved with her niece here," he said.

He'd called them boys. Shoot. Maybe they were even younger than I'd thought. In fact, maybe they were Ken's sons. Still, they were voluntarily asking me to join them for lunch. No one had talked them into it.

And maybe I wanted word to get back to Aunt Cass that I could snag some friends on my own.

"Actually, Ken, Aunt Cass has been telling me I need to get out more. I think she'd be very disappointed to find that you'd let me starve to death in her absence." I shifted my gaze back to the boys and grinned. "I'm in. What time?"

Boy-man number one informed me that they'd take their lunch break at noon, which was in about thirty minutes, and they'd meet me at the red truck out front. I nodded, smiled at Ken, and practically floated out the back door to my cottage. I had a lunch date. And I'd done it all on my own. Eat that, naysayers!

I quickly changed into clean clothing, redid my hair into its high and now somewhat flirty ponytail, and repaired my makeup. At high noon I met the two workers in front of Cass's house, as specified. They had cleaned up quite a bit, and I got my first real look at them. I was relieved to see that the first guy, flirty donut-man, was older than I'd begun to fear he was. The second really was a boy. He was tall and lean with bright red hair and a big friendly smile. A total golden retriever type. I could practically see his tail wagging as he motioned me toward the front door of the four-door truck and opened it.

"I'm Eli," he said.

I smiled at him and climbed into the cab as I offered my name in return. "I'm Kate. Nice to meet you, Eli. And thanks for getting the door for me." I buckled up as Eli closed the door and then turned to find myself staring into big hazel eyes. I sighed inside. No matter how old you get, you're never too old to get butterflies. And those hazel eyes were butterfly worthy.

"Hi, Kate. I'm Alec." Oh, Alec. Nice. It fit him. Without the dust I could see that his hair was light brown and he was, indeed, nice to look at. This day was going way up for me, considering how it had started.

"Hi, Alec. Nice to meet you too. So where are we going to go to save me from a fate worse than death?" I cheerfully smiled at Alec and then angled my head to share my smile with Eli in the back seat.

"Fate worse than death?" Eli questioned.

I nodded. "Yes, missing meals. Worse than death."

Alec laughed quietly as he started the engine, bringing it roaring to life.

"How about the Burger Stop?" Eli offered. I grinned to myself. He had to be younger than eighteen to think that the Burger Stop would be my top choice. That's where Ethan would go, though, given the option. Thinking of Ethan made me happy, and I decided that if Eli wanted a burger, we could get a burger.

"Sure, why not." I laughed. I glanced over at Alec, and we shared a look as if to say, *kids*. Then it hit me that we'd shared something, and I thought it was pretty amazing. Yes, indeed, this day was looking way, way up.

Lunch with Alec and Eli boosted my spirits. It was fun to have light conversation with two handsome men (okay, one man and one boy), get some food in my stomach, and remember that I could be totally normal.

My after-lunch dessert was that Alec asked me out for that Friday night as he walked me back to my cottage. Of course I said yes. It didn't matter that I'd been completely surprised by his asking me out. No girl on earth would have turned down that offer. Especially a girl who had something to prove. I gave him one last smile as I closed the door of my cottage behind me.

Then I noticed the wildflowers Jess had picked for me, still sitting on the kitchen counter where I'd left them the day before. Another embarrassed blush tried to rise up my neck as I once again thought about the humiliation I'd endured in exchange for those flowers. I opened the kitchen window, slid aside the screen, and returned those dratted flowers to nature. I didn't want them. I wanted nothing more to do with Jess and Cass and their little schemes. I'd landed a date on my own.

Chapter 4

Alec picked me up at six o'clock on Friday night. I smiled warmly as I opened the door and saw him standing there. He looked much cleaner than he had the last time I'd seen him, and I enjoyed taking inventory of what had been hidden from view before. Light-brown hair, hazel eyes, tanned skin. Taller than me, which if I were honest could be anyone from five foot four inches and up, and groomed nicely. The only downside was that Cass wasn't there to see my date whisk me away. A date I'd gotten on my own merit, thank you very much.

"Hey." He grinned down at me.

"Hey to you." I smiled back and turned to where Ethan was sitting on the couch playing something on the video-game system he'd conned Aunt Cass into buying him for Christmas. The teenage girl I'd hired for the night seemed to actually know what the game was, which I figured was a bonus for Ethan, although I wasn't too keen on the idea of paying her to play video games all night. Oh, well. At least they'd be happy, which would make me happy, which would make Cass eat her words . . . wait, no thoughts about that tonight. Sheesh!

"Ethan, I'll be back after your bedtime. Be good for Naomi," I called. Ethan, gentleman that he is, managed to wave a hand at me. Naomi at least had the decency to make eye contact and smile. Smart kid. She knew where the money was coming from.

"Don't worry, Mrs. Evans, we'll be fine," she said. Even though it was polite, I could have done without the "Mrs. Evans" part. I hadn't dated in years, and it made that sound so obvious, when all I wanted was to appear flirty and fun.

Alec stepped aside to let me exit the house before reaching back to close the door behind me. It was great. Over the past two years since

Charlie passed, I'd gotten used to chasing Ethan out the door and even occasionally getting shoved up against the door as Wade bolted by.

Alec and I walked to the same pickup truck that had taken us to lunch earlier in the week, and Alec, actual gentleman, opened the door for me. I smiled at him as I settled myself in the seat, smugly congratulating myself on landing such an ideal dinner partner.

"I hope you like Chinese," Alec said as we pulled onto the highway after leaving Cass's property.

"Sure." I smiled over at him demurely. I could be demure and cheerful. I could go with the flow and be a perfect little date. It was going to be lovely. There would be no explosions tonight about motives and ogling. And there would be absolutely no wilting wildflowers.

"Yeah, I thought we'd go down to Oakdale. I've heard that the Jade Flower is great," he replied.

"Oh, sure, yeah." I smiled back. Oakdale was a thirty-minute drive from Clark Springs. That would put me back later than I'd anticipated. I hoped that was okay with Naomi. Before the "mom worry" could take root, I reminded myself that I was fun, flirty, and worry free. I was a dating machine. I could totally go with the flow. Just to reassure myself, I said it out loud again. "Sounds fun. Sure." I was rewarded with a smile. Worth it. Completely. He had a very nice smile. Sure, he was no model, but his face was comfortably handsome, which was more to my taste anyhow.

"I like your outfit," Alec said into the silence.

"Wow, thanks!" I smiled back. I smoothed the flowered skirt over my knees. I bit down on my tongue to keep from sharing that I was wearing that skirt because I'd spent a bit of a time getting a stain off the sleeve of the soft, pink button-down top I'd chosen, which had necessitated wearing a cardigan to cover it. And that cardigan only went with this one skirt. Then, needing the cardigan had snowballed into wearing double deodorant, just in case my heart rate decided to rise. Nope, no sense in mentioning that.

"Whatcha thinking about over there?" he asked me.

"Oh, you know, double deodorant and all . . ." I accidentally let my inner monologue become an outer. Alec looked at me with a quirked eyebrow. "I . . . uh, um . . . uh, well, you know." I shrugged, hoping he'd drop it. He didn't.

"Like, you're hoping I wore double deodorant?" He laughed.

"Not exactly." I felt that stupid blush start rising and wanted to pull my cardigan over my head. And with that blush came the sweats and jitters that had warranted the double layering of deodorant. "Oh, man, I'm so embarrassed." I grimaced back at him.

"Don't worry about it." He continued to chuckle. "So, your boy looks nice." He tactfully changed the subject. I looked gratefully at him. Maybe I'd fall in love with him just for that.

"He is," I agreed.

"How old is he?"

"Oh, he's eight. He's in the third grade."

"Looked like he was playing *Extreme Racing*," Alec observed. I glanced back in his direction. He was serious. He knew what game Ethan had been playing. Odd. I didn't even know which one he'd had on.

"I guess," I replied noncommittally. "Do you play games a lot?"

"Sometimes back at school the guys and I would play on the weekends. *Extreme Racing* is great!" He then enthusiastically told me about the game. It was a total bummer. But, wait, I was being fun and flirty and free and flexible and any other word I could think of that made me sound like a hip and cool chick. So I smiled and oohed and aahed at all the right places. But I continued to sweat.

Alec had been right. The food at Jade Flower was delicious. And they served Coke products, which in my mind solidified them as repeatable.

The waitress, a girl named Sunshine, was just what her name tag promised. She cheerfully took our orders and served our food. When it arrived, Alec handed me a pair of chopsticks.

"Can you use these?" he asked.

"Well, not really." I gave him a little half smile meant to convey my embarrassment over being so American that I couldn't even use the right finger muscles to pinch food.

"Oh, come on, it's not that hard. Give it a try," he encouraged. He even went so far as to unwrap my chopsticks and pass them over to me. Who says chivalry is dead?

"Okay, why not." I concentrated on forming my fingers correctly. When it became obvious that my hands were useless lumps, I started to giggle to myself. Luckily, Alec smiled at me as he leaned over the table and took my fingers in his. They were warm and callused. I liked it. They felt manly.

"Here, hold them like this." He guided my stubborn fingers into the proper hold and released me.

It was at this point that the finger circus began. I had those chopsticks in the death grip of the century, terrified that if I loosened my hand even a smidgen I'd lose the correct position and never get it back. Then again, if it meant he'd hold my hand . . .

Alec chatted comfortably while I repeatedly tried to spear a piece of sweet-and-sour pork onto my chopsticks, which seemed to have developed a type of Teflon coating that prevented food from sticking. Either Alec was oblivious to my distress or he was exercising more chivalry by not mentioning my failure to procure food.

"If I was on a deserted island and given only a bowl of sweet-and-sour and some chopsticks, I'd starve to death," I grumbled, interrupting Alec's monologue about his summer job with the carpentry business handling Cass's kitchen.

"I'm sorry," he chuckled. I looked up to see that his plate was already half-empty. I was starving while he wolfed it down like a pro. He gestured at my silverware. "You gave it a good shot. Why don't you just use your fork? I don't want any date of mine to come away hungry."

"Oh, no, that's okay." I don't know that he meant it as a challenge, but it was. I glanced down at my pork, those round little breaded balls that were out to get me. "Prepare to die, pork," I said to them. I heard Alec chuckle again. Then I looked down at the chopsticks in my right hand.

My knuckles were white and my fingers were cramping. I was now down to one level of deodorant and feeling grateful for the backup. Concentrating for all I was worth, I opened up chopsticks that were shaking like a leaf from the strain and somehow, miracle of miracles, managed to pick up a piece of pork.

I raised it up, a huge grin on my face, proud of my success. Just as my eyes met Alec's, that slippery little devil shot off the end of my chopsticks.

The pork flew straight at Alec, hitting him in the face before plopping down on top of his plate of lo mein.

I wasn't sure whether to laugh or run to the bathroom and sob my heart out. Luckily, Alec solved my problem by grinning as he wiped his cheek with a napkin.

"So, a fork, huh?" I managed to squeak out.

"Seems like a good idea to me." He smiled.

"Oh, and just in case you wanted to taste some of the pork, I put a piece on your plate. That's how good I am." I laughed.

"Yes, I'll never question the master again."

After admitting defeat and picking up a fork, the rest of the meal progressed nicely. Alec made me smile by chomping down the pork I'd launched at him and giving it a thumbs-up. He continued easily maintaining the conversation while I dug into my hard-earned food.

He seamlessly picked up his story about the temporary job he held with the carpentry business while he was on a break from school. He had a few funny stories about nail guns and sandpaper that made me both cringe and smile. And if it seemed worrisome to a single mother like myself that his job seemed to be a summer thing, or that he was still trying to figure out schooling, I promptly cast those doubts aside and told myself that he was a cool, go-with-the-flow type. I smiled. He chatted.

During the drive home, he asked me more about myself, but I felt like there wasn't much to tell. Ethan, laundry, dishes, and work ran on my treadmill of life. In the end, Alec said he wanted to see me again. The deodorant had worked its magic.

"Stinking short legs!" I grumbled as I stood on a stool outside the cottage, attempting to hang a piñata from the covered parking area where my Civic typically resided. "In my next life, I'm gonna be a leggy blonde . . . no, a rich leggy blonde who has servants to hang things!"

"Hang what kinds of things? The people who annoy you?" a voice inserted into my private conversation.

The stool I was on wobbled as I turned in shock and saw Jess . . . correction, *Mr. Sullivan* . . . standing with a grin on his handsome face.

"Exactly." I smiled sweetly in answer to his question. I gave up on the piñata for a moment and chose to focus my frustration on the tall man in a dusty baseball cap and jeans who had stepped in front of the wrong she-wolf today. "I believe I'd begin with a few neighbors of mine who seem to show up at the worst possible time and aggravate me. Would you be willing to test the strength of this wood beam for me?" I pointed up at the beam I'd been attempting to hang the piñata from.

Mr. Sullivan laughed. His smile was so wonderful that it almost made me forget that I had totally embarrassed myself the last time I saw him.

"What's the piñata for?" He gestured to the brightly colored parrot in my hand.

"Last day of school. It's a surprise for Ethan." I scrunched up my nose as I gazed from the piñata to the beam and the dangling piece of rope taunting me. "The real surprise seems to be that it's impossible to stuff and behaves like a real live parrot would if you tried to tie it to a tree."

He chuckled again as he followed my gaze to the parrot. "Cool. I bet he'll like it. No kid wouldn't. You know, if you said *please* I could probably hang that up for you." He smiled sideways at me, daring me to accept his help.

I sighed and gazed toward the lane, where I expected to see Ethan walking at any moment. I really wanted to surprise him and do something fun to celebrate school letting out for the summer. I also really, really, really wanted Mr. Sullivan to stop showing up on the days when I looked like something the cat dragged in and then the dog thrashed around. However, not knowing when he was going to show up made it impossible to ever look my best. And I refused to care anyway. I was too old to be worrying about that. I shook my head and looked back at him.

He raised an eyebrow, questioning me. I shrugged and handed the parrot over. I didn't have to actually put it into words, and I cared more about Ethan being happy than getting to hang it up myself.

Mr. Sullivan walked over to where I'd been standing and kicked the stool out of the way before reaching up and quickly hanging the piñata. It cheerfully spun in circles as I again cursed my gene pool for my short stature. Of course he had to do it quickly and without height assistance. I blew a piece of loose hair out of my eyes and mumbled something that could be mistaken for either "Thank you" or "I could have done it too if I were as tall as you are," depending on how closely you listened.

"What was that?" He gave me a small grin, letting me know how closely he'd listened.

"Oh, nothing, just, you know . . ." I let it hang.

"No, I'm sorry, I don't know," he pressed, letting a full smile light up his face. "Could you repeat that?"

"Oh, just go away!" A grin slipped out as I threw my hands up and started walking down the lane to meet Ethan at the bus.

Mr. Sullivan caught up to me and matched my stride. I sped up. He matched it. I slowed down. He matched it. I thought about jogging but didn't want to risk revealing that I couldn't even make it to the road without having an attack of some sort.

Finally, I just stopped and turned to face him. "What do you want?" I grumbled.

"Actually, I was wondering how you'd feel about me taking Ethan fishing this weekend," he replied.

"Huh?" I was stumped. He wanted to pal around with Ethan?

"Fish . . . ing . . ." he mimicked, casting a line and reeling it in. I rolled my eyes.

"Where?"

"Oh, just over to the Johnsons' fish farm. I've wanted to check it out, but I don't want to look pathetic going alone. I thought Ethan might like to come along," he replied. I didn't know what to say. I was still wrapping my mind around the fact that he was worried about looking pathetic. "Look, it's not a big deal. Just a couple hours on a Saturday afternoon. What do you say?"

"Uh, well . . ." I wasn't sure how to react. I knew Ethan would love it, which made my heart soften at the idea.

"Well, I actually have a date on Saturday, so maybe we could work it out that you take Ethan while I'm on my date?"

"You have a date?" he asked.

Just then Ethan walked up and, overhearing our conversation, frowned up at me.

"You have a date again?" Ethan pouted a little bit.

"*Again?*" Mr. Sullivan mimicked Ethan but with less pout and more curiosity.

"Yes, again." I put my hands on my hips and stared them both down before changing the subject. "Mr. Sullivan has invited you to go fishing."

"Really? That would be cool!" Ethan jumped in the air and did a fist pump.

Mr. Sullivan and I both chuckled at his reaction. I looked over Ethan's head, my smile still intact. "So I'll have Ethan call you when I know what time I'm going and you boys are free to go fishing. Does that work for everyone?"

Ethan quickly gave his new fishing buddy a high five, having totally forgotten that he was supposed to be disappointed over my date. They both nodded agreement.

"Great. Now, Ethan, say goodbye. I've got a little last-day-of-school party planned." I put my arm around his shoulders and turned him toward home.

"Bye, Jess. See you tomorrow!" Ethan chirped.

"Later." Mr. Sullivan smiled at Ethan and then tipped his baseball cap at me before heading toward his property.

I was quiet on the walk down the lane, listening to Ethan chatter and fighting my own demons. In those moments when he'd been stretched out, reaching to hang the piñata, I'd been shocked to discover that maybe Mr. Sullivan wasn't the only backside ogler in these parts.

Saturday morning, despite knowing there would be no warm breakfast waiting for me, I walked to the big house to check on Cass's kitchen remodel. I laughed to myself, remembering how she'd described it as "some updating" when she'd told me about going out of town. Only Cassandra Owens would knock a kitchen to its knees and rip it from ceiling to floor and call it an "update." It was a massive overhaul. No wonder Zinn had fled to Salt Lake City. After I'd read through Cass's envelope of instructions, I'd wished she'd taken me with her.

Cass had called earlier in the week, wondering how things were going. Apparently I'd talked too much about the cutie doing the work and asked one too many questions about Zinn's family rather than giving a clear update on the actual work. I knew Cass wasn't satisfied with my report and didn't want to be bothered with answering my question about covered wagons, because she'd had Zinn call me last night and demand an update.

I unlocked the door and let myself into the kitchen. The work was progressing nicely. The new flooring was in and the cabinetry was in place. Still no countertops or appliances, but it had the skeleton of a kitchen back in place. I walked the circumference of the room and tried to remember the measurements and layout Cass's designer had drawn for me. I'd forgotten to bring my measuring tape, but it seemed to be up to scratch.

I paused in the new pantry, satisfied to see that it was larger than it had been. I couldn't wait for Zinn to stock it to the rafters. I wondered where she'd learned her amazing culinary skills. Maybe she'd done a stint with Julia Child in Paris before migrating to Salt Lake. Who knew? It was worth considering.

The phone was ringing in the cottage when I entered, and Ethan was nowhere to be seen. Probably still sleeping after our massive piñata candy binge and video-game session the night before. I picked up and was happy to find that it was Alec confirming our date for that afternoon, saying he'd pick me up at three. Apparently we'd be mini-golfing. *Swell*, I thought to myself. I hadn't mini-golfed in years. It wasn't going to be a great way to impress Alec. Mostly because I wasn't sporty at all. I put my head against the wall and banged it a time or two.

Ethan came out of his room, rubbing his eyes and looking adorably rumpled. At least he loved me, cool girl or not. I sat next to him on the couch and he leaned his head on my shoulder. We snuggled while Ethan began flipping channels at a rapid pace. I wasn't even sure how he could see the shows he was passing up. After he'd gone once around, he settled into *SpongeBob SquarePants*, and we watched quietly together. When the show was over, I nudged him and reminded him to call Mr. Sullivan about fishing. He jumped up, and I went to shower while they planned their afternoon fishing adventure.

Because I was in the bathroom busily tweaking my makeup and hair for the fiftieth time when Mr. Sullivan arrived to take Ethan fishing, I was too busy to greet him in person. I had planned it that way. I didn't need him making me feel all jittery and riling me up before my date. It felt pretty darn great that a plan of mine had worked out so well.

"Jess is here. Bye, Mom!" Ethan called. I could hear him gathering his fishing gear.

"Bye, bud. Have fun!" I called back from my sanctuary.

"Thanks, Kate," Mr. Sullivan called just before the door slammed behind the guys. I could hear their conversation for a moment before the sound of car doors shutting cut off their voices.

I gazed at myself in the mirror. I'd decided to leave my hair down for this second date. After spending what felt like hours scrubbing my hair in the shower, then blow-drying it, then dusting off the curling iron and adding some curls, my hair hung in soft waves past my shoulders. My bangs were surprising me by actually staying off to the side and out of my eyes. The amount of product I'd put in my hair to achieve this style was probably going to make my scalp bleed.

Next I checked out the makeup situation. It had been years since I'd worried about my appearance. I hadn't dated since meeting Charlie, and even then I'd been more natural. But a decade later, I needed serious updating if I was going to get back into the dating game. So I'd purchased a magazine and copied the makeup of a random model who had my same coloring. Auburn hair, brown eyes, and pale, ghastly skin. Okay, pale and ghastly was a little strong, but I didn't own an airbrush to cover up my freckled nose, and I was feeling vulnerable about getting my feet wet again in the dating world. My eyelashes weren't clumped together, so I was satisfied that things couldn't possibly get any better from the neck up.

The next, and most soul-killing, item on my list was choosing just the right outfit. I'd laid out all ten of my pants and shorts. In all honesty, only five of them fit after the binge-fest I'd gone on during the year after Charlie passed. But I couldn't admit that to myself during this stage of dating, so I'd put out all ten to give myself the illusion of having choices.

It was easy to cut the shorts out of the competition. It was only early June. I hadn't quite stepped up to the plate on shaving yet, and that meant that razor burn was a real possibility. Also, no sunlight had seen these legs in a while. Not exactly swoon worthy. The shorts went back into the closet.

Three jeans now dominated the competition. Too bad I didn't have someone to cast the final vote for me. I finally decided on the dark denim pair and slipped them on, ignoring the hitch around the hip area.

As far as tops went, I didn't have many options that weren't T-shirts. So I chose a cute little purple tunic that Aunt Cass had gotten me as a gift. I added a pair of earrings and went back to the bathroom to check out my reflection. I was pleased with the outcome. Until I looked too closely and began to overanalyze the entire outfit.

Luckily, I was saved a marathon outfit-changing session by the doorbell ringing. It was Alec. I was eager to see his reaction to the new, more stylish Kate Evans. With that in mind, I swung open the door with a happy smile on my face.

"Hey there," I chirped.

"Hey back," Alec grinned. He looked good with shorts and a polo shirt. "You ready?"

I fought to keep the smile on my face and nodded as I grabbed my purse from the hook by the door. Why hadn't he commented on my appearance? Wasn't that date etiquette 101? He had on our first date. Charlie had always had something to say while we were dating. But thinking about Charlie as I walked out the door with another man caused a pinch in my chest, and I pushed the thought back into its hiding place. Maybe if I got the ball rolling for him by complimenting him? Hey, I wasn't against fishing for a compliment. I'd been married. I got it.

"You look nice today," I hinted as he opened the door of his truck for me.

He grinned and looked down at his own outfit. "Thanks!" He shut the door.

I maintained hope as he got into the driver's side of the truck and smiled over at me, but he said nothing as we chugged down the lane to the road. It was a letdown, but not a date killer. I knew that men could be totally oblivious sometimes. I just hoped that maybe while we were swinging our golf mallets . . . no, wait, clubs . . . that he'd notice the way my free and breezy hair flowed around me in gleaming ringlets. Maybe I'd even bat my nonclumpy eyelashes at him a time or two and see how things went from there.

With those happy thoughts in my mind, I chose a green club and green golf ball and stood at the first hole with Alec. My handsome date.

The weather was beautiful this afternoon, and although there were a few other customers on the mini-golf course, it wasn't as crowded as it would get later in the evening. Alec proudly informed me that at school he'd been the reigning mini-golf champ. I wasn't great at golf in any form, but I was up for the challenge of doing something different and having a good time.

We chatted comfortably for the first half of the course. After nine holes, he was beating me by, well, by more than I'd like to admit. He seemed to appreciate that he was winning, which made me feel like the sweet and demure woman I was trying to be. I had tried a few times to whip my hair around me in a sparkling halo, but all that had resulted was that I'd choked on a few long strands and ended up with potential to develop a rat's nest. Alec said nothing. Dang it!

Hole 12 wove its way around a pond with a fountain in the middle of it. It was pretty. Apparently it was prettier than me because Alec commented on it several times while lining up his putt. It was kind of embarrassing to listen to him extol the virtues of the flowing water when I had lovely flowing hair he had yet to notice. Oh well. He putted his ball and it curved in the right places as it rolled around the edge of the pond to where the hole was.

"Your turn." He gave me a smile as he stepped to the side, his gaze caught again by the fountain. My nemesis.

"Great," I mumbled. Then my temper flared and I decided to see if I could catch his attention by pitching my ball clean over the top of the fountain to the other side, where his ball peacefully awaited him. I turned to face the pond, swung my club back as far as I could, and whacked it with all the frustration of a twenty-nine-year-old woman trying her hardest to be easy-breezy and play mini-golf while looking darling and being demure. Which means I nailed that thing. Or, more accurately, I nailed the ground next to the ball, which caused my elbows to practically bend back and my ball to bounce lightly into the pond.

"Well, that was interesting." Alec laughed at me. Oh, goody, I finally had his attention.

"Sorry." I pretended to giggle and gave him a blank look like I had no idea how on earth such a thing had happened.

"No worries. Let's see if we can fish out your ball." Alec reached for my club, but I pulled it away from him before he could get a grip on it.

"No, that's okay. I'll get it." I smiled and stepped up to the pond. As I got closer, I could hear a sucking noise and turned to ask Alec what that noise was.

"Oh, that's just the pump that takes the water from the pond into the fountain and keeps it circulating," he explained.

I nodded my understanding and bent over to see if I could spot my ball through the nasty-smelling murky water. "Someone ought to try out a little chlorine and see if they could improve the swamp-water situation here," I said to Alec over my shoulder. He chuckled.

I finally spotted my green ball lying to the right, so I stepped over and dipped my club into the water to pull the ball toward me. To my surprise and horror, I heard a giant sucking noise, then a gurgle, and then something pulled hard enough on my club to bring me to my knees. My arms from the elbow down splashed into the putrid pool, causing water to splash my face. Then the sucking noise stopped.

"Oh my gosh, Kate, are you okay? What happened?" Alec was by my side helping me up. I was still holding tightly to the club, so I bent over as I stood, water dripping from my nose. "Here, let me see that." Alec tugged the club out of my hand and gave it a hard pull.

I stood, wiping at the water on my face and pushing my wet bangs out of my eyes as I watched Alec play tug-of-war with the club. He gave one last hard pull and the sucking noise roared back to life as he freed my club from the vicious grip of the pump and lifted it from the water.

"It looks okay," I sheepishly commented, wiping at another drip from my nose. No sooner had I said that than the putter cracked almost completely in half and hung limply from Alec's hand.

"Oh, man." Alec looked from the club to me to the fountain. Then he looked again at me and started laughing. Hard. He put his hands on his knees and braced himself as he was lost in hysterics, the club a limp reminder of my embarrassment.

Soon, other laughter joined his, and I saw a couple of teenage boys who'd been playing behind us join in Alec's merriment. As I saw their laughter and watched Alec's shoulders shake, I couldn't help but join in. It really was hysterical. I could just imagine how it had looked to anyone watching. I started out chuckling but then quickly added my own laughter to theirs.

My laughter caused my bangs to slip over my eyes, a reminder that not all things go according to plan, no matter how hard we try. My attempts at being coy and stylish hadn't amounted to much. In the end, what had gotten Alec's attention had been a typical display of my clumsiness. I'd try to keep that in mind in the future. Maybe being myself was the ticket.

Chapter 5

A few days later, I tromped over to the big house to check on things and was surprised to hear voices and barking coming from the kitchen. The door was open, so I put my key back in my pocket and stepped inside. It was a madhouse. Wade was barking at Eli, who was quivering behind the half-closed pantry door. Ken was holding his baseball cap and kept glancing at the stern expression on Cass's face, and, worst of all, Alec was being verbally accosted by Zinn. Her face was pinched and her finger was practically stabbing Alec in the chest as she tore him from tip to toe. I couldn't even begin to imagine what was happening. And when did Cass and Zinn get home?

"I didn't expect you two for a few more days," I said as I purposely slammed the door behind me in what I felt was an incredible act of selflessness. My attempt to take the attention off the men worked. The voices silenced and all eyes turned in my direction. Wade thankfully stopped barking as he trotted happily to my side. Now that I had their attention, I gave a cheery smile to Cass before asking what all the hullabaloo was about.

"Katherine!" Zinn said my name like it was a curse word and gave Cass a look like she wasn't surprised at all. I mean, I'd been in trouble before, but I didn't really follow. So I looked at Cass.

"Yes, well, Zinn had specifically ordered a six-burner gas range, but there isn't a wide enough opening in the cabinetry here to fit one." Cass's voice was calm, but there was steel in it. Things weren't good when Cass slipped into her courtroom judge voice.

I knew better than to try to argue against Cass when she was trying a case, so I made what I really hoped was an apologetic face. My mistakes were never made on purpose.

"Figures," Zinn muttered.

"What figures?" I couldn't resist. Zinn focused the full weight of her displeasure on me. I wished I'd resisted a little bit. But I couldn't let her go back and attack my poor Alec. He'd never come around again, and I really needed to be dating . . . him. Yes, that's it, dating *him*. Specifically. I wasn't so desperate that I just needed to be dating anything that was male and breathed.

"Figures that you wouldn't even notice that there was a problem!" Zinn retorted.

"Well, sure. I don't cook much. So why would I have noticed that the hole should be bigger?" I put on my most cheerfully innocent expression and shrugged. Zinn just harrumphed and looked back toward Alec. No, not Alec. I had to save him.

"Well, Zinn, you're such a good cook. I mean, it isn't like you're still cooking over an open fire in Dutch ovens on the Oregon Trail. So four burners should be a cinch," I rambled off.

Zinn quirked an eyebrow and looked at Cass. "Did she just say Oregon Trail?" she asked in a confused, but still miffed, tone.

"Besides," I hurried on, "it was really Ken's job to oversee those kind of details." When all eyes swung to Ken, I felt even worse. "Plus, I'm dating Alec, so don't be mean." This announcement was met with more silence. All eyes immediately shifted back to me, including Alec's, which were now pleading with me to leave him out of this and not draw attention to him. "So, yay for me, I guess." I half raised my hands up like a strangled cheerleader and giggled a bit at the end, out of nerves.

Cass broke the silence by clearing her throat. "Okay, well, we've established that the range is incorrect and that Kate has somehow started dating one of these young men." Cass looked between Eli and Alec and then back at me. "Please tell me Alec isn't the young redhead quivering in the pantry," she stated with a somewhat twisted mouth, like she was either trying to hold in a burst of laughter or had the sudden need to regurgitate.

I giggled nervously again. "No, Alec is the one Zinn was . . . uh . . . chatting with over there." I pointed at Alec, who smiled uncomfortably and gave Cass a nod.

I wanted to tell him to man up and shake her hand or something, but I think he was afraid that Zinn would strike him like a rattlesnake if he didn't hold still. I sighed. Not the best way to introduce my family to my new romantic interest. Oh, well. At least he looked cute and manly in his T-shirt and worn jeans.

"Anyhow," Cass said, her face smoothing out as she nodded at Alec before continuing, "Ken, we need you to have the mistake corrected. I expected to find everything in order and finished when Zinn and I arrived home. It's a disappointment that it isn't. I'm not sure what we'll do for meals in the meantime."

"Honestly!" Zinn threw in.

"Dutch ovens?" I added in an attempt to lighten the situation. No one laughed. Zinn glared. I squeezed my lips together tightly to keep words from continuing to pop out.

"Mr., uh . . ." Cass gestured at Alec.

"Williams, ma'am," Alec answered.

"Williams, yes. Mr. Williams, since our Kate seems so fond of you, I'll trust that you will personally see to it that the correct items are delivered and installed." Cass lifted her chin in a haughty expression. It was a bit much.

"Yes, ma'am, of course." Alec gave her a small smile.

"Good." Cass nodded. "Now, Zinn, let's go into my study to discuss menu changes." Cass gestured to Zinn, who mumbled and shot daggers at Ken, Eli, and Alec as she left the room. I kept my eyes down, but I'm pretty sure I'd gotten a dart sent my way as well.

When Cass and Zinn were gone, Ken, Eli, and Alec seemed to sag a bit as they breathed a sigh of relief. I knew the feeling. It was one I'd experienced about a million times in my clumsy life. I gave them all a smile, letting them know I commiserated with them. Alec gestured at me to follow him out back.

When the door was closed behind us, we stepped out of view of the kitchen and around to the side of the house before speaking.

"I'm so sorry that happened." I smiled up at him, stepped closer, and took his hand in mine. I liked how his hand felt all rough and big in mine. I had missed the feeling of holding hands with a man. "What a crazy way to meet my aunt." I laughed.

"You can say that again." He blew out a breath and ran his free hand through his hair. "She was scarier than some of my professors." He laughed, and I laughed too. I mean, it had been a while, but I wasn't too old to relate to having a rough professor. "What a way for her to find out we've gone out. That was kind of embarrassing."

"Oh." I released his hand and stepped back.

"It's just, I don't want her to think that my interest in you is what made that mistake happen in the kitchen. Like I was all distracted or something." Alec glanced over my head toward the creek behind me.

"Oh."

"So . . ."

"So . . ." Now it was my turn to look anywhere but at him.

"Listen, I really like you, and I really do want to see you again. Let's just maybe try to keep things out of sight of your aunt until this all blows over." He reached out and touched my chin, making me meet his eyes, and he gave me a grin. "How does that sound?"

I gave him a small smile in return. "I can do that."

"Good. We still on for lunch next week?" He let his hand run down my arm before taking my hand back in his. It felt really, really nice. Probably the best part was that it wasn't sticky. Lately, the only hand-holding I'd done had been with eight-year-old-boy mystery stickiness attached to it.

"Yes. Ethan has a Cub Scout day camp next week, so that will work out great." I squeezed his hand. He squeezed back. Then he surprised me by leaning down and giving me a quick, soft kiss on the mouth before heading back around the house into the kitchen.

I stood where I was as the door closed behind him. Alec hadn't meant it as anything other than a sweet goodbye, but I hadn't been kissed by anyone other than Charlie in years. There hadn't been fireworks, but it had still felt new and exciting. I was trying to ignore the parts that felt disloyal and confusing. It was official—ready or not—I was back in the dating game.

The lunch date was upon me. This very hour. Sadly, I still hadn't managed to get any sunlight to hit my legs. One time I'd tried a self-tanning cream at home and I'd turned out looking like an Orange Creamsicle with the nice white and orange stripes on my legs. Charlie had laughed, insisted he liked my natural "fair" coloring, and kissed me until I'd forgotten all about my embarrassment. Somehow I doubted that exposing

Alec to that level of Kate-ness would be a good move for this early stage in our relationship. Then I was forced to wonder, *Was this a relationship?* Probably not worth exploring. For now, all my thoughts needed to go into finding something suitable to wear for a lunch date.

In keeping with my easy-breezy, fun, and flirty image I was trying to conjure up, I went for a nice black crinkly skirt that flowed around my ankles and a green V-necked T-shirt that made my eyes actually look like they had green flecks. I once again attempted the giant makeup application and then, on a whim, went all crazy and did a messy bun that only looks like you've just thrown it together, when in actuality you've twisted, pinned, and shellacked that thing until a tornado couldn't blow it out of place. All in the name of looking natural.

When the doorbell rang I hurried out of my room to answer. I paused to check my reflection in the mirror. Yep, that zit was still doing its best to form on my forehead, but the bun was in place and the mascara hadn't clumped. I was a regular beauty queen.

"Hey," I chirped as I swung the door open.

"Hi," Mr. Jess Sullivan smiled down at me. "You look cute." He grinned as he pointed down at my bare feet peeking out from my skirt. "Going somewhere?"

"What, 'cause I only look this cute if I'm going out?" I replied awkwardly, unsure about how to take a compliment from someone who confused me.

"Guess I walked into that one," he said, chuckling. Darn his good moods. They were just serving to make me look like a shrew. How could he be so calm all the time? Didn't he realize things between us were weird?

He stepped into the house even though I hadn't exactly vacated the doorway, and as he brushed by me I got a nice strong whiff of whatever outrageously manly cologne he'd put on that morning.

"Uh, come on in," I said sarcastically as he walked into the kitchen area and set a package down on the counter. I hadn't even noticed it in his hands. I left the door open and followed him to see what he had.

"When Ethan and I went fishing, we did catch and release, but he told me that he wanted to try eating a fish. So I went fishing early this morning and caught one. I brought it over for him to try."

Mr. Sullivan unwrapped a corner of the brown bag so that I could see dead fish eyeballs. It was so thoughtful of him. *Actually,* I sighed to myself, *it was.* Ethan would be really happy. He'd probably even eat the fish because Mr. Sullivan had brought it, whereas I'd never gotten him to eat anything that wasn't chicken and nuggets. Bother.

"Thanks," I said.

"No problem. If you're not going to cook it today, you'll want to freeze it," he supplied helpfully.

"Or I can take it to Zinn and let her cook it." I grinned down at the fish, pleased with myself for thinking of it.

"Sounds like a good plan to me. Want me to just walk it over there?"

"Yes . . . well . . . no. Maybe it would be better to just freeze it. Zinn isn't going to be cooking for me for a while after my crack about her cooking with a Dutch oven along the Oregon Trail." I reached hesitantly toward the fish. I didn't know if it would rub off on me, and I sure didn't want to smell like a lake trout on my lunch date. Then Alec wouldn't try to kiss me again. Maybe that's why Mr. Sullivan was wearing so much cologne, to cover up the fish smell.

"Oregon Trail? Like how the pioneers came from the east to settle the west, Oregon Trail?" He gave me a glance like he wondered if I was right in the head.

"You heard me. Zinn has to be about two hundred years old." I nodded while reaching my hand out to the fish and then pulling it back.

He started laughing. "Please tell me you didn't say that part to her face!"

I forgot the fish and glanced up at him. "Of course not. I'm no fool. I want to keep eating her cooking."

This made him laugh harder. And, obviously, that's when Alec walked in.

"Hello?" he called from the doorway.

I spun around, a slight smile on my face in greeting. Mr. Sullivan stopped laughing. I didn't look back to see what his reaction to Alec was.

"Hey there." I walked toward him and gestured for him to come in, all warmth and hospitality. "Let me just grab some shoes and I'll be ready." I reached for his hand and gave it a squeeze.

"Sure." He smiled down at me and then glanced up to see whom I'd been talking to. His smile froze in place. He looked down at me with a shocked expression.

"Yes, I know who is in my kitchen." I sighed and turned to meet Mr. Sullivan's curious look.

"Alec, this is Mr. Sullivan . . ." I began.

"Jess," my new neighbor quickly inserted and strode over to shake Alec's hand. Now I was standing in the middle of the two men. They were both taller than me by a full head, and I nervously glanced back and forth between them.

"Wow, Jess Sullivan, nice to meet you, man." Alec's face was worshipful as their hands clasped. "I'd heard you bought some property around here, but I had no idea you knew Kate. She hasn't mentioned you at all."

"Doesn't surprise me. She insists on calling me *Mr. Sullivan* after a little spat we had when I first moved here. Sadly for her, I'm pals with her boy, so she sort of tolerates me coming around." Mr. Sullivan turned his full smile wattage on Alec before looking down at me.

"You and Kate had a fight? About what? She's always so nice and easygoing. It's one of the things I like most about her." Alec seemed genuinely confused as he too looked down at me. His eyes told me he thought I was a nutjob to be fighting with a prince like Jess Sullivan.

"Oh, well, you know, I insulted her somehow. I'm sure she's usually very . . ." Mr. Sullivan couldn't seem to come up with a word to describe what characteristics I obviously didn't have in his eyes.

"Demure!" I supplied with a soft growl.

Mr. Sullivan laughed. "Yes, sure, *demure.* Perfectly describes Kate." He grinned. I glared.

Alec stared back and forth between us, but mostly he looked at me like he was trying to figure out this new facet of my personality. Shoot, I was ruining things.

"Jess is just pulling your leg." I forced out a chuckle and smiled at Alec like it was all a big joke. "We're very neighborly. In fact, he was just dropping off some fresh fish for my and Ethan's dinner. Isn't that nice of him?"

Alec nodded as his face relaxed. "Yeah, that sounds great." He was a little too enthusiastic in his praise, I thought. I'd have to watch that he didn't slip into groupie mode.

"*Jess?*" Jess, my new pal, mouthed as he gave me a knowing glance. It made me want to slap him. I had decided to call him Jess again because it was less tedious. It had nothing to do with Alec's opinion or Jess taunting me in front of my new squeeze. My life, my choice.

"Anyhow, *Jess*, buddy, we'd better get going. We've got a date and a *lady* never keeps her man waiting." I smiled up at Alec. "Let me just grab my shoes."

I hurried to my room to dig around and find sandals that wouldn't clash with my outfit. It was the longest minute of my life, wondering what they were talking about out there. I could hear their male voices, Jess's slightly deeper and slower moving, Alec's high-pitched and rapid in his excitement.

I felt flushed when I rejoined them with my strappy black sandals on. Shoot, I'd done them up too tight in my rush and the shoes were pinching my ankles. I was going to have to fix them. I gave Alec the "one minute" signal by holding up my pointer finger, and I flopped down on the couch to adjust the straps.

"Hey, Jess, would you mind putting that fish in the freezer for me?" I said cheerily while bent over my foot.

"Don't want to get stinky for your big date, huh?" Jess smiled at Alec as he headed back into the kitchen area. I could hear the paper crinkling as he moved it from the countertop into his hands.

"Kate always smells nice," Alec added. I could have kissed him smack on the lips for that. I glanced up from my feet to meet his smile and gave him a huge one in return. My hero.

When I was done fixing my sandals, I jumped up from the couch and grabbed Alec's hand, ready to go. I sent a questioning look to Jess when he didn't start walking toward the door to leave.

"I thought I'd go ahead and clean the fish for you, unless you don't trust me in your house," Jess answered my unvoiced question.

"Oh, sure. But shouldn't you do that outside?" I asked. I *was* nervous about him being in the cottage alone. What if he saw that I'd rigged my bathroom scale to a starting point of negative five pounds to give myself a little boost in the self-esteem department?

"Actually, I like to do it with some running water. I promise I'll catch the guts in a big bowl and not put them down your disposal."

"Sounds cool to me," Alec piped in. *Shut up, Alec!* Between Alec's smiling hero worship and Jess's knowing grin, I was trapped. Why was I always getting trapped around Jess?

"Sure, just, will you please lock up when you leave? You never know what kind of *crazies* will wander into your house." I gave Jess a sugary smile.

"Yep." He waved at us. "You two *kids* have a great time!" I caught his emphasis on the word and did not appreciate it one little bit.

"Thanks, Jess!" Alec waved back as I dragged him by the hand out of my cottage. It figured that Alec would jump right into a friendship with Jess. Blah!

Alec kept my hand in his on the walk to where he'd parked his truck in front of the big house. He opened the door for me and then walked around to let himself in the driver's side. He smiled over at me as he buckled up.

"Man, who'd have thought? You're friends with Jess Sullivan . . ." He shook his head and put the truck in drive.

Apparently finding out I was friends with a famous person amped up my desirability in Alec's eyes. When we arrived at the local diner for lunch, he slipped into the booth next to me rather than sitting across from me. Plus, he'd put his hand on the small of my back as we'd walked in from the parking lot. I liked that part.

What I didn't like was sitting next to someone like that when there was a perfectly good empty seat across from me. Don't even get me started on all the elbow bumping and awkwardly trying to look at someone's face when they're right next to you. Also, this newfound affection made me have to carefully evaluate what I was going to order for lunch. I loved onions and pickles and peppers, but none of those things went with close quarters. And close quarters meant the possibility of some lip locking later. So I supposed a chili dog with everything on it was out. Oh, the decisions.

Luckily for me, Alec didn't harp on the Jess situation. After placing our orders—a lightly seasoned plain chicken breast with a side of strawberries for me—he did ask how I'd met Jess, and I'd answered that he'd been at the big house one night and we'd been introduced. I left out the crushed goblets and sweatpants. Alec still didn't even know I owned a pair of sweats. That wasn't third-date material. That was like a year down the road and should come right before blowing our noses in front of each other. We had a long ways to go before that type of info would come to light.

Before I knew it, we had arrived back at my cottage and it was time for the doorstep scene. I wondered which way Alec was going to play this. He'd been affectionate throughout the meal, occasionally holding my hand or putting his arm behind me as we talked. My neck hadn't even gotten kinked from glancing his way, and I felt that I'd done right by having something so bland to eat. Ending with the sweet strawberries had been a real stroke of brilliance. He'd held my hand on the drive back. My palms were dry, and I'd covertly sucked at my teeth on the drive to make sure no food was wedged in there. I was as ready as I'd ever be.

I didn't have to wait long to find out. At the door I turned to face Alec and gazed up at him. I hoped my look said *shyly available*, but it probably said *scared witless, haven't dated in a decade*. He smiled and put his hands at my waist before pulling me into a hug.

"I had a really great time today, Kate," he said quietly against my hair.

"Me too." I relaxed my head against his chest and let my arms slide around his waist.

"I need to get back to work, but I'd like to see you again. Soon."

I was happily surprised. We'd been going a full week or so between dates, so this stepped it up quite a bit. "Sure. How about Saturday night? Come here and I'll make us dinner. You can officially meet Ethan. I mean, I know you saw him the other night, but, yeah . . ." I knew I was probably taking it too far by suggesting a relationship with my son. But he gave me a squeeze.

"Sounds great. How about seven o'clock?"

"Perfect." I didn't want to tell him how lame I was and that we usually ate dinner at five thirty while watching reruns of *Little House on the Prairie*. Nope. Let him think we were trendy and cool and dined at seven in nice clothes while discussing world events.

He lightened his hold on me, and I took a step back, but he didn't totally release me. Instead, he leaned down, and I leaned up, and he kissed me. Inside I was cheering for strawberries and plain chicken. It had been worth the sacrifice to enjoy the reward. He pulled back after a sweet moment and tucked a strand of my hair behind my ear. I refused to wonder how on earth that hair had escaped from where I'd practically hot-glued it to my head. Instead I enjoyed the moment of his hand softly caressing my face and his eyes as he smiled down at me.

I felt a few butterflies take off in my stomach. Dusty, scared little butterflies. But butterflies just the same.

Friday, the day before my dinner date with Alec, I decided to venture back over to the big house after I finished my work for the day. I was always happy to shut down my computer and put all the numbers away for the weekend.

Even though I'd happily begun sneaking food out of Zinn's newly stocked pantry on night raids, I had been avoiding going over during the day because I wanted to respect Alec's wishes to keep our relationship—*relationship!*—separate from his work at my aunt's house. Also, I wanted to stay away from Zinn's glares.

However, Alec had told me during a phone conversation—we were now talking between dates—that the proper gas range had been delivered and that the reconfiguration of the cabinets that was needed to install them was all but complete. I was curious. Also, to be honest, I wanted to see Alec in his manly work clothes. I was hoping for another hit of butterflies as a side dish too.

The kitchen was empty other than Ken, Alec, and Eli. I gave Eli and Ken a friendly wave as I walked to where Alec was working.

"Hey." He smiled at me as I approached, but it was a bit strained. I knew he was uncomfortable with me singling him out while he was working. The butterflies in my stomach flitted softly back into their cages. *Maybe next time, guys,* I thought. *Stay alert, though.*

"Hey." I smiled back. I stopped a safe distance away from him and kept my hands to themselves. "Just passing through to go see Aunt Cass, but I wanted to see the work you've done in here."

"Oh, sure." He relaxed and set down the tool he'd been working with . . . whatever it was.

"Also," I said, sneaking in a little closer and dropping my voice, "I'm going to invite Aunt Cass to join us for dinner at my place tomorrow night." I stepped back with a flirty smile on my face.

Alec's face fell. "That's tomorrow?"

I nodded. I didn't date enough that I was messing up which day I had a guy coming over for dinner.

"So, uh, something came up tomorrow. Rain check?" He had the decency to look sheepish. I sighed to myself and gave myself the pep talk about how things happen, plans change, don't stress, and blah, blah, blah.

"Sure." I managed to smile.

"Great. You're so cool!" He gave me a huge smile. I liked it. "Anyhow, about the kitchen, this is where the cabinets had to be remeasured . . ." I smiled and nodded as Alec did a quick walk-through with me. I was mostly watching the way he moved in those jeans. Yum. It made my pop-in totally worth it, especially since I wouldn't be seeing him the next night after all. One little butterfly did a happy dance in my stomach. The rest were sulking.

"It all looks wonderful." I smiled when Alec finished his tour and included Eli and Ken in the acknowledgment. "Good work, guys!" The men all smiled back at me. "Well, I'd better go find Cass. See you guys later."

I went through the swinging door, and in an effort to be somewhat mature in front of Alec, I held back from my usual karate kick, even though after having my dinner date canceled I was really geared up to give that door the beating of its life. It closed quietly behind me. *Huh.* I turned and looked at it. I had no idea it closed that softly.

At the front of the house on one side of the foyer was Cass's study. That's where I typically looked first when seeking her out. However, on the opposite side of the foyer, in the formal parlor, was where I heard voices. I recognized Cass's, and also Ethan's. He had come over earlier hoping to steal some cookies from Zinn.

It had been a major hardship for him for the past month, with Zinn gone and then the kitchen unusable. Zinn had somehow managed to whip up a batch of no-bake chocolate oatmeal cookies that afternoon, even though the kitchen still had no cooktop. I'd smelled the cookies as I'd walked into the kitchen. I was sure they were gone now that Ethan had arrived.

However, I found it odd that Cass and Ethan would be enjoying cookies in the parlor. That was a room where Ethan and food were not allowed to cohabitate. Then I heard the rumble of a lower voice that I recognized as Jess, followed by the airy laugh of a woman who was definitely a stranger to me. No women of my acquaintance laughed that way. Cass laughed daintily, and Zinn mainly scowled. We most certainly didn't trill out laughter.

I slowed my pace and peeked into the parlor, hoping to see before being seen. In the end, Wade ratted me out by hurrying over to my side with his tongue hanging out and his tail wagging.

"Hey, Mom!" Ethan waved and grinned from his seat on the sofa with a big grin. He always had a smile for me. It was one of the things that made me happiest about being his mom. That kid woke up happy. It was a gift.

"Hey, kiddo." I smiled back at him before looking around the room.

"Come in, Kate. Have a seat." Cass gestured from her seat next to Ethan. "Jess is here. And you remember Ms. Vivienne Lawson." Cass then gestured to the visitors, whose voices I'd heard a moment earlier. Figured. A Vivienne would trill, whereas a Kate would guffaw.

I offered up a smile in response to Jess and Vivienne greeting me. At least Vivienne had been warmer toward me this time. Maybe she'd forgotten about my faux pas regarding her name.

"I really don't want to interrupt." I hesitated in the doorway.

"You're not, Mom. Come in. Jess is telling Aunt Cass about his new house plans. And his friend is here to visit and see how things are going on the property." Ethan patted the empty seat next to him on the sofa.

Jess began talking again, picking up where he'd left off. I didn't listen to a word he said. I just watched him and Vivienne and Cass and Ethan interact. I was surprised to see how at ease they all seemed together. Cass didn't surprise me, really. She was always at ease in her role as a hostess when her friends popped by. She gracefully smiled regularly, making interested noises in all the right places. Vivienne took every chance she could to touch Jess on the arm, or leg or hand, as he spoke, laughing—pardon me—*trilling* as much as possible without being too awfully annoying. Ethan was clearly as happy as an eight-year-old boy could be. Even Wade was wagging his tail. I appeared to be the only one sitting stiffly, and I began to feel an odd sort of vulnerability.

It was quite obvious that I was the only one feeling awkward. Perhaps the worst realization was that it was my own fault that I wasn't able to relax around them. Well, at least with everyone but Vivienne. With their fishing trips, Jess and Ethan had been hanging around each other for weeks. Because of my initial hurt feelings and ongoing insecurities around Jess, I'd made a point to keep myself aloof.

Regret came to me slowly. My life was lonely enough without pushing away the only people around me who seemed to actually want to be part of the little life I was building.

Suddenly, Ethan's little hand slid into mine where it rested in my lap. I was surprised by the contact because I'd been so lost in my own thoughts. I looked up to meet his eyes. Not too long ago he'd come home from school so excited because he'd finally learned to truly wink without his other eye closing halfway or scrunching up. Now he threw me one of those winks and grinned. I squeezed his hand and winked at him in return. This caused him to truly smile before his gaze moved back to Jess, who was still talking. He kept his hand in mine. Maybe I did belong, just a little bit.

Chapter 6

I gave in to temptation and took a moment to snuggle with my old friend, sweatpants, pulling them on a few days after my canceled dinner date with Alec. Ethan and I were going hiking on our favorite trail, and I'd decided that since there was no chance of running into Alec up on the mountain behind Cass's house, I'd rekindle my romance with stretchy cotton.

After pulling on a worn orange tank top—which absolutely clashed with my messy pulled-up hair—I went out into the living area, where Ethan was lacing up his boots.

"Ready, buddy?" I smiled and ruffled his hair as I walked past him to where my hiking boots were waiting for me.

"Ready. I just want to go get Wade, and then I'll meet you outside." Ethan jumped up, slapped on a ball cap, and raced out the door.

Wade and Ethan were standing in the covered parking area next to my car when I came out a few minutes later. I slid a small backpack filled with water, nuts, and sunscreen over my shoulders and nodded at Ethan to lead the way. He and Wade were off like a shot, hurrying as fast as Ethan's legs could take them to the base of the trailhead.

"Wait for me before you disappear into the trees," I called. Ethan just waved back at me to let me know he'd heard.

I enjoyed the view of boy and dog running together set against the backdrop of the beautiful foothills. As we crept ever closer to the month of July, the temperature continued to rise. But the trees were blooming at the peak of their season. I could smell the fresh scent of pine as I arrived at the trailhead. Wade and Ethan were both prancing impatiently as they waited for me to catch up. I smiled to myself, constantly amazed at the level of energy an eight-year-old boy could exude. I remembered a time when I'd had that level of energy. But that had been before . . .

"Can we go ahead now, Mom? We'll wait at the burnt tree!" Ethan interrupted my thoughts, and I was grateful.

"I thought the plan was to hike *together* today," I teased him.

"Please? After that I'll stick with you."

"That's fine. But stay on the path; no wandering off. I don't want to have to call the Boy Scouts to find you." I winked at him. It was a running joke with us that the Boy Scout troops in the area would lose you before they found you.

"Wade, let's go, boy." Ethan patted Wade on the head before they took off again and disappeared into the trees. I could hear Ethan's boots crunching on pine needles and old leaves as they ran off. His happy voice kept up a running monologue to the dog.

I followed at a more sedate, but steady, pace up the hillside. The start of the path was a slight incline, but then it zigged back and became steeper as I left the foothills for higher terrain. The day was glorious. My sweats were comfy, the sun was shining on my shoulders, and my hair wasn't making my neck sweat. The only thing that could have improved the day would have been Alec's company.

Just thinking about him made me want to see him again. We had settled into a comfortable, pressure-free situation, where we saw each other about once a week. My mind knew it was perfect for my first feeble steps back into the dating world, and yet, at times I found myself disappointed that we didn't see each other more. I went back and forth on that teeter-totter a lot.

As the burnt tree came into sight about fifteen minutes later, I was caught up in imagining Alec's dark hair shining in the morning light filtering through the trees. I'd definitely insist on walking behind him on a trail like this. I had a feeling I'd like the view.

I looked up to see Ethan using a rock to scrape at the charred bark of the old tree. It had been hit by lightning at some point in the past. All that was left was a huge forked stump that rose up about five feet out of the ground. There were no branches or leaves, and never any new growth, but that stump sat like a scarred sentinel on the trail. From where the burnt tree stood, a gap in the foliage allowed us to see down to Cass's house.

As I gazed down the hill, I was once again amazed at all that Cass had accomplished in her life. She'd never married, which had been a disappointment to her, but she'd had a very successful law career that had spanned more than four decades before she became a legal consultant to Colorado's elite. Heck, some of America's elite. She still had visitors come and seek her counsel, but I thought it was more for her hospitality and Zinn's cooking than actual legal needs.

"Ready for a drink, buddy?" I asked as I approached Ethan and Wade, my thoughts dragged back to the present.

"Sure." Ethan jumped up and headed to meet me as I swung the backpack off my shoulders and sat it in the shade of an aspen. I pulled out his water bottle and then a little dish for Wade, along with the dog's water bottle. Cass always insisted I treat her dog with the same care as I'd treat my son. Thus I always found myself carrying water and a dish for poor, pampered Wade. I'd prefer he just drink out of one of the little streams. But Ethan would rat me out if I didn't follow directions.

With boy and dog drinking quietly, I uncapped my own water bottle and took a few swigs. The water felt nice and cool. Even though it was only mid-morning, the temperature was rising. And my sweats, though comfy, were beginning to feel a little sticky on my legs.

"So what do you think about Alec?" I asked Ethan as we capped our bottles and shook out Wade's dish.

"He's cool." Ethan shrugged. Typical. He was such a boy.

"You okay with me dating him?" I zipped the pack closed and swung it back into place.

"Yep."

"Just yep?" I laughed and lightly pinched Ethan's rib cage.

"Stop." He wiggled away from me with a laugh. "Yep." He grinned.

"Okay. Well, if you have any questions, you can ask me," I said, getting serious again.

Ethan was quiet for a minute. "Well, Jess says you like Alec and are having fun, so I should just be happy for you."

It took me a moment to find my voice over the surprise in my throat: "He said that, huh?"

"Yeah. I think he's probably right. I mean, I have fun with Jess and you don't make a big deal out of it. So I just do the same thing for you and Alec."

"Well, thanks, buddy." I stared at Ethan as he looked down toward Cass's house. When had my sweet little boy gotten so grown up? His baby cheeks had leaned out and his hair had gotten darker. His limbs weren't pudgy but were starting to get gangly. His shoes looked way too big for the rest of his body. If I saw a zit I was gonna freak. Luckily his skin was still baby smooth. I couldn't resist the urge to pull him into my arms and kiss his little face. He landed on my lap with a grunt and turned his face under the onslaught of my kisses. He was getting too big for this treatment, and he seriously had the sharpest little butt bone in the world. But he allowed me my moment.

After I put him back on the ground, he began screwing and unscrewing the lid on his water bottle and staring at it like it was the most interesting thing in the world.

"Just one question?" He turned back to face me.

"Shoot."

"Do you guys kiss?"

I laughed. "Yes." Slight exaggeration. We'd shared two small kisses. I was totally counting them.

"That's gross." Ethan shook his head, stood up, and walked away to rejoin the trail.

"Someday you won't think so," I called as I caught up to him.

The next thirty minutes to the halfway point of the trail were hiked mostly in silence. I enjoyed watching Ethan and Wade run back and forth across the trail and into the denser brush and trees to chase a squirrel or look closer at a spiderweb or flower. Our progress wasn't fast, but it was peaceful. I loved summers with Ethan. No school and no schedule other than what I imposed on us for my job. We hiked, and on the rare day when I had the gumption, I'd even take him to the swimming pool.

After hauling him onto my lap earlier and feeling how big he'd grown, I tried not to watch the scene through tears. How grateful I was for that little guy. I sometimes thought Ethan had saved my life after Charlie passed. He'd given me the only real reason to get up each day. He'd needed me at a time when I needed someone to expect something from me. If not for him, I would have shriveled up from grief. I tried not to think about how much I'd probably let him down that first year. Those thoughts were best left alone.

At the high point of our hike, there was a flat meadow area, higher than the tree line below it, where we could see for miles. It seemed like all of Clark Springs was open to our view. Wade and Ethan were both panting by the time we found a shady spot on the side of the meadow and sat down. First thing I did was kick off my shoes and socks and pull my sweats up to my knees. It felt good to air out those puppies. Who cared if I hadn't shaved my legs since Saturday? The beasts of the mountains were all hairy too. Besides, Ethan wouldn't know the first thing about how my legs were supposed to look. I opened my pack and more water was passed around. Then I got out the bag of nuts and we began chomping away at our snack.

"Nuts wasn't my best idea," I mumbled to Ethan as I took another swig of water. "The salt is making my mouth dry."

"You should have packed oranges or apples," Ethan helpfully offered.

"Thanks for the tip, buddy. Where were you when I was packing the food?"

"Probably playing video games." Ethan gave me a grin that had gotten him out of a lot of trouble in the past.

"I do believe you're right." I flashed him a grin back.

Suddenly Wade's ears pricked up in the direction of the trail. Before long we heard the rumble of an ATV engine climbing closer to us.

"I wonder who that is," I said.

"Probably Jess. I don't know anyone else who uses this trail," Ethan replied. He stood up and began walking toward the sound. Oh, super. I wasn't even safe to wear sweats on my own mountain anymore.

"Ethan, wait. Let's just make sure," I hedged. I knew it was Jess. There's no way it wouldn't be. I was dressed like a pumpkin. With any luck he'd have Vivienne and a camera crew trailing along.

Ethan looked back at me like he thought I was worrying too much, but he stopped his progress and waited. I was grateful. At least my kid was obedient . . . this time.

Sure enough, it was Jess. I recognized him even with a baseball cap and sunglasses hiding his face and hair. His long, lean limbs looked at ease as he drove his four-wheeler through the clearing. His smile could have blinded me if I hadn't had my glasses on. *Good grief, I think there may just be such a thing as overbleaching your teeth*, I grumbled silently before mentally telling myself to get a grip and stop being so snarky.

In the throes of hero worship, Ethan and Wade were racing toward the intruder before he'd even come to a full stop.

Dust swirled around them as Jess stopped, but it didn't block my view of him jumping gracefully off the machine and giving Ethan a high five. Then he looked up and gave me a smile as he and Ethan began walking my way. Well, technically, you could call Jess's gait more of a saunter. It was ridiculous. Like a panther. I was pretty sure someone had taught him how to walk like that. I bet he never tripped or fell down the stairs like I did.

I quickly began tugging the cuffs of my sweatpants down to my ankles and praying that the sunlight hadn't been glinting off my stumpy leg hair.

"Hey, Kate." Jess's voice reached me before his body did.

"Mom, see, it *is* Jess." Ethan was smiling up at Jess. Wade's tail was wagging as he too looked up at the man of the hour.

"Hey, neighbor." I was proud of myself for achieving a cheerful-sounding greeting. He had, after all, told Ethan to be nice to Alec. So I owed him one. "Where's Vivienne Lawson?" I asked, calling her by her full name in a way that wasn't strange at all. Sigh.

"Oh, she's not really into riding ATVs. So she's relaxing back at the trailer," Jess replied with a smile. "I ran over to the big house to see Cass, and she told me you two had taken off up here. Hope it's okay that I chased you down." Jess folded his long body into the shade next to me and pulled off his ball cap as he sat. He ran his hands through his hair. I was somewhat happy to see that he got hat head like normal people do.

"Uh, no, that's fine," I managed. I tried to slide over a hair without Jess noticing. The shade wasn't exactly spacious, and he had sat down a little close for comfort. He noticed. And he winked. I wanted to shout at him that no one winks outside of the movies. It's cheesy. But I kept my cool.

"You look nice," he commented as he took off his sunglasses and gave me a once-over.

"Sure I do." I made my lips into a thin line and gave him the stink eye. I looked horrible. I couldn't get a compliment on my appearance from the guy I was dating, but this one was always mentioning it. What was up with that? It frazzled me. "I look like a pumpkin today and you know it," I said.

He laughed. "I would never have thought that. But now that you mention it . . ." He leaned back and gave me a second look.

I swatted at his arm, and he chuckled again. I quickly drew my hand back, shocked at what I had done. I had actually reached out to touch him. I looked him in the eye, trying to figure out what was happening. He met my perusal with a raised eyebrow. I wanted to swat him again.

Then I remembered last week's awkward scene in the parlor, where I had felt so left out. I had decided to try to make nice with everyone so I could be part of the group. For some reason, my discomfort around him always dove straight into moodiness. I sighed and attempted to redirect my feelings.

"Can I get a ride on your four-wheeler sometime?" Ethan interrupted the silent conversation Jess and I had been having. I can tell you that, for once, the interruption was welcome.

"Sure, buddy." Jess's eyes left my face and rested on Ethan.

"Okay." Ethan smiled and ran back over to the four-wheeler with Wade.

"What's up?" I asked when Jess's attention was back on me. I reached down and started plucking at the wild grass next to me so I didn't have to look so closely at those eyes.

"I need to leave town for a while," Jess began. "I'm up for a movie role that I wanted, which is cool, but construction has started on my new house, which makes the timing hard. I need a contact person here who can actually go to the homesite a couple times a week to check on the progress. I'd like someone who will give me honest feedback and information."

I looked up to see he'd been watching me as I pulled the grass into small pieces. "Okay. What did Cass say?"

"Cass?" Jess gave me a confused look.

"You said you'd gone to the big house," I explained.

"Oh, right. I was just stopping in to say hi to her. I was hoping *you* could help me with the contact person here in town."

"Oh, okay." Not okay. I didn't know the first thing about the topic, nor did I understand why I hadn't put on at least a smidge of mascara that morning. And why *me* when Cass knew literally every person in Clark Springs? "Well, let me think."

I picked up some more grass and began listing people in my head who would be good options for Jess to call. They had to be honest and knowledgeable about construction. Someone with the free time to go to his property a few times a week and make phone calls to Jess. I remembered Alec's reaction when he met Jess. Alec would probably love me forever if I got him hooked up with that kind of deal.

A smile lit my features as I looked back to where Jess was sitting, his eyes still resting on me. "I've got it. How about Alec?" I chirped.

"Alec?" Jess frowned. "That guy you're dating?"

"Sure. He'd be great. He's honest, he knows about construction, he could go over in the evenings, and I know he'd get a kick out of doing it for you." I clapped my hands together at my level of genius.

Jess looked slightly amused by my enthusiasm even as he said, "Well, Alec isn't exactly who I had in mind."

"Oh? If you had someone in mind, then why are you asking me for help?" I huffed a bit. I felt a little let down that I couldn't hand this present to Alec all wrapped up with a big bow.

"I'm asking *you* to do it." He shook his head and grinned like I was the thickest post in the fence. Maybe I was.

"Oh."

"So what do you think? Would you be able, and willing, to help me out? Be my point of contact while I'm in Los Angeles?" His gaze wandered back to his four-wheeler, which Ethan was now sitting on while pretending to ride it like a horse. The corners of Jess's mouth pulled up, but his eyes still looked serious. He almost acted like he cared what I said.

"Why?" I asked. I wasn't sure why he'd ask me. He slid his gaze back over to me. It made me nervous, so I did what I always do when nervous and let words come pouring out of my mouth. "I know nothing about construction. I've been a pain from the moment we met, and I'm a walking disaster. I wear sweatpants when I think no one is looking. I'm short. I get zits sometimes. My hair completely clashes with this tank top. I trip on things and spill things and say things I don't mean . . ."

Jess finally held up a hand to stop my monologue and started smiling again. "Easy," he chuckled. "I'm asking you because I know that you'll be honest with me. Everyone else around here just wants to please me, so they'll tell me what they think I want to hear. You, on the other hand, will just lay it out there. I need someone who doesn't care who I am."

"Well, I definitely don't care," I agreed softly while nodding my head thoughtfully.

Jess laughed. "That's exactly the kind of thing I'm talking about."

I opened my mouth in a shocked little *O* when I realized what I'd said. It made Jess laugh harder.

"I'm sorry."

"Don't be. Just be yourself and tell me the truth about how things are going here," Jess encouraged.

"Don't you have a foreman or a construction leader guy who should be doing that?" I hedged. "I mean, you did hear about how I messed up Cass's new kitchen, right?"

"Oh, I heard." He grinned. "And yes, I do have the best *'construction leader guy'* around." I gave in to the urge to roll my eyes. "He'll give me regular updates and keep me in the loop," Jess continued. "But I want a second set of eyes to tell me if he really painted the kitchen aqua when he said it was blue. Or if they put a closet in the bathroom rather than a toilet stall."

"I don't know, Jess . . ." I broke our eye contact and picked up more grass. I needed to think.

"Well, at least you're calling me 'Jess' now. That's a start."

"We can go back to Mr. Sullivan anytime. Don't push it," I retorted with a raise of my eyebrows.

After a few moments of silence, I shifted my gaze to Ethan and Wade. I was pretty sure they were doing some sort of Indian rain dance around the four-wheeler. It made me smile.

"I'm willing to pay if it will sway you," Jess broke into my thoughts.

I grinned and looked back at him. "I'll do it for twenty-five thousand dollars."

Now it was Jess's turn to huff. "What on earth would you do with twenty-five thousand dollars?"

"I'd buy all the pink sweatpants and orange tank tops that I can find," I stated.

He smiled. "That would sure be sad for all the women out there who want to copy your look."

I nodded. "I know. You're probably right. How about I do it for fifteen thousand dollars and not be quite so greedy."

Jess pretended to think about it for a while before turning back to me. "Okay, how about I pay you five hundred dollars per week *and* all the fish I can catch when I'm back in town?"

Now it was my turn to think about it. "I suppose that would be fair . . . as long as you're gone for at least ten months or so. I have my wardrobe to consider!"

Jess laughed out loud. "I don't think that's going to happen."

"Fine. I'll just do it for all the four-wheeler rides that Ethan can stand when you're in town. You can keep your stinky fish and your money."

"I really am willing to pay you, Kate." Jess grew serious once again.

I shrugged. "Don't worry about it. Ethan will probably cost you fifteen thousand dollars in gas."

"Deal!" Jess offered his hand to shake on it. I hesitated before offering mine in return. His was warm—and large and callused. Just like Alec's. I didn't like the comparison.

He stood up and casually dusted off his pants before putting his hat and sunglasses back on. "Well, thanks. I'll drop off some information before I leave town," he said. I looked up at him and nodded.

He strode toward Ethan, and I couldn't hear their conversation over the hum of the ATV as he started it again. I watched as he gave Ethan another high five and then headed back down the mountain in a cloud of dust.

I wasn't proud of it, but the next Saturday I ate three chocolate-frosted cake donuts for breakfast. With sprinkles. I washed them down with a cola. No, not diet cola. Full-strength, high-octane, diabetes-courting cola. Alec was taking Ethan and me to a water park in Oakdale that day. I considered it carbo-loading. Doing a colon cleanse, fat cleanse, or some sort of diuretic would have made sense. But this was an emotionally charged situation, and I couldn't think straight. Donuts it was.

Ethan was in heaven as he licked frosting from his fingertips. I knew a crash would come later in the day after our breakfast of champions left us hanging, but there was no getting around it now. Besides, I totally needed the artificial high to keep my shaky smile in place. I just could not be fun and flirty in a swimsuit if I didn't have donuts and caffeine backing me up.

I was determined not to mention my worries about looking chubby because I'd recently read a magazine article that listed things men hate hearing women complain about. Surprise, surprise, "looking fat" was on that list. Yep. I was gonna keep my lips sealed. At least in front of Alec. In front of Ethan, the fly in my living area, the creatures of the forest, and my reflection in the mirror, all bets were off.

As I zipped from room to room gathering suntan lotion, beach towels, flip-flops, and sunglasses, I mumbled about how I was sure my thighs were jiggling and my chest would escape the suit at some point. I had no idea what on earth had prompted me to say yes. It was moments like these that I truly, madly, deeply missed the comfort of being married and knowing the man was yours regardless of how much wiggle was in your step.

Finally, Ethan had had enough. "Mom, stop it!" He even went so far as to turn away from the TV and glare at me. "You look fine. You are the only one who cares how you look. Let's just go have fun." Having given his super-adult-like speech, he turned back to his show.

I froze for a few moments and gaped at my little man-boy. Those words were something Charlie would have said to me on just such an occasion. Charlie had always laughed or rolled his eyes when I complained about my body.

"Honey," he'd say. *"A guy likes a little something to snuggle without worrying about it poking his eye out. Your curves make you womanly. Those models may be skinny, but they don't look healthy and real like you do."* I'd always smiled at him and appreciated his efforts, all the while wishing I was just a few pounds lighter.

But hearing Ethan tell me to just relax and have fun made me pause and think for a moment. Maybe I'd have to try a little harder to accept my curves and just enjoy life. Besides, some of those curves had come from the birth of that great kid who was smearing chocolate on his face right now.

I heard a knock at the door and glanced at the clock. It was still about ten minutes before I expected Alec, and he wasn't known to run early, so I figured it was probably Cass. I glanced down at my slightly peach-colored legs—an improvement over winter's pasty white—and took a second to wonder if I should grab my cover-up before answering the door. At this moment I was in nothing more than my Hawaiian-print one-piece. No bikini for me. It didn't make sense to show off the stomach if I was so worried about the thighs.

"Who do you think is at the door?" I said to Ethan as I tried to decide if I should answer the door or return to my room for the cover-up. Ethan shrugged helpfully. "Thanks, buddy." I ruffled his hair and headed for the door. Worst-case scenario, it was Alec. And Alec would see me in my suit at some point, anyhow. May as well get the shock factor over now.

I swung open the door and realized that worst-case scenario would actually have been preferable to the horror show that was upon me in the form of Jess. With Vivienne. I hurriedly backed up and only opened the door partially, keeping my lower half hidden behind the door. Jess grinned, and Vivienne gave me a cool little smile.

I cleared my throat. "Uh, hi there, neighbor."

"Hey. I'm on my way to the airport to catch my flight back to LA. I wanted to drop off a few things."

"Uh-huh." I stood as still as possible, awkwardly bent in half, everything from the waist down firmly in hiding. I realized it was childish to cower like that. I just did not care.

"Hey, Jess." Ethan joined me at the door and gave me a funny look as he tried to elbow the door open wider. I held firm, which only served to annoy Ethan and amuse Jess. Vivienne's face was emotionless.

"Hey, pal. How you doing?" Jess smiled at Ethan.

"Good. Getting ready to go to the water park with Mom's friend, Alec," Ethan replied.

"That sounds fun."

"Like a date?" Vivienne asked. I couldn't tell if she was surprised I was dating or mocking me for having a date at a water park. Either way, it was rude.

"Yep, so we've got to hurry," I inserted before Ethan could get all chummy and invite them in. "What did you want to drop off?"

"She's not even going to invite us in," Vivienne stage-whispered to Jess. It was like she'd read my mind. Was she a vampire? With her uber-thin build, emotionless expression, and perfect skin, I could make a case for it.

I met her gaze when she turned away from Jess's ear. She didn't like me. I'd realized that before, but I just couldn't figure out why. I was hiding behind a door in my swimsuit, thighs quivering in horror, while she stood on my doorstep looking like she'd stepped straight out of a salon. What on earth did she have to worry about as far as I was concerned?

"Viv," Jess said, giving her a look and turning back to Ethan and me. He held a folder out. Taking it would mean I had to peel one of my hands off the side of the door and risk letting it swing from its current position. This was a problem. I looked to Ethan and tipped my head in the direction of Jess's hand, suggesting he grab the folder for me.

"Uh . . ." Ethan scrunched up his face in concentration before Jess chuckled and handed the folder to Ethan. The sound of Jess's amusement made Vivienne's brows draw together and her lips purse. Sadly, it didn't do anything to detract from her looks. It just made her appear pouty and perfectly kissable.

"*Anyhoooo*." Jess elongated the word in a way that acknowledged how awkward this situation was. It made me grin before I could stop it. My grin made Jess grin, which made Vivienne pout, and I was worried Ethan was going to get a neck cramp from looking back and forth between the intruders on the doorstep and his seriously demented mother hiding behind the door.

"Those the papers for the construction project?" I finally managed.

"Yep." Jess nodded as Ethan looked down at the folder in his hand. "There's a construction schedule in there listing the order of projects and when they are expected to be completed. There's also a page of details such as what type of wood to use for cabinets, paint colors, and flooring selections."

"You sure you want me to do this?" I bit my lip as I looked at the folder in Ethan's grip. I wasn't sure I wanted this level of responsibility or involvement in Jess's affairs. I felt like we came from such different worlds, and despite his serious physical appeal, I wasn't sure I wanted to enter that world. I liked my safe little everyday small-town life.

"Baby, I tried to tell you to ask someone else," Vivienne said in a whiny, pouty way. *Baby?* Yuck.

I glanced up from the folder and gave her my best icy smile, the one I liked to pretend I used on girls in high school who were mean to me, but which I really only used when practicing in the mirror. I had no way of knowing how it looked when used on a live human. Judging by the sudden catch in Jess's breathing and the narrowing of Vivienne's eyes, I achieved something. But the fact that Jess had looked away and started coughing as though covering a laugh was not good.

"I'm sure it will be fine!" I chirped, suddenly incredibly eager to dive into the war. My embarrassment faded in a rush that felt a little like nausea. It had nothing to do with donuts and everything to do with Vivienne. In a bold move, I threw the door wide, stepped out, and grabbed the folder from Ethan's hands. I may not be as dainty as Vivienne, and no one would pay money to see me in a swimsuit, but my size had an advantage in this situation. I'd crush her stick-thin little body like a twig.

Jess's grin faltered at the look on my face. Or maybe it faltered at the look of me in a bathing suit. No, it was definitely the fire in my eyes. He hurriedly put an arm around Vivienne's slender shoulders as she took a step toward me. I wished I'd been wearing five-inch heels so that we could at least be looking eye to eye during our standoff.

"Well, thanks again, Kate. I'll be in touch." Jess half dragged Vivienne away as she started talking animatedly and kept looking over her shoulder at me. I was fairly sure I heard her say something about me being crazy and her not trusting me at all. I pointed two of my fingers at my own eyes and then darted them back toward her in the "I'll be watching you" sign. If she thought I was crazy, then I may as well act the part. I had the satisfaction of seeing her mouth drop open before she turned to Jess and began squawking again.

I was just about to slam the door closed when I saw Alec walk around the side of the big house headed in our direction. Super. His progress came to a screeching halt when he saw Jess and Vivienne walking toward him. His face broke out in a huge smile, and he stepped toward Jess with his hand out. Jess shook his hand, and the two men began talking, but I couldn't hear what they were saying from my vantage point.

Vivienne, clearly in no mood to be social, continued stalking around the big house to the front area, where the car was parked. Jess slapped Alec on the back in a buddy-buddy way before following his poor, dear, pouty-lipped little vampire. I hoped she burned to a crisp in the sunlight.

After Jess disappeared from sight, Alec turned to me, his grin still huge, and jogged the distance to my front door. "Man, I will never get used to seeing Jess Sullivan hanging around here." He laughed. He pushed past me into the house and turned to finish his gushing. "And Vivienne Lawson right there with him. Wow. Wait until I tell my buddies." He smiled again as I closed the door. "Although, she sure didn't seem very happy. What happened?" he asked.

"It can be very painful to have such a big head," I replied sweetly before crossing to the kitchen and setting the folder down on the counter.

I turned back to face Alec and caught him giving me a slow perusal. Oh, yes, that's right, I was in a swimsuit. Guess the time for worrying about his reaction was past. Here he was now, and he was reacting. When his eyes made it back up to my face, I could feel the pulse of mortification in my hairline and the heat of my face turning red.

"Nice." Alec nodded in what appeared to be approval. Well, that was new, and kind of nice. He typically didn't notice a thing about how I looked.

"Thanks." I let my lips curve in what I hoped was a gracious smile. Inside, my stomach flipped and threatened to throw chocolate-donut goodness out of my mouth. I could hardly breathe for fear of my stomach lunging out of its holding pattern and wiping that flirty look off his face.

"I'm glad you said that," Ethan piped up. Ethan, who I'd forgotten was standing there watching everything. "'Cause all morning Mom's been saying how fat she looks in her swimsuit. I think she looks fine." Ethan, who was going to be grounded for life and never play a video game again. Was it possible to die of embarrassment? Was it possible for your face to explode from blushing?

Luckily, Alec laughed and looked back at me, that smile warming me even more, if that was possible. "Nah, your mom looks great in that suit." He winked at me. Jess had winked at me once and I'd thought it ridiculous. Alec's wink made me want to soar to the moon.

I was hard-pressed not to strut a little as I excused myself to get the bag of dry clothing, sunscreen, and towels I had packed for the day. In my newfound confidence, I was tempted to not even wear my wrap in the car on the ride to the water park. Luckily, I remembered that legs standing up look much better than legs sitting down and pressed together on a seat. So I wrapped it up, and we hit the road, leaving Vivienne and her pouty lips in the dust.

The water park in Oakdale was good sized for a relatively small town. The park itself was run-of-the-mill, with various slides, a lazy river, splash pad, and wave pool. Yep, a typical park, but not a typical day. The last time I'd gone to a water park was as a teenager, pre-children, pre-widowhood, and in the glory days of living life sag-free. If only I had appreciated those days more.

There was nothing typical about me in a swimsuit on a date, with my son in tow. In fact, the whole thing felt more and more odd to me as I watched Alec pay for the tickets. My newly acquired confidence struggled to bear up under the picture my mind was painting in fascinating detail of the various viewpoints Alec would have of me throughout the day. It was all I could do to keep my hands still at my sides rather than try to pull my wrap tighter around me and slink back to the car.

Any true water park lover knows that item number one upon gaining entrance is to find the perfect spot to lay out towels and establish your little oasis among the bikini dwellers. It was with that in mind that I dutifully hoofed around behind Alec and Ethan, who were acting a little overeager for my taste. They were laughing and pointing out possible locations, taking stock of the slides and planning an order. For an uneasy moment, I felt like the mom following along behind my sons. *Well, young is as young does*, I told myself, *so get to skipping!*

After managing to find a spot with a shade canopy, we spread out our towels, and it was time for the unveiling. Yes, technically the unveiling had happened in my kitchen already. And, yes, Alec had given me no reason to think I should feel awkward about my body. But that little scene had happened about forty minutes earlier, and as I was operating under the theory that most men suffer from short-term memory loss, I was sure he'd already forgotten giving me the thumbs-up. Another cause for concern was all the teenage girls tossing their hair and giggling as they strutted about the park. I wasn't sure I'd look quite as appealing in a side-by-side comparison.

I had forgotten how insecure a person could feel while dating! With that thought came the familiar ping of missing Charlie. This all would have been so much easier if it were Charlie, Ethan, and I out for a day as a family. I shook the thought away. In the end, as my fingers trembled uselessly at the tie to my wrap, I was saved by Ethan.

"Mom, I want to start on the big slide over there." Ethan pointed toward a huge slide, probably the one the park featured in its advertisements, and gave me a huge smile. He was bouncing on his toes.

"I'll take him." Alec's beaming smile matched Ethan's. "Why don't you finish getting settled, and we'll come back for you after our run?"

Oh, well. "Okay." I gave a little smile to *my boys* and waved them off. They didn't spare me a glance. At this point, my fingers magically overcame their urge to tremble, and I whipped that wrap off in a move that would make any stage performer jealous. I stood watching Alec and Ethan bound away like two eager puppies before my eye was caught by another woman standing nearby, laying out towels.

"Looks like your boys are going to have a great time today!" she chirped.

I felt a blush start to rise as I gave her a smile in return before turning my back to her and busying myself with setting out towels and sunscreen. How humiliating. I was only twenty-nine years old, for heaven's sake. Certainly not old enough to be Alec's mother!

By the time Ethan and Alec had returned, dripping water and smiling to rival the glorious sunshine, I was ready to claim my rightful place as a member of the group, not the mommy.

"That was awesome. We want to go on another. Are you ready, Mom?" Ethan asked.

"I'm ready!" I practically growled between slightly clenched teeth. "Let's do this thing!" And I stalked off toward the nearest slide I could find.

After an hour of riding slides, lounging on tubes down the lazy river, and cleverly avoiding the wave pool, I was exhausted. Water parks are not for the faint of heart. Nor are they for women who only exercise every third Wednesday, if they're in the mood. Water parks are for those with endless energy. I couldn't press on and suggested we retire to the towels for a snack. If I just happened to pass out and sleep for the next five hours, well, the boys could carry on without me.

Thankfully, the boys agreed that they were starving—'cause are boys ever not starving?—and we trudged back to our home away from home. Okay, I trudged. Alec and Ethan seemed to have no problem bouncing along. It was peculiar, but the more energetic Alec proved to be, the less appealing he became. It was obvious that he'd never be happy lounging with me in sweats and eating pints of Ben & Jerry's while the world rolled along. Bummer. 'Cause he looked so good all lean and muscled in his board shorts. I should have known it was too good to be true.

After a brief rest—really, fifteen minutes is all?—Alec and Ethan begged me to join them on an enclosed tube slide that twisted and turned all over before splashing into the pool below. The "cool" part about this slide was that it was made of black tubing and was basically pitch-black inside, even in the middle of the day. The "extra cool" part was that you were allowed to go down in a group, forming a sort of train by wrapping your legs around the person in front of you.

I didn't see the appeal of such a situation. "Wouldn't the dark coloring make it really hot inside?" I hedged. "Doesn't it hurt to get banged all around with someone else's legs wrapped around you?"

Ethan and Alec met each other's gaze as though seeing if the other understood what, exactly, my objection was.

Alec lost the battle and turned to me. "I think it's kind of romantic!" He winked. Well, odd, winking had seemed pretty great this morning, but winking was definitely not working for me this afternoon.

"Nice try." I attempted a laugh, hoping he wasn't serious about thinking it was romantic.

Alec and Ethan once again exchanged a look, and this time Alec shrugged. This would be the sign for Ethan to take over.

"Please, Mom. I mean, how often do we get to come here? It'll be fun!" Ethan turned those striking brown eyes on me and, despite the laws of human nature, I swear he was able to make them grow and become more round. It was ridiculous, but effective.

"Fine," I mumbled as I pushed to a stand.

"What happened to *'Let's do this thing'*?" Alec teased as he took my hand in his. I smiled up at him. At least he'd held my hand rather than scampering off without me this time. I squeezed his hand and started walking.

After scaling at least ten flights of stairs, I began to understand why all the people at water parks are skinny. When we reached the top, I was breathing hard but trying to appear cool and unruffled, which just made for a sort of strangled noise and an odd rise and fall of my chest with every breath I took. Alec gave me a slightly concerned glance, which was nothing compared to the look I got from the water park employee, who was about two seconds away from calling an ambulance. I gave him a curt nod, letting him know that if he made that call he may as well call for two ambulances, because I'd take him down with me. He nodded back at me. Clearly I wasn't the first crazed nearly thirty-year-old to come to the park and attempt to relive the flirty days of adolescence while expecting death at any moment.

I could have kissed that water park employee when he let a few people go before us. He made it sound like it was protocol, but I knew from the sly look he gave me that he was doing it for me. He was on my good list, and I'd have told him so, but this little exchange was on the down-low, and Alec didn't need to see me as the lethargic couch lover I really was.

When it was our turn, Alec suggested I go first, followed by Ethan, with him bringing up the rear. I had no reason to object to this arrangement. It protected Ethan and meant that I didn't have to wrap my legs around anyone. With how much tribulation I had experienced that day, I was sure to have regrown a few leg hairs. Adding *scruffy* to the list of adjectives Alec used to describe me wasn't on the top on my list.

As I entered the tube and sat down, waiting for Ethan to wrap his little legs around my waist, I was hit by a hot puff of air coming from inside the tube. Swell. I was right in my worries that it would be like sliding down a stovepipe.

When Alec was settled, the water park employee, who would be getting a Christmas card from me, counted us down before Alec pushed us off of the ledge.

It really was pitch-black inside. I couldn't even see my hand in front of my face. In a way, this was freeing, because while I still needed to keep my screams silent, I was able to make a grotesque face of fear without worrying about Alec seeing it.

I could hear Ethan whooping and Alec laughing as we twisted and turned down the tunnel at what felt like warp speed. Occasionally, a turn was so sharp that we'd fall to our sides or our backs, landing in the lap of the person behind us.

The ride felt like it took a long time. I was finally relaxing into it and beginning to feel my expression ease into a smile when I suddenly pounded into something with the force of a steam engine. I felt a heavy thud on my chest, followed by my eye and forehead. And then that something was lying on top of me. I screamed, and when I heard a return scream, I realized that it was a person.

I pushed at the body—a male, judging by the fact that my struggling hands met with flesh—and instead of screaming began yelling words like "get off," "move," and "ouch!"

At this point, I would have been flat on my back while this guy used my body for a sled, except that poor Ethan was attached to me and I was using his stomach as a pillow. Ethan was no longer whooping but yelling "Mom! Mom!" as we continued to hurtle down the slide.

Alec was calling my name, which added to the chaos, and I felt my legs connect with a bony knee, or foot, or something as my mystery guest tried to push away from me. It caused me to squeak in distress.

"When does this ride end?" I screamed at the top of my lungs.

Luckily, the universe heard my call, because I saw a point of light up ahead. That light gave me the extra energy I needed to give the guy a hard shove, which only caused him to scoot up my body further, bashing my head again.

I knew in that moment that all hope was lost of coming away from that park looking like someone who'd had a great time and was "totally game" for these types of adventures. Instead, I would be leaving the park on a stretcher, begging to wake up and find out it had all been a dream. I was young at heart but seriously too old for this junk.

I groaned in relief as my body splashed into the pool and the weight of the guy lifted off me. I was tempted to stay submerged for a while, floating and pretending it was all a dream, but strong arms grabbed me beneath the armpits and hauled me up. I gasped for air as I surfaced. Alec was there, wrapping his arms around me and dragging me toward the edge of the pool while I heard poor Ethan yelling for a lifeguard in a voice that haunted me.

"Ethan, Ethan," I gasped out, desperate to stop his yelling and let him know I was okay.

"Shhh, Ethan's fine," Alec said close to my ear, misinterpreting my concern. "He's getting some help."

"I'm okay," I insisted, trying to stand.

"No, you're not." Alec's voice was as firm as his arms as we stepped from the water and I was immediately laid on the ground. "You need someone to check you out."

"I thought you already did that," I tried to joke, but Alec's face was serious.

Alec's head suddenly turned, and he yelled, "HEY!" as he released me and stood up. I turned my aching head—wow, it really was starting to ache—in the direction Alec was facing to see a guy walking toward us with a bloody nose. "Who climbs *up* a water slide at a water park? Are you stupid?" Alec pointed a finger at him. "People go *down* slides!"

The guy stopped by my side and knelt down next to me. "Sorry, lady," he said.

"You should be. That was idiotic of you," I replied in an annoyed voice, unwilling to really yell at him, but angry all the same. "And it hurt too." I gestured toward his nose, and he shrugged a shoulder.

"You look worse," he replied.

"What?" I looked to Alec for clarification, but he was pushed out of the way as the lifeguard finally arrived on scene with his first-aid kit, followed closely by Ethan, who had tears in his eyes.

Oh, great, it was my best friend, the park employee from the top of the slide. In fact, the entire slide had been shut down while I was tended to. I couldn't help but notice that he was breathing heavily after his rush down the ten flights of stairs. Excellent. Maybe worth getting hurt to see.

"You're in serious trouble, buddy!" the park employee said to the teen, who was still kneeling by me.

"Yep," he replied.

"Park security is coming to get you as soon as I take a look at your face," the park employee went on as he clicked open his kit and began rummaging around. I noticed his name badge said *Justin*.

"I hope your mom grounds you," I added. Justin chuckled, which made me feel a little better.

We were all silent as Justin cleaned up the perp's blood and handed him some gauze before letting security take him away. Then it was my turn. I hadn't seen a mirror yet, but judging by the amount of places Justin cleaned and how badly my head ached, I was pretty sure I'd lost the tube-slide war.

When Justin had done all he could, he clicked his box shut and turned to Alec. "You'll probably want to watch her for any signs of concussion," he said. Alec nodded. Then Justin turned to me. "When you feel ready, let's get you off this cement and back to a shady area where you can rest. I'm afraid you'll have to call it a day after this." His gaze strayed away before he looked back at me. "You're gonna have quite a shiner." His mouth lifted as though he wanted to smile.

"I'm tough." I grinned. Ouch, it hurt to grin.

"Yep," Justin said as he put an arm around my back to help me to a sitting position. "First thing I thought when I saw you."

Somehow I appreciated his humor when all I wanted to do was hide. The crowd was dispersing, and as soon as I released Justin, the water slide would be back up and running.

Alec jumped in and helped me stand, and Ethan replaced Justin, wrapping a small arm around my waist. Poor Ethan. He looked worried and kept glancing away from my face. That could not be a good sign. Then again, maybe he'd never ask me to take him to a water park again. Every cloud has a silver lining.

By Monday morning, my headache had finally passed, but my left eye was swollen and turning a startling shade of greenish blue. I looked like I'd been attacked by someone in a dark tube slide—wait, I had! My nose was tender, the cut on my lip was scabbing over, and my knees had bruises where that kid and I had pummeled each other on our descent.

Alec had called the big house on our way home to tell Cass what had happened, and Zinn had jumped in like a good little nursing soldier. I'd been fed like a queen for the past two days, which had been a real treat. Alec had called to check in on me, although I tried not to feel bad about knowing that he'd been finishing up at Cass's house and hadn't stopped by in person. Ethan had done a splendid job of playing nurse and even agreed to sit through the whole BBC *Pride and Prejudice* miniseries with me on Sunday.

Now it was Tuesday morning, and my phone was ringing. I glanced from my place on the couch to see where the phone had ended up. Great. It was on the kitchen counter. I had begun the achy process of heaving myself off the couch when Ethan trotted out from his bedroom, where he'd been playing with his train set.

"I got it, Mom." He smiled over at me. I returned his smile gratefully and leaned back into the cushions.

I could hear his mumbled greeting, and then his face lit up and he began speed-talking like only an eight-year-old can. I felt bad for whoever was on the receiving end of one of his hyperspeed monologues. Trying to get a word in edgewise was like attempting to stop a speeding locomotive. You were kind of along for the ride.

After he wound down, I heard his footsteps as he brought the phone to me. I had zoned back into the talk show I was watching and forgotten all about the phone call and the person Ethan was monopolizing. Watching other people's trashy lives can do that to a girl. Ethan handed me the phone without clueing me in to who it was and then hustled back to his room, eager to get back to his game. Even without him telling me who the caller was, I was pretty sure I knew. Only a few people got that kind of cheery reaction out of Ethan.

"Hello?"

"Hey, Kate. It's Jess." I was right.

"Hey, Jess. How's it going?" I mumbled. Not purposely. It's just that on the television, Jenny was about to find out if Bill or Sam was her baby daddy. It was a pivotal moment, and I had watched them fight for the last twenty minutes in order to get here.

"Happy to hear from me, as always." Jess chuckled.

"Sorry. It's just that I've been waiting to find out who the father is and they're telling us now," I explained.

Jess was silent on his end for a moment. Probably trying to digest that information. "Uh, do I want to ask?" he finally said.

"Long story. Can you give me one second . . ." was my distracted reply as I watched the host tear open the envelope in front of a teary Jenny. Bill and Sam both wore stoic expressions. "Wow, she's freaking out!" I said out loud.

"Who's freaking out?" Jess asked.

"Jenny!"

"Should I call you back later?" he teased.

"No, just hold on. Sorry. He's opening the . . ." I didn't finish the sentence and watched entranced as the host said the name of the father. The audience went wild. Jenny was sobbing, and a relieved Sam, not the father, was led offstage. Bill was just staring in shock while Jenny yelled in his face. It was a gratifying moment.

"Okay, what's up?" I clicked off the TV and licked my lip where my smile had stretched my skin a bit.

"Well, maybe I should ask you that. Ethan says you were in some kind of accident this weekend and have been lying on the couch—and now you're involved in some sort of paternity testing?"

"Oh." I laughed at what Jess must be thinking. "I was watching a trashy talk show. Bill is the father. But Jenny is angry about it 'cause she loved Sam. But Sam really dodged a bullet on that one, 'cause Jenny is kind of a freak show. Like circus level." I smiled even though he couldn't see it.

"Poor Bill," Jess said dryly.

"Indeed!"

"And the accident?"

"Oh, that . . ." This time I hedged. I wasn't exactly out to impress Jess, mostly because I'd already made several crazy impressions and didn't hold out any hope of undoing his opinion of me. Still, that didn't mean I needed him to know that I'd been hanging at a water park and gotten attacked in a tube slide.

"Would you believe I was saving a baby in a runaway stroller?" I asked.

"Nope."

"Well, how about saving children in a runaway car? I had to chase it down and jump in and apply the brakes."

"Still doesn't ring true to me."

"Okay, fine. You want the truth?"

"I really do, Kate." Jess sounded serious. Oddly serious. It was time to whip out the big guns.

"Fine. There was this really sweet older woman walking across the street when a group of road cyclists came by and didn't see her. They were about to plow her down, so I ran to grab her and they got me instead. Really banged me up. My eye is black and blue, my lip is scabbed over, my nose is swollen, and my knees are bruised. But it was worth it to keep her from getting hurt."

"Wow."

"I know, huh?"

"Just, wow."

"Right?" Oops, I may have sounded smug on that last one.

"I just . . . really . . . don't believe you." Odd how I could actually hear Jess's silent laughter through the phone.

"Well," I huffed dramatically, "that's your own problem. I'm sure your Hollywood lifestyle has made you cynical and afraid to trust." Good one. Point me. Zing!

"How about I tell you what I think happened?"

"Fine. Whatever." I purposely used a bored voice.

"I think you and Ethan went to a water park with your super hunky new boyfriend, Alec. You were on a tube slide and a kid was climbing up from the bottom and you crashed into him. The injuries you got from 'saving the old woman' sound accurate, though." He chuckled.

I sighed loudly. "Who told you?"

"Ethan. About two seconds ago. Wasn't he standing near you while he talked?"

"Do you honestly think I listen to every Ethan monologue?" I joked.

"Especially when there's the matter of a paternity test to steal your attention away," Jess replied.

"Yes, well, of course. I have my priorities." I finally laughed. Jess joined me. It was a nice moment. Unexpectedly so.

"Are you really okay? What a crazy accident," Jess said when our laughter stopped.

"Yes. A little sore, but fine."

"I bet Alec feels awful."

"Probably." I shrugged even though he couldn't see me.

"What do you mean, 'probably'? Hasn't he been by to check on you?" Jess sounded surprised and maybe a little annoyed.

"Well, it's just . . ." I sighed, unsure of what to say when I didn't fully understand myself why he hadn't been by.

"Just what?" Jess pressed.

"Don't worry about it. You're a busy guy. What did you need?" I decided evasion was the best tactic. There was entirely too much focus on me, and I needed that to end.

Jess was quiet for a moment before he replied. "Fine," he said, even though his tone said he wasn't fine with dropping it. "I was wondering if you'd had a chance to drop by my place. They were supposed to be finishing the foundation yesterday and today. But it sounds like you've been busy recovering."

"Oh, man. Sorry." I meant it.

"Don't apologize. Recovering from a tube-slide terrorist attack isn't something to take lightly." His joking tone was back.

"Obviously. Not to mention that finding out who the father of your child is should be taken seriously," I returned.

"Obviously," Jess said, using my own words in reply.

"Honestly, it's just been really painful to walk. I promise I'll get over there tomorrow and check on things after I'm done working," I offered. "How is LA treating you?"

"Good. I got a callback on that part I was after." He sounded happy.

"That's great."

After a moment of silence that was all the more awkward because the rest of the conversation had been flowing nicely, I cleared my throat.

"Yeah, well, I really hope you feel better quickly, Kate," Jess spoke into the silence.

"Thanks."

"I don't suppose you want to send me a picture of that black eye. Ethan says it's pretty amazing. I could show it to the makeup crew on my next set, give them some pointers," he teased.

I didn't know how to react. My first thought was to bluster angrily, but instead I heard myself saying, "Why not?"

Jess must have been surprised, because there was another moment of silence before he said goodbye. I clicked off without a word and pressed the camera button on my cell. Before I could give it a second thought, I took a close-up picture of my eye and sent it off to Jess with the caption *Just glad that sweet old woman is okay!*

Chapter 7

A few weeks later, my black eye had finally healed, and I found myself on Jess's property, giving him another update. This time we were video-chatting as I walked around the property, letting him see the changes for himself.

During our conversation, he informed me that he'd be bringing his family back to Clark Springs the next week to spend some time touring his property and relaxing together. His younger brother, Jack, was engaged and was considering having his wedding at Jess's new place. In addition to the house being built on the property, Jess had hired a landscape architect who would begin drawing up plans. Jack and his fiancée wanted to see the land in person before deciding for sure. In my opinion, it would definitely be a beautiful place for a wedding when it was all done.

It would also be a great way to introduce his family and friends to his new sprawling country estate. Okay, those were my words. Jess referred to his new home as his *cabin*. If it were a cabin, then I was the queen of Timbuktu, and someone had better start treating me as such.

"That'll be nice to spend some time with your family," I said as I got into my car to head back home. "The property is really coming together nicely. The house isn't quite livable, though. Are you all going to stay in the RV?" I asked, referring to the trailer Jess lived in while in town.

"Yes. We camped a lot as kids, so it shouldn't be hard. Although Zara might not like it."

"Zara?" I asked.

"Yeah, Jack's fiancée. I don't know if she's camped or anything before. I'm sure Jack would tell me if it were going to be a problem," Jess reasoned.

"Do you know if Jack has even asked Zara about staying in an RV?"

"No. That's for him to worry about, not me." Jess sounded oddly defensive.

"Okay." I decided to drop it. His family's level of comfy cozy was not any of my concern. "Just shoot me a text when you know what day your family will be arriving so that I don't accidently crash any parties." I paused while waiting for a car to pass so I could make a left onto Cass's drive. "I'd hate to be the crazy neighbor wandering in uninvited."

"Okay, but honestly, is this something I need to be worrying about?" he asked in a slightly uncertain tone.

I laughed as I turned onto Cass's property and drove up to my cottage. "You know what happens when you assume, don't you?"

He made a noise that told me he knew exactly where I was going with that. "Fine. I'll call Jack."

I told him goodbye and good luck. I didn't know Zara, but I did know that no good came out of unasked questions.

As luck would have it, when the Sullivan family did arrive in town, Zara turned out to be perfectly perfect in every way. A regular Mary Poppins. I would have been genetically coded to hate her guts, except that she was also perfectly nice and had a perfectly lovely sense of humor. On principle I decided that I'd have to at least 10 percent hate her. I had no choice, really.

Jess had called Aunt Cass and invited her, Ethan, and me to a lunch barbeque on his property. He wanted us to meet his family and for his family to meet his neighbors. Cass had immediately accepted his invitation on behalf of all of us. I couldn't quite believe how nervous I was.

I'd asked if I could bring Alec. It would score me total bonus points with him and also allow me the pleasure of not being alone. Cass had shut me down cold. I was pretty sure that Alec wasn't scoring points with Cass because I hadn't seen his face for over a week after the water-park incident. He'd called, sure, but no visits and no chocolates for the injured. If I was honest, he wasn't scoring points with me, either. But in my desperation—excuse me, newly flexible attitudes about dating—I was trying not to hold it against him . . . even if the two times we'd gone out since had felt a little hollow somehow.

So here I found myself, dateless and standing in the dirt outside of Jess's RV while meeting more beautiful people than one family should have. I tried to stand up straight and smile pretty for the new faces while watching Ethan run around Jess like a puppy who hadn't seen his master in too long.

Smoke, delicious-smelling smoke, rose from a barbeque grill that had been set up a few feet from the RV. On a table under the shade awning were all sorts of delightful-looking foods.

The men of the Sullivan clan were getting chairs set up and bringing food out of the RV. I had a chance to observe them for a moment before introductions. Clearly, they were made from the same mold. Tall, dark, and delectable. They were okay, if you went for that sort of look.

Their mother, Sharon, was a cheerful little raven-haired general, shouting out directions for the "boys" to move this, set up that, and generally jump to. Somehow she did it all with a sparkle in her eye. Perhaps my favorite thing about Sharon Sullivan was that she was about the same height as me. If that little sprite of a woman could get those strapping boys to quiver like a bunch of little bunny rabbits, then I was sure I'd be her biggest fan.

Zara remained in the RV when we first arrived, but she soon joined the chaos of the gathering, carrying a large bowl of salad in her slender arms. She was also raven haired and had big, cheerful blue eyes. She was, of course, "thrilled" to meet us and just "loving" the adventure of camping out in the "wilds of Colorado." Then, as if to add an exclamation point to her chipper greeting, she set down the bowl of salad, closed her eyes, and drew in a deep breath.

My gaze shot to Jess. As if on their own, my eyebrows shot up into my hairline. I was sure Jess understood my meaning without me actually saying "Is she for real?" out loud. He nodded, and one side of his mouth pulled up.

Introductions were made and soon heaps of juicy deliciousness bathed in barbecue sauce and falling off the bone were steaming on my plate. I managed to do a fine job of keeping my mouth stuffed with food in order to avoid having to speak too much. I wasn't above irritating Jess, but I didn't want his family to think of me as some kind of harpy he had to deal with. When I did catch Jess's eye, he always managed to have an amused look on his face.

After the meal, which Cass and I graciously thanked the Sullivan family for providing, Matthew Sullivan, patriarch, challenged me to a game of Scrabble.

"Oh, brother! You and that game." Sharon waved a dismissive and slightly perturbed hand at Matthew as she cleared plates. "You leave that nice Kate alone and find someone else to bother."

I caught Jess's eye at that moment, and he mouthed "Nice Kate?" with a fake confused look on his face. I couldn't hold back a tiny smile.

"I'm sure Kate would love to play with you, Dad," Jess supplied helpfully.

"That's great!" Matthew jumped up from the table and ran into the RV.

Jess laughed as his dad disappeared inside.

"Thanks, pal," I said in a sugary voice.

He chuckled. "Anytime, friend."

In an instant, Matthew was back out and guiding me to a table where the remnants of salad, fruit, and chips were still sitting. "Jack, get this stuff out of our way, would you?" he called to the younger Sullivan son.

"Sure, Dad." Jack smiled cheerfully and hurried over.

To me, how quickly Jack began moving dishes looked suspicious. Even more suspicious was how helpfully Sharon and Jess abandoned the dirty dishes to clear the serving table and make space for me to play with Matthew.

"Let me get you some comfy chairs." Jess practically darted to the eating area and came back before I'd even had a chance to process.

"Thanks, son." Matthew nodded once at Jess and gestured for me to take a chair.

"I'll just get a rag to wipe the table down first." Sharon disappeared inside the RV.

"Can I help?" Zara poked her head out of the RV, where she'd begun washing utensils. Jack just shook his head and pushed her back inside as he moved through the doorway with bowls of fruit. Almost like he was keeping her from becoming a victim of something.

"Allow me to help you get settled." Jess held the empty chair for me, and as I sent a startled glance his way it seemed like his eyes were dancing with barely restrained glee.

"Uh, thanks?" I sat down, and Jess slid my chair into place. I looked around to find Cass and Ethan off to the side, watching the entire exchange with interested, and confused, looks on their faces. "Jess?" I turned before he walked away and motioned for him to lean down. When he did, I got as close to his ear as I dared and whispered, "Why do I feel like I've just signed a deal with the devil?"

Jess turned his head, and I couldn't help but pull back a little as our eyes met. I also couldn't help but notice how he smelled. Clean and fresh, like laundry detergent and mountain air. It made me forget what I was doing.

"It was nice knowing ya." Jess chuckled and pulled away quickly to walk to where Cass and Ethan were standing. I could hear him chatting quietly with them before they disappeared over to the construction site to walk around a bit.

Matthew cleared his throat, and I realized that the table was cleaned off and the Scrabble board had been set up. "Best two out of three, dear?" he asked.

"Uh, okay," I said.

He rubbed his slightly wrinkled hands together. "Excellent. You first."

I had probably only played Scrabble one time in my life. And that had been on a computer. But I was up to the challenge, and it prevented me from having to figure out how to chat more with Jess or Zara, who I was beginning to think was a real-life Disney princess.

I can honestly say that the hours playing Scrabble with Matthew passed quickly. Yes, I said *hours*. As in plural. Matthew turned out to be a clever and witty conversationalist, and when the second game ended in a tie, I was pleased and even slightly eager to go to the third round. By the end of the third round, Matthew and I were old friends, laughing and teasing each other, even occasionally goading each other about attempting to use made-up words. It was fun.

After the third game, I finally stretched and looked around. "Oh my gosh!" I pushed back my chair and scanned the area for other human life-forms. “How long have we been playing?” I said, shocked to find that the light was beginning to dim as the afternoon moved toward evening.

“About two hours,” a feminine voice supplied from behind me. I turned to find Zara standing near. “I was just coming to rescue you.” She laughed. Her laugh surprised me, and I found myself laughing along. It came from her belly. It wasn’t trilling or breathy or anything annoying. It was a great laugh.

“No need for a rescue, dear.” Matthew cracked a few joints as he stood. “We had a lovely time.”

Zara looked back at me with a raised eyebrow, as if questioning the truth of Matthew’s statement.

I laughed again. “It’s true!” I shrugged and held out my hands in a helpless gesture. “I believe he’s turned me into a Scrabble junkie.” Matthew’s laugh joined mine, and he came around the table to give me a quick one-armed squeeze.

“Well played, Kate. I’ll look forward to a rematch another time.” Matthew squeezed again and then released me to begin gathering up the Scrabble board and letters.

I looked past Zara, hoping to catch sight of Ethan and Cass. “Ethan and Cass must be dying to get home by now,” I said.

“Oh, Jess took them home about an hour ago. I was hoping you’d stay and play a round of croquet before it gets too dark,” Zara replied.

“Um . . .” I didn’t know what to say.

“Cass said to go ahead and stay.” Zara grabbed my wrist and began pulling me gently toward an open field area. “I could really use a partner. Playing Jack and Jess can get chilling.”

“But . . . I should be home for Ethan,” I argued, unsure about engaging in another game with this group. I also felt guilty that I had deserted Ethan, and I didn’t want to be here for another couple of hours. I had no idea how long their croquet game would take, and my mom guilt was raging at the moment.

“Cass is watching him. Please stay! If you don’t play, then I’m stuck with the Sullivan brothers. They think they’re the kings of croquet, and it’s so annoying to be the third wheel in their oddball competitions. If you’ll stay and play with me, then we can give them a run for their money.” Zara gave me a big cheesy grin that had me smiling with her.

"I don't know. I've already taken up so much of your day," I hedged, guilt about my extra-long Scrabble game keeping me from saying yes.

"I cheat." Zara stopped and released my arm.

I couldn't help but laugh. "What?"

"I do. I totally cheat. I'm sneaky so that Jack and Jess can't prove it, but I win sometimes, and it makes them crazy."

"You do?"

"Yes. I'll help you cheat too." Zara waggled her eyebrows at me.

"Cass has Ethan?" I began to waver, the idea of cheating Jess Sullivan somehow tantalizing.

"She does."

"Okay, I'm in." I laughed.

Zara grabbed my wrist again, but this time she didn't have to drag me along. This time I was willing and even eager to do my very best to cheat my way to victory.

Jess and Jack were standing in the field holding croquet mallets and balls, wearing practically identical grins. Their grins said they thought this would be an easy win. I stopped in front of them and lifted my chin a bit higher.

"You're in?" Jess asked me. I just nodded. "Great." His grin widened, and he shared a glance with his brother.

"Boys against girls, or couples?" Jack turned to look back at Zara and me. I wanted to point out to Jack that Jess and I were not in any way a couple, but Zara stepped in.

"I have complete faith in Kate. We're gonna take you two to the cleaners," she replied.

Jack and Jess grinned at each other again and chuckled. "You're on," Jess said. They high-fived. I gave them a look.

"Don't you think that's a bit premature?" I asked.

"Nope." Jack chuckled, and Jess joined in.

The guys handed Zara and me each a ball and mallet and then explained the course, pointing out each hoop. They made use of the entire field by spacing the hoops far apart and in incredibly odd places, a sure sign that Jack and Jess thought they were awfully clever. Zara looked at me and rolled her eyes. I smiled in return.

Before I realized what was happening, we were being hustled to the starting peg and Jack was busily explaining the rules.

"Should I be listening to this?" I whispered to Zara.

"Not really. It's mostly for Jess and Jack so that they have something to argue about during the game."

"Also, we won't be following these rules." I slanted her a look.

"Exactly." She winked.

"Ladies first," Jack said as Zara and I joined them.

"Oh, gee. Thanks, honey." Zara smiled lovingly at her soon-to-be husband, and it was all I could do not to snort at the genuine smile on her face. Jack's face flushed a bit, as though he was embarrassed, and he smiled down at Zara.

"Sure, babe," he mumbled just before stealing a little kiss.

I was in awe of the awesomeness of Zara. Too bad that I could only ninety-percent commit to liking her, 'cause at that moment she could have been my new best friend.

"Kate?" Jess took my attention from the couple and gestured for me to join Zara at the starting post.

"Oh, thanks," I said, unable to perform as eloquently as Zara had.

Jess just nodded. I almost laughed at the difference between us and the loving couple.

Zara lined up her ball and swung at the post, somehow managing to swing wide and miss it. That was when I was privileged to see her next performance. She stomped her foot and gave the post a little kick. "I don't care how many times you make me play this game, Jack Sullivan. I'm never going to be any good." She turned and huffed past me to stand grumpily by Jack, who put his arm around her. It was all I could do to keep my jaw from hitting the dirt.

I had wondered how Zara would make anyone believe that she was inept at the game of croquet when she was clearly such an athletic and graceful person. She was all long, sleek lines, strolling through the beautiful forest areas while I spent much of my life stumbling into trees and bushes with my lumbering gate. But when I saw her performance, I wondered if Jess should hand over the actor title to Zara. Amazing.

"Your turn, Kate," Jess said from behind me.

I shook off my shock and walked up to the post, where I bent a little to swing my mallet.

"I promise not to look at your rear end," Jess inserted right as I took a swing. His comment made my spine snap, and I, too, missed the ball.

Unlike Zara, however, I really was annoyed and turned to give Jess a glare. "Oh, too bad, Kate. Looks like you ladies aren't off to a good start." He smiled innocently.

I moved out of the way for Jess, who was up. Just as his mallet arced above his head—really, who on earth swings their croquet mallet that high?—I said in my most chipper voice, "I never promised not to look at your rear end, though."

Jess made a satisfying error and just barely struck the post. His ball moved, but not far, and he turned to glare at me. It was my turn to smile innocently as Jack walked past me for his turn.

"That one has some fire in her," Jack said as he slapped Jess on the back and took his place at the starting post. Jack was the only one to make a nice clean hit and get his ball firmly into play and on its way to the first hoop, which was barely noticeable in the tall grass.

As we moved through the first few hoops, Zara and I got further and further behind. By the time the guys were sailing through the fifth hoop, they were small figures in the distance—just how far apart *had* they put the hoops?—and I was beginning to doubt Zara's claims that we could successfully cheat them out of a victory. I was about to say something to that effect when Zara looked at me and rubbed her hands together like a villain from an old black-and-white movie.

"Okay, they're far enough away. Let's get going." She smacked her ball gracefully and right on target at the same time that Jack was hitting his ball. The crack of her mallet was disguised by the same cracking noise coming from Jack hitting his ball. As the guys watched Jack's ball sail through the grass, Zara and I watched her ball make it halfway to the next hoop and roll to a soft stop in the grass. Zara walked quickly to her ball while Jess gave Jack a high five. Neither of the men had seen it. Zara made a show of clapping for Jack, who had also had a nice hit and made it through the fifth hoop. He waved back at her and gestured for Zara to go, as it was actually her turn at that point.

Zara raised her club to an awkward angle and drove it partially into the grass, causing a huge clump of dirt to fly and her ball to move a short distance. Jack loyally clapped for her while Jess just laughed. I clapped for her, too, and said encouraging words loudly enough for Jack and Jess to hear.

My turn was next. Following Zara's example, I let some dirt fly and my ball made hardly any progress. Zara ran back to me while cheering for my "failure," pretending to show a united front with me.

She flung an arm around my shoulder and said quietly, "Watch Jess. When he goes, you go. Try to time your hit with his so that the guys don't notice it. Never, never swing your mallet up in the air. Try to keep your mallet down at your side and swing it in a way that makes it look like you're just swinging it by your side while you're waiting your turn. While your ball is rolling walk with it. But make sure you stop before they turn to see your reaction."

I nodded.

She stepped away, and I watched Jess closely as he lined up his shot. As his mallet rose up, again above his shoulders, I swung mine back and cracked it at the same time as Jack. Both of us got clean hits, and I scrambled to move up with my ball while Jack and Jess cheered.

Zara started clapping for Jess, and I joined in as they glanced back at us to gauge our reactions. Jess appeared confused for a moment, and it looked like he was counting hoops, wondering if he'd just been mistaken about where Zara and I were on the course. But Jack slapped him on the back and his worried frown turned into a grin as they walked up to Jess's ball.

Over the course of the next few rounds, Zara and I steadily, and in our minds stealthily, closed the gap between us and the boys. But we had to put a stop to our cheating while the men were headed back in our direction, having completed the last hoop and begun the loop back, returning to what was now the end post. We had managed to cut the distance to only one hoop behind, and while the guys were justifiably confused, Zara maintained such an air of innocence that they didn't dare question her.

Jess walked over to stand close to me as we both arrived at the next hoop. Too close. He obviously smelled something fishy and wanted to observe what was happening.

"It's the strangest thing, the way Zara always suddenly seems to catch up to us when we play croquet. For someone so obviously bad at the game, she holds her own," he mumbled, half to me and half to himself. I just made a noncommittal sound in return and kept my eyes on Jack, whose turn it was. "And you, where did you come from?" He turned the full weight of his stare on me.

Inside I was squirming under the intensity of that gaze, but I turned to look him in the eye and hoped that I was the picture of confused innocence when I said, "Denver."

"What?" Jess look perplexed. Excellent.

"You asked where I'm from. Denver." Then I chuckled and added, "You sure picked a strange time to get interested in my past," before stepping up to take my swing. I missed. Surprise. When I looked back to where Jess was still standing, he was wearing a grin, and when our eyes met, he shook his head before wandering up to his ball.

"I, too, have found that the ditzy approach always throws them off the trail." Zara laughed as she walked to where I was standing.

"It's a classic," I replied, laughing myself.

Zara and I continued to make steady progress, our cheating becoming flawless as we neared the end. Whenever the men would look our way, we would giggle at each other and twist our hair with our fingers. When they'd look away, we'd casually tap our balls forward before starting to giggle and chatter again.

We were on hoop three, or whatever it would be on the way back, and the guys were on hoop two when Zara suddenly got a ferocious look on her face and asked me if I was ready to turn our little game of croquet into more of a polo match.

"Huh?" was all I managed.

"Can you sprint?" she pressed.

"Uh, no . . ."

"Today is the day you learn, then, I'm afraid." I swear her eyes got all beady and suspicious as she took in the lay of the land around us. Finally, her eyes met mine again and the gleam in them made me believe that she would see this thing to the end, throwing me over her shoulder and carrying my ball and mallet in her own two hands if I didn't make it.

"I don't get . . ."

"When their backs are turned, we go for it," she said, intensity burning in her every word. "We make them pay for all those stupid jokes about us and how many times I had to giggle and twirl my hair. You ready?"

"No! I'm not. I have no idea what we're doing." I was getting a bit anxious now, feeling like someone had poured a jar of wasps down my throat.

"When I say 'three,' you start running as fast as you can, hitting your ball as you go along. Just keep going. Taking turns is over. You sprint through each hoop, cracking that ball with every step, until we reach that post. I'm hoping we'll have the element of surprise on our side. If we're lucky, they'll just stare at us until we pass them. More likely, they'll catch on and it'll be a race to the end." Her voice was quiet and kind of rough and low. I kept expecting her to call me *soldier*. My palms were getting sweaty. I kind of liked it.

"Have you done this before?" I asked, a smile pulling at the edges of my mouth.

"Yes." She pushed hair out of her face.

"Did it work?"

"Not really." Her mouth finally lifted on one side. "You in?"

I nodded, a full grin lighting my face. She started to laugh but reined it in and looked to where the men were. Jack was lining up his shot.

"One . . ." Zara began. Jack swung his mallet back. "Two . . ." Jack swung his mallet down. "Three!" Zara shouted right as Jack connected with the ball.

We were off like two zebras being chased by hyenas. The sound of our mallets repeatedly hitting our balls echoed through the clearing. We ran bent over, as quickly as we could. We were through the second-to-last hoop and had caught up to the boys before they reacted. I was afraid to look at their faces, but I could hear their voices over the pounding of my heart and my own breathing.

"What the . . ." Jack yelled.

"Get them!" Jess replied.

More *cracks* filled the air. The boys were yelling and as Zara and I neared the last hoop she began doing a war cry that I was positive she'd learned from some Native American ancestor.

I could hear Jess and Jack pounding up behind us, making up the difference. I pushed myself harder. Giggles began to burst out of me, made airy and light by my lack of breath as I ran faster than I'd ever thought possible while hitting a croquet ball.

"Zara! You're gonna pay for this!" Jack yelled.

"Kate . . ." Jess began.

"Eat dirt!" I yelled back to him without breaking stride.

Zara laughed at my reply and our eyes met for a wild, fanatical moment. Then laughter, full and round, burst out of both of us. I clutched my side, still running, practically spent.

"They're catching us," I said to Zara between cracks.

"They always do," she huffed between giggles.

Then the boys were on our heels. The post was only ten feet away. I could feel victory lighting up my face into a brilliant smile. Too bad that the klutz in me kicked in at that moment and my foot caught, sending me sprawling to the earth, flat on my poor belly. Zara ground to a halt and reached out a hand for me.

"No . . . just take my ball. Take my ball!" I yelled. She nodded as Jess and Jack overtook me. Zara picked up my ball and held it in one hand as she continued to hit her ball along, trying to gain back the lead.

Jess and Jack beat her to the post by half a second. I let my head fall to the earth as I took in huge lungfuls of air. I could hear Jess and Jack whooping and hollering and yelling about how they'd still won even though we had cheated.

Zara's soft footfalls landed close to my ear, just before her body plopped down next to mine.

"You okay?" she asked.

I turned my face so that I could see her. "Yep."

"We lost." She looked up at the sky and let her head fall back.

I rolled onto my back and ignored the aching in my hands where I'd tried to catch myself. "Yep." I sighed.

"Stinks!" Zara huffed. I started to laugh quietly. Zara joined in, our shoulders shaking, and lay down next to me on the soft grass.

We just lay there, gasping and laughing until Jack and Jess joined us, arms crossed and identical looks of reproach on their faces. After a moment, they both reached out to help us up.

As I reached for Jess's hand, he said, "You still lost."

"It was totally worth it." I smiled as he pulled me to my feet. His hand was warm and strong, and he held on to mine as he looked over my face.

"I can see you're pleased with yourself." His voice was stern, but his hold on my hand was gentle.

I just nodded like a dummy, grinning from ear to ear, feeling more laughter bubbling up. I looked to where Zara and Jack were standing, Zara grinning and Jack trying to be serious as he spoke softly to her. The sight made the last of my restraint break, and my laughter burst out of me in a loud rush.

I released Jess's hand to wrap my arms around my stomach. "You should've seen your faces," I said breathlessly to him.

This time Jess nodded and looked away over my shoulder, but not before I'd seen the amusement in his eyes.

When my laughter quieted down he looked back at me, allowing a smile to form. "You do realize that this calls for a rematch," he stated, as though that was the only obvious way to right the wrong we cheaters had caused.

"Why?" Zara inserted from where she and Jack were standing, hand in hand, having finished their quiet exchange. "You guys won, so no harm done."

"You can't call that a win!" Jack replied, seemingly shocked by what his fiancée was suggesting. "At least not an honest win." Jess nodded his agreement.

"Well, it's not going to be today, I'm afraid," I said. "I need to get home to Ethan." I turned and began walking back toward where the cars were parked.

"When then?" Jack pressed as the others fell into step with me.

"Uh . . ." I pretended to think about it for a moment. "How about when pigs fly?"

Jess finally allowed himself a small chuckle. "With Kate around, that will be any day now."

The way he said it made me glance at him. He was looking back at me. I didn't want to analyze the look too much, but it seemed he hadn't meant it as an insult. I allowed the warmth of that discovery to seep into me as the three of them walked me to my car.

Chapter 8

It was with relief that I accepted Alec's invitation to go on another date the next week. I needed to get back on firm footing after the terrific day I'd spent with the Sullivan family. That day had been a step out of real life. I didn't belong in that movie-star circle, and I needed to come back to earth.

Alec had suggested Ethan join us again. I silently congratulated myself for finding a guy who wanted to spend time with Ethan. Score one for me. I was a little less congratulatory when Alec suggested a roller-skating rink. Sigh. When I was twelve, I'd have been thrilled with that suggestion. If I were honest, even at age twenty, I would have loved the idea of holding hands with my romantic partner, gliding effortlessly in the darkened room and clinging to his arm as I pretended to be inept at skating. Looking up at him and batting my eyes a little.

At twenty-nine, there was no more pretending. I really was inept at roller-skating, having not done it for at least ten years. I was convinced my ankles would snap from the pressure of holding up my unsteady body. Also, I was worried about sweat from the effort of skating. Another concern was the safety of any toddlers in my vicinity and fellow mothers on the sidelines wondering who I thought I was.

"Let me ask Ethan," I'd replied, hoping Ethan would have no idea what skating was and shoot the idea down for me. But Ethan had been "pumped" about trying something new, which is how I found myself bumping along in Alec's truck.

I was grateful that I didn't have to say much, as Alec and Ethan kept the conversation alive by swapping tricks on how to win that video game they both liked. Yes, I should have known the name of it. I was, in fact, pretty sure I'd been told the name. But my mind stored only so much knowledge and released the rest. Video-game trivia was always immediately purged.

Alec must have noticed my silence because his hand crept across the distance between us and he twined his fingers with mine. I glanced up at him, and he squeezed my hand as Ethan kept chattering away. I smiled. He wasn't a bad guy. Even though some of his date ideas were kind of juvenile, it had been fun to be more carefree, and Ethan had sure enjoyed the water park. Well, until I'd had my unfortunate tube-slide accident. I was determined that no such accidents would happen today.

I was also determined to not be outdone by Alec and Ethan. I wasn't even thirty years old, surely too young to sit on the sidelines. I was still relevant enough to lace up those size sevens and be cheerfully flexible the entire time. I would glide and smile, I would hold hands with Alec, and I would *not* crash, I would *not* cry, and I would *not* get sweaty palms! And when it was time for the couple's skate, I would be ready to rock and roll.

Thirty-five minutes later, I had to take a break. I had crashed twice. My palms were so sweaty that I couldn't have even held on to Alec's hand without a glue stick to keep us together, and I could feel moisture gathering behind my eyes begging to be set free. I was way too old to be crying in a roller-skating rink, but there it was. Time to make a little getaway and regroup.

I excused myself to use the ladies' room and rolled away from Ethan and Alec with a cheerful wave. I went straight into the bathroom and ran my shaking hands under cold water, hoping the shock of it would help settle me. My cell phone began to ring, the jaunty little tune filling the bathroom as it echoed off the walls.

I dried my hands and answered without checking the caller ID.

"Yes?" I said, my voice quivering and thick with the desire to cry.

"Kate?" It was Jess. He was back in California and probably had business to discuss with me. For some reason, the sound of his voice made me want to break down.

"Mm-hmm," I whimpered, trying my best to swallow down the large lump and shove the tears away before they could make any real progress.

"Kate?" Jess's voice sounded more intense. I was sniffling and shaking, annoyed with my weakness. "Are you there? What's going on?" His voice was rising. "What's wrong?"

"My palms are sweaty!" I whined.

My announcement was met with silence while Jess tried to process what I'd said and why I would be so upset about it.

"And I've crashed twice!" I continued.

"You crashed?" Now he sounded worried. "Where are you?" he asked.

"At Happy's Roller Skating Rink."

"Come again?"

"You know, that little roller rink by the movie theater," I pushed out past the lump.

"You crashed in the parking lot?" Jess was desperately trying to get a grip on the conversation.

"No, inside. The floor is hard!" I whispered.

There was another lengthy silence where the only sound was my sniffling as the urge to cry began to lift.

"Kate, are you telling me that you're inside the rink and you've crashed twice on roller skates?" Jess finally asked.

"Yes," I said miserably.

"Who are you there with?" Jess sounded relieved, but still concerned. Although not concerned for my safety—more like he thought I'd cracked.

"Alec and Ethan."

"On a date," he clarified.

"Yes."

"And you're crying with sweaty palms?" he continued. His voice sounded lighter now.

"I'm not crying!" I defended. "I'm just in the bathroom."

"That would explain the echo," Jess mumbled. We were both quiet for a moment. I used the time to take a few deep breaths and get back under control. "Where is Alec now?" Jess finally asked.

"Well, he's not in the ladies' room," I retorted in a stronger voice.

"So one thing is going right, then." Jess chuckled. "Does he know you're in there upset?"

"Are you kidding me? No!" I retorted, stung a little. "It's bad enough that my palms are sweaty and my knees are bruising from crashing on that rock-hard floor. I'd never let him see me like this!"

"Why did he think roller-skating would be a good date?" Jess asked.

"Because . . . well, I'm pretty sure he's a college student or something," I mumbled.

"He's a what?"

I chose not to repeat it and moved on. "Also, I'm cheerfully flexible and fun." A leftover sniffle punctuated just how fun and cheerful I was at that moment.

"I see," he said, as though he really did see what was going on. "Kate, you really should tell Alec when his ideas are bogus."

"Says the guy who plays death-match croquet!" I flung back.

"Hey, that was a family cookout. Not a date," he defended himself.

I was quiet for a moment. He had a point. I huffed. "Fine. What did you call about?"

"In the face of your current crisis, it doesn't seem as important. It can wait. Are you sure you're okay?"

"This is hardly a crisis," I retorted, stung by him basically calling me hysterical when I was patting myself on the back for keeping it together. "Of course, I'm fine," I insisted.

"Okay. I'll call you back later. And Kate, make sure your helmet is on tight." He chuckled softly.

He hung up before I could reply to his seriously unwarranted advice. I shoved my phone back into my pocket and splashed my entire face with cold water. Then I held my hands on my closed eyes, hoping to cool down the burn and possibly reduce swelling. I toweled off my face and hands before looking into the mirror.

Somehow my easy-breezy good-times ponytail had gotten messed up. Something I've never understood is how getting upset messes up your hair. I hadn't even cried, really. I had crashed a few times, but I didn't have any recollection of my hair getting snagged on anything.

I pulled the rubber band out of my hair and did my best to finger-comb it back into place. With my hair fixed, I tried to pretend that Alec wouldn't notice my sudden lack of excitement. I had used some flirty glimmer eye shadow that day, and the only traces left were now glimmering halfway down my face. I sighed. I wasn't sure how many more adventurous dates I could go on. I needed a good dinner-and-a-movie date to soothe my weary soul. Dating hadn't been this hard before.

When I left the bathroom, I found Alec and Ethan hanging out at the snack bar. They were each sipping a soda and sharing a plate of nachos. Food of adventurers everywhere. A third drink sat in front of an empty seat, and my heart lifted a little at the knowledge that they had thought to get me something.

I pulled out the empty chair, wincing at the attention the scraping noise drew to me.

"Hey, there she is." Alec smiled up at me. His smile faded a bit as I flopped into my seat.

"Here she is." I tried my best to grin back at him.

"Uh, you okay?" he asked.

"Yeah, Mom, you were in the bathroom, like, forever," Ethan inserted.

I smiled down at him. "Yeah, sorry. I had a phone call, and so I was gone longer than I expected." I smiled and took a large gulp of my soda. It was orange flavored. The only thing that would have been more pre-pubescent would have been grape soda. I choked it down, trying not to be disappointed that the soda wasn't a more adult, cola-flavored offering.

"Who called?" Ethan asked. I was grateful that he bit and I could change the subject away from myself.

"Oh, it was just Jess. Looking for an update on the cabin. I told him I was busy on a date with my two best guys, so he tried to keep it short." I reached out and mussed Ethan's hair in a gesture of affection. I wasn't sure *best guys* had been the right thing to say, but Alec didn't seem weirded out by it.

"Jess, huh?" Alec seemed thoughtful. Then his eyes took on a sudden gleam and his gaze zeroed in on me. "You think he and his girlfriend would ever want to double with us?" He was clearly enthused by the idea. My stomach plopped down to wallow in orange fizz.

"I don't know," I said aloud. My insides were screaming that the last thing I needed was to invite Jess and Ms. Vivienne Gorgeous-Ice-Queen Lawson on one of my superfun dates.

"It could be really cool," Alec continued, almost to himself.

"Well, you know, Jess is in California getting ready to shoot a movie. I don't really know when he'll be back in town," I replied.

"You talk to him all the time, though. Maybe you could just mention it next time you talk," Alec pushed.

I tried to smile, but my lips felt stiff and my palms were beginning to sweat again. I tried to brush it off with a shaky laugh. "I can't make any promises."

"Jess would love to go skating. This has been fun!" Ethan helpfully added.

"You think?" Alec looked at me for confirmation of his greatest hopes.

"I doubt skating is his thing," I replied gently, remembering that Jess's exact word regarding roller-skating had been "bogus."

Alec reached over and lay his hand on mine, giving it a squeeze and leaning closer to me. "Just ask, okay? For me?" Alec then half stood and planted a kiss on my lips before sitting back in his seat. I hadn't kissed him back. I was in too much shock.

He wanted to double with Jess and Vivienne. He'd just kissed me in front of Ethan, who looked a little perplexed by the exchange, and I was sipping orange soda in a roller rink. It was all I could do not to excuse myself and go back to the bathroom for hysterics round two.

A few days later, Alec sent me a bouquet of daisies. They just happened to be my favorite flower. I was fairly sure they were his way of saying sorry about the bummer time I'd had at the roller rink. I was gazing at them with a happy smile when a knock at the front door interrupted Ethan and me making an incredible dinner from a box. Ethan rushed to the door and threw it open wide.

Aunt Cass walked purposefully in with a smile for Ethan. She was always smiling at the things Ethan did. If I'd thrown the door open like that I would have been given the pursed-lip look, but Cass loved Ethan's "enthusiasm for life." Her smile faded a bit as she saw Alec's flowers, which caused me to frown.

"Are those flowers from Alec?" she asked. I nodded. "You're still dating him?" I turned to Ethan.

"Ethan, buddy, will you go to your room for a minute so I can visit with Auntie Cass?" I said in a kind but stern voice. Ethan, nobody's fool, quickly obeyed.

"Yes, I'm still dating him." I gestured for her to have a seat on the couch and then sat on the chair facing her.

"Even after that water-slide accident?" Cass raised an eyebrow. How do people do that? I've always wanted to be able to raise one eyebrow. It has so many uses and can literally speak a sentence without the person opening their mouth.

"Of course. You don't stop dating someone because of a freak accident," I said practically.

"Yes, that's true. But you also don't keep dating a person who doesn't have the decency to visit you afterward."

"He brought me flowers then too!" I defended.

"Did he?" Cass's voice said she was highly skeptical.

Did he? my own voice echoed. The bad news was that I honestly couldn't remember if he'd brought me flowers after the tube-slide disaster. The good news was that I was stubborn enough to nod convincingly in the face of Cass's skepticism.

"And what are these flowers for?" She pointed to the beautiful arrangement on the countertop.

"An apology . . ." I started to say, but when Cass's gaze whipped to mine, I realized my tactical error.

"Hmm . . ." was all she said.

"Anyway, what has you coming my way this evening?" I redirected. Cass gave me a small smile, well aware of my maneuvering. I was grateful she was apparently willing to let it drop.

"Actually, I'm thinking of going to Aspen for a few days to visit my dear friend Ellie." Her smile softened as she thought of her friend. "You do remember her, of course," she stated rather than asked.

"Yes." I smiled too.

Ellie had been a sort of adopted aunt to me over the years. She and Cass had been friends since they were children growing up together. During Cass's working years, before she moved to Clark Springs full time, the big house had been her summer retreat, and Ellie's visits had often overlapped mine. While Cass had never married, Ellie had gone on to marry and then to raise three children. Those three children occasionally came on her visits, and I had fond memories of adventures spent together.

"That sounds great. But weren't you just gone to Utah? Feeling the travel bug lately?" I inquired.

Cass was thoughtful for a moment. "I suppose you could say that. Do you realize I'm turning seventy-five on my next birthday?"

I wasn't expecting that curveball and wasn't sure where Cass was going with it. "Oh, yeah?" was all I had to offer in reply.

"Yes. Well, Ellie is my best friend, and it's been a while. So I thought, why not?" Her eyes sparkled as they met mine.

"I think it's a great idea. Do you need anything from me while you're gone, or is Zinn running the show?"

At this Cass stood up, prepared to wrap up our discussion. "Zinn will be fine. I just wanted to let you know. I'll leave in the morning and be gone about a week." Cass walked toward the door and opened it to let herself out.

"Have a great trip," I said. Then, before she could walk out, I grabbed her arm and pulled her into a hug. "I love you, Cass," I whispered into her ear, "even though you are an opinionated old woman."

I could tell by the way her body stiffened that I'd taken her by surprise. But she quickly relaxed and squeezed me back. "I love you too, dear," she said, patting me, "even though no one manages to step into more disasters than you do." She chuckled, and then she was gone on a breeze of floral perfume.

Chapter 9

With Cass heading out to visit her oldest chum, I was hoping Zinn would be willing to watch Ethan while I went on a date with Alec on Friday night. I was excited to go on an Ethan-free date, hoping upon hope that meant it would be a more grown-up setting. But getting Zinn to tend to Ethan would require some buttering up. Oh, Zinn loved to feed him and visit with him, but actual babysitting was not on her list of services she provided. So far I hadn't ever managed to find Zinn's particular currency. I was fairly sure there was nothing in this world she cared that much about, except Cass. I didn't figure threatening Cass's life in order to get a favor out of Zinn would pan out, so I was left with nothing to barter with. I decided to try something I was very good at harnessing: desperation.

Zinn was easily found in her new kitchen, and I wondered for a moment if she ever left it. Maybe in the back of the pantry there was a trapdoor that swung open and contained her bed. She was probably comfortable in small spaces near kitchens, having grown up as a scullery maid in Great Britain. It was a new theory I was chewing on.

"Hey there, Zinn!" I plastered a big smile on my face.

She looked up from where she'd been wiping down the spotless countertops. "What do you need?" she asked, cutting right to the point in a very Zinn-like manner.

"Well, you know, I've been very lonely over the past few years, and I've recently started seeing someone . . ." I began, letting my eyes droop down to the floor and kind of swishing my foot around.

"Yes, I know." She slapped her rag back down on the countertop and began scrubbing again. "Ethan isn't enough company for you? You have to go and rob a cradle to find company?"

I pulled a face at the back of her head. This wasn't going well at all. Robbing cradles? Please. Alec was an adult! Anyone with eyes could see he was all grown up. So what that he never got a five o'clock shadow? And who cared that sometimes his pants sagged a bit and I'd been considering getting him a belt. That was beside the point.

"Of course Ethan is great company, and I am so lucky to have him." I stalled for a moment, wondering what angle to approach from. "Ethan sure loves you, Zinn."

Zinn turned and looked at me in her special *you deserve a straitjacket* way before replying, "This boy you keep going on dates with, he took you to a roller-skating rink?"

Oh, no, this was not going well. I was looking at a possible mission abort. Time to speed up my departure.

"You are a cougar," Zinn spoke again before I could. I froze.

"I'm sorry? What?" I was shocked to hear Zinn call me that.

"You know, those older women that date younger men. You are a cougar." Zinn looked me straight on as she said it.

"Um, Zinn, I think I'd have to be like sixty years old or something and dating a twenty-year-old to be called a cougar. I don't think Alec is that much younger than me." I was desperate to leave.

"No, you're wrong. It doesn't matter your age, only that he is much younger than you."

"Zinn, I don't think he's all that much younger than me." That fact had been something I'd banked on, telling myself that I was young enough to be dating someone still working on his schooling.

"Tell me again where you went on your date."

I clamped my lips tight. Answering would mean immediate amputation to any leg I had to stand on. Zinn did a dry laugh as she saw my expression. That alone floored me, and I looked closely at her. I wasn't sure I'd ever heard Zinn laugh.

"It's worse than I thought." Her shoulders were shaking, and she was making a strange sound. "You are definitely a cougar." At this, she shuffled past me into the pantry while I stood frozen in shock.

The worst part was I wasn't even sure if I had a sitter or not. But I wasn't about to ask.

On Friday afternoon, like a boy shot out of a cannon, Ethan came running in the front door from the big house. I had been working in the silence, and the slamming of the door startled me enough that I had to delete a few digits.

"Jess will be here any second!" Ethan shouted at me as he ran down the hall. I quickly saved my file and caught up to him as he changed out of his nicer shorts into some old cutoff jean shorts that I reserved for more outdoorsy times.

"What? Jess? Is he back in town?" I couldn't quite keep up.

"Yes, and we're going fishing down at the fish farm. Then we'll cook them up for dinner." Ethan was all grins as he flew back down the hall toward the front door to get his muddy boots.

"Wait! You are eight! You don't get to make plans without me being involved. Besides, I have a date with Alec tonight. Zinn is watching you." I stuttered along as I followed him, fingers crossed behind my back as I told the little fib. I had no idea if Zinn was planning to watch him or not. I had not, in fact, actually asked her.

"Zinn is watching me? Cool! She'll cook the fish way better than you would." Ethan pumped a fist in the air as if he'd just won a great prize. It was not flattering, to say the least, and I was forced to put my hands on my hips and stand directly in front of him.

"Ethan. Stop." He slowed for a moment in the face of my mom-ness and looked up at me. "First of all, you really need to find some friends your own age. You can't be hanging around with Jess every second he's here." I was finding it hard to believe that my eight-year-old knew when Jess was in town and had planned an outing with him without my knowing anything about it. It was a sign of parenting failure that I just was not having.

"Jess called me. I don't even have a phone, Mom. So I can't invite him anywhere. He does it." Ethan stated this slowly, as if he were talking to a three-year-old. I flatlined my lips and stepped it up.

"You're right, you don't have a phone. So how did Jess call you?"

"At the big house. He said he just called a couple of numbers until he found me." Ethan shrugged and bolted around me to grab a bucket to put worms in. I found it highly suspicious that one of those numbers Jess called didn't ring my phone.

"Nobody told me!" I threw my hands in the air.

"Because it just barely happened like two seconds ago." Ethan turned back to give me a look that was so Charlie it stopped me in my tracks. The look that said, "Have you even listened to a word I've been saying?" It stopped me long enough for there to be a knock at the door and for Ethan to zip around me and throw it open in his exuberant way.

My mouth must have been hanging open to my chest because Jess, framed in the doorway, just smiled when he saw me. "Surprised?" he asked.

I snapped my mouth shut. "Hardly," I retorted, miffed that I'd been left out of the discussion about where *my* son would be going and with whom. "Whenever Ethan starts scrambling around acting like a puppy whose favorite chew toy is being dangled in front of him, I figure you're involved somehow." I turned back to the kitchen area, where Ethan was rummaging around in the fridge. Jess let himself in and closed the door behind him.

"What are you looking for now?" I asked Ethan's back.

"A snack!" Ethan's voice was muffled.

"You're at the wrong house for that," I replied before turning back to Jess. "You and I need to have a little chat about making plans with my son before asking his mother." I gave Jess the same hands-on-hips mom look I'd given Ethan a minute earlier.

He had the smarts to look apologetic. "You're right. Sorry. I forget he's so young because he's just my little buddy." I pulled a face. "Okay, message received. I'll call you first from here on out." I nodded, which made him smile. "You should come with us, Kate."

"I don't think so," I replied.

He just smiled bigger. "Why not?"

I really just wanted to snap back. I wanted the satisfaction of getting under his skin like he got under mine. I was choosing not to analyze the feeling.

"Yeah, Mom. Why not? You should totally come. It'll be fun." Ethan closed the fridge, a new prey in view, and hurried over to Jess's side. Solidarity is highly overrated.

"I have a date tonight," I replied, as though that would explain everything.

"Just makes sense to me that an adventurous girl like you, who likes water slides and roller-skating, would be up for a little fishing." Jess said this with a totally serious face, like his statement was legitimate and based on fact.

I scowled. Jess's acting skills gave him the advantage, as he was able to maintain his innocent look in the face of my disbelief and under Ethan's scrutiny as he gazed back and forth between us.

"Now why on earth would you think that a *lady* like me would want to spend the afternoon with some smelly fish?" I turned and headed back toward the couch, where I planned to regally plop down in dismissal.

"Jess is right, Mom!" Ethan's happy voice stopped me, and I turned back to look at him. "You have been so fun lately with all the new things you've been doing. You would probably like fishing!"

I turned to Jess, who wisely looked at the ceiling and began whistling like he wasn't even a part of this conversation. It had gotten ugly. Somehow he had suckered my sweet boy into using the most powerful tool in his arsenal. Mom guilt.

"I don't want to smell like fish on my date," I hedged. Jess was grinning now even though he was still looking anywhere but at me.

"Alec wouldn't mind," Ethan assured me. I had no choice but to smile at that one. At his age, Ethan didn't mind any smell at all. I had yet to hear him tell me something was disgusting.

"In fact, why don't we invite Alec along too?" Jess threw this out like he was telling Ethan there was a toy store opening in our backyard and everything would be free.

I had to put an immediate stop to this. No way was Alec going anywhere near Jess. It was bad enough that Alec kept asking me to get Jess to double with us.

"He's busy this afternoon," I replied quickly.

"Oh, too bad." Ethan shrugged, over it already.

"We can be fast if you need time to primp before your date tonight." Jess's innocent act was back on. Ugh.

"Really, Mom, please come! You'll love it. You don't even have to worry, 'cuz there are fences everywhere to keep you from falling in." Ethan hurried over and grabbed my hand while his eyes did their little pleading dance. We had gone full DEFCON 2 on this. The only thing missing was a pouty lip.

"Now why would you think I'd fall in?" I laughed down at Ethan. Rather than replying, he laughed back and squeezed my hand. I knew why he thought I'd fall in. Because nothing in his life experience with me had suggested otherwise. "I have to be back by five. No later!" I warned, even though I had never in my life taken two hours to get ready for something.

"We can do that," Ethan assured me and then looked over his shoulder at Jess to make sure it wouldn't be a problem.

I sighed. I knew when a battle was lost. "I don't have any fishing gear."

"That's fine. You can share with Ethan and me," Jess said, rejoining the conversation. "Now hurry and change into something you don't mind getting a little dirty. Something like those favorite sweats of yours . . ." Jess didn't get to finish that statement because I'd hurled a couch pillow at him. Leave it to him to mention my stupid sweatpants. Nothing good ever came from wearing them.

Ninety minutes later and the fish weren't biting. At a fish farm. Is that even possible? I had asked and was assured by the manager that it was indeed very rare to catch zero fish at a fish farm. Luckily for Jess, I only 12 percent wanted to kill him for inviting me. The other 88 percent was dreaming about Alec and our date that night and the fact that I was glad in a twisted way that I hadn't managed to wrangle in a fish. I still smelled fine, and I hadn't gotten any fish guts on my jeans. I was out in the sun with my sweet Ethan, who was over the moon that I'd agreed to leave my cottage and venture out once again into the wide, wide world. Yes, things were going better than I'd expected.

"Mom, just try one more time." He came up to my side and handed me his fishing pole. "I'll even bait the hook!" I glanced around to see that Jess had wandered quite a distance away and was chatting it up with some apparent groupies. I was pretty certain I even heard some giggling, and they were all men. I congratulated myself for managing to steer clear of becoming a member of his fan club. It seemed like a great time to have some one-on-one time with Ethan.

"Okay." I smiled in my cheerfully flexible turning-over-a-new-leaf kind of way. "Put that bait on and let's give it a go."

Ethan scrambled to bait the hook, probably relieved that I wasn't going all crazed badger over fishing and goop and my total failure as an angler.

"It's ready, Mom." He grinned up at me and pointed to the water.

I was at a fish farm and didn't even need to cast, because there were literally hundreds of slimy water dwellers who just hung around next to the fencing with their mouths open waiting for food to drop in. I certainly didn't have to tease them by going all real nature on them. But I was feeling upbeat about how well things were going and the promise of an evening spent with a hunky guy, so I cast that line as well as I could across the pond. It landed with a satisfying plop and no damage to anyone near me. Yep, life was good. Ethan even clapped, and I ruffled his hair.

Surprisingly, something tugged at my line. Normally, actually catching a fish at a fish farm wasn't that surprising. For me, it was. "What the . . ." I turned to Ethan. "Something is actually tugging my line." I laughed. He laughed with me.

"Reel it in, Mom. Reel it in!" He started jumping up and down, rooting for me like you would when you're watching the underdog have a shining moment and you're just so happy for them and their glimmer of success. This underdog was loving it.

It didn't take long to drag the line across the lake, and as I was about to reel it out of the water, I practically crowed, "Dinner's on me tonight, boys!"

Dinner turned about to be a three-inch-long baby bigmouth bass about the size of my pointer finger. Or at least that's what the manager said from behind my back.

"Don't even know how that little guy got in there. He should be in the other pond until he's grown." He reached over my shoulder, intent on freeing that tiny thing from my hook and tossing him into a pail of water nearby.

I swung the pole out of reach and looked him dead in the eye. "I need a picture first," I said, holding my chin up and keeping my face totally serious. "This is the catch of the day as far as I am concerned, and I want to remember it."

Ethan began to giggle. I heard more laughter around me and realized that for some reason a small group had gathered to see my triumph, probably because Jess had returned. He stepped up next to us, and his smile was ear to ear. That smile made my insides do a strange wiggle as my eyes locked with his.

"Well, ma'am, I'm mighty impressed by that fish. He's a real keeper." He drawled it out with a Southern accent he'd probably learned on set somewhere. It made me laugh.

"She wants a picture with it," the manager grumbled at Jess, apparently hoping to get some support in the face of my stubbornness.

"By all means, let's capture this moment for her!" Jess laughed.

"Yay, Mom!" Ethan cheered.

My face cracked into a broad grin as I started to laugh, and before I had a chance to get ready, Jess had taken out his phone and snapped a picture.

The manager eventually got the fish from me and put him in the pail, saving his life for another day, while Ethan danced around me and people began to file away. I couldn't stop laughing to myself as we gathered up the actual keepers that Ethan and Jess had caught and headed for the car.

Jess finally showed me the picture on the drive home. My hair was whipping around my head with the sun shining through it, making my head look like flames were licking out of it. My smile was practically cracking my cheeks, and I was staring at that little micro-fish like it was the biggest prize in the world. I looked at it for a moment while Jess laughed in the seat next to me. Ethan was cheerfully babbling in the back seat, and the only thing that kept running through my mind was, *It's good to see you again.*

When we got back home, I sent the boys out to the creek to clean their fish before taking them up to Zinn for dinner. I wasn't taking any chances of them stinking up my house, which might then stink up me. Not to mention that Zinn would go all World War II fighter pilot on them if they gutted fish in her kitchen.

I waved a quick goodbye and headed straight to the cottage. As I turned on the shower to get the steam going, I was still feeling quite satisfied with myself for not only indulging Ethan and going fishing, but handling the situation of the baby bass with humor and goodwill. There was a small chance I was maturing. Or reemerging, maybe.

The last time I remembered fishing had been with my parents. I think even Charlie would have been surprised to see me today, casting and laughing and participating with more than just a quiet but cheerful presence. Today reminded me of my life as a young girl, hair always wild, grin always wide. It had been almost strange to see the picture. When was the last time I had looked like that? Had Charlie ever seen me so carefree? I did know that Charlie would have been surprised to see the way I was always arguing with Jess. With Charlie, there had been no real arguments or annoyances.

Thinking about life before Charlie was dangerous, so I stepped into the shower and scrubbed. I didn't want to take a chance that some trout-pond smell had stuck in my hair or something, so I lathered profusely. When I got out of the shower, my skin was pink and gleaming. Even my freckles looked clean.

It didn't take two hours to get ready, but I took my time, pampering myself and listening to classic rock turned up way too loud. There's just something about a little Aerosmith to get you ready for a night out.

Eventually, seven rolled around, and as I was packing up my purse, I realized my phone battery had died. I plugged it in and saw a text from Alec canceling our date. I wasn't sure how I felt. Partially annoyed, sure. I mean, a girl doesn't spend all that time getting ready to just sit at home. But I was a bit relieved too. I had been thinking a lot about Zinn's cougar comment, and the fact that Alec canceled with a text message didn't exactly ease my worries.

In the end, I shook off my serious thoughts, fluffed my hair up again, and ran up to the big house to join the others for a fish dinner. I wouldn't overthink it. Who knew where we would have gone anyhow. Probably an arcade, with my luck.

Chapter 10

Tuesday morning I stood in my cottage living space, hands on my hips, my gaze traveling around as I took stock of the place. I'd had much too much thinking time over the past few days, and it was time for a nice distraction. Even my bookkeeping couldn't keep my mind engaged. It only made sense that painting would be the answer to my quandaries about if I had, indeed, become a cougar.

It had nothing to do with the fact that painting was the only skill I had aside from embarrassing myself and rocking a ponytail. I had considered crochet, but taking up a new hobby sounded frustrating. Every woman knows that when you are deliberating over something as troubling as relationships, you don't up and start a new hobby. That adds frustration to doubts, which whips up a nice batch of angry. Then throw in needles, or crochet hooks, or whatever they are called, and you are brewing up a disaster. Painting it was.

"I'm thinking a soothing blue," I said to an oblivious Ethan. I tugged on my lower lip and looked around some more. "Yes, blue. Nothing too dark. We want to open up the space and make it feel relaxing. Don't want it to feel like you're trapped in a sunken ship and going to drown!" I clapped my hands and turned to where Ethan was sitting on the couch. "You like blue, right?" I asked.

He didn't bother to look away from his comic book as he replied, "Does Auntie Cass?"

"I haven't asked her," I replied, feeling a little flustered at the oversight. Man, my mind really was all tied up.

"You probably should." He looked up at me. Being reminded by an eight-year-old that I should ask permission made me feel as big as the bass I'd reeled in a few days before. It also made my heart swell for my sweet boy.

"Have I told you what a great kid you are?" I walked over and ruffled his hair. He smiled in reply.

My cell phone rang its happy little jingle on the couch next to Ethan, and I asked him to grab it. I was doing my best to make him talk on the phone so that despite his electronic generation, he'd have half a chance of having an actual conversation as an adult. Typically, this involved a lot of me coaching and him giving me dirty looks while saying nothing into the phone that could actually be understood. Nevertheless, I pressed on in my motherly duties.

"Yep?" he said. I turned to him in horror. *Yep* was not a word we had approved for answering phone calls. He looked up at me with a fake innocent expression. I just knew Jess was behind that look. Another thing mother was not approving.

I walked around the couch and sat directly in front of him on the coffee table, ready to begin our counseling session.

"Uh, this is Ethan?" He said it as a question. I rolled my eyes and nodded at him. Yes, you are Ethan. Come on, this is Knowledge 101 here, buddy. You have to know your name. Own it. "Uh-huh. Oh, wait, are you one of those salespeople my mom doesn't like to talk to?" Oh man, this was bad. Good if the person was indeed a solicitor, bad if it was any other member of society.

"Ask who's calling!" I mouthed.

He gave me a look before mumbling something like "Cn ak who callng?" I groaned and put my face in my hands. Public speaking struck off the list of talents. "Yeah, my mom is here."

I didn't blame whoever was on the phone for bypassing him. No fool would continue down that path. He passed the phone to me upside down and shrugged. Maybe one of these days he'd get it. The Wright brothers didn't fly on their first try.

"Hello?" I said very politely while smiling at Ethan and making a thumbs-up sign. "How may I help you?" I enunciated every word clearly and kept that smile on while making big eyes to show Ethan how great I was doing at this talking-on-the-phone bit.

"Yes, hello, is this Katherine Evans?" a man's voice asked.

"Yes, I *am* Katherine." I again looked to Ethan. See, stating my name with confidence.

"I'm calling from St. Ann's Hospital in Glenwood Springs," he began. My blood turned to ice. Glenwood Springs was on the way from Aspen to our home in Clark Springs. Aunt Cass was driving home today. "I am told you are the closest family of Cassandra Owens?"

It took a minute to work my voice out around the fear, but I finally squeaked out, "Yes, that's right. I'm her niece."

Ethan, alerted by my tone of voice, sat up from his slouching position and watched my face. I could feel tears building behind my eyes. My hands were shaking and my legs felt tingly. *Not again, not Cass. I cannot lose another person.* That same cold fear that had trickled over me the other two times I'd gotten this kind of phone call began its icy climb.

"I'm sorry to tell you that Ms. Owens was in a car accident today on Interstate 70 outside of our city. She was transported by ambulance to our hospital and is currently in surgery."

"So she's . . ."

"She's still alive, ma'am. Yes." He'd obviously had to make many of these types of calls, because he knew just what I was trying to ask. "However, she is in serious condition. She broke her leg and arm, and they need to be reset before they can be cast. There was some internal bleeding as well. All are being addressed in surgery. We are hopeful but can never make any definite promises in situations like this. I'm sorry."

I heard everything he said. Really, I did. My brain, however, didn't register much past broken bones, internal bleeding, and surgery. Somehow through the fog I managed to ask him when the accident had happened and how long she'd be in surgery. He told me that the accident had happened about an hour before and that he had no answers on the surgery.

"I would advise you to come to the hospital and bring any family members that you feel would be appropriate." I freaked a little more when he said that. That's the stuff you say to the family of dying people.

"I understand. We will be there as soon as we possibly can."

"When you arrive, you'll want to go to the ER first, and they can direct you to where she's currently located."

"Thank you." I hung up.

"Mom?" Ethan pushed through the foggy feeling with his sharp voice. "What's going on with Auntie Cass?"

I abruptly stood up and practically ran to my bedroom with Ethan rushing behind me. "Aunt Cass has been in an accident. Pack an overnight bag and meet me back in the kitchen. We have to go to the hospital." I didn't wait to see if he obeyed. I knew he would because there was fear in my voice and we were talking about his beloved great-aunt.

In my room, I shoved open my closet and grabbed an old backpack off the floor. Then I grabbed jeans, a T-shirt, a set of clean underwear, and some socks. Next were basic toiletries. I'm talking toothbrush, deodorant, and hair band, end of story. I was back in the kitchen before I'd even finished zipping the pack.

I heard Ethan rifling through his room and didn't even care what he was packing as I began searching through cupboards for snacks to take. The cupboards were pretty bare. I'd have to run up to the big house to get something to tide us over for the hours we could be sitting in a hospital waiting room.

The big house! I immediately stopped and gazed out the front window toward it. Zinn. I had to tell Zinn. My heart sank even lower. Tears threatened, but I took a big breath and muscled them back down. No tears. The last time, when it was Charlie, I had crumbled. I'd always wished I had handled it better. This time would be different. I was determined to be the strong one and get Zinn, Ethan, and me through whatever lay ahead.

"Ethan!" I called toward the back of the cottage. He popped his head out of the doorway. "I have to tell Zinn and get some snacks. When you're done packing, bring your bag, lock up the cottage, and come to the big house." Ethan nodded and disappeared again.

I shouldered my backpack and ran up to the big house. This was no time to saunter. I needed to get to Cass. In my rush, I blew through the back door like a tornado and found Zinn sitting at the table sipping something out of a delicate little teacup. Huh. The scene caught me off guard enough that for a moment I forgot why I was there. I didn't think Zinn took tea. This discovery pushed her life story in a new direction that . . . I did not have time for!

"Rushing around as usual, Kate?" Zinn said calmly as she took a sip. "At least close the door behind you."

"Forget the door! Aunt Cass has been in an accident. She's in emergency surgery at a hospital in Glenwood Springs. We're going there right now. Pack a bag and meet me out back in five minutes!"

I turned and dove for the pantry, not watching to see what she would do. I never questioned whether Zinn was family or not. In my mind, she was as much a part of this ragtag group as I was.

While I was digging around for granola bars and fruit that we could take easily, I heard Zinn's chair scrape back, followed by the banging of the swinging door as Zinn rushed out. Turns out even Zinn can karate chop a swinging door when there's a crisis.

The two-hour drive to Glenwood Springs dragged by. Two hours is a decent drive in the best of circumstances. In a silent car rushing to see a seriously injured loved one, it is torture. None of us could talk. Every conversation dead-ended after five minutes. Our minds couldn't stay focused. Playing travel tunes somehow felt disrespectful of our situation. So we drove in heavy, heavy silence, each of us praying in our hearts for Aunt Cass to stay with us.

Once we arrived at the hospital, we were told Aunt Cass was still in surgery. Her surgery was going well, at least according to the information a staff member read us off a computer screen. After surgery, she would be in recovery for a bit, and then she would be moved to a room in ICU. We were directed to the ICU waiting room and told we would be contacted there.

Waiting room was an appropriate name for the small, desperation-filled lounge area. Several couches and chairs were already filled with people waiting for news. I knew Aunt Cass's surgery would be at least thirty more minutes, because the kind lady in the ER told us that. After that, probably another thirty in recovery before being moved to her room. A full hour of waiting after two interminable hours of driving. I would explode if I had to just sit some more.

I decided to try to reach Alec. I was feeling anxious and scared, and I needed to be strong for Zinn and Ethan, but I felt weak for myself. I wanted to hear his voice and feel less alone.

"I'm going to go find a restroom and get a drink," I told Zinn and Ethan as I stood. "Can you guys watch my pack? I'll be back as fast as

I can." Zinn nodded and reached over to hold Ethan's hand so that he wouldn't feel alone. Bless her.

I tucked my phone in my pocket and walked as sedately as I could out of the waiting room and into the corridor beyond. I didn't think it would look good to run out of there even though my skin felt like it was crawling.

As soon as I was away from Zinn and Ethan, those darn tears that I'd held so firmly at bay began to reproduce at an alarming rate. Before I'd even fully committed to crying, they were leaking out of my eyes and running down my cheeks. I angrily swatted at them but had no control to stop them.

I found a little side hallway that looked fairly deserted and dialed Alec. I had no idea what I wanted him to do. Nothing really, just answer. No luck. I got his voice mail. It didn't feel like the thing to leave on a message, so I hung up.

After finding a bathroom and a drinking fountain, I harnessed those tears back into place and tried calling him again. Still no answer. The lack of an answer made the tears well up again. I knew it wasn't totally rational to be seeking Alec at a time like this. We'd dated a bit, we'd kissed a bit, we'd held hands, but we hadn't crossed into the territory of sharing life's woes with each other. I even knew in the back of my head that calling him my boyfriend was pushing it, but darn it, I wanted to talk to him and I wanted him now!

I tried a third time, definitely reaching stalker status, before giving up and shooting a quick text asking him to call me when he could. I even put a 911 on the end of the text, hoping to convey that it was an emergency and I wasn't crazy.

I leaned up against the wall in the little side hallway and looked at the screen of my phone, hoping a magic fairy godmother would pop out and make it all better. Nothing happened. The phone didn't ring. I sniffled. At that moment, I hated that phone. It was really letting me down. I needed at least one thing to do its job today.

I closed my eyes and slid down the wall, putting my head on my knees and letting my arms flop to my side. I wasn't ready to face the waiting room again. I just needed a few more minutes to be alone. Obviously, this is exactly when I heard footsteps coming toward me in the main hallway. I desperately hoped they would pass, because I was pretty sure I wasn't supposed to be camped out there. They didn't. Instead, the footsteps paused, and I heard a voice that shocked me to the core.

"Kate?" It was Jess.

My head popped up almost violently to see him standing there looking slightly unsure, wondering if it was actually me or someone else. When he saw my face, he turned and began walking toward me. Something about seeing him broke all barriers. The dam collapsed, and the river flooded its banks. I let my head flop back down onto my knees and just sobbed my heart out.

"Yep, it's definitely you." Jess's voice held a smile as he slid down to sit next to me. He sat close enough to me that our shoulders were touching.

"Shut up," I moaned. "Not funny." The contact of his body against mine felt so nice right then, but I would never have admitted it.

"Ken told me about Cass when I stopped by the big house. I came as quickly as I could. Why didn't you call me? I would have driven you."

I just shrugged. I couldn't answer. I was crying too hard. I had even begun making a slurping moaning noise that definitely belonged in the animal kingdom.

Jess apparently realized I wasn't sane at that moment, so he dropped that line of questioning and put his arm around my shoulders. "Hey, it's going to be fine. Cass is a strong woman." He gave my shoulders a squeeze. I turned in his arm and put my head against his shoulder, letting his shirt have the honor of soaking up my tears and probably my snot too.

"I'm sure you're right, but what if you're wrong?" I whispered, tearing the words out of me from my scared place and hoping for a good reply. "My parents died in a car accident when I was in college. My husband collapsed at work and was rushed to the hospital before he died. I'm experiencing some major déjà vu here." The last came out on a hiccup.

Jess started stroking my hair and neck in a way that was soothing as he answered. "I didn't know that. I'm sorry. No wonder you're so upset about Cass." My breathing began to slow as the warmth and comfort of him worked its way through me. "I do think she'll be okay, though. I'm not just saying that."

I sniffled. "Thanks." For some reason I felt compelled to add, "Alec didn't answer his phone." Jess just made a noise, letting me know he'd heard me and wasn't surprised. But he held off from saying anything, and I was glad, as I doubted it would have been kind.

We sat there for a few moments, him playing lightly with my hair and me getting myself under control. I appreciated that he didn't try to break the silence. I needed the time to restore myself. Finally, I sat up, pulling away from him, and stood. Jess followed suit.

"I already saw Ethan and Zinn. They seem to be holding up a little better than you are," he teased.

"They usually do," I responded with a grumpy face.

Jess chuckled as he gestured for me to lead the way back to the waiting room. When I got to the corner where the main hall intersected, I waited for him to come walk next to me. Together, we made our way back.

A word of advice: If you ever have to visit a family member in the hospital, leave America's greatest heartthrob at home. The madness that greeted us in the waiting room would have been comical if it hadn't been so downright annoying. Jess held the door open for me as we entered. As soon as Ethan spotted Jess, he jumped up and ran to him, making a sort of squealing noise. Zinn also smiled but waited patiently in her chair for Jess to make his way toward her.

That wasn't odd. Jess was popular around our house. However, the entire rest of the waiting room stopped what they were doing, and all turned to face Jess with zombie-like looks on their faces. Like their brains had been zapped and they were being controlled by remote. Jess paused and looked around at all those people rotating at his entrance and then looked over to me with a bemused expression.

The rest of the people in the waiting room were absolutely silent. They clearly felt that they were in the presence of greatness. I immediately started across the room, and Jess quickly stepped in behind me, walking with his arm around Ethan's shoulders to where Zinn was waiting. I could tell all the eyes on him unnerved him, which surprised me. I would have assumed that a Hollywood guy would love the attention.

As Jess walked through the room, everyone pivoted in their seats so that they were facing him at all times. When we got to our chairs, the adoring public was still staring. Jess again looked at me, and I dipped into a curtsy, which made him laugh and made Zinn pinch my arm.

My curtsy, along with the sound of Jess's laugh, broke the spell, and people began looking at their toes or the ceiling or wherever they expected that their dignity had gotten off to. Jess tried to play it cool by giving a little wave to anyone in the room who was still looking his way. I snorted. It was so red carpet. Zinn pinched me again. I sat with a huff as conversations around us began to hum again.

"Any word on Cass?" Jess asked Zinn as he joined Ethan on a couch.

"A nurse told us that she is out of surgery. Moving to a recovery room. The surgeon should come see us soon," Zinn replied. I wondered how long I had been moping in the hallway. The question had me turning on my phone to see if Alec had texted back yet. Nothing. I huffed again.

"Did the nurse say how the surgery went?" Jess asked.

"Just that it went as well as can be expected . . ."

". . . in situations like these," I interrupted and pulled a face. I'd heard that phrase one too many times. This time I saw Zinn's little pinchers coming and dodged her.

"Well, hopefully we won't have to wait long," Jess piped back up.

We didn't have to wait at all. Word of Jess's arrival and his connection to Cassandra Owens had sped through the hospital like wildfire. Hospital staff were casually strolling past the waiting room and innocently glancing through the glass wall to catch a glimpse. Soon a surgeon, still in his scrubs and with sweat on his forehead, entered the room. He didn't even call out the last name and wait for a family to approach him. He came straight to us. Surprise, surprise. We all stood to greet him.

"I'm Dr. Selby," he greeted us. "I wanted to let you know that Ms. Owens is stable now. She had a broken ankle, knee, and elbow. We have made repairs and reset the bones. She had some internal bleeding in her abdomen, which we were able to also repair. She will require a lot of rest, but we expect her to recover normally."

I was surprised to find tears filling my eyes at the news that Cass would recover. The sudden swell of emotion clogged my throat, and when I opened my mouth to thank the surgeon, I was unable to get any words out. I looked to Zinn, but she seemed to have lost her voice as well and was looking at her clasped hands. Jess, who had been standing next to me, put a hand on my shoulder and squeezed it once before reaching out to shake the surgeon's hand and thank him for all he had done on behalf of Cass.

Another drawn-out hour passed before we were allowed to see Cass. I pulled rank and insisted on going in first. I was blood and I was an adult, so it was going to be me, and Zinn could just wait. It almost got ugly, the two of us staring at each other while the poor nurse waited to escort whoever won the wordless war back to Cass's room. In the end, Zinn's eyes were spitting fire, but she gave a short nod and turned back to her seat.

I followed the nurse on shaky legs to the room where Cass would be situated for the next couple of days while her recovery was watched closely by the staff. I didn't know whether to be relieved or upset that she was sleeping. The nurse explained to me that the aftereffects of the anesthesia, combined with the trauma and the pain medications they were giving her, were basically knocking her out cold. It was probably for the best. I didn't want her suffering just so that I could speak with her.

I nodded my understanding to the nurse and thanked her for her help before pulling a chair up next to the bed and taking Cass's hand gently in mine. IVs jutted out of her hand, and tubes and wires tracking everything were hooked up all over. Her normally pristine white hair was flying around her head in a crazed halo. I reached up and smoothed it down so that she wouldn't be upset when she woke to find herself in disarray.

I lay my head on the bed next to her arm and held her hand for a little while, the beeping of the machines and our soft breathing combining in a soothing rhythm.

Alec still wasn't answering. It was now almost ten o'clock at night. I had been at the hospital since noon and couldn't imagine where on earth he could be. His work day was certainly over at this point. It was a Tuesday, so my guess was he wasn't out doing much. Still, no text, no answer. Without realizing it, I had decided to focus all my fear and frustration over Cass toward Alec's lack of availability. I was steaming mad. I had sent him several strongly worded text messages and was most likely hovering on the edge of becoming a full-on harpy. I didn't care one bit.

We had spent the last bazillion hours taking turns visiting Cass, trying to find some dinner, but mostly just waiting and sitting. To make matters worse, Zinn was exhausted, Ethan was exhausted, and the fan parade for the amazing Jess Sullivan had continued as shift changes occurred and new families came and went from the waiting room. I was a bundle of nerves.

"Kate?" Jess's voice pulled me from my internal debate over which method of torture would get my message across most clearly to Alec. I glanced to the couch where he was sitting with a dozing Ethan. "Zinn and Ethan are pretty wiped. Honestly, I am too. What were you thinking for sleeping arrangements tonight?"

I hadn't thought for one second about sleeping arrangements other than that I knew we wouldn't be sleeping at home and had thought to bring overnight supplies. I shrugged. "You don't have to stay if you need to get home."

Jess rubbed his hand over his face and looked at the clock on the wall. I was sure he could feel the range of emotions radiating out from me and was trying to clamp down on his own frustration. He took a deep breath and pushed it out.

"I was thinking that I could look into getting a hotel room for the night so that everyone can get some rest. We can come back tomorrow morning to see how Cass is doing and make plans from there."

I was quiet for a moment because I wasn't even sure I could afford a hotel room. I was too embarrassed to mention that to him and have him think I was asking for money. Yet he was there and offering. I looked to see Ethan snuggled up to his side, and I knew how much Cass and Zinn liked him. I took a deep breath and forced myself to accept his kindness.

"That would be good," I replied quietly.

Jess stopped his face rubbing and looked at me like I'd suddenly sprouted three heads. "Really? You're okay with that?"

"Am I really usually that difficult?" A slight pulling up of my lips occurred as I saw his surprise that I'd gone down without a fight.

"I'm not going to answer that question." Jess's lips pulled up too. Then we were smiling at each other. "I'll go ask one of the staff members if they have a recommendation for somewhere to book a room."

"How about you let me do that? Otherwise you can bet that the room they recommend will be in the same house they'll be sleeping in tonight." I sighed dramatically and stood from my seat, reaching my arms high above my head and stretching my legs. I caught Jess watching me stretch and nervously glanced down at my phone screen again.

"Still no Alec?" Jess asked. I shook my head as I tucked my phone into my back pocket and headed out of the waiting room. I thought I heard Jess whisper "jerk" under his breath. I chose not to acknowledge it, even if he had voiced what was becoming my own opinion.

It wasn't hard to find lodging in town, and I sent Ethan and Zinn off with Jess in his car to get settled for the night. I wanted to make sure everything was fine with Cass before I joined them. Plus, I still felt too strung out to settle down.

I sat with Cass for an hour after they left, feeling terribly grateful to hear her breathing and see that her coloring was good. I couldn't help comparing her to how my parents had looked, how Charlie had looked. They'd had the paleness and stiffness of death. Their bodies had looked like a shell, their spirits gone to the next life. I was so grateful for that pulse under Cass's skin.

Feelings that I thought I had worked through and accepted wanted to push to the surface. The actual physical ache in my chest, the nausea, the numbness in my head. It seemed like those feelings constantly lurked in my mind, just waiting for an opening. Feelings of grief were strange that way, always present but becoming more bearable until something opened the door for them. I allowed them their moment before firmly squashing them back down with a reminder that looking forward was the only option.

Eventually, the nursing staff gently kicked me out. I shuffled out to my car and got in. The interior of the car was quiet. The night was dark, and I took a moment to roll my shoulders and take deep breaths. Cass was fine. Ethan and Zinn were resting under the care of Jess. It was going to be okay.

I flipped open my phone and saw that it was just after eleven. Still nothing from Alec. I briefly wondered if I had been dumped and this was how I was going to find out about it. His lack of communication made my hurt feelings roar back to life. How dare he not be around when I needed him.

I started my car with more vigor than was needed and all but laid a strip of rubber pulling out of the parking lot. It felt good to give physical release to my mental anguish. I blasted my radio as I drove through the deserted streets to the hotel before slamming my car into the parking space. I jammed the gear shift into park and turned off the engine. I was still mad. I didn't feel like I could go into the hotel this angry. I had Zinn and Ethan to think about. After a couple of deep breaths, I got out of my car and stood next to it for a moment, letting the cooler night breeze blow across my overly warm body.

I pulled my hair out of its messy ponytail and tilted my head back, letting the air catch at it before rubbing at the achy spot I always got from putting my thick hair up. I leaned back against my car and let my head hang forward, arching my back and neck to stretch out the achiness, my hair swirling in front of my face while I took a few more deep breaths and tried to remember how grateful I was that Cass was okay. How Zinn had cared for all of us today by making sure we had food and water and anything else we might need. How kind Jess had been to me, entertaining Ethan and making sure the hospital staff kept us in the loop. Alec shouldn't matter. My family was here, and we were going to be okay.

When I opened my eyes and stood up straight, I saw Jess a few paces away. I was surprised, but kind of not surprised too. He'd been popping up all day. I gave him a small smile as he finished approaching me.

"Hey, everything okay with Cass?" he asked. His eyes were following my hair as it waved uninhibited around my face. I was too tired to care that I probably looked like I'd been zapped with electricity.

"Yes, she's settled for the night. What are you doing out here?" We both spoke quietly, something about the darkness making it feel necessary even though we were alone.

"I was watching for you. Wanted to make sure you got here all right. When I saw your car pull in, I thought I'd come walk you up."

Something about that was just so darn wonderful that I suddenly found tears rising up. I had thought all my tears were gone after the hallway scene earlier, but apparently they weren't. "That's just so nice of you," I said, sniffling.

Suddenly Jess's arms were around me and he was pulling me close. I buried myself in the warmth and strength of him, letting my arms go around his waist and holding on tight. I hadn't been held just for the comfort of it in a long time. It felt amazing. Jess's hands were just the right amount of warm on my back, his chin resting lightly on the top of my head. I was sure my hair was tickling his face, but he didn't seem bothered.

"I can't stand this," I whispered thickly.

"I know."

"I'm so everything right now. Angry, sad, frustrated, scared, grateful. The emotions are bouncing around inside of me like ping-pong balls in gym class."

I felt Jess's chest vibrate as he chuckled at my description. "It'll be okay, Kate."

I loved hearing him say my name. I hated that I loved hearing him say my name. I hated that his arms felt so perfect around me, holding me firmly in place. I hated it so much that I raised my head a little and snuggled my face up under his chin so that I could feel the skin of his neck against my cheek, seeking closer contact.

"I know," I replied.

Then Jess brushed back my hair from my face and tilted his head a bit before giving me a kiss on my forehead. The spot tingled after he moved. "I'm here for whatever you need," he whispered against my hair. He hesitated, almost like he was holding himself back, before adding, "I care about Cass too."

We stood together for a few more moments before I finally let go. His arms were slow to release me, letting his hands run down my arms as he did so. Eventually, he stepped back and looked down into my face. Our gazes held, and something bright and alive began to grow in my chest. I could see something alight in his gaze as well. Jess reached a hand toward me as if he were going to pull me close again, but it was all so frightening and lovely and just too much at that moment, so I broke eye contact and looked behind him to the building.

"I guess we'd better get to bed. It's been a long day," I said as I turned back to the car and leaned in to grab my backpack. He mumbled his agreement as we walked toward the building. We didn't say anything else to each other as we made our way to the room. Jess had booked us a two-bedroom suite, for which I was grateful as I closed my door behind me. Zinn on the bed and Ethan on a rollaway were already breathing the deep and steady rhythms of sleep as I entered our room. It didn't take long to ready myself to join them.

It was too bad that sleep didn't come easily. I obsessively checked my phone once more before getting under the covers. Still nothing. When I closed my eyes, two sets of eyes floated restlessly through my mind even though my body was drained. One hazel, one a startling green.

Chapter 11

The next day, I sent Zinn and Ethan home with Jess in the evening. It was pointless for us to all be there. I knew Zinn would take great care of Ethan, and I seriously doubted Jess didn't have better things to do than sit around a hospital and pay for our hotel room another night. Then again, he could probably write off his stint at the hospital as marketing. He'd sure drummed up some fans in the waiting rooms. I had been torn between amusement and discomfort at seeing such a blatant example of his fame.

Alec had finally texted me back on Friday with this spectacular little gem: *Hey, what's up?* When the text came in, I couldn't help but yell "Really?" at the phone and slam it shut. I hadn't responded. I was pleased with my restraint in not throwing the phone across the room.

On Sunday, after four days in the hospital, I was finally able to drive Cass home to Clark Springs. It had been a long week for all of us. I had desperately missed Ethan, having never been apart from him for more than a night. But it had been especially hard on Cass, who did not appreciate the inconvenience of having gotten in an accident.

Now here we were: Jess and Ken the handyman on either side of Aunt Cass, helping her up the grand staircase to her suite of rooms, Ethan encouraging her from a few steps ahead, and Zinn hovering behind her as if to catch her should the men fail in their duty. I ran ahead, making sure every pillow was fluffed and all was in order for her return. Zinn and I had practically come to blows when I had insisted on checking everything out before the men brought Cass in.

"In all my time here I have never . . ." Zinn had mumbled as she'd shadowed my every move, her hands punctuating her disgust with my questioning her.

It had been worth it when Cass had struggled around the corner into her bedroom and the worry lines and creases had dissolved as she'd gazed around her pristine room. "It's good to be home." She'd glanced to both Zinn and me and given us a tiny smile. Ethan had clapped for her and made us all laugh. In a spontaneous moment, I'd grabbed Zinn's gnarled hand and given it a squeeze before dropping it again.

Ken slipped away as soon as we got Cass on the bed, but Jess and Ethan hovered in the doorway as Zinn fluffed pillows and I arranged blankets over Cass. I worked my way to the bookshelf and began randomly grabbing anything I thought might interest Cass while Zinn was stirring some mystery tea.

As I sat the books down, Cass waved me away. "Kate, honestly, I'm fine. Besides, I'm much too tired to read. You've done enough already." She sounded tired, but I knew she was grateful.

I was all but humbly bowing before her and offering to do anything in the world to make her comfortable when the doorbell chimed. Zinn looked downright apoplectic over the interruption to her fussing, so I scurried off to get it.

It was Alec, hat in hand, literally. I was so caught off guard by the return of my estranged boyfriend that I was momentarily speechless, as though I had to rummage through my brain and figure out who he was and what words would be appropriate. In the end, he broke the awkward silence.

"Hey, Kate." He smiled at me. I liked that smile. I really did. I just didn't particularly like the person attached to it right then.

"Yep" was my curt reply.

"I tried you at the cottage, but you weren't there, so I thought I'd try you here. I haven't heard from you for a bit and wanted to check in." He had the decency to look uncomfortable. When I didn't pipe in, he tried again. "You haven't responded to any of my phone calls or text messages, and I was getting a little worried."

That was absolutely the most ludicrous thing he could have said. I was 100 percent sure I felt something in my brain pop, and I took a step out of the doorway onto the porch, forcing him to take a step backward.

"I didn't realize we were obligated to respond to each other's phone calls and text messages!" I hammered at him. "I was under the impression that we would get back to each other when we had a chance." Something on my face began twitching. This was not good. Hurricane Kate was going to wash away any chance of a relationship with Alec. I did not care.

"Yeah, about that. I'm real sorry . . ."

"Sorry?" I screeched. Oh boy, I was screeching. This wasn't good at all. As I went to take another step forward, I felt a hand on my elbow holding me back. I swung my head around, prepared to let spittle fly, and saw Jess standing slightly behind me. He wasn't looking at me but at Alec as he stepped up so that he was standing next to me.

"Hey, man," Jess said. He let his hand drop from my elbow, but instead of leaving me completely, he moved it to the small of my back and let it rest there. Normally, the presumption would have irritated me beyond belief, but in that moment it felt incredibly comforting. Like I was on a team. Warmth radiated out from the place his hand was resting lightly and seemed to wash away some of my temper.

"Hey," Alec perked up as he raised his eyebrows and then shot a look toward me. Guy code for *This girl is crazy, am I right, dude?* "I was just dropping by to check in with Kate. I haven't heard from her for a bit," he said.

"So you didn't get her text messages?" Jess asked.

Alec again looked a little sheepish and stared to the side for a minute before looking back to Jess. "Not really. I mean, I haven't been in town, and my phone has been acting up."

"Huh, so nothing? All week?"

Alec just shrugged, which for some reason made Jess's hand tense on my back. It had me glancing away from Alec and looking to his face. Jess was always so easygoing, and I was surprised to see his eyes tighten up. I had done a lot of aggravating things to Jess and never seen him react like that. Something about Jess's irritation made me supremely happy. I'd hoped he'd been taught some super ninja moves on one of his movie sets and I'd get to see him use them on Alec.

Instead, Jess kind of rolled his shoulders before glancing down at me. In his gaze was something I couldn't quite discern. Our eyes locked, and I felt his thumb draw a slow circle on my back, almost like Jess had forgotten Alec was there and, well, and I didn't know what.

"Seems to me if I had a girl like Kate, I wouldn't be missing her calls," Jess responded to Alec while still looking at me. Of its own free will, my body slightly turned toward Jess, as if to get closer.

Alec cleared his throat, and the spell was broken as both Jess and I looked back toward him, standing there, hat being crushed in his hands. "I'm really sorry. I heard Miss Cass was in an accident?" he fished.

This time I did step forward again, and Jess didn't stop me. His warm hand dropped from my back. I felt the loss, and it fueled my anger. "Yes, Cass was hurt—badly. I've been with her in the hospital for days. I've texted and called a million times." I punctuated the last bit by throwing my hands in the air.

"I'm really sorry." Alec didn't step back but instead stepped forward and put his arms around me before pulling me in close. "That must have been awful," he soothed. But nothing about his hold was soothing, and I pushed away.

"It was awful," I replied. "I was upset and terrified, and you couldn't be bothered to respond," I huffed out and turned away from him, only to find that Jess had slipped back into the house. I hated that he was gone. Even more than that, I hated that I cared.

I kept my back to Alec and said, "I don't think we should keep dating."

Alec stepped up behind me but refrained from trying to touch me again. "I guess this always had to end anyhow." I turned and gave him a questioning look. "School is starting back up soon, and I don't do long-distance."

"School?" I almost gagged on the word. "I thought you were on a break from school!"

"Yeah, I was. But that's where I've been the past couple of days. I decided to start back up at Colorado State and had to get all registered, you know?"

I just shook my head, too shocked to utter a word. That felt like a big decision to not have told me about.

Alec grinned. "Yeah, so I'll be going back soon, and I . . . I just had such a great summer hanging with you and Ethan. And a little kissing on the side wasn't so bad, was it?" When I remained quiet, he added, "I really thought you knew that I was thinking about going back."

"I definitely did not," I whispered.

He laughed again, probably his way of dealing with the awkward moment. "Sorry." That was it. All he was going to offer. Sorry I didn't tell you I was going away, sorry you thought this relationship was more than it was, sorry I didn't help you out during your emergency.

I felt myself deflate as I stood there, his sorry hanging between us. There was nothing left to say or do, and we both knew it.

"Well, good luck with school," I said flatly before walking away and shutting Cass's big front door behind me. I was too horrified to find it at all amusing that I, Katherine Evans, had been nothing more than a summer fling. I should have felt flattered, and maybe in time I would, but in the moment all I could hear was Zinn's accusing voice telling me I was a cougar. She was right.

Later that night, in the privacy of my cottage bedroom, I shed a tear for Alec. He hadn't been my Prince Charming. He had barely even been a boyfriend, but he had been something to me. If nothing else, he had been the one to show me that I could date again . . . that it was okay to dust myself off and shine.

Chapter 12

The sweat on my back made my shirt sticky as I sat on the little porch of my cottage a few nights later. It had been a long day. My pink sweats were back, along with a purple-ish tank that clung in all the wrong places. My hair had been French braided at one point, but wisps had fallen out and were curling around my face and ears.

Over the past week, Cass had turned out to be a demanding patient. Even though Zinn kept the house spotless, in her current caged situation, Cass wanted even more done. Better books, fluffier pillows, warmer tea, colder water, a softer sponge for her sponge bath. I had dusted, moved furniture, and basically carried Cass from her bed to a lounge chair a million times that day. Not to mention giving her my version of a sponge bath and a massage that was completely ineffective, according to my darling aunt. I was just plain beat.

Ethan had eventually announced that he was going to bed, and I had barely had a minute to chase him down, give him a hug, and tuck him in before heading back up to the big house. I felt guilty for missing yet another summer day with him. I made a note to remember to reward him for being a stellar human. Ice cream usually did the trick.

I had kicked off my shoes and slumped down into one of the patio chairs, letting my legs flop to the side and my head hang back, wishing upon a star that even a trickle of a breeze would come across the creek to cool my skin. Cass had decided that she was freezing cold that day—never mind that it was high summer—and had cranked the heat on.

My mind leafed slowly through the day, thinking on things Cass had said, images of Zinn flittering about trying to make herself useful, Ethan peeking in the door every now and then, his hand on Wade's head, Wade's entire body wagging at the sight of all his people in one room.

My mind kept sticking on something I had overheard Cass discussing with Zinn while I'd been under her bed trying to plug in a charger for her phone.

"Jess told me he found out about a theater in Aspen that is closing its doors. He's thinking of reopening it and building up a community theater," Cass had half whispered to Zinn. "I just can't understand why he'd give up his movie career and settle for something small potatoes like that." Zinn had apparently indicated some sort of agreement, because Cass had pressed on. "A man like that, in his prime, successful and in demand, doesn't just walk away. I can't figure him out. I always thought Jess was more sensible than that. There will be time later to settle down."

At that point I had popped out from under the bed, and the subject was dropped like a hot stick. I let my mind chug on it for a bit, wondering what Jess's plans were and why. I had thought about it more than I cared to admit while doing the mindless tasks involved in housekeeping. I agreed with Cass. I couldn't figure him out.

Another few days passed before I saw the subject of my thoughts appear. I hadn't seen or heard from him for over a week. Not since he'd walked away during my conversation with Alec. When I saw him enter the kitchen, where I was preparing a tray for Cass, I felt an unbidden blush rise to my cheeks. Out of nowhere I remembered the feeling of his hand on my back, tracking its slow circle, the way his hands had played with my hair at the hospital, the way he had held me in the dark parking lot of the hotel. I forced out a deep breath and tried to smile casually.

"Hey," he said, walking to where I was standing. "How's my friend Cinderella doing today?"

A genuine smile replaced my timid one as I replied, "Wishing for a fairy godmother." I gestured with my free hand to my grubby clothing and flyaway hair before laughing.

"Cass hasn't been the easiest patient, I hear. At least according to Ethan. Even Zinn complained to me yesterday when I went in to say hello." Jess took the tray from me as I began to lift it, and he motioned for me to lead the way.

"Are you sure you want to go back in there?" I asked, standing in my spot.

"Maybe if we gang up on her she won't bite?" Jess stated it like a question, which had me smiling again.

"Forward march!" I replied like a drill sergeant. I spun in a tight circle and began marching my way out of the kitchen. Jess chuckled again behind me.

"So what brings you here today?" I asked as we reached the staircase and began climbing side by side.

"I'm leaving town again tomorrow. I needed to talk with you before I go."

"Sure. Let me get Cass settled and we'll go outside. The cool air will do me good."

"Cool air? It's at least ninety degrees out there today."

"Wait until you get to Cass's room. It's probably ninety degrees in here today too," I grumbled before taking the tray from him and slipping into the sauna.

When Cass saw Jess in the doorway waiting for me, she suddenly became a model patient.

"Oh, dear, you shouldn't keep Jess waiting. You've worked so hard, and this tray looks so lovely. Why don't you take a little break. I'll call Zinn if I need anything." She sweetly patted my hand with her good one and gave Jess a smile.

I wanted to strangle her. Even more than imagining her slow and painful demise, I wanted out of the house. Not one to question a gift, I gave her a quick kiss on the cheek and bolted toward the door. I was half jogging by the time I made it across the large suite to Jess. I grabbed his arm and catapulted both of us out of the room and down the stairs, never letting go of him.

"Run for it! There's not a second to lose," I stage-whispered as we reached the bottom of the stairs. I spun on my stocking feet around the corner of the banister and ran down the hallway into the kitchen. Jess was right behind me, still holding tightly to my hand as I dragged him along.

By the time we blew out the back door onto the covered patio, both of us were laughing.

"I think we're clear, Captain." Jess released my hand and saluted me.

I flopped down onto a padded swing, and the motion got it rocking. I pulled my socks off and threw them to the ground before pulling my hair out of its high bun and running my fingers through it. It felt wonderful to be outside.

Jess surprised me by sitting on the swing next to me. I noticed him watching me finger-comb my hair out of the side of his eyes with a small smile on his lips. For the first time, I truly didn't care. Oh, I still knew I was no Vivienne Lawson. I was still short and a little round. My hair was still frizzy and thick and, darn it, I was still sporting some awful fashion. Nothing about me had changed. All that had changed was how I felt about Jess. Sometime in the past weeks he had become just Jess, and I was just Kate, and it was all fine.

The thought startled me. I looked to where Jess was sitting, our shoulders nearly touching as he gazed out across the gardens toward the mountain beyond. The moment I'd realized I was comfortable with Jess was the moment I became royally uncomfortable.

Jess looked back to me. "So I feel like I just rescued the damsel from the dragon. I'm hoping that means you'll do me a favor." He was grinning.

"Shoot," I replied.

"I'm heading out of town again, like I said, and I could still use your help keeping tabs on the work being done at my place. If you can believe it, Jack and Zara have decided for sure that my cabin would be the perfect setting for their wedding." He seemed a bit confused by that, which made me smile.

"It's a beautiful property. I can see why they'd want to have their wedding there."

"It is pretty, yes, but it's also far away from any family and friends they have. I'd think that they'd prefer something local to them." He shrugged. He was a man who didn't understand how dreams of a beautiful wedding could make you choose to leave your local area. "Anyhow, that's going to require some serious landscaping. I had those plans drawn up but haven't moved forward on them because I thought maybe Zara had changed her mind. I was wrong. Luckily, the house itself is almost done. Maybe another couple of weeks. After that I am hoping the landscaping crew can do their job in a month or two as well. Doesn't make sense to start landscaping when we still have work being done on the house. They'd kill any grass or flowers that were planted."

"Sure." I smiled to myself at the serious look on his face.

"I have to do this photo shoot in Arizona this weekend, and then I'm off to London to film some more on the movie. I'll probably be gone about two months." Jess seemed slightly bothered by the amount of time he was committed to being away. His gaze drifted back to the mountains and, unless I was mistaken, there were new lines on his face. He looked worn out. Our new friendship and the memories of his recent kindness toward me made my heart pinch at the sight.

"I thought you liked all that stuff," I said softly. "The travel, the glitz and glamour."

Jess looked directly at me for a moment before he answered. "I used to. I thought it was what I wanted. Some things have changed. I don't think I can do this forever," he replied. We were silent for a moment, the squeaking of the swing as he lazily pushed it with one toe the only sound. The moment felt heavy with undercurrents and importance, but I couldn't put my finger on why.

"Is there anything I can do to help?" I ventured. Caring about Jess at all was new territory, and I wasn't sure how to play this.

He shook his head slowly and replied, "Thanks for the offer. But helping me out again by keeping an eye on things while I'm gone will be enough."

My sympathies rose at the weariness in his tone, and I reached out to lay my hand on his forearm. He flinched a bit at the contact, probably as shocked as I was that I'd initiated it, but he didn't pull away and kept the swing steadily going. We were quiet for a few moments. It was nice. So nice I was scared by it.

"Where are you going?" I asked.

"Arizona. A place called Sedona. Going to do a photo shoot for a magazine cover," Jess replied.

"Sounds cool." I gave his arm a squeeze. I was being so darn friendly.

"Yeah. It really is a cool town. Lots of art places and shops, great little restaurants, and a place called Slide Rock where you can ride down natural rock formations like water slides into little pools. I hear it's a lot of fun. I thought about checking it out while I was there. Ethan would probably love it," he said somewhat absently. "Man, I wish you guys could come." His eyes swung to mine with a glimmer of hope, like he was thinking about moving ahead with that thought.

Speaking of rocks, I felt like one had plunged down to the bottom of my stomach at the idea of him inviting Ethan and me to join him on his photo shoot. I would absolutely not fit in that world. Plus, we were just becoming friends and nowhere near the point of traveling together. Add in the fact that it was one thing for him and Ethan to go fishing and pal around the property, but totally another for Ethan to see Jess as more than he was in our lives.

I pulled my hand off his arm and fisted it in my lap. "Jess, I . . ." I started, needing to head this off before it turned into an actual conversation.

He raised his hand and smiled before I could say anything. "Don't sweat it. It was a spontaneous thought. Although I do think it would be fun for you and Ethan to get away. And I don't think I'd be horrible company. I would have enjoyed a friendly face to kill the time with."

I smiled at him as I realized he wasn't going to push me. The tension drifted out of my body. "I hope you have a good trip."

"I'll talk to you soon?" He smiled back.

I shrugged as I hopped off the swing. "If I don't get any better offers," I shot back over my shoulder jokingly. His laugh was the last thing I heard before the house door closed behind me.

With Ethan back in school, I was able to spend more time with Cass and give Zinn a break. Her recovery was coming along nicely. Her arm was now in a sling rather than a cast, and her leg had been changed to a walking cast with a boot, so she had gained some independence and mobility. It had helped her mood tremendously.

After lunch, I helped Cass down to the main floor and out to the patio with a magazine to read and some cool lemonade. I got Cass settled comfortably in her chair while I took up my favorite position on the swing. Wade was seated on the patio floor next to Cass's chair. The poor hunk of fur had been mopey ever since school started back up. He missed Ethan. It was obvious that Wade considered Ethan a littermate.

"Have you seen this magazine article about Jess?" Cass asked, whipping out the magazine she'd brought down with her.

I reluctantly took it out of her hand. There was Jess on the cover, standing against a backdrop of red rock and green bushes. He looked so happy and at home, a wide smile on his face, his eyes looking straight at the camera. My heart gave a little flutter. He was seriously striking. How on earth could he have thought it would be a good idea to have me along on that trip? We were total opposites. I was so glad I hadn't gone. I flipped to the story about Jess inside the magazine.

The first thing that caught my eye was a picture of him sliding down rocks into a pool beyond. The caption on the pictures labeled it as Slide Rock. It did look fun. Maybe I would take Ethan sometime. But then another picture caught my eye: Jess dining at a little table with a beautiful, leggy, perfectly dressed blonde.

I fought against a jumble of emotions that flared up as I looked at him and Vivienne. I was angry without reason, sad without reason, and hurt without reason. They made an incredibly attractive couple. "America's Sweethearts," the caption read. Indeed. I couldn't imagine Jess with anyone more ideal.

I handed the magazine back to Cass without reading any more. I couldn't understand my feelings. I was so jumbled up, and I didn't like it. Jess should be with someone who matched him and could live his lifestyle. I had been foolish to think he'd been disappointed about Ethan and me not going with him. Apparently, he'd just been after any friendly face, and he'd found one.

"I heard what happened with Alec," Cass stated into the stillness. I simply nodded. No surprise there. Between Zinn, Jess, and Ethan, someone was bound to tell her. "Well, I hate to say I told you so, but . . ."

"Then please, Cass, don't." I held up a hand to keep her from going on.

Cass quickly regained her momentum, never one to be kept from saying what was on her mind. "Fine, well, I don't think that means you should give up dating altogether."

"Oh?" I mumbled, because I knew she required some kind of response that proved I was listening, even if it wasn't sincere interest.

"Yes. I had my doubts about Alec, but I was happy to see you dating again after Charlie. You've always been such a social little thing, and it was good to see you out again." I didn't know what to say to that, so I just nodded to encourage her to proceed.

"I met a nice man at my doctor's appointment yesterday. He's got two daughters. His name is Nate Carmichael. I gave him your number."

"What? Cass!" I glared at her. "You can't just give out my number to any strange man you meet!"

"He isn't strange, Katherine. He's a very nice man."

"That you met at the doctor's office! He could have been there for anything. Did you see lice crawling on his head? Did he have something swollen and pus-filled anywhere?" I pushed my foot down and made the swing fly back in my frustration.

"As usual, you are completely overreacting," Cass huffed. She hated to be told her ideas were anything other than perfect. Being a mother would have been a real disappointment to her, seeing as kids always think your ideas are bad. "I don't know why I put up with you sometimes," she added under her breath. I scowled to let her know I'd heard. She responded with a little laugh, the tension broken.

"Then why was he at a doctor's office?" I questioned.

"He had one of his sweet little girls there. She was being treated for strep throat. He seemed to be a very caring father." She gave me an angelic smile.

"Fine. But did you really give him my number? I don't know anything about him. Is he expecting a date or something?"

"Well, that is the general idea when you give a man a woman's number," Cass replied.

"What does he look like? Please tell me he's not the creature from the Black Lagoon. The missing link? Was he all hunched and hairy?"

Cass laughed at my ranting before waving her hand for me to stop. "Please, Kate. I wouldn't set you up with a monster. Honestly. He's a perfectly normal-looking man. I'd guess midthirties. Divorced. He lives and works in Oakdale. Shares custody with his ex-wife."

"Is he shorter than me?"

"That would be difficult, dear."

Point Cass. Rudely attained, but point. "What did you tell him about me?"

"I told him you were widowed with a son. That you grump around the place in sweatpants and flip-flops all day long and I'd appreciate it if he could take you off my hands for a little while, if only because it would mean you'd change into something more presentable."

When I opened my mouth to retort, Cass started laughing again. "Kate, please. I have lived and loved a lot more than you give me credit for. I showed him your picture and told him you are a lovely person. He seemed interested in getting to know you. I believe he'll call soon."

I was quiet as I pushed the swing back and forth, considering. What harm could come of going on a blind date? At least I'd get out of the house. Jess was off having adventures across the globe with Vivienne Lawson, not that I cared. Alec was off at school doing who knew what. So maybe I should step into the ring too. A new ring, though—not that dating a young person had been all bad, just that I would like to enter the adult dating ring.

Cass must have sensed my capitulation, because she smiled softly and said, "You'll answer if he calls?"

"I'll answer if he calls," I confirmed.

That night, Jess called. It was late. Too late for phone calls. I didn't even say a word as I answered the phone. It was more of a croak.

"Kate?"

"Midnight," I croaked.

"You'd like me to call you 'Midnight' now? Did you join a gang while I was away?"

"Yes. We go around beating up people who call other people at horrible times of the night," I replied.

Jess chuckled. "Sorry. With the time difference, I get mixed up sometimes. I was hoping it wasn't too late there. Should I call another time?"

I thought about telling him yes, I really did. "You'll just manage to screw it up again. I'm awake now, so go ahead."

"Are you still in bed?"

"A gentleman never asks that question," I said as I shuffled to a sitting position, my back against the headboard.

I could hear the smile in his voice as he replied, "I'm worried you'll fall back asleep while I'm talking to you."

"It would be good for your ego. You're probably used to all the women hanging off your every word," I cracked.

"All but one," he joked.

"I'm sitting up now. The hard wood of the headboard is digging into my back. Is that good enough?" I asked.

"That'll do. Hey, I just wanted an update on the house and how things are going with Cass."

We spent the next fifteen minutes talking about Jess's house and Cass's recovery and Ethan starting school. The cabin was close to being done. The workers were down to the finishing touches that would make his cabin something amazing. I didn't tell him how much I'd liked walking around the past few days, checking in and seeing the progress. I'd paused at windows and watched Ethan and Wade running near the hillside where the ground hadn't been cut up by machinery. I could see how it would be to live there. It felt welcoming. He'd done a great job designing the space, and the workers he'd hired were quality.

As our conversation was winding down, that picture of Jess dining in Sedona with Vivienne suddenly formed in my mind. Without a moment's thought, I blurted out, "Cass gave my number to some guy she met at her doctor's office. Guess I'm blind-dating now."

I expected Jess to laugh. Instead, he was quiet for a minute. "Really?" was all he said.

"Yes. I'm supposed to expect his call soon. I don't know what that means. Soon could be tomorrow. Soon could be in October."

"I don't think you can say October is soon. That's like a month and a half away. It's a pretty safe bet he'll call before then."

"Stop being literal," I huffed.

"Stop being dramatic," he countered.

"This from the actor?" I joked. "But seriously, what if he shows up and smells like tuna fish?"

"Has that happened before?"

"Only the first time you came to my cottage," I teased. Jess laughed again. "But I told Cass I'd answer if he calls. I can't say no to that evil woman."

"I seem to have the same problem. Listen, I'm sure the date will be fine. Want some advice?"

I was surprised by the offer. "Um, sure?"

"Make sure you wash your sweatpants tomorrow, and then don't wear them again until he calls. That way they'll be ready for your hot date, no matter what."

"You're dumb," I retorted, but I was smiling. I knew Jess could hear the smile in my voice over the phone.

"I should let you get back to bed," he said softly, after a pause.

"Yes, you should."

"Okay. I'll call you again soon."

"So should I be expecting another call tomorrow . . . or not until October?" I pretended to be seriously curious. Jess's laugh was the last sound I heard before the phone went silent.

Chapter 13

Nate Carmichael, divorced dad and perfectly lovely fellow, was at my door just a few days later. He definitely did not smell like tuna fish. Nor was he a monster of a man. He was exactly as Cass had described him: a normal-looking man in his midthirties. He had kind eyes and a nice smile. He wasn't shorter than me, but he wasn't overly tall either. He was comfortable.

We had spoken on the phone the night before for thirty minutes. He seemed pleasant and down-to-earth. He'd laughed at my jokes and even made a few himself. I liked that he had experienced some things in his life. It made him relatable in a way that I realized Alec never had been. I wouldn't have to try too hard with Nate to be the perfect little date. Nate knew that life was messy and that people had opinions and that part of growing up was being less willing to try stupid stuff. I found that attractive in and of itself.

I had been a little surprised when Nate had suggested we go out the very next night. I had agreed, though, and arranged for Cass to keep an eye on Ethan. She was being ridiculously supportive of my date.

Nate walked me around to the front of the big house, where his sedan was parked, and opened my door. Points for gentlemanly behavior. He had suggested we start with dinner together, and I had readily agreed. A girl had to eat. Why not do it with a man who may be interesting?

We managed to keep up conversation in the car. He told me about his girls, Ally and Liz, ages ten and six. The younger one was recovering from her strep. So that was good. He had a dog too, of which, oddly enough, he shared custody with his ex-wife. That was strange, because I'd always thought of dogs as pets, not exactly something you'd arrange custody of. Whether I understood it or not, I figured it showed that he loved animals, and animal lovers aren't usually homicidal maniacs. So that was good too.

He took me to an Italian place run out of a tiny shed, with all its dining tables outside under big red-and-white-striped umbrellas. It was a perfect choice in that Italian was a safe bet, while dining alfresco showed he could do something different. Frankly, I would have eaten it out of a bin behind the restaurant. I was that big a fan of Italian food wizardry.

As we got settled and ordered our food, I couldn't help but compare this with my first date with Alec. "Do you ever use chopsticks?" I asked randomly.

Nate gave me a confused look and replied, "When I'm eating Chinese food, yes."

"Huh. I've never really gotten the hang of them. Italian was a good choice." I smiled, and he returned the smile. It was all very nice.

Dinner was delicious. Great huge helpings of melty cheese, pasta, and sauces that made you think maybe, just maybe, your ancestors were Italian and your soul was recognizing its own.

"I think I was Italian in a past life," I said around a delectable meatball.

I was satisfied to hear Nate laugh. "I ask my mom each year on my birthday if she wants this year to be the year that she admits I was born in Italy."

I loved that he joined right in. "Sometimes I try to speak Italian around the house, but Ethan tells me to stop, that I am too old to pull it off. I'm definitely sure I should be offended by him saying that."

"I wonder if we could find an Italian family to adopt us. They could teach us their food secrets, and you could dye your hair black and spray on a fake tan and go on TV!" Nate chuckled.

"I've always wanted to be rich *and* a good cook!" I pointed my fork in the air. "It's so disappointing that each morning I wake up and am neither of those things, no matter how many stars I wish upon."

"Jiminy Cricket was a liar," Nate added, and we both laughed.

We talked TV shows we were into, movies we'd like to see, music we weren't sure we understood, and the general exploits that went along with parenting. He was cautious about mentioning his ex-wife, and I was grateful for that. He clearly wasn't hung up on her, but he also didn't want to go about disparaging her.

I was dating a grown-up. This made me so happy that I ordered dessert and smiled at him the entire time I ate it. Cass had made a good call with Nate. I'd see him again if he asked.

"So how was your date?" Jess asked across the line when I answered the next morning.

"Just jumping straight to that?" I laughed. Then I thought about it for a minute. "Wait, how did you know I went out?"

"I just figured that he'd call sooner than later." Jess said this like it was the most obvious thing in the world.

"Yeah, right. One of your local spies must have told you. Probably the little one with the big mouth."

"Ethan didn't say anything. I took a wild guess, and I was right. So how was it?"

"No way you guessed that accurately." I wasn't willing to give it up just yet. "Honestly, how on earth did you know?" I pressed.

"I figured Cass showed him your picture and he was interested enough to call sooner than later. It had been a couple of days, a respectable, nonstalker amount of time. So the phone call had to have happened. A divorced dad isn't going to have time to waste with his busy life, so I figured a quick ask. I was right."

"All from one picture of a garden gnome?" I laughed.

"Stop. You can't honestly think you look like a garden gnome." Jess's voice sounded annoyed. Like if I could see him his lips would be pinched and his eyes would have rolled back into his head.

I was too bemused to respond. Were we treading on serious ground here? I was not about to discuss my perception of myself with Mr. American Hunk of the Year.

"You've never cared to ask about any of my other dates. Why this one?" I purposely kept my voice light.

Jess sighed so dramatically I could practically feel his disgruntled vibes through the phone line. "Look, Kate, someone should have told you a long time ago that you're beautiful. And you should have been told that enough times to believe it." We were both quiet after that startling bit of information. I had no idea how to respond.

Jess Sullivan thought I was beautiful. I couldn't have come up with a response if my life had depended on it. My silence must have been misinterpreted across the miles because Jess sighed again. I could practically see him running his hand across his face like he did when I had really bugged him.

"I was calling to check up on the house, but my time is up. I'll call again soon." And he hung up. I was stumped. How was he out of time when we had only been talking for a total of three minutes, tops? Not to mention that my brain still felt dizzy with the revelation that he thought I was pretty.

In all honesty, Charlie had told me a million times that I was beautiful. Somehow I'd always thought that he sort of *had* to tell me that because he was my husband. Jess Sullivan, however, had absolutely no obligation to tell me any such thing.

I set the phone down and went down the hall to the bathroom, where I closed the door and looked at myself in the mirror. I saw all the same things I'd always seen. A slightly short, curvy redhead. This time I forced myself to look closer to try to see what Jess was saying he saw . . . what maybe Nate had seen when Cass had shown him my picture.

I stood in front of that mirror for a long time.

Nate did ask to see me again. Because of time commitments with his girls, we would have to wait until another weekend rolled around, but in the meantime, I was pleased with myself for snagging a second date.

I decided such success deserved exercise. While Ethan and I cleaned up from dinner, I suggested we take a hike that led through the lower foothills, eventually ending at Jess's property. I needed to check up on the house and have something ready to report to Jess when he called again. I hadn't heard from him for a few days. Not since his little *beautiful* bomb had been dropped. I couldn't say I was sad about the silence from across the ocean. Things were a little awkward. You can't unsay some things. Trust me, I know.

Ethan was thrilled to get a hike in during the cooler evening hours. He quickly changed and ran to get Wade from the big house to go with us. I saw Cass hobble out to the patio and wave as Wade ran toward us with Ethan not far behind. I waved back at Cass and waited for Ethan and Wade to get to me. They both barely paused as they darted past me toward the trailhead. I laughed to myself and turned to follow at a more sedate pace.

Clark Springs in late August to early September was a great place to live. The evenings usually cooled down into the seventies and the sun stayed out later. It made for pleasant hours to enjoy the forest and hills around Cass's property. I lost sight of Ethan and his best pal pretty quickly, but I could hear Ethan's cheerful chatter ahead of me on the trail and Wade's occasional bark as he warned off squirrels and birds, letting them know something fierce was in the forest.

It wasn't a terribly long hike to Jess's. When we got there, the workers were working on hanging outside lights. They waved at me as I emerged from the trees and began crossing the open space toward them. The lawn was finished, and many of the decorative flower beds were being filled in. A few finishing touches and the place would be perfect for Jack and Zara's wedding.

The cabin, as Jess still stubbornly insisted on calling the place, was just about done. I had been given a key, and I called to Ethan to stay nearby while I had a look around inside. Jess had especially wanted me to give him a report on the finishes and details. I had tried to suggest he find someone more keen on looking at details, but he'd insisted I could handle the job.

I motioned with my key to let the workers know I'd be going in before I unlocked the back door and kicked off my shoes. The flooring was all down, the painting all done. Light fixtures were being hung, and then window coverings would go up. It really felt like a home at this point. I ran my hand along the kitchen countertop, wishing I cooked a little more. Cooking in this kitchen would be a pleasure. Cleaning up would still totally be the pits, though.

I wandered aimlessly, looking at every nook and cranny, memorizing details to report back. Occasionally, I could hear Ethan call out or Wade bark. I could hear the laughter and chatter of the workmen outside. It was so incredibly peaceful, almost like the sounds of family life, that I suddenly felt more alone than I had since Charlie passed. I wasn't sure exactly when it had become normal for me to be without a companion, but in that moment I felt such a sense of loneliness and loss that I was nearly brought to tears.

I made my way into the master bedroom and decided to take advantage of the large window seat. I climbed up, pulled me knees up to my chin, and watched Ethan run and run around the beautiful foothills. I smiled at the sight of him. I only wished I could have a tenth of the energy that he had.

". . . has some money left after building this house. I don't think that theater will make him much."

I caught the tail end of a sentence as two workers made their way around the end of the house near where I was sitting. They were carrying a ladder and some boxes. At the mention of the theater, I all but pressed my ear to the windowpanes. I didn't want to smear the clean glass, but I would if I had to. I needed to know what was going on with that theater.

"I think he's made enough to live on for the rest of his life, whether that theater works out or not. I'm just surprised he would give up his fame to run a local theater," the second man said, entering the conversation.

"Maybe his name alone will draw people to it," Man One suggested. Man Two shrugged and nodded as they rounded the corner out of sight.

What on earth? I thought. *What is Jess up to?*

In the end, Nate had to cancel our plans for a second date. After which I had to cancel. Then his daughter got sick. Then Ethan got sick. I'm pretty sure even his dog got sick. Oh, welcome back, school year. How we loved the germ exchange brought on by many sticky hands using very little soap.

Luckily for me, I was surprised one early evening by a knock on my cottage door. When I opened it, I was greeted by Zara's cheerful face. Her smile looked a little apologetic as she stood there waiting for me to get over my shock.

"Zara! Come in," I said, laughing and throwing the door wide.

"Thanks." She laughed too and gave me a brief hug after I'd closed the door behind her. "I'm so sorry to drop in on you, but I don't have your number and can't seem to get Jess. I've been in town and over at his property working with my wedding planner to make sure all the arrangements have been finalized. We wrapped up this afternoon, but my flight doesn't leave until tomorrow morning. I wondered if you'd want to have dinner with me?"

I didn't even need two seconds to think about it. "I'd love to. Ethan is up at the big house playing fetch with Wade. I just need to call Cass and see if she minds if he stays for a while longer. Have a seat."

Zara sat gracefully on the couch while I hunted down my phone and placed a call to the big house. Cass was more than happy to watch Ethan, and I reported the good news to Zara.

"Did you have anything particular in mind?" I asked. "Like, are we talking takeout with stretchy pants, or should I have shaved my legs this morning?"

Zara laughed. "I really don't care at all." I took a moment to give her a once-over. She looked tired under her smile. My mind was made up.

"You look pretty fancy for takeout," I teased. Zara looked down at herself in a burgundy pantsuit with a black silk top and pulled a silly face. Suddenly a thought hit me. "Do you even own a pair of sweats?"

"Sweats?" she asked, obviously thinking she'd heard me wrong. "Like what you wear in gym class or at summer camp?" At my nod, she shook her head.

"That's what I thought. Well, you introduced me to killer croquet, so I'm going to introduce you to sweats. We're staying in tonight. Come with me." I motioned for her to follow me, and she chuckled as she stood to obey.

The problem I should have foreseen but managed to avoid was that Zara's legs were several inches longer and possibly tighter than mine. Like nothing on her body jiggled. I had a feeling she'd actually make sweatpants look attractive. I didn't let that sad thought distract me from my mission.

She sat on the edge of my bed while I pulled a few clean, worn pairs of sweats out and put them next to her. "As my guest, you get first choice." I teasingly smiled.

She rubbed her hand over each of them as though feeling for the quality of material. Either that or she needed her hands to tell her what her eyes weren't believing. She was about to dress like her middle school gym teacher.

"They're soft." She smiled up at me.

"This is true." I grinned.

"I don't think they'll match my silk shirt." She laughed as she picked up a gray pair.

"No worries. I'm sure I can find a windbreaker for you to wear," I teased. She laughed. I went to another drawer and pulled out a soft white T-shirt and handed it to her. "It's going to be too big, but that's okay. Stretchy clothes are perfect for what I've got in mind tonight."

"I think I like where you're going with this." She smiled.

"Oh, stick with me, kid," I replied as I gestured to the bathroom where she could change. "By the time I'm done with you, you'll never want to wear silk, tailored clothing again."

I had been right about two things. Zara made sweats look good, even if the fitted cuff of mine were hitting her mid-calf. And Zara was tired. She flopped on my couch and gratefully took the afghan I offered her, snuggling in the corner and leaning her head back.

"I took the liberty of ordering pizza while you were changing," I said as I sat opposite her and tucked my shorter legs under me to keep them from dangling out of reach of the floor.

"Please tell me you got all the meats." She sighed as she let her eyes close for a minute.

"Your arteries are about to be spectacularly clogged," I replied. She laughed. "Tell me about the wedding."

She opened her eyes and pulled a face. "Would you mind terribly if we talked about anything else? I'm about weddinged out."

"Okay, do you prefer dogs or cats?" I asked.

She didn't miss a beat, but just went along with the abrupt change of direction. "Um, cats. Less maintenance. They don't bark. They don't get that weird dog smell. They don't rub in their own messes." She sat up a bit, her eyes sparkling.

"I disagree with you that cats are better, but you're the guest here, so we'll move on. If you could, would you want the power to read minds?"

She thought about this one for a second. "No. I don't want to know what people are really thinking. I prefer to assume good."

"Me too. I'm already like 73 percent sure people are irritated with the things I do. I find that living with that small bit of doubt keeps me going. If I knew 100 percent, then I'd just be bummed all the time."

Zara laughed. "Okay, my turn. If you had to stay one age for the rest of your life, what would it be?"

"Well, so far my twenties have been a bit of a disappointment." I pulled a face. "I mean, other than having Ethan, of course."

"Goes without saying." Zara nodded.

"So I'm going to hope my thirties are better and throw out the number thirty-five. Old enough to keep things together better, young enough to still have my natural hair color. You?"

"Oh, I think forty. Everyone says that you spend your thirties getting to know yourself and by forty you feel confident."

"Forty is the new twenty, I hear," I said in a pseudo-wise way. Zara smiled.

The pizza arrived a short time later—total benefit of living in a small town—and we continued our question-and-answer session, laughing, good-naturedly debating, and talking until Ethan finally stumbled home holding Cass's hand and ready for bed.

I thanked Cass and walked my sweet sleepy boy to his room to get into pajamas. As I tucked him in and said prayers with him, I could hear Zara cleaning up our mess.

When I returned to the main living area, the kitchen was clean and Zara was once again wearing her beautiful pantsuit. I was happy to see that she looked more relaxed.

"Kate, thank you so much for tonight." She hugged me. "I really needed this."

I squeezed her tight and stepped back. "Me too," I replied. And it was true. I'd forgotten how relaxing and fun it could be to share an evening laughing with a woman my own age.

I watched her walk to her car and get in, waving one last time as she pulled away. It had been a huge surprise to see Zara at my door. But how much fun we'd had together that night hadn't surprised me one bit. She was a keeper.

Chapter 14

By the time Nate and I were able to meet up again, it had been just over a month and we were about to slide into October. We'd had some nice phone conversations, but I was happy to be actually getting together. I jokingly told him I'd be the girl wearing the red rose pinned to her lapel. He asked what a lapel was, as he didn't want to be looking at the wrong parts of a girl. I laughed. It was going to be nice to see him again.

We agreed to meet up in Oakdale this time. He didn't have long without his girls, and I was happy to make the drive down and get to spend more time on the date that way. He had suggested an upscale steak house, and I happily complied.

I arrived a little early, which had surprised me more than anyone else. Usually, I ran late when trying to look dazzling, but for some reason everything had come together for me that evening. Ethan hadn't complained about me going out. I hadn't had to buy his cooperation with pizza and ice cream. My hair was smooth and waving nicely down my back, my skirt was snug enough to give a hint of my curves without advertising them, and best of all my shoes didn't pinch. I was looking forward to a lovely meal with an interesting man.

I stepped into the waiting area of the steak house and looked around me to find that Nate wasn't there. I told the maître d' that I was waiting for my date to arrive, and as I took a seat I heard someone call my name. I looked up to see Jess's father, Matthew, striding toward me, his hands outstretched. My entire face practically split, my smile was so big. I really liked Matthew, regardless of how confused my feelings for his son were at the moment.

"Well, what a surprise!" I stood back up to greet him and was swallowed in a warm embrace before being given a peck on the cheek.

"A pleasant one, I hope." He smiled down at me. I nodded. "Come, everyone will want to say hello." He grabbed my hand in his large one and began leading me around the corner to where his family was seated. They were all looking at me with smiles as I approached. Jack stood and shook my hand, while Sharon and Zara remained seated. They all looked polished and happy.

"We thought we saw you come in." Zara beamed, pointing at the sidewalk just outside their window. "How pretty you look tonight. What brings you here?"

I felt a slight blush rise to my cheeks and laughingly answered, "I'm here on a hot date."

"Ooh, those are the very best kind." Sharon laughed with me.

"What are you all doing here?" I asked.

Jack put an arm around Zara as he replied. "We're just getting the last details for the wedding finalized. Can't believe it's next week!" Zara was smiling up at him and then turned to me and nodded her agreement.

"Next week? Wow, time really got away from me. How wonderful!" I clapped my hands together and gave a little cheer as quietly as possible so as not to offend fellow diners.

"You didn't know it was next week?" Matthew inserted. "Jess didn't tell you?"

Sharon and Zara exchanged questioning looks before Sharon looked to me. "But you're his date, right? He RSVP'd plus one and, well . . ." She let the sentence hang out there, apparently realizing too late that I was not actually the plus one.

"I'm so sorry, Kate. I just assumed Jess was bringing you, or else I would have personally called," Zara stated uncomfortably.

"Oh . . . no. It's fine." I knew how crazy planning a wedding was, and even though I really liked Zara, I was a relatively new person in her life. I didn't want her to feel guilty for the totally innocent oversight. I was completely okay. "Jess and I are only like 10 percent friends." The Sullivans all laughed a bit too loudly at my joke. My face heated yet again. Traitorous pale skin!

"Well, even if you aren't his date to the wedding, I hope you'll let me challenge you to another game of Scrabble." Matthew, bless his heart, saved the day by changing the subject.

"Absolutely. It was the best game of Scrabble I've ever played." I reached up and gave his shoulder a squeeze. "In fact, I do believe you've ruined me, because I'll never want to play anyone else again." At this, the laughs were more genuine, and Matthew returned my smile.

"What is she doing here?" a voice interrupted from behind me in a fake whisper. All eyes at the table shifted as Matthew and I turned slightly. "And what does she mean, playing Scrabble with your father?"

I abruptly met the cool eyes of Vivienne Lawson. There was some serious frost there. I had to admit that she looked amazing. She wore a formfitting cherry-red dress with matching heels. Her white-blonde hair swirled artfully around her face, and her makeup was absolute perfection. I resisted the urge to slump down and slink away. Instead, I gathered my newfound confidence and drew out a smile. She may be va-va-voom, but I had recently been told that I wasn't too shabby.

"Hello, Vivienne." I put all the cheerfulness I possibly could into my voice.

"Hey, Kate." Jess's voice drew my attention as he stepped from my peripheral vision. He looked pretty amazing himself, all cleaned up for dinner, but I squashed down the thought and gave him a half smile before looking back to Vivienne.

"Matthew and I enjoy playing Scrabble together," I said to Vivienne. Then I shrugged like it was no big thing, because I knew it would drive her mad. It did, and I gave myself a little high five in my head.

"Well, Matthew, I didn't know you were such a big Scrabble fan. I'd love to play you while you're in town." Vivienne looked around me and flashed Matthew her megawatt star smile before her eyes turned back to me. She opened her mouth to say something, but Jess jumped in before she could.

"What brings you here tonight?" he asked me, trying to find a safe topic.

"I'm meeting a date," I said. I turned back to the table and gave them all a genuine smile. "In fact, if you'll all excuse me, I don't want to keep him waiting. So fun to see you all. Zara and Jack, I wish you all the best."

"We'd really love for you to come to the wedding," Zara stated quickly as I started to turn away. I glanced up at Vivienne to see how Zara's request had been received. Not well. She was obviously mentally envisioning ways to permanently remove me from the picture.

I turned back to Zara and gave her a smile. "I'm sure it's going to be a beautiful day," I replied, carefully avoiding any kind of commitment. Another thing I avoided was glancing toward Jess as I left the table and made my way back to the entrance of the restaurant.

Nate still wasn't there. I found an empty seat and sat down, grateful that I couldn't see the Sullivan family from where I was sitting. I hoped that when Nate did show up, we'd be seated far away.

"Kate?" Jess came around the corner into the waiting room. His face was serious, his eyes strained. I looked up at him when he stopped in front of me. "I'm sorry about Vivienne."

"No big deal. She's just a big territorial jungle cat and wanted me out." I half smiled.

Jess looked away and then back down at me. "The thing is, it's not really her territory, you know? My family likes you. I'm sorry she was so rude."

"Don't sweat it." I waved my hand to show him how cool I was with it even though on the inside I was seriously not cool. Vivienne had a gift for getting under my skin. "I didn't know you were back in town."

"Yeah. Got back this morning."

"Well, welcome back." I just looked at him. I had nothing else to say. The whole time I kept thinking, *He thinks I'm beautiful; he said I'm beautiful.* It made me feel shy and squirmy, and I just wanted him to go away.

"Listen, Kate, about the wedding . . ."

"Oh, there's my date." I stood quickly as I saw Nate pull open the door. "Have a great night." I didn't let Jess finish. I didn't want to hear it. He didn't owe me any sort of explanation. I wasn't family, and I had always done my best to maintain distance between us, afraid to let myself care for him, regardless of how small that distance had grown recently. The entire encounter had been a good reminder to stay where I belonged and let him do the same.

I left him standing there while I went to Nate. Nate leaned down and gave me a hug before I tucked my hand through his arm, and we made our way to the maître d's stand to be taken to our seat. Out of the corner of my eye, I saw Jess walk around the corner back to his family.

Unfortunately, we did get seated within eyesight of the Sullivan family. We were across the restaurant, but I could still see them from my seat. In a stroke of bad luck, Nate had his back to them. If only I'd chosen that chair to sit in. Instead, I found myself occasionally catching Jess's eye. It annoyed me greatly. I decided that if he was going to insist on watching the whole date, then I would pour it on thick for his viewing pleasure.

I made sure to laugh and smile at everything that came out of Nate's mouth. It seemed to be bothering Jess, which was a point for me. But it seemed to be making Nate question my sanity, which put me back a point.

Jess and I hadn't spoken, aside from a few brief updates in recent weeks. We hadn't fought; we hadn't even joked. We'd been all business. Despite wanting him at arm's length, I was bugged to have actually been kept there. Regardless of all logic, I wanted to set him off-balance the way I felt off-balance around him.

"Have you ever wanted to bug someone just because they're bugging you?" I blurted out to Nate.

He looked a bit caught off guard. I had probably interrupted him in the middle of a sentence. He gamely changed to my topic. "Yes. Definitely. Sometimes it's kind of fun to embarrass your kids to get back at them for all the sleepless nights." He laughed at his joke. I did too. It was a good one. Parenting jokes, they were the meat of our relationship.

"True, true." I let my smile linger. I was pretty sure Jess was looking our way again. "Tell me about how it was with your ex-wife when you first met."

Nate hedged. I didn't blame him. It was pretty personal stuff. Poor Nate. He tugged at his collar and looked down at his plate. I stared at him, waiting for his reply. He had no idea what I wanted from him, and it showed.

"I'm sorry. Just forget I asked. It's really not a big deal." I shrugged, laughed in what I hoped was a casual way, and went back to eating.

Nate didn't have much to say after that, and we finished our meal in relative silence. We didn't order dessert. I think we both knew that dinner had been awkward. My grinning so much the entire time had made my face hurt. Not to mention Nate being dragged through crazy town. I felt bad. I couldn't tell him that I'd done it all to annoy the big movie star across the room. Even I knew it sounded full-scale nutso.

My car was parked right in front of the restaurant, on the street. Nate walked me to my car, and I turned to face him as I leaned against my car door. "Hey, look, I know it was all insane asylum in there tonight. I'm sorry. I ran into someone before you came, and it stirred up some emotions that made me act strange. I hope you can forgive me," I said.

Nate smiled kindly at me, his face finally relaxed. "I wondered what was going on."

This time I laughed for real. "I bet you did. I am so sorry. You're so great. You deserve to not have your one free night spent with someone who should be in a straitjacket."

Nate surprised me by stepping closer. We were practically eye to eye with me wearing heels, and I could see the laughter in his. "You definitely need to make it up to me," he said.

I couldn't decide if the line creeped me out or not. I was not about to make the mistake of asking what he had in mind for making up. That would be too much. So I played it safe by nodding. "Maybe next time dinner can be on me?" I offered.

Nate took another step closer. Now I could feel the heat coming off his body and the warmth of his breath on my face. It wasn't such a bad feeling. "That sounds like an offer I'll take you up on." He smiled again.

Nate lightly kneaded my shoulders before letting his hands slide around to my back. He pulled me close for a full-body hug. I didn't fight him. I'm a hugger. Hugging is good. Ethan says I hug him too much. I let my arms go around Nate and hugged him back. He was a nice guy. He hadn't run away screaming even though I wasn't great company that night.

He then leaned back away from me a bit and kissed me full on the mouth. I didn't have time to react much other than to think, *Oh, so we're having our first kiss here, in the street?* Just as I had accepted that idea and went to kiss him back, he pulled away. I hadn't even had time to decide if I was enjoying him kissing me.

"Drive safe." He gave my hand a squeeze before turning to walk away.

I pressed two fingertips to my mouth, sort of wondering about the whole exchange, when I heard voices coming from the entrance of the restaurant. I wasn't sure what it was about the voices that drew my attention, but I turned to see the Sullivan family exiting. They were all coupled up as they walked out, not aware that I was there.

Except Jess. He was looking straight at me while Vivienne tugged on his arm. I couldn't read his expression clearly from where I stood, but I couldn't seem to break the eye contact, either. My fingers felt glued to my lips, my face void of expression. He made a move as though he was going to come over to where I stood, but Vivienne tugged again, saying something to him. He shook his head and closed his eyes for a brief moment before turning and following his family.

Chapter 15

The day of Jack and Zara's wedding dawned with perfection. The sky was a clear silky blue as the sun shone pinkish over the mountain. The grass was a sparkling green with morning dew, the birds were chirping, and I felt like it was a morning fit for a princess. How I wished I were one and my fairy godmother would whisk me away from all the emotions churning inside of me.

I sat on the patio of the big house, wrapped in an oversized fuzzy cardigan, drinking some hot cocoa and taking it all in. Sadly, the peaceful, beautiful morning was in stark contrast to what was happening inside my mind and body. It seemed like everything on my inside wanted to be on my outside.

I heard the door close behind me and turned to see Cass padding out in her robe and slippers. Her walking had improved, but she still had a slight limp as she made her way over to me. It surprised me to see her in anything other than a perfectly put-together outfit.

"Scoot." Cass motioned for me to make room for her on the deeply cushioned swing. Even more surprised, I did so. I tucked my shorter legs up under me and let Cass take over pushing the swing with her uninjured leg. We enjoyed the slow motion in silence for a few minutes before Cass got to her reason for coming out.

"I hear Zara called and asked you to come to the wedding," she said quietly.

I cringed as I remembered that phone call. It had happened the day after we'd met in the restaurant. She had been so sweet and sincere in wanting me there. It was so kind of her. And I really, really wanted to support her and Jack. I just didn't know if I could face Jess after things had been so awkward at the restaurant. Or I could face Vivienne and her steely looks. Still, five days later I was going back and forth.

"I don't know what to do," I replied.

"You go. A friend asks you to her wedding, you go," Cass stated as though it were the simplest thing in the world. It was, sure, if you hadn't told the entire Sullivan family that you were only 10 percent friendly with their son. Not to mention then being eyeball tasered by his girlfriend, all after him awkwardly telling you he found you pleasant to look at. Oh, hey, and don't forget the fact that the festivities were going to take place at his house, so there would be no avoiding him.

"There are just going to be so many beautiful people there," I hedged. Cass turned to look at me with her signature eyebrow raise.

"What on earth does that have to do with anything?" she asked.

"I don't know. Nothing and everything," I replied. "I worry about that stuff. You've met the Sullivans. Next to them I'm the country bumpkin neighbor who shows up in her out-of-date clothing with her ratty hair and her unplucked eyebrows."

Cass chuckled. "You've never cared about your unplucked eyebrows before."

I scowled at her. "And you've never mentioned that you thought they needed plucking before!" I retorted. It made Cass actually laugh. I quietly waited for her to finish enjoying herself so much.

"Kate, what is the real problem? You're a lovely woman, and the Sullivan family likes you. You aren't the type of girl to miss a friend's wedding. It's been too long since you had a girlfriend, so why cast her away like it doesn't matter?" she asked.

Well, poop. She had me between a rock and a hard place on that one. So I did what every child does when being questioned by a parental figure; I shrugged.

Cass respected my privacy and unwillingness to answer for about three seconds before she pushed. "You must have a pretty good reason for disappointing Zara on her wedding day."

I took a deep breath and threw my hands up. "It's Jess, okay?" I blew out a hard breath.

For some reason Cass smiled to herself. A secret little smile like she'd just eaten the last chocolate in the house before anyone else realized what had happened. It irked me. "I thought maybe it was about Jess," she said.

"What? Why would you possibly think that? Not everything is about Jess!" I shot back.

"I agree. For me it isn't. But it does seem to be that way for you. If you are missing your friend's wedding because you had some sort of disagreement with her soon-to-be brother-in-law, then you have made it all about you and him. By doing that, you have taken her day away from her."

"I sometimes honestly wish you were more of a simpleton," I huffed. Cass laughed again. Then she patiently waited for me to stop fuming and start thinking. This process wasn't always fast. Luckily, Cass was experienced in the art of dealing with me.

"You're probably right," I finally said, sighing. "I should go and help Zara have a good day. I don't have to interact with Jess if I don't want to. I can be nice and get through a few hours without causing a scene." I stood up from the swing. "I'll be so good it'll be like I wasn't even there."

Cass stood next to me and patted my back. "I doubt you'll be perfect at blending in, but just do your best to not steal the spotlight."

"I don't know what you're talking about," I protested.

"There was a time, dear, when you were all about the spotlight. And it seems to me that that girl is making a comeback."

She laughed as she walked back into the house. I rolled my eyes at her retreating form and turned to the cottage. There was some serious work to do if I was going to attend this wedding . . . starting with my eyebrows.

To say Jack and Zara's wedding was the most amazing thing I'd ever attended wouldn't tell the half of it. It was spectacular in its simplicity, understated yet somehow extravagant. My theory, as I looked over the setup, was that rich people know how to make things look like they just fell together and everything was super easy. Kind of like how some girls put on gobs of makeup to look natural. Whatever it was, Zara and her wedding planner had done it amazingly well.

I had arrived as primped and pressed as I could possibly be about half an hour before the ceremony was supposed to start. I hadn't had time to shop for a new dress, but luckily I still had some nicer clothes from my past life. I dug out a navy-blue cocktail dress and strappy matching sandals that had always made me feel fancy.

My hands had been shaking so badly that it was a total miracle I hadn't cut myself shaving. I had even managed to avoid singeing my ears while curling my hair into loose ringlets before pinning some of it up. Knowing Jess's house as I did, I was able to sneak in a side door and get through the house without being noticed. I liked to tell myself I was a very stealthy girl, but probably no one in the house was focused on anyone but themselves and their job.

I had assumed the bridal setup would happen in the master. With its enormous size and spacious bathroom, it seemed a natural fit. I made my way there and knocked on the door. I was rewarded with a smile when Sharon peeked out the big double doors. I smiled in relief, happy my assumption had played out.

"Kate!" She reached out one manicured hand and pulled me in, never stepping out from behind the door herself. "You came! Zara, look who's here," Sharon chirped as she shut the door behind us. I glanced to the side at Sharon to smile back at her and saw she was in her slip and pearls, but nothing else. That explained the hiding behind the door. She pulled me into a hug before I could move another step, patting my back warmly.

"Kate!" Zara squealed from the other side of the room, where she was sitting in front of a large vanity that had presumably been brought in for the event. A pretty brunette in wedding colors stood behind her with a curling iron in her hands. "My cousin Stephanie has my head attached to this curling iron, but trust me, I am jumping up and down on the inside." She laughed. Cousin Stephanie pulled a face at me that made me smile.

As we laughed, Zara reached out one hand and waved me over. I obeyed and took her offered hand, giving it a friendly squeeze.

"You look so pretty! All the guys will be drooling over you today. I only hope I'll get some of the attention," Zara said cheerfully.

"Would this be a bad time to tell you I brought my croquet mallet and am planning on giving a demo of my special skill sets today?" I smiled and batted my eyelashes playfully at her. I was rewarded with one of Zara's contagious laughs.

"In that case, I say we abandon this whole thing and stage a huge game on the new lawn. I don't think Jack would mind if we pushed things back a day or two."

I pretended to think it over, scratching at my chin and making *hmm* noises. "You know, it doesn't have to be all about the game. I think it's probably part of any good training routine to take breaks for fun. It helps you stay loose and relaxed. We don't want to risk burnout." I sighed, twisting my face into the type of smile that someone who is trying really hard to be happy about something would wear.

Sharon and Zara both laughed out loud. "Hey, I won't argue with the master. Someone of your caliber obviously knows what she's doing." Zara chuckled. When we had stopped laughing, Zara said, "I'm really glad you came, Kate. I don't have a lot of people here today—curse of destination weddings—and it's good to feel like I have a friend." She lifted her hand again, and I held on to it.

I couldn't help but notice the absence of Zara's mother or more family and friends helping her get ready. I wasn't about to ask about it. And, actually, in a strange way it helped me to relax, knowing I could provide her with some of the support she needed today.

Sharon turned and went into the bathroom to finish her makeup. As she rounded the corner out of sight, Zara tugged on my hand and pulled me closer. "Listen, I need to explain why Vivienne is here," she said in a low voice.

"No, you don't. It's fine. I know she and Jess are dating."

"Actually . . . well, that's up to Jess to tell you, 'cause it's his business, but Vivienne was invited *before*, you know? And she was really upset when Jess suggested she not come. She'll do anything to attach herself to what she sees as his star power. So she's here, but she's not really *here*, okay?"

I could not have been more confused if she'd explained the entire thing to me in Chinese. Unwilling to ask questions and risk more of a discussion, I simply smiled and shrugged, showing her it was no biggie to me. Who Jess was dating, and who was attached to his star power, was none of my concern. I was there for Zara.

The ceremony itself was everything a ceremony should be. It took place inside one of three enormous white tents that had been dotted around Jess's property. Inside, the tent had been transformed so it felt like a chapel. Rows of chairs with flower garlands, a raised stand at the front, even somehow an organ. As a bonus, well-concealed heaters lent comfort to the otherwise chilly October day. My eyes all but popped out of my head at the beauty of it. It felt like we'd left Jess's rural retreat behind and entered a new realm.

It was obvious that Jack and Zara were crazy about each other. His face was glowing as his love walked down the aisle on the arm of an older gentleman dressed in a smart suit. Matthew, Sharon, Jess, and Vivienne were all smiling as well, turned toward the back of the seats as Zara appeared. There was a lean, dark-haired older woman across the aisle from them, also dressed in wedding colors, standing next to Cousin Stephanie, who I assumed was related to Zara, although I had yet to meet any of her family.

I had slipped quietly into an empty seat on the back row and had tried to blend in. I did not want to cause a scene. Heck, I hardly wanted to be there other than to make Zara's smile remain. I breathed a sigh of relief when neither Jess nor Vivienne seemed to see me and instead had eyes only for Zara. Soon enough, everyone was once again facing front and watching the ceremony unfold.

I don't think someone who has been married can ever attend a wedding without thinking back on their own. For me, it was bittersweet hearing those traditional words spoken aloud. Words of uniting and love and promises. I thought of how handsome Charlie had looked at our simple wedding. Of how nervous I had been. I remembered him whispering in my ear before the pastor had started, saying how I was so beautiful and that I was all he'd wanted. Charlie had sweet-talked me into marriage. I had been a little hesitant and unsure. We had met soon after my parents had died, and I wasn't feeling very brave about loving anyone just then. Charlie had been patience itself as he helped me move forward.

Charlie hadn't been perfect, of course, but neither had I. We hadn't really ever fought, but I had definitely made mistakes. I thought of when we found out we'd be having a baby, and then of when we brought Ethan home from the hospital. Priceless days of togetherness. It was emotional to remember all that happiness now that Charlie was gone, yet somehow time was doing its job of blunting the edges of the pain and making it feel more nostalgic.

I listened closely as Jack and Zara made their promises. Their vows were full of hope for their future together. I crossed my fingers for them in my lap, and then I crossed my toes in my shoes, adding my hope to theirs that nothing would mar their forever.

After the ceremony, the wedding party moved to another tented section of the property for a dinner before the big bash to really celebrate the event. I trailed behind the majority of the group, ducking my head whenever there was a possibility for eye contact with a certain member of the Sullivan clan. It seemed to be working. I felt ridiculously proud of myself as I took an empty chair at the table farthest from where the family was seated. So far so good.

It wasn't hard to spot Jess in the small group. He was at the head table with the bride and groom. He was all smiles as he spoke with guests and ate his meal. Vivienne's light coloring was the perfect contrast for his dark coloring and dark tux. He looked as delicious as the food I was being served. I mentally slapped myself for that thought and turned my full attention to visiting with some friends of the Sullivan family. They had made me laugh with stories about Jack and Zara's meeting and courtship, and it eased the stress I was feeling.

I couldn't help but notice when Jess stood up to leave the tent. Just before he walked out, he looked in my direction, making it clear he'd known I was there all along. He gave me a small nod and raised one hand in a slight wave, one side of his mouth angled up in a half smile. My pulse began to race. I wasn't sure where we stood or what he was thinking. I didn't appreciate him looking so amazing. I did, however, give him a small smile back. He paused for a second, and his smile grew as our eyes held. Mine grew to match his before he gave me one more nod and exited the tent.

Unfortunately for me, the moment I glanced away from where I'd been smiling at Jess my eyes collided with Vivienne's. She'd seen the entire thing, and she was not happy.

I can't scientifically confirm this, but it felt like the temperature in the entire city of Clark Springs suddenly dropped ten degrees, and I could feel a hush fall over the crowd when Vivienne stood and began stalking toward me.

She quickly reached my side and glared down at me. “I know for a fact that you were not invited. Is wedding-crashing a local country tradition?” she sneered. I heard someone at the table gasp. It was strange to hear such hateful things out of such a pretty face.

I squared my shoulders. If there was one thing that middle school with carrot hair and squatty legs had taught me, it was to look strong and the bullies won’t bully. This wasn’t the time to focus on the success rate of that particular thought process.

“Oh Vivienne, didn’t you know that Zara personally called and asked me to come?” I smiled a syrupy sweet smile back at her.

“Your lies won’t save you. I’m going to get someone to escort you out.”

“I don’t think causing a scene like this at Zara and Jack’s wedding is the best way to get Jess to keep you around,” I stage-whispered behind my hand. Vivienne’s eyes widened. I returned to my normal volume as I slowly pushed my chair back and stood up, praying my shaking legs would carry me off in grand style. “I for one wouldn’t dream of making their guests feel uncomfortable.”

“What are you doing?” Vivienne stiffened as I stood to face her.

“I think maybe I’ll go freshen up a bit.” I threw her a tight smile, spun on my heel, and headed out of the tent toward the house. It was time to make my exit. There was no way I was going to be involved in a scene and hurt Zara in any way.

In fact, as I walked out of the tent, my simple plan to go freshen up suddenly morphed into a new plan involving jumping straight into my car and driving until I ran out of gas. Then I’d live off of cupcakes and beef jerky until I stopped shaking and could figure out my life. It was a solid plan. I even had a cardigan in my car somewhere in case the night got chilly.

Sadly, I didn’t take into account other people. Like Zara and Sharon.

“Kate, wait!” I heard Sharon’s voice from behind me. There was no way I was going to ignore that woman. I liked her too much. So I stopped a few paces outside the tented area and waited for her to catch up, Zara close behind. It made my heart clench to see the look on Zara’s face and her frustration as she tried to move quickly in her beautiful gown. I could not ruin this for her. I pasted on a smile as they approached.

“You’re not leaving, are you?” Sharon asked as she caught me.

“Well . . .” I hedged, unsure of how to answer.

"Kate, oh my gosh, I saw Vivienne talking to you." Zara was puffing slightly as she grabbed my arm. "I'll kill her, I swear I will. I don't think anyone would blame me on my wedding day if I went a little Bridezilla and took out that psycho!" She was really agitated. I needed to calm her down before her makeup was ruined and I was somehow blamed for the big raccoon-eye fiasco.

"No, no, that was nothing," I said, trying somewhat successfully to laugh it off.

"Not based on the looks people at the table were giving you two," Sharon stated flatly.

"Oh, so you saw that. Well, there's a perfectly good explanation." I fished within my mind for a great story while Sharon and Zara waited to see what I'd come up with. "You see, Vivienne came up to, uh, welcome me and ask how my dinner was. But I needed to go to the bathroom, so I stood to excuse myself, not realizing I'd be coming off rude, because, see, I kind of interrupted her when I stood. So now I'm just on my way to the bathroom to freshen up a bit." I gave them a dazzling smile as I summed up the encounter.

"Bull," Zara stated. Something about her wholly emotionless face and her one-word response totally cracked me up. I couldn't help the giggle that burst out of me.

"I'm sorry, but what part of that story didn't sound true?" I giggled while trying to maintain a straight face.

"I don't know about Zara, but for me it was the part about you interrupting Vivienne and getting away with it. If you'd actually done that, you wouldn't have lived to be telling us about it." Sharon almost got the words out before she cracked a grin.

A smile broke out on Zara's face too, and pretty soon the three of us were holding onto each other's hands and laughing hysterically. Jack made his way over to our little trio, alerted by his bride running away and the sound of our joined laughter ringing through the evening air.

"What on earth is happening over here?" He smiled as he joined us and put an arm around Zara.

She smiled up at him, wiping away the tears that had formed. "Oh, not much. Kate just really needs to use the bathroom."

"Really, really needs to!" Sharon smiled at her son.

“Worse than I’ve ever needed to in my entire life!” I laughed. “In fact, I’m sorry to interrupt you, but I’d better be off.”

Jack had no reply to that. His baffled expression set off another round of laughter among the three of us. Jack just shook his head. When I didn’t move from the circle, he finally gave me a questioning look and said, “Kate, didn’t you need to use the bathroom?” Which, of course, made me laugh so hard that I really *did* need to find it—and soon.

As I turned away from the group to go find the restroom, Zara called after me, “Dancing starts in ten minutes, Kate. I’ll see you on the floor. Bring your best moves!”

Somehow, in the ten minutes I’d been gone, night had managed to fully encompass the affair. The group had moved to a dance floor that had been set up in yet another tent. Inside, beautiful rows of twinkly lights dangled above the floor on clear strings, somehow looking like fireflies and bringing just the right amount of light to give the area a romantic ambiance. Heaters puffed out warm air, and everything felt cozy and happy.

A DJ was stationed at one end of the floor, and liquid refreshment was on the other. On either side were seating sections for those taking a break or just enjoying watching. I had danced once with Matthew, once with Jack, and once with a man seated by me at dinner. Other than that, I had spent most of the time sitting on a white sofa, sipping cola, and watching the couples and groups dance to the music. I was happy there, watching and relaxing.

Vivienne had probably taken dance lessons, based on the way she twirled elegantly around the floor in the arms of every male over the age of fifteen. I added it to my list of things about Vivienne that were just the worst. On principle, I couldn’t like someone who looked that good while doing hard things and whom all men wanted to hang around. It wasn’t natural.

Jack and Zara were completely wrapped up in each other, and Matthew and Sharon were making some pretty impressive dance moves of their own. I realized after a few minutes that Jess wasn’t on the floor. I wondered where he had gotten off to. Maybe he didn’t dance much. I had seen him out there a few times, but . . . maybe I shouldn't care. I took another sip of my cola.

I felt someone sit next to me on the couch before I had even noticed anyone approaching. I turned, surprised and hoping my drink hadn't spilled, to see Jess. He was looking closely down at my face, his eyes roaming over me, most likely wondering if we were still fighting or if we were friends. For some reason, his searching look made me smile.

"At ease, soldier," I said. "I've holstered the gun tonight."

He smiled and leaned fully back into the couch as he looked toward the dance floor. "It's been a great day," he said, his eyes following the newlyweds.

"Agreed. Even better because I didn't spill my drink when you flopped down next to me with no warning." Jess looked back at me, and I gestured to my spotless dress and my still-full cup. His eyes crinkled as he looked back at the dancers.

"It definitely is my lucky day."

He put his arm along the back of the couch as he relaxed more into his seat. I could feel a couple of his fingertips resting on my shoulder. It was strangely nice. I wasn't sure I liked it. I wanted to move back for more contact, but I was too busy trying to decide if I should sit up straighter out of his way. It was exhausting to be so turned up inside whenever Jess was around.

"Why aren't you dancing with Vivienne?" I blurted into the silence. "She's a good dancer. I bet you two would look great out there together."

Jess shrugged. "I'm not as good as she is. It would only annoy her."

"So better not to dance at all than to dance with her?" Even I could hear the cynicism in my voice. I would have to work on my attitude problems. But she'd started it.

"Sure, something like that." Jess chuckled.

His chuckle decided it for me, and I pushed farther back into the couch and maybe even edged a little closer to his side. I liked the warmth of his leg against mine. I wasn't sure if it was my imagination or not, but it felt like he pressed a little closer to me too.

"Why aren't you dancing anymore?" he asked. I made a noncommittal noise. "You looked like you were having fun earlier." He turned his head and smiled at me as I did the same. Oh, we were closer than I'd realized. Those eyes were seriously green. I looked away. I did not, however, slide away. My body somehow craved the closeness. This was dangerous in the extreme.

"I decided I'd rather sip a drink and sit on a comfy sofa than make everyone feel bad by showing off my impressive kitchen-dancing skills. It's Jack and Zara's special day, and I promised Cass I wouldn't steal the spotlight," I stated.

"Cass was worried about that?"

"Yep."

"Kitchen-dancing skills?" Jess asked.

"You know, the moves you do when you're at home listening to music and you dance along, but you'd never in a million years actually let anyone see you doing that? It usually involves serving spoons and a dish towel."

"Ah, yes. For me those are bathroom-dancing skills."

"I'm sure you can appreciate my restraint in not stealing the show tonight. I had done all the boring normal dancing I could do, and I could feel the beast wanting to be released. I got it under control only by staying off the dance floor and offering it some cola."

"You are very kind," he chuckled. I could tell he was looking at me again, but I kept my gaze firmly fixed on the dancers.

He raised up a couple of those fingers that were grazing my shoulder and began twirling a strand of my hair. Butterflies, big time, took flight. This was very, very bad, but I couldn't have moved despite how much I wanted to run. I felt heat creeping into my face as I flushed from the contact. I hoped he wouldn't notice and sighed in relief when he looked back to the people dancing.

We sat in silence for a few minutes. It was pleasurable torture. The warmth of him along my side, the fingers playing in my hair, the twinkling lights, the laughter and conversations of the people celebrating. It felt like time had stopped, and things were shifting and changing in ways I couldn't understand. Weren't Jess and I in a fight, or stalemate, or something? Didn't I only like him 10 percent? Hadn't we been successfully ignoring each other all day? Heck, all month?

"You could dance with *me*," Jess said, finally breaking the silence, his voice low enough to barely reach my ears. I could tell he had turned to look at me again. I wasn't brave enough to look back. I felt like my face would crack and he'd be able to see inside to those parts that were equally terrified and excited.

"Think you can handle that?" I joked, trying to release the tension in my bones. My lungs somehow felt frozen as his knuckles grazed my neck.

"Kate, I'm pretty sure I can handle whatever you throw at me," he replied in a soft voice that had the hairs on my neck standing up. I had a feeling we were talking about more than dancing. All I knew was that I was going to come apart if we kept sitting there, so I jumped up.

"Okay, let's see what you've got," I said.

Jess stood up and took my hand, leading me to the dance floor. Just my luck, a slow song came on. I didn't know whether to be horrified or relieved. Fast dancing was not part of my skill set. I could slow dance, sure, but did I really want to be slow dancing with Jess? It felt like a huge mistake somehow, a step in a direction I didn't want to go, down a path I had violently ignored.

I mentally shook away those thoughts. Jess had a girlfriend. Jess was my friend. This didn't need to be any different than dancing with Jack or Matthew. Friends can dance.

Jess opened his arms, and I stepped into them, placing one hand in his and my other on his shoulder. He began leading me in slow circles around the dance floor. I met eyes with Zara and Sharon as we weaved our way around. Both gave me a big smile, and Zara gave me a thumbs-up. It made me smile and relax.

"You look really beautiful today, Kate." Jess broke the quiet by bending close to my ear as he gave me the compliment. "I saw you when you were sneaking in to see Zara before the ceremony."

I was surprised and pulled back to meet his eyes. "You did?" I asked. "I thought I'd been so sneaky."

Jess smiled. "Nope, I saw you and thought you looked great."

I looked behind him again and leaned in close to avoid his eyes. Two compliments in one conversation? Polite behavior dictated that I return it. And the truth was he did look amazing, tall and lean in his tux. The black somehow brought out his suntanned skin and made his eyes a vibrant green. He'd been smiling all day, or so I assumed, because I certainly hadn't been obsessively watching him all day long. He and Vivienne had made such a striking, perfectly beautiful couple. It had almost been painful to see.

"You look good today too, Jess," I said as awkwardly as I possibly could have. It made Jess's shoulder shake under my hand as he chuckled lightly.

"Thanks. It's amazing what a bar of soap and some water will do for a guy."

We went back to silently dancing. Everything about it was perfect—or would have been if I could have relaxed at all. I felt like I'd been put on a roller coaster and was emotionally hanging on for dear life. His hand on my back firmly guiding me and pressing me close to him felt like heaven. Yet I wanted to shake it off and run for it. I sighed.

That sigh must have communicated a world of feeling to Jess, because he placed my other hand on his shoulder and put both of his arms around me, pulling me in closer, like he knew I wanted to bolt. He pressed his cheek against my hair and held me as we circled the floor.

I was surprised that we fit together as well as we did despite our height difference. It felt like he was tucking me into some safe place and surrounding me. My heart was beating so hard I thought it would flop out of my chest.

"Easy, Kate," Jess murmured against my hair. One of his hands caressed my back, and the skin under it all but shuddered.

The song was ending. I lightly pulled against Jess's hold, ready to have some space and get some control back. I needed to think. I needed some air. Jess didn't care what I needed, and he held me close until the very last note, only then relaxing his hold and letting me step back.

Another song was starting already as we looked at each other. We were no longer touching, but somehow whatever it was that had held us together during that dance was still there. Tangible and real. Jess's eyes were blazing, more green than usual. I didn't know what he saw in my expression. I felt powerless to move or speak or do anything to break that spell.

He reached for me as the next song picked up, and I was back in his arms. The standard dance form was forgotten as I put my arms around him and his wrapped around me. His head rested on mine and we were swaying and spinning our way around the room. I could feel his heart beat against my cheek. Every now and then he would run a hand up my back or caress it in a small circle. Then he was nuzzling against my hair, moving it away from my face, planting a feather-light kiss by my ear. I couldn't breathe. I was suffocating and soaring at the same time. My heart was in my throat, and my legs were fully rubber. How could I be flying and sinking at the same time? Tears pricked my eyes and a lump clogged my throat.

When the song ended, I couldn't meet his eyes. We were slow to part again. He kept hold of my hands, keeping me grounded and a little trapped near him. I just did not think I could handle another moment of connection. I was scared and confused and somehow so happy I thought I would die. *Friends don't dance like that*, I thought.

"Kate?" Jess's voice was soft and husky and warm and questioning, asking me to look up and meet his gaze. I took a deep breath and shook my head a little, eyes firmly on the ground, begging him for reprieve.

"Kate!" It was Sharon. She took my hands out of Jess's and was laughing and babbling about something as she pulled me along behind her. I didn't hear a word of it. Nor did I look back to Jess as I let her drag me away, grateful that she was saving me.

Eventually, I came to understand that it was time for Zara to throw her bouquet. I tried to clear my head and stumbled into a huddle with the other single ladies, who would also try to catch it. My heart wasn't in it, especially when I noticed Vivienne standing nearby with a look of determination. Zara was standing on the stairs that led up to Jess's back deck and had her toss-away bouquet in hand. She searched the group until she saw me, and then her smile grew. She was happy I was there, so I smiled back at her and gave her a thumbs-up sign. Once everyone was ready, she turned and threw the bouquet.

It took a second before I realized she had specifically aimed it in my direction. I halfheartedly lunged for it, trying to put on a good show. Three girls around me were shrieking and diving, desperate for some unknown reason to grab the prize. I was not willing to sacrifice myself for the honor, so I attempted to step back. However, another girl had lunged forward from behind me and nailed me in the back. Her momentum carried me forward, and I went flying into the fray.

As I flew forward, I managed to stumble over yet another girl, planting myself in the grass flat on my stomach. My fall managed to start an entire dog-pile situation, and I was the lucky bottom dog. Girls were laughing and wiggling, trying to get out of the pile while I grunted and groaned beneath them, bouquet forgotten and survival becoming vitally important. Someone was screeching particularly loudly, and I kept getting jabbed by sharp elbows. Finally, I decided to give up and play dead while they all untangled themselves. I flopped my arms out to the side, face down in spread-eagle formation.

My left hand made contact with something and I heard a voice yell gleefully, "Kate got it! Kate got the bouquet!" It was Zara, and she sounded a little too happy that my hand had accidentally flopped against the flowers. I groaned again.

"No fair! No fair!" someone was yelling while the other girls started laughing again. Pretty soon hands started reaching and lifting girls off me. Everyone seemed to think it was quite hilarious to end up in a dog pile over a wedding bouquet. Yep, pretty funny unless you're bottom dog. I was fairly sure my dress would have grass stains and my hair would have some sort of nature in it. I would consider myself lucky to not have a smear of some sort on my forehead.

Someone was complaining about my "win" as I was finally helped to my feet and dusted off by Matthew before being presented with the bouquet. I looked at it in confusion, a dumb smile on my face. Zara grabbed the hand holding it and lifted it into the air in the sign of victory.

"Next to get married is Kate!" Zara laughed.

Everyone cheered. Well, not everyone. Vivienne sure didn't cheer. In fact, she stepped forward, mouth open and ready to start complaining. Jess materialized from somewhere and put a hand on her arm. She turned to face him, and I used that second to find Jack in the crowd and motion for him to come over.

"Oh, look, there's Jack," I said cheerfully. "I think it's time for the happy couple to head off on their honeymoon."

Jack quickly joined Zara and put his arms around her, giving her a passionate kiss and fully distracting everyone from the bouquet situation. After the kiss, he swung her up in his arms and began walking around to the front of the house.

Everyone followed to see them off. Everyone but me. This night needed to be over for me. Watching Jess walk off with Vivienne toward the front of the house was like a bee's sting straight to the heart after our shared moments dancing. I was going to sneak off another way and go home. I walked up the stairs where Zara had been standing and into the back door of the house. I had left my purse in the master bedroom. As I passed through the kitchen, I sat the much-coveted bouquet on the table.

I found my purse sitting on Jess's bed and caught my reflection in the mirror as I turned to leave. Noticing the grass in my hair, I paused, trying to decide if I should pick it out or just go. While I debated, someone came into the room behind me. Our eyes met in the mirror. Jess. *Oh no, oh no, oh no.*

"Congrats on catching the bouquet?" he joked, making it sound like a question. I smiled warily at his reflection. I noticed that his tux jacket and bow tie were gone, his shirtsleeves rolled up, his collar open. He looked a little rumpled, but as beautiful as I'd ever seen him. I swallowed nervously.

"Maybe you should congratulate me on surviving that dog pile. I could have died down there." I turned to face him and began walking to the door, holding my purse to my chest, avoiding eye contact, intent on getting out. Out of this room, out of this house, maybe out of this town. Far, far away.

"You left your bouquet on the kitchen table." Jess took a step toward me, meeting me inside the room and successfully stopping my progress.

"I don't want it. Zara wanted me to have it, but I don't care about those things. Vivienne can have it. Please give it to her. She was so mad," I replied.

Jess took another step closer. I felt my heart rate increase and those dang butterflies got in holding position, ready to fly at any moment. I put a hand up to stop him from coming any closer. "Jess . . ." was all I managed to get out. I didn't know what I wanted to say. I just knew that he was hazardous to my health today. Well, really, he always had been in one way or another. I couldn't trust my feelings around him.

Instead of moving away, Jess took the hand I was holding up and held it in his own. He used that traitorous hand to pull me closer so that we were inches away from each other.

"You have grass in your hair," he whispered. I couldn't have spoken if I'd wanted to, so I just nodded. "Did you get hurt being bottom dog?" he asked. I shook my head, even though I knew that in the morning I'd have a bruise or two where the other girls' knees and elbows had hit.

He closed that tiny space between us and put his arms around me, cradling me against him. For a long moment he held me close. I could almost feel him willing me to slow down and let go. What he didn't seem to understand was that he was the reason I was wound up and humming inside. I wanted to have a good cry over the unfairness of it all. He was asking me for things I didn't know how to give.

Before I could do anything to stop it, he reached up and caressed my cheek, moving my hair away again and bending down to kiss my forehead. I involuntarily, and I do mean involuntarily, raised my head to give him easier access. I was terribly disappointed in my body right then. He used that access to plant a kiss on my eyebrow and then the corner of my mouth. My eyes were closed tightly. My purse dropped from tingling fingers and hit the floor as my arms came up to circle his neck. I was wearing heels, but even then I raised to my tiptoes and pressed closer. It was like I couldn't stop this; it was out of my control entirely.

"Kate, let me, just let me . . ." Jess breathed before using his hand to lift my chin and pressing his lips to mine. Softly, so softly. I didn't fight him, but at first I didn't kiss him back. His second kiss was more firm, and before I really understood how it happened, I was responding. And I was soaring. I hadn't felt anything so good, so perfect, so astonishing in a long, long time. My heart was singing inside my chest. I thought I would burst.

I didn't want him to stop kissing me. I wanted it to go on forever and ever. Forget the cupcakes and jerky. I would take Jess with me and I'd live off his kisses. Why had I ever thought I was indifferent to this man? I couldn't remember why I didn't want him close to me. I was spinning, spinning, spinning.

"Jess?" a voice down the hall called. "Jess?"

Jess broke the kiss, but he didn't step away. He kept holding me tight as he tipped his forehead against mine. Neither of us said a word.

"Jess?" It was Matthew. This time I recognized the voice. I pulled away hard, planting my feet back on the ground and quickly turned back toward the vanity to hide my face. I was flushed, and I knew my lips would be swollen. I didn't want Matthew to see me.

"Jess?" Matthew was getting closer.

I heard Jess mumble under his breath before responding. "Yeah, Dad. I'll be right there." Something about hearing his voice so ragged caused my blush to deepen even further. Had we really just done that? I pressed my hands to my lips, the evidence too real to disregard.

"Listen, Kate . . ." Jess said.

"No, don't, please," I interrupted. "Just go see what your dad wants before he comes in here and finds . . . this."

"Will you wait? I think we should talk. There are things . . ."

I knew he was looking my way, so I shook my head as I interrupted him. "I don't think so. Your family and your *date* are waiting for you." As soon as I said the word *date* I felt a lump grow in my throat. It was a miracle that I could even breathe. I felt tears gathering behind my eyes.

"I can get rid of them. I need to . . ." Jess began.

"Jess? Son, where are you?" Matthew called again, this time a little impatiently as his footsteps neared.

"Please, Jess. Go see what he wants!" I pleaded around the lump. I finally turned around and allowed Jess to see my face. I knew my eyes were sparkling with tears and I probably looked desperate. I hoped it would be the motivation he needed to leave. I truly needed him to leave.

Jess gave a groan of frustration before he spun and walked out of the room. I waited until I could hear his and Matthew's voices leave the house before I sank down on the edge of his bed. What had I done? I couldn't just pretend that away. Perhaps the worst part was how much I had loved it and how at home I had felt.

Chapter 16

I successfully dodged all of Jess's attempts at contact for the next full week. He had flown back to LA the morning after the wedding to finish his press tour promoting his movie. I used his absence to my advantage. It made me feel terribly guilty to listen to his voice mails and read his text messages, pleading with me to call him, to return his texts, begging me not to shut him out. Yet it was comforting to know that he couldn't physically track me down.

I went over and over it in my mind, and no matter how I looked at it, I didn't see what choice I had. Jess was a movie star. At the end of the day, he was loved by a nation . . . and honestly probably some international places too. He was wined and dined and catered to. I could not in any way compete with that. I would lose that battle. I wasn't worldly. I didn't understand glitz and glamour. I wasn't sure what he wanted from me, but I was completely sure that I couldn't give it to him. The worst part was knowing that eventually he'd figure it out for himself. On that day, I would be relieved that I'd protected my heart.

I was grateful for the distraction of work, Ethan, and Nate. In that order. I worked longer hours than were necessary during the day. In the evenings, I parented the heck out of Ethan. And Nate, he was a real down-to-earth man whom I could have an actual future with. I spent hours building up that future with him in my mind. We would live in a little town and raise our children together. We would get pizza on Friday nights and rent movies. We would go to bed early and make school lunches. It wouldn't make my heart soar like thoughts of Jess did, but it would be comfortable.

In the dark hours when I was honest with myself, I wondered exactly why I felt so lonely when I had Nate. When had it changed? *Why* had it changed?

It was with that in mind that I went out with Nate two times in the week Jess was gone. I was desperate to spend time with him, to prove to myself that I was right to disregard Jess and go with the sure thing. The problem was that the sure thing didn't feel so great anymore.

For our first date after Jess left, I suggested a movie. It was something I didn't typically like to do when newly dating because you couldn't get to know a person in a quiet theater. That was kind of my point that night. I just needed to sit next to him and have him hold my hand. He did hold my hand. His hand was big, and warm, and totally comfortable . . . even if it was oddly soft. We didn't talk much, but I didn't actually want to talk, so it was fine.

When we walked to my car, he kissed me good night. I pressed into him and gave it my all, kissing him back and hugging him close. He responded in kind. It was nice. Yet somehow the fact that it was *nice* made it terrible. When I broke contact, I kept my eyes down, trying to keep him from seeing what I was afraid he'd see. Heartache. Why did kissing Nate bring heartache?

For the second date, Nate took me bowling. I liked bowling, and it was a fun way to spend time together. I had suggested bringing our kids along, but Nate had been hesitant, saying he'd like to date a little longer before getting kids involved. I respected his decision but felt a little hurt by it too. In my mind, Nate was my alternative to Jess. I had twisted things and was needlessly putting pressure on our fledgling relationship. I bowled the highest score of my life. I decided it was a sign and even more frantically clung to the idea of Nate.

"Jess is back today, you know," Zinn stated at breakfast a week after the wedding.

"Yes!" Ethan pumped his fist in the air and did a little dance next to his chair before sitting down.

I remained silent. I was totally sure Zinn knew I had been steering clear of contact with or mention of Jess Sullivan.

"We are always happy when he comes home," Zinn pressed.

"Yep. Hey, care to watch Ethan while I go out with Nate again this weekend?" I smiled sweetly at Zinn, letting her know I saw right through her ploy. She harrumphed at me.

"I don't see why you date that man." She gave me the stink eye.

"Ethan, go get your backpack ready and shoes on," I said to the side, not wanting him here for this conversation. When he was clear of the room, I turned back to Zinn. "Who would you have me date then, Zinn?" I threw up my hands, frustrated. Zinn clamped her lips tight and glared at me. "Jess? Is that who?" I pressed. "Guess what, he would grow bored of me in two days. He is a big-time movie star. What on earth could he possibly see or want in a regular girl like me?" I pushed back from the table and grabbed my dishes.

"You are better than that Vivienne Lawson he hangs around," Zinn stated.

I sighed. "Zinn, that's nice of you to say, but it's not true. She is elegant and beautiful and all Jess would want."

"Oh, careers, they change." Zinn waved her hand as though casting off my worries. "Jess is too smart to end up with a woman like Vivienne. She's mean. He won't be a movie star forever, you know. Plus, you make his eyes sparkle when he looks at you."

"What?" I whispered.

"You heard me." Zinn looked to me again.

Our eyes held, and I began to wonder what Zinn saw when Jess and I were together. What did Zinn know of romance or who belonged together? Was she a matchmaker in her former life? The Dolly Levi of ancient times?

"You need to get Ethan to the bus. Now go." Zinn shooed me out the door, but not before she gave me a nod and a small smile.

Ethan was in the big house's front hall, where he'd stationed his shoes and backpack. I walked toward him slowly, my thoughts spinning out of control. I made Jess's eyes sparkle? Well, he made my everything sparkle. I couldn't stand thinking about it, knowing I was setting myself up for heartache. Jess was a risk I just couldn't take.

As I walked Ethan to the bus, I spent the time listing reasons why I could not ever be with Jess Sullivan.

One—I was a walking disaster. Spills, tripping, saying the wrong thing. I would embarrass him.

Two—I was too short for him, and although my curves weren't the worst thing in the world, it would be nice if my chest were where it had started rather than creeping toward my lap. Vivienne's chest was perky.

Three—I had crazy hair. Never sleek or in place, always waving about my head and looking all Medusa. It would clash with the red carpet.

Four—I was temperamental. I took everything wrong, overreacted, had crazy moments.

Five—I had a bad habit of wearing sweats. Bet he didn't even know where sweatpants were sold.

It gave me a strange sort of comfort to list my flaws, as though somehow I were making it my choice to stay away from Jess. Like I was pre-rejecting myself for him. I knew it was twisted, but it was my twisted.

Ethan was rambling on about a new boy at school as we stood at the bus stop. I was happy that he was making a new friend and being kind to the new kid. Ethan was the best. He didn't stop talking until he was on the bus, and then he just transferred his monologue to whomever he was seated by. He waved at me through the window, and I blew him a kiss and watched until the bus rounded the corner.

I turned to walk back to the cottage and was shocked to find Mr. Sullivan himself, Mr. Hunky Hunkerton, standing directly behind me. I squealed in surprise. He didn't laugh. His expression was unyielding. I was in major trouble.

So I did what any girl would do when faced with that, well, face. I pasted on my biggest, cheeriest smile, gave him a brief greeting, and did my best to walk around him and head home. And just like any other girl, I failed.

"I don't think so. We need to talk, and you can't avoid me anymore." Jess snagged my arm in a firm, but gentle, grip as I tried to skirt around him.

I looked up into his face. Those green, green eyes were not dancing anymore. He was seriously ticked off. I sighed.

"Fine, but can we not do it standing out on the street?" I asked.

Jess let go of me and gestured toward the cottage. We started walking. I had absolutely nothing to say. Asking how his press tour had gone seemed wrong. Asking after his family also seemed wrong. Small talk was not going to do me any favors. So I waited. I was proud of my self-control when all I wanted to do was babble nervously.

Finally we passed the big house and were almost to the cottage. I hesitated at the front door, not sure if I should invite him in or if we should talk on the porch. Wouldn't that be like the whole Big Bad Wolf thing? I believed I was in danger of being eaten.

Jess had no patience. He reached around me, pushed open the door, and herded me inside before closing the door behind him and leaning against it. I turned to look at him.

"You look good," he said, finally breaking the silence. "I'm glad, seeing as at one point I wondered if you were dying in a hospital somewhere." Uh-oh, sarcasm alert.

I gave a little smile. "Nope, I'm fine."

Jess pushed away from the door and started walking to where I was standing. I shifted over and put the couch between us. Jess's lips raised a bit into a sort of smile.

"So enough about me. How have you been?" I offered in a shaky voice.

"Oh, no. No. I'm much more interested in talking about how you've been," Jess insisted, coming to a stop with his knees touching the couch cushions.

"Oh, me? Really not much to report. Just the usual. Number crunching, homework, laundry, dishes." I laughed nervously. Trying to play cool was super hard.

"Maybe you'd like to join me on the couch for a little chat?" He gestured to one of the seats.

"You know, you go ahead and sit on the couch. I really like the chair best." I hurried to scoot around the couch, but Jess turned and I miscalculated and, well, that was disappointing because now we were standing very close, both of us frozen in place.

I could feel his body almost touching mine. I did not at all appreciate how it was making me feel. Even though I knew it was bad form, I looked down and started chanting *Nate, Nate, Nate* to myself as a reminder of what I really wanted. I couldn't afford to be distracted by Jess. Not when all those paths led to heartache.

Jess obviously had no idea at all what was going on in my head, because he reached up and brushed back a strand of my hair that had fallen forward as I was looking at our feet and chanting another man's name. The contact was electric. I looked up before I could help it. He brushed his thumb across my cheekbone as our gazes met. I was pretty sure I was going to be a puddle.

"Kate?" he murmured. I made a little sound. "Care to tell me why you left me hanging for the past week?" I shook my head, but I couldn't stop looking into those eyes. I noticed his eyes crinkle up a bit at the corners as he realized how I was reacting to him. It annoyed me enough that I pulled away and flopped quickly in the chair. He sat down on the couch with a slight smile on his face.

"Look, I don't know what to tell you. I've been really busy." I delivered my excuse as airily as I could.

"I've been pretty busy too, but I still called."

I had no reply to that, so I just sat silently, holding his gaze.

"Kate." Jess sighed and rubbed his face. He was frustrated. It made me smile to myself that he wasn't as in control as he was acting. "I don't think we can just pretend nothing happened between us at the wedding."

"I agree. We both know something did happen. We both also know that things like that happen at weddings all the time." I tucked my feet under me and propped my chin on my hand while I spoke. I really, really wanted to look like I'd thought this out and was totally casual about it. I was in no way the kind of girl who *ever* did something like that at weddings. Ever. He didn't need to know that.

Jess didn't seem to like the direction I was going with this. He scowled. "What are you trying to say?"

"Oh, you know, just that we don't really need to worry about it or talk about it. I'm dating someone; you're dating someone. Let's not blow this thing out of proportion. So we kissed? No big deal. We are both adults, and we got caught up in the romance of a wedding. It's totally understandable. No reason we can't still be friends." I finished with a benevolent smile. I was trying to make him think that I was chalking it up to a little meaningless moment and kindly letting him off the hook.

Jess did not return that smile. Instead, he leaned forward on the edge of his seat. "We can be friends?"

I nodded, glad he was seeing it my way.

"You're dating that guy still?"

Um, his voice seemed to be rising a bit. I nodded again, my smile fading.

"That kiss was no big deal?"

Shoot, even I knew three questions in a row was a bad thing. My casual air was quickly turning to apprehension. I began to check my exit options.

Jess stared at me. Then he did something so unexpected that I hadn't a moment to block it. He moved forward, dropped to his knees in front of me where I sat, put his hands on my face, and kissed me. Full-on kissing. This wasn't gentle; it was demanding. Eight long days of frustration were delivered in that kiss.

Darn it if I didn't respond in kind. I was entirely on fire. I had thought of little else besides kissing him for the past week, no matter how hard I'd tried to distract myself. I slid to the edge of my chair as my arms wove around his neck and pulled him closer, fingers grabbing his hair and holding tight. Days and days of telling myself no had done nothing to curb my longing for this.

He abruptly broke it off and met my gaze. My fingers were still in his hair, our noses touching and our breath mingling. I could hear my heart thundering in my ears, begging for more. I wanted to pull him back, but I knew it would be unwelcome.

"Kate," he finally said, almost against my lips. "You are not my friend."

Then he released me, stood up, and strode right out the front door, slamming it behind him.

Chapter 17

After the dramatic reunion with Jess, I was grateful that a date with Nate had already been set up for the next night. Thanks to some seriously inspired internet searches on quick and easy updos, I was feeling confident when he picked me up. He was taking me to an art gallery opening in a trendy tourist town neighboring Oakdale. I knew exactly zero about art, well, true art. I looked at something and either liked it or didn't, but I didn't interpret art or care much about what the artist was trying to communicate. However, I thought it would be fun to do something different, in my flirty dress with my smooth legs and seductive hair.

Things were going to happen tonight. Good things, maybe even life-changing things. It was time to throw myself in with Nate and ride that train to the end of the line. Hopefully, he felt the same way. I just wished that the thought of Jess holding my face in his hands and kissing me like a madman would leave me alone.

Nate held my hand on the drive, and we chatted amiably. It was very sweet. Not exciting, not blood humming, but sweet and safe and exactly what I was looking for.

"Okay," he whispered close to my ear shortly after entering the gallery, "the trick to these things is to swirl your drink while looking at each picture. Then take a sip and either say it's trash or it's spectacular. Never let them know that the only art you own is that picture of two cats that Ethan drew you." I laughed, charmed that he remembered me telling him about Ethan's cat picture. More proof that he really listened and cared.

Nate and I went to the canapés table first and got ourselves tiny plates of finger food and a drink of sparkling water. Then we chose an end to start on and began perusing art. Yep, there I was, fancy dress, canapés in hand, perusing art in a trendy gallery. This was great. I was definitely exactly where I wanted to be. I was with a great guy, living life to the fullest. I probably told myself that about fifteen times over the course of the evening.

"What do you think of this piece?" a man's voice interrupted my swirling and perusing about twenty minutes in. I turned to see an older man dressed all in black with his gray hair spiked and a blue jeweled nose ring. I was honestly more interested in the nose ring than in the painting I'd been looking at.

I turned my attention back to the monster hanging on the wall, blazing lights making it seem alive somehow. The splashes of red overlaying some dark shape felt unformed and dangerous. "Um, I suppose I find it disturbing," I said honestly. I heard Nate stifle a laugh next to me. That couldn't be a good sign.

The nose-ring guy made a thoughtful sound. "Disturbing? In what way?" he pressed as though he were actually considering my words.

I was staring desperately at the painting, trying to come up with an answer. "Well, for one thing, it would scare the bejeebers out of me every time I walked past it in the dark," I finally stated.

Nate snorted a bit and put his hand on my back as he leaned around me to address the man. "This is her first time in an art gallery," he soothed. He made it sound like I'd just been let off the farm for the day. I felt somehow disgraced as a flush began to rise. Lucky for me, my temper rose to meet it.

"Actually, I stand by it," I said to the man and Nate.

The man's eyes scrunched up, and he broke into a smile. "It is a terrifying painting. You're just the first person to admit that." He reached out a hand to shake mine. "Henry Watkins." He held my hand firmly. "The gallery owner."

"Well, that's better than having said that to the artist, then." I smiled back at him as he gave my hand a final squeeze and released it.

"Yes," he agreed with a soft chuckle. "I'm very pleased to meet you tonight, Mrs. . . . ?"

Oh, he thought Nate and I were married. And why wouldn't he after Nate apologized for me like I was his little lady?

"I'm Kate Evans. This is my date, Nate Carmichael."

"Oh, your date. I'm sorry for the assumption."

"No apologies necessary. I don't mind one bit." Nate squeezed my waist and gave me a wink.

"Well, I'm glad you came. I hope you find other pieces that are more to your liking." Henry gave us one last smile before venturing out to mingle in the crowd.

I felt a little less relaxed as Nate and I went back to swishing and perusing. Even though I was mostly enjoying my first time at an art gallery, I had begun to feel disillusioned with my date.

"I had a great time tonight," Nate said as we stepped up to my door a couple of hours later. "You look so nice in that dress, showing off those great curves. You're a seriously attractive little woman." He smiled and pulled me into a hug, kissing my forehead before he moved to my mouth.

As I kissed him I felt tears welling up, and I willed them back down. His hands roamed my back, and with each caress and each kiss I knew, I just *knew*, it would never work with Nate. It wasn't anything he'd done. He was great. We had a lot in common. But I finally admitted to myself that I had been forcing the connection. If I hadn't called him and pestered him, then it probably would have just fizzled naturally, or we would have become good friends. Instead, I'd stirred him up and given him hope, and all that hope was kissing me on my doorstep, running his hot hands over me, thinking I was his little woman, and not even realizing this was goodbye.

After a few short moments, I broke the kiss and stepped out of his embrace.

"That was nice, Kate." He used a finger to move some hair behind my ear and then tilted my chin up. "I think you know I really like you."

I held up a hand before he could go further and make it worse. "I like you too, Nate. A lot." He leaned in to renew our kissing, thinking we were on the same page. I felt a prick to my heart, knowing I'd done this to him. "Listen, Nate." I turned my head.

"I know, it's late. School night and all that. I'll let you go. Next time maybe you could come back to my place?" he interrupted and snuck another kiss while I stood gaping at his invitation.

"Actually, Nate, I'm not sure there should be a next time." I hurried and spit it out before I could chicken out.

"Why?" he asked, obviously shocked.

I used the moment to pull out of his embrace and wrap my arms around myself like a shield. "I can't give you a great reason, Nate. I like you. We have a lot in common. I'm just thinking we'd be better friends than . . ."

"Significant others," Nate finished softly. Maybe he felt it too? I nodded. "Does it count for anything that I'm really attracted to you?" he asked.

"Sure it does. It's flattering. It's just that for me I can't see it going the distance," I replied quietly. I hated that I was hurting him and giving up my safe relationship in the process.

Nate nodded again. He looked once more into my eyes and then just turned and walked away. I watched him round the corner of the big house before I let myself in.

The TV was on in the cottage living room even though the other lights were out, and I could see the back of Cass's head out of the corner of my eye as I kicked off my shoes and prepared to mope.

"I'm back now. Thanks so much for watching Ethan," I said to Cass.

"Oh, hey, Cass had to go, so I'm here." Jess turned to face me.

Seeing him there, at that exact moment, felt like a kick in the stomach.

"No, no, no. Not you. You can*not* be here right now!" I stared in horror at him. This was his fault. It was totally his fault that I had broken up with a perfectly lovely man. His fault because he'd shown me what heart-pounding attraction felt like and ruined everything. His fault because I'd thought of him all night. I couldn't have him, and I couldn't have someone else. He'd made a huge mess of my heart.

Jess turned off the TV and stood up. "What do you mean? Are you okay? Where were you tonight?"

"I was out with Nate, and no, I'm not okay. I am definitely not okay." My voice grew more and more strained as the tears threatened to fall. "I'm not okay at all. You need to go, just go!" I turned and hurried to my room, closing the door behind me and locking it.

I went into my closet and angrily threw off my jacket and unzipped my dress. As I hung it up, tears began to fall down my face. Jess knocked softly and called my name. I slammed open my dresser drawers and grabbed leggings and a long T-shirt, pulling them on angrily while sobbing my heart out. I didn't care that I wasn't crying silently. I liked that Jess could hear my anguish.

I had gotten out and dated this year. I'd left the safe cocoon of widowhood and put myself out there. I'd had a summer fling and an actual grown-up relationship. I was tired. I was going to take Ethan back to Denver and never think about stupid Jess Sullivan again. I could find someone there who would make my heart soar and be totally practical at the same time. It didn't have to be just one or the other.

That stupid Jess Sullivan was knocking on my locked door again, asking me to let him in and tell him what was going on.

"Is it Nate? Did he do something?" he was saying.

"No. Go home, Jess," I retorted through the closed door before wandering to my laundry pile and digging out fuzzy comfort socks.

"Kate, sweetheart, you're killing me. Please let me in."

"Do not call me *sweetheart.* I am not your sweetheart. I will never be your sweetheart. I'll never be anyone's sweetheart again!" I raged while pulling on my fuzzy socks. I sounded like a twelve-year-old and I knew it. I just didn't care. Sometimes only a good hysterical meltdown would do.

I began pulling out the pins that had kept my hair styled so nicely and slapping them down on the dresser while Jess was still knocking and saying my name. Even though Ethan slept the deep sleep of childhood, I knew with my luck that Jess would wake him. I stomped to my door and flung it open with renewed frustration. The last thing I needed was Ethan awake to witness his mom falling apart.

"Go away, Jess!" I whisper-yelled through the tears. "You're going to wake up Ethan, and then I'll really kill you. Don't give me another reason to!" I started to shut the door again, but he caught it before I could and slipped into my room, closing it softly behind him.

Jess leaned against the door, and we stood facing each other, me a mess, him unsure of what was going on. He was looking at me like he was facing down a wild animal and had no clue if he'd live or die.

"What happened tonight?" he asked cautiously.

I wiped my hand sloppily across my face. "I looked really, really great in that dress!" I blubbered, pointing to my closet and a dress he couldn't possibly see.

"I didn't get a chance to see it, but I'm sure you did. You always look great," he soothed. "Did Nate not like it?"

"I do not always look great. I'm upset, not an idiot!" I snarled.

"Agree to disagree on that," Jess mumbled under his breath.

"Nate loved my dress. He loved it a lot. He wanted me to come to his place. That's how much he liked it." With my hair finally free and floating wildly around me, I paced to the window and looked out over the foothills beyond, bathed in moonlight.

"He wanted to . . . Wait, Kate, did he push you or hurt you or something?" Jess came and stood next to me, facing me and watching me closely. His voice sounded oddly angry.

I shook my head. "No. He kissed me, but he stopped when I told him to." I sniffed and hugged my arms around myself.

I felt Jess put his hand on my back and rub gently. "I don't understand what happened. Why are you so upset?"

I spun to face him and stepped out of his reach, arms hugging myself tightly, tears still falling, makeup destroyed. "You ruined everything. Everything. I can't date Nate because of you. I don't know what to do because of you!"

Jess looked at me carefully, trying to understand what I was saying. He rubbed his face and shook his head. "I don't understand what I did. I would never hurt you like this, Kate."

"You kissed me!" I wailed.

Jess's head shot up. "I kissed you?"

I nodded. "Twice. It ruined everything."

Without warning, I found myself in his arms. I didn't think I'd ever been held so tightly. He was talking nonsense words as he wrapped his arms around me. He seemed in some way as anxious as I was feeling.

I sank into his embrace, wrapping my arms around his waist and laying my head on his chest. I was tired of fighting.

"Kate, I didn't know . . . I'm so sorry, sweetheart," he was saying as he stroked my back and hair. I was slowly settling down, warming to him, seeking the comfort I craved from only him even though he was the one causing the pain. "I didn't realize you cared so much about Nate."

"Oh, Jess, I don't want Nate," I finally said, sniffling. He stopped his caressing and held very still. It felt like his body was suddenly on high alert.

"Then I don't understand," he probed.

"You can't understand something that I don't even understand. I'm all jumbled up inside." I was transitioning into the calm after the storm, and I felt myself deflating.

"Kate . . ." He breathed my name in a way that had me looking up at him. Those eyes caught the moonlight from the window. I loved his eyes.

This time I initiated the kiss. I stood on tiptoe and pressed my lips firmly to his. He hesitantly kissed me back before he stepped away and broke the contact, his face unreadable.

"Kate?" he asked. I tried to push out of his arms, but he held me firm. "Look at me, please," he whispered.

"I don't think that would be a good idea," I replied, dazed and upset and a little shocked at myself.

In true Jess form, he guided my face back to his. "Kate, are you telling me that *you* broke it off with Nate? Not the other way around?"

I nodded, and Jess let out a big breath that he'd been holding and crushed me to him. His lips were on mine again, and it was bliss. How I loved it, soaring and tumbling and feeling so filled up with light that I could hardly stand it. He was everywhere, surrounding me, comforting me, protecting me. He was exactly what I needed, and it was sweet torment.

I didn't understand how it could be this way with him. I hadn't felt this level of emotion with Charlie. Everything with Charlie had been steady and soft and comfortable, like a warm blanket being wrapped around me by loving arms. Jess was a rocket to the moon, hanging on for dear life, praying you could withstand the fall.

We kissed in the darkness, saying nothing at all. I was content to be close to him for whatever time I had tonight. I knew that the time was coming to leave this behind. I would carry him as a cherished memory and never think of what might have been. I knew too well that those dreams couldn't come true. He was meant to orbit the sun.

Before things could get out of hand, Jess stepped back from me, but he held my hands tightly. "Kate, I'm going crazy over you," he shocked me by saying.

"I . . ." I hesitated as I looked into those eyes. He looked so sincere and a little vulnerable. Nothing at all like I expected Jess to ever look. He looked so normal, stripped bare, just a regular man.

"I'm mad for you," he stated simply. "I think about you all the time."

"I'm too short and curvy and way too clumsy," I stuttered. "I say strange things and have a temper. I wear horrible clothes."

"You're perfect, Kate," he interrupted. "You're full of life. You're beautiful to me," he insisted. "I want to be with you." He whispered the last part into the darkness. His sincerity brought another round of tears to my eyes.

I was speechless. I never thought I'd hear those words from anyone again after Charlie, but especially not from someone like Jess. I fretted and worried about what to say. My mind felt foggy and frozen. In the silence, he kissed me again, softly and briefly, still holding my hands.

"It's too much, Jess. I need to breathe," I finally asserted as I pulled back.

He nodded, seeming to understand. He didn't understand, but I wasn't going to press that tonight. Instead, I leaned forward and wove my arms around his waist, enjoying the sweet feeling of his body next to mine as we held each other.

After one last moment, I stepped back and released him. "Good night, Jess," I said.

He smiled down at me. "Good night, Kate."

I watched as he walked out of my room and out the front door of the cottage before I crawled into bed and let the tears return. Goodbyes were so hard, and I already missed the feel of his arms around me.

Chapter 18

Halloween rolled around a couple of days later. I had been so busy thinking about my breakup with Nate and that heated exchange with Jess in the darkness of my bedroom that I was grateful I'd prepared early.

Jess called or dropped by each day. He had a permanent smile on his face. I loved that smile so much. That smile made me start to believe in things that couldn't be. That smile promised something good was coming my way. I spent a lot of time reminding myself that that smile couldn't possibly last forever.

I had managed to avoid any alone moments with Jess, never answering the door or phone when Ethan was away at school, even going so far as to wear headphones while I worked. It was a scaredy-cat way of holding him at arm's length. However, despite my best tactics, Jess was going to come trick-or-treating with Ethan and me that night. Ethan had invited him. I was once again trapped by my love for that little boy.

Ethan looked absolutely adorable in a cowboy costume that Zinn had sewn for him. I drew on a great mustache and had even found a horse costume for Wade online. I only took about 168 pictures of them in various poses before Ethan started whining. They looked hilarious together.

After we went up to the big house to show Cass and Zinn the finished costumes, we drove to Jess's property to find him waiting at the end of the lane. He was dressed up like a mobster, with a crisp, well-tailored black suit and a white fedora. It was a swoon-worthy situation. He was made for that type of clothes.

I was dressed up in the most pathetic of costumes. A bathrobe, slippers, and shower cap. I'd spent so much time planning and searching for Ethan's costume that mine got pushed back. Oh well, at least I was dressed up at all given my current state of affairs.

Jess got in the passenger seat and surprised me by leaning over and greeting me with a kiss on the cheek before turning back to Ethan and giving his costume a once-over.

"You look awesome, buddy!" he said, giving Ethan a high five. "Extra points for dressing up Wade. He looks hysterical." Jess chuckled, and the sight of his smile, along with the sound of his laugh, went straight to my stomach, where it flipped around for a while. It made me miserable. I was terrified and tied up in knots. I was falling for this man, who was as dangerous to me as his costume portrayed.

"Let's go." Ethan tapped my shoulder, breaking me out of my stupor. Jess turned back to me, and our faces were close for a moment before I whipped to face forward again.

"Candy waits for no one." Jess laughed again.

Cass's house was located outside of the main city limits of Clark Springs, so we drove a few miles into town, where there were more houses for Ethan to beg candy from. I parked my car in a familiar subdivision and we all piled out.

"Can I go, Mom?" Ethan asked as we all stood on the sidewalk.

"Yes, but we need to be able to see each other at all times, so don't get too far ahead." I didn't have to fake a smile as I watched Ethan bounce on his feet, ready to get all the free candy he wanted.

"Okay, deal." And he was off, Wade's leash in one hand and his candy bag in the other.

"Too bad he doesn't realize that parents are paying a ton of money for their kids to get free candy. When I lived in Denver, I spent a lot of money on candy for trick-or-treaters." I smiled fondly at the memory.

"One year I had a pillowcase to fill and somewhere along the way a small hole got torn in the bottom corner. So I left a trail of candy all the way home and had hardly any left when I got there." Jess laughed.

"I'm glad to see you overcame your difficult childhood experiences." I gestured to the sidewalk in the direction Ethan was headed, and we began walking side by side, occasionally dodging excited candy hunters as we strolled along, keeping an eye on Ethan.

Jess reached for my hand and twined his fingers with mine as we walked. I knew mine were shaky and a little sweaty, but I held on anyway, wanting this contact. I couldn't understand how I could want something so badly but be so terrified of it at the same time.

Jess managed to make the rest of the evening perfect. He kept up light and easy chitchat as we walked the streets hand in hand. He was playful and kind to Ethan, as he always was. It felt so normal and lovely that it almost hurt.

After trick-or-treating, Jess asked if we could pop by his cabin before going back to the cottage. There he'd set up a surprise Halloween party for Ethan and me. The kitchen was decorated with orange and black balloons, and there were pumpkins and carving tools and a scary-but-not-too-scary movie to watch afterward. My heart pounded in my throat as I watched this beautiful man and my son together. He loved Ethan. Even *I* could see that through my haze of self-doubt and worry.

Ethan, of course, fell asleep halfway through the movie. He'd had a very busy night. Jess saw this as an opportunity and moved his little sleeping body to another couch before coming to sit next to me. He put an arm around my shoulders and pulled me up against his side. I tugged off my itchy shower cap and leaned into him. It was a night for indulgences.

Jess's fingers played lightly with the skin on the back of my neck and under my ear. I relaxed inch by inch into his side until I was as firmly pressed up against him as I could be. I let my head flop onto his shoulder. It felt amazing. I was trying to remember what about this had been such a bad idea.

"Kate?"

"Hmm?"

"Kate?" he asked again.

This time I leaned back and tilted my face to look at him. His eyes were strained, but tender. I knew I had put that strained look there with my anti-conversations campaign. I saw the questions in his eyes and knew he wanted to find the answers. I also knew I was the one who had the wall to tear down. I found myself suddenly terrified.

"We probably need to talk," I breathed, the fear stealing my voice.

"Finally." He smiled at me and let me go so that we were a normal distance apart again.

"I know . . . well, I mean, I think . . ."

Jess reached out and picked my hand out of my lap. "Let's start with the easy stuff. Kate, I really, really care about you. I have for a long time," he stated clearly and easily. How I wished I could express myself like that. "I love Ethan, and I would never do anything that would hurt him."

"I know that. But I have to be careful about dating because of him."

Jess's lips got flat and he gave me a look of disbelief. "That doesn't hold much water, considering you dated two men this past year."

Oops. My bad. Wrong thing to say. I tried to save it. "Yes, but they weren't serious." I kind of smiled.

"Could have fooled me with all the kissing and referring to them as your boyfriend. I seem to remember one of them even invited you to his place."

Um, so, I didn't have much defense there. I'd have to try another avenue. "What about Vivienne?"

"What about her?"

"You dated her."

"Yes, I did. I'm not trying to say I didn't," Jess replied.

"Well, um, shouldn't you want to date more people like her?" I asked.

"If I wanted to date people like Vivienne, I would have kept dating Vivienne." He was so logical it was disgusting. "Also, Vivienne and I wanted different things." I really had nothing to reply with, so I looked down at our hands sitting in my lap. I loved his hands. I wasn't sure how manicured movie-star hands could look so masculine, but they were. I got distracted and began tracing the shape of them with one of my fingers, loving the roughness of his skin against the softness of mine.

"We're getting off track here," Jess finally stated after watching me trace his fingers for a while. He sounded annoyed, so I looked back up and met his eyes. I nodded.

"That happens a lot with me." I grinned.

Jess immediately grinned back. Something about that grin and how he just kind of dealt with me made me feel suddenly warm inside. I could feel it heating up my face, rushing up my neck and into my cheeks. He leaned toward me, closing the distance, looking at my mouth.

I let go of his hands and leaned back, shaking my head. "No, no. We won't get anywhere if you start that up," I said firmly.

Jess smiled again and put both his hands in the air. "Fine, fine." Then he took a deep breath and said, "Kate, you know how I feel about you.

I've been falling for you since the moment I first saw you, wearing those amazing sweatpants, all ruffled and scattered, knocking glasses on the floor of Cass's house and making Zinn so mad. Something about you pulls me in. I want more of that."

Wow, now we were getting somewhere, but he'd taken the wrong fork in the road. This was supposed to be the conversation where we agreed to just be friends and everyone would be happy. Mostly me. I'd be happy. That was the important end point I was trying to reach, even if I knew I wouldn't be *that* happy.

"I don't know what to say," I admitted.

"It's really very simple. Do you care about me?"

I refocused on his face and smiled up at him. "Yes."

He seemed to let out a breath he'd been holding. "Good. So can we please just finally be together?" He reached out for my hands.

"No." I pulled them back slightly out of reach.

He stopped smiling and leaned back, making the distance between us greater. "Why?"

"We wouldn't make each other happy." I decided that blaming both of us would be better than my taking all the blame.

I knew it was a lie. I knew that for as long as I was with Jess, I'd be happy. It was when he left—or even worse, was taken from me—that I'd be very, very unhappy.

"What? Why?" he asked again.

"You're the tetherball post and I'm the tetherball." I put my hands up in a helpless gesture.

He shook his head and closed his eyes for a moment. Finally, he puffed out a big breath and looked directly at me again. "I'm the pole and you're the ball?" He leaned his back against a cushion and folded his arms across his chest. "So in your mind I'm firmly grounded and you're kind of all over the place?" I nodded, and he smiled a little. "Is that a problem?"

"It's not just that. I'm too old," I finally said.

He blinked slowly at me. "I'm older than you are."

Rats. "I'm a mother and that takes up a lot of time."

"Didn't keep you from dating Alec and Nate. Besides, I already love Ethan."

Drat. "I wear sweatpants."

"I've known that for some time now and come to peace with it."

Shoot. "I can get kind of grumpy."

"Again, no surprise there."

"Sometimes I do strange things or get myself in weird situations."

"Life with you would never be boring."

Humph. "My hair would clash with the red carpet, and I wouldn't fit in there."

"I've bought a theater in Aspen and am going to quit doing movies and run that theater. No more red carpet. Also, how is your hair clashing with the red carpet even a thing?" His facial expression on that last bit was so hilarious I almost cracked. I held firm.

Stalemate. He'd actually announced it. He was going to quit Hollywood and be more local. Or at least as local as Aspen was.

"You w-what?" I sputtered out.

He saw my weakened moment and leaned in closer. "I'm quitting movies and Hollywood and all that travel. I want something here more." It felt like he was alluding to me being what he wanted more than Hollywood. I felt myself both expanding with happiness and shrinking under the weight of being enough for him.

"You can't give that all up for me," I squeaked out. "I can't take that kind of pressure."

Jess put his arms around me and pulled me softly into his body, hugging me close but not holding me tight. "Don't take this the wrong way, love, but I didn't do it all for you."

Oddly, that made me relax a little bit.

"I've been thinking about it for a while, and it was something that I planned when I found this land and built my house. Kind of a long-term goal. But then I met you and Ethan and Cass and Zinn, and suddenly, well, it felt like maybe I should hurry that goal along a little bit."

"Oh," I stated. "So you're more in love with my old aunt and her housekeeper than with Hollywood?" I joked in a shaky voice.

"You caught me." He chuckled softly against me. I felt the vibration of it down to my toes.

"You said Vivienne didn't want the same things you wanted. Is that why you broke up? Because she wanted to stay in Hollywood and you didn't?" I asked.

"No, Kate. The thing I wanted was you."

His words were overpowering. "But you won't want me forever," I finally whispered, getting to the root of the problem.

"Ah," he said, acknowledging that we were getting to the point. "What makes you think that?"

"Jess, you have a mirror and eyeballs. Men like you who are handsome and wealthy and famous do not have relationships with women like me. You'll always be around beautiful women, and they will be tempting. I'll get older and crankier and rounder with age, and you'll tire of me. I don't think I can go through that . . . having you leave me." I continued to whisper, my throat clogging with tears that I was holding back.

"Have you noticed that men's ears and noses never stop growing?" Jess asked.

"Um, no?" I had no idea where he was going with that.

"Yep. I'm going to say that's scientific. Point is, someday I'll have a big hairy nose and big ears and my eyebrows will start growing really long and strange. I'll start wearing my pants pulled too high and socks with sandals. Men really do get worse with age. In fact, I've probably peaked at this point. I'm hoping that you'll be able to overlook that and still want to be with me."

I looked up at him and gave him a little half smile. "But why me? How on earth could someone like you find something worth having in me?"

He kissed me softly on the forehead before saying, "I keep asking myself the same question. 'How on earth can I hope that Kate will see something worth having in me?'"

I laid my head back under his chin, and we were quiet for a few moments. I didn't know what to think. He said he wanted this to become a relationship. I was still scared. He made some good arguments, and I had told him my fears. My head and my heart were in a major battle.

"I need some time and space to think, Jess. Can you give me that?"

"I feel like that's all I do is give you space." He chuckled in a frustrated way. "But I'll try."

It's kind of amazing how long two days can feel when you're thinking over something. Two things had become painfully clear. First, I wanted to be with Jess. My hands shook from wanting to touch him and hold him. My mouth ached from wanting to talk and tell him that we should be together. Still, I held back because of the second thing, which was the big speed bump in my life. I was terrified. Over the course of those days, I'd come to realize how deeply my feelings for Jess ran, and I was completely sure I wouldn't survive it if I lost him. I'd lost so many I loved already. He could give up Hollywood, but could he promise he'd never get sick or hurt? I needed forever, and there was no guarantee printed on his side.

On the third morning, while I was working in the cottage, I heard thudding and cracking sounds coming from around back. I walked down the hall and peeked through Ethan's bedroom window. Outside, Jess and another man were chopping wood and stacking it against my cottage. It was so nice. The guilt I felt over him doing nice things for me when I only made things hard for him sparked my temper.

I pushed my feet into boots and put on my big coat before stomping around the side of the cottage to where they were busily working. I was momentarily distracted by the sight of Jess playing lumberjack. It was the stuff of fantasies. Wood chopping is primal ancestral stuff. I shivered in my coat, and it wasn't just from the frosty air.

They noticed my presence and turned to face me. Despite my frustration, a big smile broke out on my face when I saw that it was Jack chopping with him. I hurried forward and held out my hands to him for a quick greeting. He squeezed my hands and bent to kiss my cheek, telling me how good it was to see me.

"What brings you to town?" I asked Jack as Jess pushed the head of the ax he was using into the wood stump and tucked his hands into his coat pockets.

"Just a quick visit on our way home from the honeymoon. Zara and I thought we'd help Jess with a few projects around his place, seeing as he was nice enough to host our wedding. We'll be here for about two days. Mom and Dad are flying in this afternoon to pitch in as well, and I know that Zara would love to see you. You should come over tonight if you're free," Jack invited.

I turned to face Jess, and he gave me a look, letting me know it was my call. I wasn't sure that I should spend more time building relationships in his family, but I really liked them. I took a deep breath and fought back my fears.

"Okay, thanks." Then I remembered why I was out there and I turned to Jess. "What are you doing?"

He pointed at the ax and then the woodpile. I couldn't help the grin that formed at his short, silent answer. "Well, you really don't need to do that."

"It was getting low, and I don't want you to be cold," Jess replied concisely. His frustration with me was evident in his stance, and I felt guilt creep back in.

"Oh, you don't need to worry. We have a furnace in there. I just keep the wood for fires occasionally." I forced a smile in Jack's direction. Jack didn't smile back. He was a man who was reading the vibes and wasn't about to get in the middle of this. He looked away as if a tree in the distance held great interest for him.

"If it snows too much and the power goes out, it would be good for you to have some wood," Jess tried again, but his face was taut.

"I'll just go up to the big house. I'm sure Cass is prepared." I shrugged and waved a hand in the air.

"Well, then, if Cass isn't prepared, you will be," Jess insisted, bending over and grabbing the ax back out of the stump to start up again.

"Jess, you don't need to do nice things for me!" My emotions were starting to build again. I had so much happening inside of me.

Jack glanced between Jess and me with the confused and somewhat embarrassed look of a person who has innocently stumbled into something that they have no business being a part of. Smart man he was, he didn't even bother saying goodbye. He just turned and walked back to the path he and Jess had taken through the woods to my cottage. Jack was out. The Sullivans would be hearing about this pretty soon.

"Chopping my wood isn't giving me space!" I pressed.

"Katherine Evans, I can't handle any more space. I have been a gentleman, and I'm done!" He set the ax back down and took a step toward me.

Being touched by him was the last thing I wanted, so I backed up a couple of steps until I was stopped by the woodpile itself. My heart was racing with a strange excitement as I both watched and heard his footsteps crunching in the snow toward me.

"I've kept up my end of the bargain and given you time! Do you have any idea how that feels to a man, to just wait around like an idiot? You need to knock down that wall and start talking," he stated. A sense of dread crept up when I realized he meant business. It made my knees weak.

"No, Jess. Just stop. I need more time."

"Time is up, sweetheart," he said as he stopped directly in front of me, trapping me, pressing close so I couldn't move.

"Jess, please." My voice shook. "Can't you see that I'm afraid?" I whispered.

His demeanor instantly changed. He relaxed and searched my face before taking a slow deep breath and a small step back, giving us both room to handle this new information.

"What are you afraid of?" he asked quietly.

His entire expression seemed to be saying, *Finally*. Finally he was going to get some answers. The realization that he had been fighting a battle against something he didn't understand was the motivation I needed to open up.

I almost choked on the words that I knew he needed to hear. "I hate this space as much you do. But I have lost so many people that I love! How could I bear to let myself love you if loss is going to be the end result?"

"I know you've lost so much, and I'm sorry you've had to go through that," he replied. I was grateful that he didn't try to argue with me but simply acknowledged my feelings. "I don't know what the future holds. But I do know that if you can't take the risk, then we'll never find out."

I nodded at the truth of his words. Yet to someone like me, who'd lost so much, sometimes true statements took a while to sink in.

It was my turn to make the first move. It was the most terrifying thing in the world to take a step toward him and wrap my arms around his waist. He put his arms around my back and held me close. I felt his relief and pleasure at the contact. His body relaxed into mine, his arms tightening around me, his chin coming to rest on my head.

"Will you really come over tonight?" he asked.

"Yes," I responded.

"Good." He gave me a squeeze and kissed the top of my head. "I can handle small steps, sweetheart. All I ask is that you trust me enough to try." All I could do was nod.

We stood quietly holding each other in the frosty air for a few more minutes before he quickly kissed my forehead and went back to finish the wood chopping. I watched him for a second before I turned back to the cottage and sought its safe warmth. This time, with each strike of the ax, I felt a part of my shell splitting apart too.

Chapter 19

That evening found me at Jess's cabin as promised. Jess had greeted me warmly with a smile and a light, friendly kiss on the cheek, keeping his promise to take small steps. Our eyes had caught as he'd helped me take off my coat and hang it on the coatrack, and I'd felt the vulnerability and newness between us. His eyes were back to their normal smiling steadiness, and I'd longed to wrap myself in their comfort.

I'd had to smile when I'd followed Jess into the large gathering area and found the family sitting around a cozy circular breakfast table. The table was stacked with pretzels, chocolates, peanuts, licorice, and popcorn. Next to the table on a stand was a bowl of ice with sodas and water bottles waiting to be had. In the center of the table sat an open Monopoly game board.

"This looks dangerously like an all-nighter," I joked as I made my way to the collection of people sitting around the table. "I thought only Scrabble games went that long." Everyone laughed, standing up to give me hugs and exchange greetings.

"Kate, you look absolutely darling!" Sharon smiled as she hugged me close. I squeezed her back.

A chair next to Jess had been left open for me, and I sat down, excited to see how this night would go. Last time I'd played games with the Sullivan family, it had been anything but boring.

"Okay, here is the situation with Monopoly." Zara leaned over and pulled me close to whisper in my ear. "It's not quite as bad as croquet, because Sharon is playing, and she won't let the boys get too out of hand. But don't be fooled by her either. She's out to win."

I nodded my understanding. "Do we cheat?" It was a valid question.

Zara grinned. "Is there ever a time when the answer to that question is no?"

I laughed, accidentally drawing the gazes of everyone else. "Just telling Zara a story about Ethan." I smiled in what I hoped was a proud-mother way.

Jess and Jack gave each other knowing looks before going back to setting up the board.

"So there are some things we can do with the money. You're going to get really itchy a few times and put them up your sleeve. A favorite of mine is to take some to the fridge and pretend to be looking for something to add to the table, but really you leave a couple of bills inside. Then go back and get it when you need it. Armpits also work well for money storage."

"Am I going to be handling armpit money during this game?" I giggled quietly.

"Yes. Most definitely. That money has probably been all over the place. You can't be a wimp when you're up against this family."

"Should I be wearing rubber gloves?" I teased.

"My advice is simple. Never, never, and I mean never, sniff the money," she replied. It made both of us laugh again, drawing more unwanted attention.

"What kind of failing plot are you two hatching over there?" Matthew pushed his way into our conversation.

"Nothing at all, Matthew. Zara and I haven't seen each other since the wedding. We have a lot to catch up on." I smiled innocently at him. He gave me a very skeptical eye before motioning to Jack to start the game.

"We're wasting time and I'm getting old. Let's play!" he said.

And just like that, the most enjoyable hours I'd spent in a long time flew by. The Sullivan family were clever, underhanded, and downright sinister in their gameplay. Their theory seemed to be that the only time cheating was wrong was when you got caught. Cheating without being caught wasn't technically cheating; rather, it was playing the game well.

People were all over the room. Going to the bathroom, excusing themselves to get a knife, popping more popcorn even though there was still some left. Everyone apparently had been attacked by mosquitoes with all the scratching of heads under hats, legs, arms, and, yes, even armpits.

In the giddy atmosphere, it didn't take long for Jess and me to relax and begin to really enjoy each other. Somehow, he and I became a team instead of Zara and me. We whispered schemes, hid money for each other, agreed on whom to sink. Over the course of the night, our chairs and our heads drew closer as we laughed and talked. Soon his arm was draped casually over the back of my chair, and he would occasionally play with a lock of the hair I'd left down or absentmindedly draw a lazy pattern on my shoulders, neck, or back.

It was a pleasure to be entirely relaxed and friendly. I realized how much I really liked Jess. His sense of humor, his willingness to be flexible and see where certain roads led. How he didn't have to have all the answers before taking a step forward. It got me thinking about other aspects of his personality that I liked. I liked that he worked hard, that he loved his family, that he was kind and helpful, that he was dependable and available when needed. I liked that he let me be me and just rolled with it.

It was oddly nerve-racking to discover that aside from my physical attraction to Jess, there was an emotional and mental attachment too. The barriers inside of me that had begun to crack the day before were slipping away, and I was helpless to shore them up. The final straw was thoughts of him with Ethan. Ethan adored Jess. Ethan needed a man in his life, and Jess had filled that gap. Jess had filled all the gaps, even sneaking in where I didn't want him. I'd been fighting so hard, but I was seriously in trouble here. I was falling in love with Jess. Who was I kidding . . . I was already half in love with him. It would only take the smallest nudge to push me over to the place of no return.

What if he left me? What if he died like Charlie and my parents had? Could I live through that again? Wasn't it better to leave like I'd been planning? I'd never had the courage to actually do it, but I had been looking casually at apartments in Denver. Maybe it was time, now that I knew how I felt about Jess and how much it would tear me apart to lose him. I would leave him first, choose the pain rather than having it forced on me by him later.

I felt bad thinking about walking away. Surely he would bounce back quickly. Someone as strong, talented, kind, and handsome as Jess would easily find another woman to love. But the idea of another woman in his life made my stomach plunge to my toes.

All these thoughts must have flitted across my face, because the room became suddenly quiet.

"Kate?" Sharon's voice broke through my thoughts. My eyes refocused, and I looked around to see all five sets of eyes on me, concerned, watching.

I tried to smile and shook my head. "Sorry. Just got distracted."

"Are you sure? You looked upset," Matthew responded kindly.

"Well, I'm pretty sure that I'm losing, and I just realized I have no way to win. That's disappointing." I forced a laugh and gestured at my part of the board. I was indeed losing. But it wasn't the battle on the board; it was the battle in my heart.

Jess gave my shoulder a squeeze. "I think I'll bow out too. Kate and I are hopelessly behind. Who wants to make me a deal on our properties?" he asked.

Jack and Zara began to haggle for our properties, waving their hands and shouting in a way that got me laughing again and helped me put my worries behind me for the moment.

After Jess got our properties evenly divided between the four remaining players, he suggested we put on our coats and go out front to look at the stars. I agreed, being a glutton for punishment and all that. He held my coat while I put my arms in it, and I smiled at his kind gesture.

The stars were amazing on such a clear, cold night. As I stared up at them, I knew what I needed to do. And I needed to do it now. I needed answers, and I wouldn't find them here, with him always close by.

"I'm glad I came tonight." I smiled toward the sky.

"Me too," he said.

"Jess, you need to know that I really like you," I said, diving in. I turned away from the stars to face him. Looking up into his eyes gave me a jolt, and I felt those blasted butterflies in my stomach as he gazed back down at me. His face was relaxed and he had a slight smile.

"I really, really like you too, Kate." He pushed a flyaway piece of hair behind my ear. His touch was electric.

"No, I mean, I like you. As a person, as a friend, as someone to spend time with," I pushed on.

His face fell. "Only as a friend?" he asked.

I dodged the question and went on. "I just think it's important that you know that you aren't only someone to date . . . or whatever. That I actually like you on a friendship level too."

His lips pulled up into a smile. "I feel that way about you too."

"Tonight was fun," I said. He nodded. "I'm glad. We needed to just have fun."

"Kate, I've been thinking a lot about what you said yesterday about being scared." He turned to face me. "I understand being scared. I've been scared over you for months now."

I chuckled at this revelation. "This has been one interesting ride."

"Understatement." He puffed out a laugh too. "I don't know exactly what I'm trying to say, but I want you to know that you aren't alone. You have me. We could be scared together."

I reached my cold hands up to pull his head down to mine and kiss him. I was kissing him for being so wonderful and kind and patient with me. It was a thank-you kiss.

"I think I'll head out," I said when we parted.

He smiled at me, not pressing me for any more. "Good night."

And then, like a true yellow-bellied chicken, I got in my car and ran away.

It was surprisingly easy to get out of town without being questioned. In the end, I told Ethan I was surprising him with a visit to his grandparents, my in-laws, just outside of Denver. It was unlike me to take Ethan out of school, which made the whole thing that much more exciting to him.

I had loaded up the car very late after getting home from Jess's house, and we hit the road before first light. Not wanting to discuss anything with the very astute Cass or the POW interrogator Zinn, I left them a note on the kitchen table of the big house, telling them I was off on an adventure. I kept it light and fun, like I'd had a moment of spontaneity. I didn't even call Charlie's parents until we'd been driving for an hour.

As I suspected, Charlie's parents, Carl and Margaret, were surprised but more than willing to have us pop in for a few days. Charlie's sister was in town with her three kids, and "Wouldn't it just be the best to have all the grandkids together for a few days?" My stomach sank a bit when I realized I wouldn't have much alone time with Carl and Margaret to work some things out. But I kept it happy for Ethan, who was genuinely thrilled to see Grandpa and Grandma.

The drive to Charlie's childhood home would take about four hours. I could have stretched it into five if I stopped several times, but Ethan was anxious and completely oblivious that we were on a life-changing mission.

For the entire night I had thought about my plans. What would I say to Carl and Margaret? Where would I go? What was my end plan? The light of day, however, had me questioning my resolve. Was this really the right choice? How did I think running away from Jess would make things easier? I knew from experiencing Charlie's death that leaving didn't make you suddenly forget.

Yet back in Clark Springs, I felt I had no options. I was too close to the problem. He was there every day, popping up all the time, chopping my wood. I needed some real space, time to think, options. I was hoping Denver would give me those options.

Jess texted once on the drive, asking what Ethan and I were up to that day. He wondered if we wanted to have lunch with his family. I hated myself for doing it, but I deleted the text without answering it. The entire point of running away was to be, well, away.

Pulling up to Charlie's parents' house felt strange to me. Almost like revisiting another life. It wasn't that it had been that long since I'd been there. Charlie had only been gone for a little over two years at this point. I hadn't kept Ethan from them and had been back a couple of times. But it had been at least six months or more, and I felt like an entirely different person. Things had changed inside of me. Not to mention that this time my heart was stubbornly trying to wrap itself around another man. It almost felt like I had betrayed Charlie somehow and his parents would see right through me.

"Mom! What's taking so long?" Ethan popped out of the car and ran up to the front door before I said a word. Carl and Margaret were holding him in a loving embrace by the time I met them with our bags in hand and an unsure smile on my face.

"We're so glad you're here." Margaret beamed at me. "Carl, take the bags. They can have Charlie's old room," she instructed. Carl, quiet as always, took my bags and disappeared into the house.

Three black-haired children streaked past Carl and all but mowed Ethan down in their glee. They were jumping up and down and talking about a million miles a minute. Cousins were each other's biggest fans. They gathered Ethan into their group and hurtled back into the house.

Margaret laughed with me at their antics and put her arm around my back, gently guiding me inside. I felt unsteady as I let her lead me into where her daughter, Kelly, was sitting with her husband, Rob. They greeted me kindly as I sank into a seat.

"We'll have lunch soon, but why don't you tell us what you and Ethan have been up to before that." Margaret sat down close to me just as Carl joined us.

I felt frozen inside. I didn't know what to tell them. I didn't think kicking it off with the tale of how I was losing my mind would be the best idea. There was so much to tell, but so much of it was about dating three men. Alec, Nate, Jess. I just couldn't imagine sharing all my misadventures with my dead husband's family. In the end, I just kind of shook my head and laughed.

"I guess the answer is life. I've been up to life."

Luckily, Kelly laughed and jumped right in. "That's what I always tell my girlfriends when we finally see each other. I have nothing new to report. Same stuff every day."

It was best to let her think that, so I smiled and agreed. United in our mom-ness. It was safe and easy. No rocking the boat.

After lunch, the kids went off to play again. I was happy to see Ethan having such a great time with his cousins. It made me feel a little less nervous about what I was planning to do. Ethan would miss Jess, but he would have friends here. As I was helping Margaret and Kelly clean up, my phone chimed with a new message. I slipped the phone out of my pocket and checked.

Jess again. *Didn't hear back from you this morning. Missed lunch. Dinner plans?*

I deleted it again, determined to have not just space, but distance. Yet pushing the delete button felt like a little stab in my heart. I realized how unkind and unfair I was being to the man who just wanted to be part of my life. Being so torn all the time was exhausting.

Margaret's kitchen was warm and safe and quiet. Ironically, it grated on me. Where was the life? Had it always been this way here? When had I started wanting more? As we washed up, I found myself wishing I was cleaning up with Sharon and Zara, coming up with ways to cheat the boys, Matthew begging for a game of Scrabble, everyone moaning and rolling their eyes. I missed Zinn and Cass's conversation and karate chopping the kitchen door.

As soon as the dishes were put away, I quietly asked Margaret if I could speak with her and Carl in private. Kelly and Margaret exchanged a quick glance before Margaret gave me a smile and we went to find Carl in his office.

The door was closed and I was seated carefully on a chair before I spoke. I wasn't sure how they would react to my wanting to move back to Denver. I was scared to ask for their help. I didn't know how to tell them that I was seeking refuge so that I could decide if I wanted to take the risk of being with another man. It felt disloyal, yet necessary.

"Thank you so much for letting Ethan and me pop in unexpectedly!" I smiled warmly at both of them. They had always been kind to me. I had probably abused it—maybe, I don't know. Oddly, I didn't think much about my relationship with them. They were just kind of there. Always pleasant, always helpful, steady and easy.

"Of course. We're always happy to see you and our sweet grandson." Margaret smiled again. Like I said, always pleasant.

"Well, I was hoping you'd do me a favor," I began, steeling myself, hoping they'd provide a temporary living place while I got my life on a new track. Yet when I opened my mouth, another question popped out unexpectedly. "I need to ask you about my relationship with Charlie."

Oh shoot, oh shoot! What just happened? I was a bit panicked on the inside. I mean, I had been thinking about it but didn't mean to actually ask it at this point. This conversation was supposed to happen in a few weeks when I was settled firmly in my pondering phase.

They looked puzzled, rotating their glances between me and each other. "What do you mean?" Carl finally asked.

Well, in for a penny, in for a pound. "I mean, from your perspective, what did you see in my relationship with Charlie?" I asked.

Carl nodded at Margaret to take this one. She straightened up and looked at me for a moment. I was sure she could see right through me. She seemed to settle on something and nodded to herself before speaking.

"Kate, since you're asking, I'm going to be very candid with you," she said somewhat unsurely. I smiled my encouragement. "I was against Charlie marrying you."

Well, that was not what I'd been expecting to hear. I slouched back in my seat. "Oh" was all I said for a moment. "Can you tell me why?" I asked.

"Yes. If I remember the timing correctly, you and Charlie met just a few months after your parents had passed away," Margaret began. She looked to me for confirmation, and I nodded. That was true. Charlie had come into my life during the dark early days. "You were clearly grieving. Charlie was such a steady boy, always cheerful and responsible. I was worried that you would somehow swallow him up in that grief you were fighting."

"Do you think I did?" I whispered as I saw meeting Charlie through their eyes. How sullen I had been, barely eking out a life. Orphaned and an only child, so alone.

"No, I don't," Carl inserted.

Margaret smiled at me to show she agreed with him. "It seemed more like Charlie became your new lifeline. You . . . what's the word for it . . . revolved around him. Like he was your sun and you were rotating around him, getting strength from him. You became happier, and Charlie was happy too."

"So then why were you against us marrying?" I asked again.

"Well, it's hard to explain . . ." Margaret hesitated as she looked for words.

"You didn't seem to be you," Carl stated bluntly. "Like we were just waiting for you to become someone else."

"Like Bruce Banner and the Hulk?" I joked.

They laughed, helping to ease the hurt I was feeling, rational or not.

"No, no, not like that." Margaret took a deep breath. "But Carl is right. I saw something inside of you that you were holding back. We were worried that maybe Charlie didn't know the real you. He married a version of you, but not the whole Kate."

I was shocked by their statements. I sat fully back in my chair and looked to the ceiling, letting their words roll through my brain and settle in. It recolored my memories.

"Did you ever tell Charlie this?" I asked finally.

"No. He never asked if we thought he should marry you. He was so in love he couldn't see what we saw," Carl stated.

"But you were against it all along?"

"No, dear. We were at first, but we grew to love you. You were a good wife to Charlie and a lovely mother for Ethan. We are grateful for that," Margaret inserted quickly.

I looked down at my lap. So many words warred in my head for release. "Charlie and I had a perfect marriage," I finally blurted out.

"Yes, it looked like that from the outside," Margaret agreed.

"We never fought. We were happy, and I was always cheerful," I added.

Neither of them said anything but just made affirmative sounds.

"I'm not sure that's normal?" The last came out as a question.

This time Carl laughed out loud, and Margaret joined him. "In our experience, you're right. It's not normal to never argue."

"Is that what you meant by you felt I was holding part of myself back?" I ventured to ask.

They both thought that over before Margaret broke the silence. "Yes, that's probably it. You had just lost your parents and were so alone. I think you wanted so desperately to belong somewhere that you did whatever it took to be pleasant and accommodating. You took on so many of Charlie's likes and interests. I wondered where Kate existed as her own person. There were occasional glimpses of something sort of . . . fierce, I guess . . . underneath all that sunshine, but we never saw it break free. We didn't know if Charlie saw that fire, and we were worried about that."

"I've changed lately. And I've met someone," I blurted again. I couldn't seem to help vomiting words out. What had happened to *I want to move back to Denver; can we stay here for a bit?*

"Oh?" Carl said.

I nodded, avoiding their eyes. I was worried about what they'd see there. "We definitely argue. I'm always getting into ridiculous situations. I ignore him, and then I pull him close. My life feels like a roller coaster that I stepped onto without realizing it was happening. I don't recognize myself in a lot of ways." I got teary just thinking of it. "With Charlie I was so easygoing and so happy."

"We didn't know you before you met Charlie, but maybe all those things you've been holding in for so long are popping out." Margaret's voice was soothing, and she reached out to hold my hand. "It can't be easy while those things shift around."

They both sat quietly, patiently waiting, Margaret holding my hand and Carl reaching out a hand to my shoulder. I felt so comforted by them, these people who had loved me even though they were afraid for their son. I admired them for raising Charlie to love so well. I also found myself wondering about my marriage to Charlie. Could we have gone the distance? Would I have always been so pleasant, or would this other side of me have eventually reared her flaming red head? I suddenly found myself asking the same questions that Carl and Margaret had been asking for years.

I felt hollowed out by my visit with Carl and Margaret. They kindly suggested I rest in my room until dinner time. I gladly complied after checking in to find Ethan having a great time while building a snowman in the backyard with his three cousins.

I needed to rethink my move to Denver for perhaps the millionth time. I needed to ask different questions than I'd thought I needed to ask. Time to process and regroup. Somehow my plan had jumped ahead to step ten when I thought I'd be on step one here. Was running away really the right thing to do?

As I lay down on the bed, I got another chime on my phone. Jess. My heart nearly burst from seeing his name on the screen. This man who was at the mercy of all my turbulent emotions and still just wanted me to let him love me.

Are you OK? was all it said. No, I wasn't. I felt blindsided by the revelations of the afternoon. I also felt grateful to see things in a new light. I somehow felt a little crushed and a little lighter at the same time. Was I relieved or upset that my plans had changed with the words exchanged today?

I will be, I finally texted back.

Can I help? His text came back mere seconds later.

I wished he could. I sighed. I didn't know how to answer that question. As I hesitated, another text chimed.

Where are you? he asked.

I ran away.

From me?

Mostly from myself, I sent, realizing the truth of that statement even as I sent it. It hadn't been Jess I was running from after all.

Can I help you find your way back?

Just leave a light on for me. I let my fingers hover over the screen, wanting to say so much more but knowing the words needed to be said in person.

Chapter 20

Saturday morning I left Ethan with his grandparents. In order to follow the next part of my new and improved plan, I really needed to be alone. It was a beautiful morning. The snow was crisp on the lawns, and the light coming off of the snow was blinding. It would have been a perfect morning to sit near a window looking outside and sipping something warm. Too bad it wasn't that day for me.

I had determined to take myself on a *This Is Your Life*–type tour through the Denver area. The apartment where I'd lived when I met Charlie, our first apartment together, and finally our home. The place where Ethan joined our family and where we were living at the time of Charlie's death.

My motivation for revisiting all things Charlie had come to me like a comet to the earth while lying in his old bedroom the night before. I realized I was still mad at him. I still felt betrayed by his passing. But there was more than that. Because of that betrayal, I couldn't seem to trust that Jess would stay with me, and fear had become my biggest motivator. Fear had me running, and until I faced it down, I would never be free of it.

Charlie and I hadn't fought at all, about anything, ever. I had always felt like our marriage had been strong and secure. Yet I couldn't help wondering, particularly given Margaret's and Carl's statements the day before, if maybe Charlie had been married to a version of me who was entirely different from who I was now. Would Charlie even recognize me? And if I wasn't the same anymore, then I had no idea how to be in a relationship. Would Jess be willing to accept that I was learning about myself and go along for the ride? More than that even, did I want Jess along for the ride? Was I brave enough?

All I knew was that the thought of losing Jess made me feel even worse than the thought of taking a chance on him made me feel. Even if I couldn't admit it to him, or even verbalize it to myself, he made my heart pound and my stomach swoop and every feeling in the world come alive inside of me.

And what about sweet Ethan? That kid deserved to have a man in his life who spent time with him and loved him and taught him about manhood. In the absence of Charlie, he couldn't have asked for a better role model than Jess.

I had much to ponder as I drove for hours around Denver. Jess, of course, texted a few times. My answers were always short, just enough to keep him from flipping his lid.

How are you today? and *Ready to tell me where you are?* and *Can I help?* He must have asked me that last one at least five times. I knew this was hard on him. He didn't deserve any of this. It was hard on me as well. I ignored most of them until early afternoon, when I finally sent a quick response and then silenced my phone.

I'm trying to find myself again was all I said. It would have to be enough.

My last stop was the home where Charlie and I had lived. A new family was in residence. It was clear that they had children from the play set in the side yard and a standard scarf-wearing snowman in the front. For a moment, I was blindsided by jealousy. *That should have been us!* I screamed in my head. Ethan should have had siblings by now.

On a day like this, Charlie would have made pancakes for breakfast, played with the children outside while I did laundry and tidied up around the house. In the evening, we would have had soup for dinner and cuddled up on the couch to watch a movie. Charlie and I would have gotten the children to bed and then crawled into our own bed and talked into the darkness of the night. We would have made plans for our future and held each other closely.

In that house, life had been idyllic. I had been Charlie's docile little wife, and he had been my rescuer from loneliness. Had he ever seen glimpses of what his parents saw? Had he ever wondered about a fire that lurked behind my eyes? There was no doubt that he had come into my life at a time when I truly needed him. I had truly loved him. I knew it. Our love for each other was real, even if there were parts of me that I had unwittingly kept hidden.

But maybe it wasn't all my fault. I had been so young when we'd met. A freshman in college, only nineteen years old. I had just lost my parents and had no idea how to go about life. I had been scared and so desperate to create a new family that once I'd finally trusted in Charlie I had jumped right in. Married at twenty and a mother to Ethan by twenty-one. Looking back at it, Charlie and I had practically been babies having a baby.

I saw the front-porch light come on and a man step out, taking a closer look at my parked car. I realized I must have been sitting there for a while. They were probably about to call the police, and I didn't need an encounter with the cops to add to my list of harebrained schemes. I pulled out of my old neighborhood, saying a stinging goodbye forever, and drove to a grocery-store parking lot. I parked as far away from the store as I could to allow myself some privacy before making two phone calls.

The first was to Margaret to check in on Ethan and let her know that I was doing all right. I would be home by bedtime to tuck him in.

Then I made my second phone call.

"Owens residence," Zinn answered crisply.

"Hi, Zinn." I knew my voice sounded worn out.

"Hello, Kate," Zinn replied. "Jess and his family came for dinner. He is worried about you." She stated it in a way that said an entire paragraph about how I, Kate, had wronged her darling Jess and she was put out with me.

"Sorry." I didn't feel like I needed to apologize for taking a time-out for myself, but not apologizing for vexing Zinn wasn't a good move.

"Yes, well, I told him you are fine. We don't worry too much when you disappear," she huffed.

"Thanks." She made an unintelligible sound. "Out of curiosity, is there a scenario where you do worry about me disappearing?" I wondered.

"Yes. If I come downstairs one morning and find the donuts still in their box, then I will know something terrible has happened to you."

I couldn't help a little smile at her reply. "Fair enough. Um, you didn't tell Jess where I am, did you?"

Zinn sighed loudly. Clearly I had maligned her honor. "No, of course not. I'm no gossip."

I almost laughed despite my heartache. Zinn could have single-handedly run the Underground Railroad with the way that lady knew who was where doing what at all times.

"Can I please speak with Aunt Cass?"

"Yes, I'll get her." I heard a thunk as Zinn set down the phone on the countertop. Even though it was cordless, Zinn couldn't ever manage to understand that she could walk away with it. She pretended that she wanted it to always stay in the kitchen, but I knew the truth. She thought it was attached with an invisible wire and I was trying to prank her to see if she'd actually walk with it.

A few moments later, Cass's voice came on the line. "Kate, dear?"

I smiled at the familiarity of her voice. She'd been such a lifeline to me over the years. It made my throat swell and my voice came out in a wobble. "Yes, it's me."

"How are you?"

"I'm okay."

"How is my Ethan?" Her voice was warm as she said his name.

"Ethan is having fun with his grandparents and cousins."

"Good. And you?"

"I'm okay," I replied.

"Good. How's the weather down there?"

"Uh, fine. Winter has arrived. It's been snowy."

"How are Carl and Margaret doing?" Dang it, Cass was doing small talk. She probably wondered why on earth I'd called.

"They're fine. Listen, Cass, I didn't really call to shoot the breeze," I stated.

"Well, thank goodness. I was running out of questions." She laughed.

I couldn't help but laugh too. "Speaking of questions, the reason I'm calling is, well, I need you to answer some for me."

"Oh, okay." I had caught her by surprise.

"I need you to tell me what I was like before Mom and Dad died." My voice had gotten soft and vulnerable. I both needed and dreaded her answer.

"Well . . ." I could practically hear the wheels turning in her impeccably styled little gray head. I pictured her gazing off into the background, a finger resting on her lips as she thought. I waited patiently for her answer, knowing better than to rush her.

"Well, Kate, I'd say you were really something else. You were wonderful!" she finally stated.

"Wonderful?" I wasn't sure I'd heard her correctly.

"Oh, yes," she confirmed.

"She's right," I heard Zinn's voice pop up. That little eavesdropper had stayed on the other line.

"Zinn!" I said her name on a burst of laughter.

"What? I would feel bad, but you both knew I was going to listen in, so I don't," Zinn stated matter-of-factly. Both Cass and I chuckled at that.

"Can you explain what you mean?" I asked.

"You were as unruly and unmanageable as that hair of yours." Cass's voice was tender with nostalgia. "You were constantly running about, always ready for an adventure, getting into scrapes and disasters one after another. And always so happy about it."

"You were so moody. Happy one moment, crying the next moment, yelling at someone a minute later. Nothing about you was predictable," Zinn inserted. "Nearly drove me over the edge."

"That doesn't sound wonderful," I asserted.

"Well, the thing is, you did it all in a way that somehow brought that excitement for life to everyone around you. We watched you, and you kept us on our toes all the time. Even when you'd have an outburst or get angry, you bounced back quickly. It was like you were so full of life that you couldn't contain it all, so it just burst out of you before you moved on to something else," Cass explained.

"You were a total pain," Zinn added.

Cass chuckled. "You loved it when Kate came to visit," she said to Zinn.

Zinn made a noise, but she didn't argue.

"And after my parents died?" I questioned.

They were both quiet again. I felt the weight of their silence, their unwillingness to hurt me, their desire to help me even while unsure how answering the question would help.

"Come on, you two. You just finished telling me what a pain I was before they died. Why can't you tell me how I was after?" I pressed.

"You get this one," Zinn said to Cass. "I'm only the hired help."

Cass scoffed. "Hired help when it suits you."

"Aunt Cass? Please?" I begged.

Cass took a deep breath. "I'm not sure exactly what you're asking, Kate, so I hope this will answer it. When your parents died, the spark inside of you seemed to be blown out. You still looked like our Kate, but you stopped acting like our Kate. You bottled up everything and started behaving. We hardly recognized you when you first came to visit after the funeral."

"What about my marriage to Charlie? What did you think about that?"

"I was very happy when you met Charlie, and so soon after your parents' death. He was such a nice man, and I knew he would help you heal," Cass answered.

"Did he? Help me heal, I mean?"

"Of course he did," Zinn said.

"He helped you a great deal and did a wonderful job of caring for you," Cass expounded.

"Was it all a lie?" I whispered.

"What do you mean?" Cass asked.

"Well, if I wasn't me and was all bottled up, then who was Charlie married to?"

"Charlie was married to you, you foolish girl," Zinn stated, unwilling as usual to entertain any sign of self-pity.

"But, I mean, was our marriage a sham?" I felt so defenseless asking that question to these two strong women.

"No. You loved him, and he loved you, no matter which version of yourself you gave to him. He would have loved this side of you too. Charlie was a good man," Cass answered.

"He lied to me," I said softly.

"He loved you and didn't want to hurt you," Cass replied. She had always tried to help me see things from Charlie's side. I was never truly sure if she agreed with what he'd done or if she was simply trying to help me forgive and move on.

"He made it hard for me to believe," I was whispering now.

"Believe in what?" Zinn asked.

But Cass understood. "Ah," she said in a low voice. "So that's why you've run away."

I nodded but realized they couldn't see me. "Yes," I murmured. "What if he lies to me, breaks my heart, hurts me like Charlie did? What if he can't accept me as I am? What if he dies? I don't know that I could stand it."

"No one ever knows how long they have on this earth, but I do know that life with you is never dull. Jess would never grow bored of you," Cass soothed.

"Jess? You're running from Jess? You really are a foolish girl," Zinn grumbled, and there was a sorrow in her tone I'd never heard before. I was surprised as she continued. "I made many mistakes in my life, but running away from a man who wanted to love me was the biggest. I had a chance just like you once. I was too stubborn to accept it. I wanted adventure away from the little town where I was raised. So I ran away to start a new life, and he found another woman to love. I didn't find adventure waiting for me. I found loneliness. I was embarrassed, and I cut off all ties with my family and became lost. I'm lucky that Cass found me and gave me a home. Don't repeat my mistakes." I heard a beep as she shut off her connection.

I processed all Zinn had said. Maybe I would never know Zinn's true story. And maybe that was fine. I was finally learning that we don't always have to have all the answers. I knew the important truths about Zinn. She was loyal, dependable, and someone I loved. At the end of the day, that was enough. I now also knew that her past held pain and heartache and that it was time for me to stop digging around in it. I was grateful in that moment that Zinn loved me enough to warn me against making a mistake.

"Do you think I'm foolish?" I asked Cass as I returned to the conversation.

"No, dear. I think you're scared and you're hurting and you're vulnerable. You've lost a lot of people in your life."

"What should I do about Jess?"

"What does Jess say?"

"He wants to be with me." I said quietly, hardly believing I was saying the words out loud for the first time. "But Cass, he's a full-on famous movie star. He's so handsome. He could have any woman he wanted."

"Jess is a grown man, intelligent and successful. Have you talked to him about this?"

"A little," I admitted.

"So, again, what does Jess say?"

I breathed out a laugh as I repeated the same answer. "He wants to be with me."

"Only you can decide for sure what you want, but I can tell you that something has stirred you back up and you're acting more like yourself again. We see signs of our girl coming back to us. It's been a long time. I don't know if we should give Jess all the credit, or if it was simply time for you to find your way back. The Kate I knew would have grasped firmly to life and not thought twice about it. You just need to decide if New Kate feels the same way and if Jess is the thing you want to grab on to."

I thought for a moment. "I'm a little afraid," I admitted. "I was going to move to Denver and never come back."

Cass made a soft noise, letting me know she had suspected as much, but she didn't openly address the move.

"I'm also a little afraid of the person I'm becoming."

"Well, you shouldn't be afraid. I've known her a long time, and she's wonderful if you'll give her a chance," Cass replied.

I wished I could hug her right then. We weren't overly affectionate that way, but I would have given anything to wrap my arms around her and thank her for everything. For putting up with both Crazy Kate and Grieving Kate. For giving me a home and love and a family to anchor myself to. But mostly for thinking I was wonderful.

I barely slept Saturday night. I tossed and turned, conversations and revelations floating around my mind like a dryer full of laundry. I must have opened my phone thirty-two times wanting to text Jess, wanting even more to call him and tell him to wait just a little longer, to not give up on me now.

I had finally caved at around 4 a.m. and sent a text that said, *Did you leave that light on for me?*

To which he'd replied, *Always.*

Sunday morning was another beauty. I enjoyed a quiet breakfast with Carl, Margaret, Kelly, and Rob while the kids got in more play time before they had to say goodbye to each other. Ethan had school the next day, but my motivation to get back home wasn't only based on that.

The conversation flowed comfortably, with no one asking questions about where I'd gone and what I'd done the day before. How different it was from Cass and Zinn, who practically demanded to know everything. I wondered how I'd never noticed that in some ways Charlie's family were strangers to me. We were so polite and cordial with each other, but we acted more like business acquaintances. The conversation I'd had with Carl and Margaret two days earlier had probably been the most real discussion we'd ever had. How sad that I'd held myself bottled up so tightly for the entire time I was married to their son. I'd have to try to fix that in the future.

"So what does today hold for you, Kate?" Kelly asked. I smiled to myself, thinking how two days ago that answer had been very different. Two days ago I was going to move back to Denver and ask Carl and Margaret if Ethan and I could stay with them while I looked for a job and an apartment. I was going to run away from Jess and never look back. I had been nothing but scared.

The answer this morning was different. I had asked the questions I'd needed to ask, and their answers hadn't been what I'd expected. They had taken me in a new direction. If possible, I was even more scared.

I had driven past my old stomping grounds and found that they weren't calling to me like I thought they would. Instead, I had felt homesick. I missed my cottage and the two old ladies I lived with. I missed Jess. I missed laughing and arguing with someone and feeling that sense of excitement. I missed the way he met me at every turn, the way he pushed and took and kept coming back for more.

"I thought maybe I'd go past Charlie's grave before we head back home." I smiled at Kelly. "It's been a while, and I think it would be good for Ethan to go visit."

Carl nodded and Margaret gave me a pat on the arm. "I think that's a great idea. When do you think you'll leave?"

"Actually," I said, laughing at the joy that radiated out from me at the thought of running back to where I belonged, "I think I'm ready to go now." I pushed my chair away from the table and cleared my dishes, the others following suit.

When we were done, I gave Carl and Margaret the most sincere hug I'd ever given them.

"Thank you for what you said to me," I told them while Kelly watched from the side.

"We were worried we'd said too much," Margaret admitted, squeezing me back.

"No, it was just what I needed. You've helped me so much."

"Don't stay away too long this time," Carl admonished kindly.

"I won't," I promised.

Then I whisked Ethan and our luggage out to the car, and we headed to the cemetery for one last goodbye.

Our visit to the cemetery was quick, with only a few brief tugs at my heart reminding me that I had faith in Charlie. I somehow knew that morning, standing in the light snowfall and looking up into the sky, that had I shown him this new side of me, he would have loved me anyhow. I wished I had been brave enough to let him in all the way.

Ethan, unsure about how to act, had been quiet and just let his gaze wander over the headstones near Charlie's. I cleaned the snow from his name and got rid of the now sticky and wet autumn leaves that hadn't been blown away by the winter storms.

In the end, we didn't stay long, because there was nothing to say. I loved him. Old Kate would be Charlie's forever. New Kate, well, her future was wide open.

As we sat in our car before pulling out of the cemetery for the drive home, I finally shot off a text of my own to Jess.

I'm coming was all it said. He didn't reply, and I didn't let it bother me. I was going home, and we would figure it out.

Chapter 21

There's a slight chance I broke some laws getting home that morning. My heart seemed to have dropped down to my foot and was pushing harder on the gas pedal than my mind would have allowed. Ethan kept looking at the speedometer from the back seat and making disapproving sounds, letting me know he wasn't sure I should be going that fast.

Finally, after the tenth time of him looking and then mumbling something, I reached back and tickled his knee.

"No coppy, no stoppy. Right, buddy?" I teased. He squirmed away and gave a resigned sigh in a dramatic way that let me know he'd thought I was being odd but he'd just deal with it. I tickled him again, and we fell into silence as a few more miles sped by. Well, at least as silent as it can be with Van Halen blaring from the radio.

As we reached the halfway point of the drive, I turned off the radio and met Ethan's questioning eyes in the rearview mirror.

"Listen, buddy, I wanted to talk to you about something. You know I've been going out on dates a little bit lately?" Ethan nodded. "Well, I'm thinking I'd like to go on some dates with Jess." I smiled as the words warmed my heart.

Ethan's smile grew larger. "Really?"

"Yes, I really like him."

"I do too. That would be okay," Ethan replied.

"Are you sure? Because he was your friend first, and I don't want you to feel weird."

"Why would I feel weird?"

I chuckled to myself at little-boy logic. Where had he been over the past weeks of me torturing myself over every little decision? I shrugged casually.

"Will he still take me fishing?"

"You bet." I smiled again at him.

"Okay. Then that's cool."

And just like that, it really was cool.

It was still afternoon when we got home, and everything was quiet in the stillness of the snow. I eased the car into the carport next to the cottage, my fingers drumming on the steering wheel in nervous anticipation. I was beginning to wonder if I'd come down with a flu or something, because I hadn't been able to eat lunch and I was feeling the beginnings of perspiration. Then again, facing the man who may think you've scorned him can do that to a girl. Was this how Jess had felt over the last months as he watched and waited and hoped I'd come around?

My mind was running in circles wondering how it would all play out. Was Jess at home? Would he accept my phone call, or should I just drop by? Would Ethan feel ditched if I told him to go hang out with Cass while I tried to put the puzzle pieces of my love life together?

My hands began to shake as I popped the trunk of my car open and bent in to retrieve our suitcases. As I stood up with bags in hand and turned around, I saw a very familiar figure come around the side of the big house. Nothing had ever looked more like home to me than seeing him walking toward me at that moment.

Pure adrenaline kicked in as I dropped the bags right there and ran toward him.

"Jess!" I was so happy I thought I would burst. It didn't matter that his face had looked slightly hesitant, or that I wasn't sure how he would receive me. I just threw myself straight at him, trusting that he would catch me. He'd once said he could handle anything I threw at him . . .

"Hey," he said, laughing, his arms coming around me as he lifted me off my feet and hugged me close.

"I'm so, so sorry," I whispered in his ear. His only response was to squeeze me closer. "I came back," I added.

"I can see that." He smiled against my cheek before easing my feet back to the ground.

We kept our arms around each other as we looked each other over, communicating silently, all our hopes and fears coming together in the stillness between us.

"Hi, Jess," Ethan interrupted.

Jess and I stepped away from each other as Ethan looked back and forth with an assessing glance. Even though I'd told him about wanting to date Jess, he still hadn't actually seen us together. This was new for everyone.

"Hey, buddy. How was your trip?" Jess said.

Ethan finally pulled a silly face. To eight-year-old boys, love was pretty gross, and Ethan wasn't wanting to stick around to watch. "You know what, I'm going to go see what Zinn has to eat," he said. "I'll see you later." Jess and I chuckled.

Jess picked up our bags as I led the way into the cottage. When he set the bags next to the door and closed it, I suddenly felt shy, standing there facing him with my entire heart on my sleeve. Before, I had always been so guarded, and he had been so open. Our roles had reversed. I wasn't sure what to do.

"I really am so sorry, Jess," I felt compelled to say again. "For everything I've put you through." I felt emotion start to build as he watched my face. I desperately hoped he still wanted to be with me after all I'd done to push him away.

"Why did you leave?" he finally asked quietly.

"I was scared," I admitted.

"And now?"

I took a deep breath and let it out slowly. How to explain to him everything that had happened, all that I'd learned and how I felt now. It was overwhelming.

"Still scared," I breathed out on a laugh. "But hopeful."

He came slowly to me and helped me out of my coat, all the while looking me over, trying to assess what had happened. Maybe he could see the change in me.

After he hung up our coats, we stayed standing. I can't really explain why; maybe it felt like sitting would be too casual for all that needed to be said.

"Can you tell me?" he asked as we stood facing each other.

I nodded and plunged in with both feet. I told him of my plans to move to Denver, to be a chicken, to run away. How I'd hoped that distance would make things easier. I told him what Carl and Margaret had said and about my conversation with Cass and Zinn. I told him about my fears of losing him. He shook his head at that and started to move forward, to touch me, to try to calm my fears, but I took a step back. He couldn't touch me during this part.

"I was so afraid, and I still am a little, that if you saw me . . . the real me . . . that I wouldn't be enough for you and you'd leave me," I finally finished haltingly, laying it all out for him to sort through.

"Kate, love, that's where you're wrong," he said quietly. "I've always seen you. This whole time I've seen the real you. And Cass was right. You're wonderful."

He closed the space between us slowly, and then I was in his arms, for the first time with openness between us.

"I love you, Jess," I whispered against his ear, relieved to finally tell the truth to both of us.

"I've loved you forever," he replied, lightly brushing his lips across my cheek.

After a few more minutes of stillness together, I suggested we head up to the big house. We did so hand in hand, words flying between us quickly, so much to be said. So much happiness. I couldn't wait to tell Cass and Zinn that New Kate was going to grab on with both hands and enjoy the ride.

Epilogue

The snow is falling gently on the hills backing our property, but it doesn't touch me where I am, snugly wrapped up on a couch in front of the window. Jess is behind me, his arms around me, my head resting on his chest as he caresses my growing belly, waiting for movement from this little girl who will be coming in just two more months.

So much has happened, so much has changed in the past year. Yet right now everything is quiet. Sometimes I think I'll burst from the happiness of being Jess's wife. Living here in Jess's cabin—our cabin—with Jess and Ethan, is everything I thought it would be. We fight, we tease, we love, we hide nothing . . . we are a family.

"I have a present for you," I say to Jess as I struggle out of his arms and make my way across the room to where our Christmas tree is standing. I find the gift I'm searching for and hurry back to his warmth.

"Christmas isn't until next week." He raises his eyebrow at me.

"Open it." I smile as I sit facing him.

He unwraps it quickly and pulls out a pair of bright sky-blue sweatpants. His laugh immediately fills the room, and my laughter joins in. "I've never had a pair of these before," he chuckles.

"I think you're going to really like them," I reply. "In fact, I bet you'll never want to wear anything else."

He leans in and kisses me. "I love you, Kate Sullivan."

I know he does. I really know it. And I love him too.

Acknowledgments

My parents have to get top billing here. They taught me that imperfect people are worth giving perfect love to, that words have power, and that laughter can heal. Thanks for being the parents everyone else wishes they had.

My four beautiful children. Dreams do come true! I know, 'cuz you're mine.

My two sisters, who share all my moments, whether they are big or small. My angel brother—I know you're cheering me on! Sara, who is living proof of the promise of new beginnings.

My in-laws, who I hope will allow me to stay in the will. Thank you for just accepting me for me. Dibs on the chips and dip!

My extended family far and wide, who have always shown me the power of knowing where you belong. I've been so blessed to be surrounded by amazing adventurers and gifted storytellers.

My truly priceless and talented friends. No girl has ever been as lucky as I am.

My "DC Ladies," for starting a book club in an effort to see each other regularly, and then letting it fade into an eating and gabbing club that we all love! Thank you for the twenty-five-plus years of escapades—several of which made it into this book. I look forward to many, many more!

Wade—a loyal friend—who said if he wasn't in the book it wouldn't be worth reading. I hope you enjoy your central role. I'll see you at DQ, buddy.

The lovely people at Cedar Fort Publishing. Briana and Kaitlin for endlessly and kindly answering my questions. Jessilyn and James taught me so much through the editing process, and this book is better because of their efforts. And Wes, thank you for this beautiful cover!

And last, but in no way least, I'd like to thank my beta readers. R. B., C. H., and E. T. (not the alien). They took my little fledgling book and gave me the courage to leap from the nest.

About the Author

Aspen Marie Hadley loves nothing more than a great story. She has been supplied with endless fodder for those stories through her work at a dry cleaners', as a waitress, as a dental office manager, executive assistant, transcriptionist, and working on an 800- line taking customer messages while attending Utah State University. She loves people and the crazy, romantic, defiant, dumb, risky, wonderful things they do. Aspen shares her life with a patient husband, four hilarious children, one grumpy dog, and two incredibly loud birds. *Simply Starstruck* is Aspen's debut novel. You can find her on Facebook at facebook.com/aspenthewriter and Instagram @aspenhadley_author.

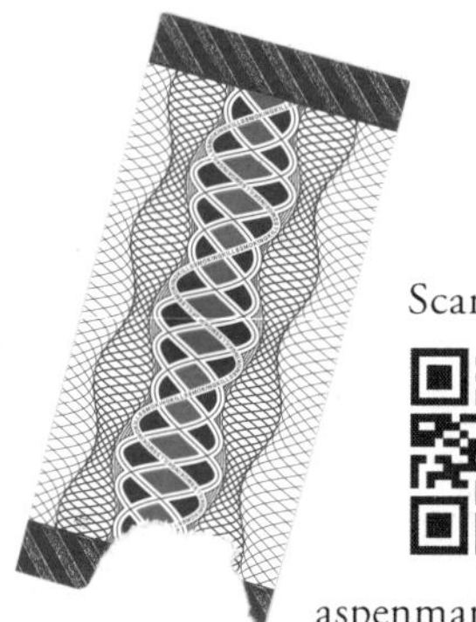

Scan to visit

aspenmariehadley.com